TRASH DADDY

JENNI TAYLA

When I first started dreaming up Trash Daddy, I was told by another writer that I owed the world's daughters better literature.

To which I said... have you met some of the world's daughters?

So this is for you, the daughters who love red flag, skeezy, daddy types, that should definitely be in prison.

Enjoy.

Playlist

"Sex, Drugs, Etc." by Beach Weather

"Little Deaths" Sir Sly

"Neon Signs" Suki Waterhouse

"Wet Dream" Wet Leg

"Summer Vibe" Forrest Nolan

"Pineapple Sunrise" Beach Weather

"Dreamin'" Skinny Dyck

"Juice" New Beat Fund

"Swoon" Beach Weather

"Maraschino Love" EZI

"Come Here" Dominic Fike

"Dead Inside" Younger Hunger

"Mol y Sol" Hugo Brijs

"Too Late" The Happy Fits

"Want You So Bad" The Vaccines

"Sharp As a Knife" Danny Ayer

"Bathroom" Montell Fish

"Galaxy" Hensonn

"John Doe" Adam Jensen

"drowning" Vague003, Sadistik

"HAUNTED" Isabel LaRosa

"Shot It-Club Mix" KVPV

"Intro" The xx

"In and Out" Blonder

This playlist is available on Spotify.
https://open.spotify.com/playlist/0uWwz8KfuC7zLJqXs8xb4F?si=26n
1mWUGSr2owxJaOnhqGw

Content Advisory

Please be aware that despite the cheery book cover, this book falls firmly in the dark romance genre. For the record, this story is a work of fiction, and I do not condone any situation or actions that take place between these characters. If you wish to go in blind to this story, then continue to chapter one. If you don't want to go in blind, please read the trigger warnings list, which can be found on my linktree: https://linktr.ee/jennitaylabooks

Author's Note

Trash Daddy came to me as a spark of inspiration while driving down the coast during a family vacation with my partner and children. That spark, with a little imagination and a lot of wicked, inappropriate humor, took on a life of its own. Some stories demand attention and essentially write themselves. This was most certainly the case with Luke and Carmella. Trash Daddy wasn't the first book I was supposed to publish, but here we are.

Nothing about this book is to be taken seriously (not that anyone would ever take Luke seriously); it is purely for your dirty, smutty entertainment. It is an adult contemporary dark romance that contains mature and graphic content. Reader discretion is advised. You know what you can handle, so please practice self-care.

CONTENTS

Oooof, Maybe This Was Too Spicy

LUKE

Dainty chains on a gothic miniskirt slap against my hands in tandem with my balls slapping against her slit. Dim fluorescent lights hum and flicker overhead while heavy-metal music blares through the old wooden door, masking the breathy moans of the chick I'm balls deep in.

Not my typical scene for sure, but variety is the spice of life. And I like my life spicy.

A shiny, pink pussy grips my cock. I pull out and slam into this chick's cunt. *Damn, that hole is good.*

The living-dead girl moans and swivels her hips on my fuckstick, shooting licks of arousal into my groin. I press us against the discolored water-stained vanity top, pinning her fishnet-wrapped thighs. Black-rimmed and filthy, the bathroom sink lurks under her slim stomach. My hands smooth up her ribcage, lifting the black crop top to fondle her tits. Her nipples create little buds, tight with arousal; I slip them between my fingertips and squeeze, making her groan. Dark purple and black hair spills over my arm, and her head falls back as she fucks herself on my dick.

Our eyes meet in the filthy mirror. "You feel fucking amazing; you know that?" I grunt.

The goth girl gives me a little smile and bites her bottom lip. Her big green eyes flutter closed.

"So." I thrust hard, and her slick heat grips my cock. I grind deeper into her.

"Fucking." Wednesday yelps as I shove her face into the mirror.

"Tight." The vanity shakes violently as I drive into her. Pieces of dry, rotted caulking drop to the floor.

She cries out, grabbing onto the faucet and towel dispenser. "It hurts."

Panting in her ear, I smooth back her straight purple-black hair. "It hurts, huh? Thought that was your thing, Wednesday?"

"It is. Do it harder." Her pink tongue flicks out over her lips. She gives me a wolfish grin.

Laughter slips from between my lips. *The Addams Family* tune pops into my head, and I fuck to the rhythm. It's been a while since I've had this much fun. Lust reaches a fever pitch as I watch my cock slide into her rosy pussy.

The bathroom door swings open, and some spike-headed dipshit with parachute pants stumbles in carrying an empty beer bottle.

"Do you fucking mind? I'm trying to nut here," I snap, not bothering to stop ramming myself into Hot Topic. My balls ache. *I've been slapping them against this slut for too long.*

He freezes upon seeing us, jaw slackening. I'm sure we make quite the picture: me with my ass peeking out from under my baby-blue linen jacket, matching slacks bunched around my knees, and Wednesday bent over the sink with her head crammed against the mirror, ass up and bouncing perkily on my cock. *God damn, does her ass ever bounce.* My eyes flick over her pink puckered asshole.

Twisting to see who I'm talking to, Wednesday realizes we have an audience. Gasping, she tries to push down her skirt and shove her tits back into the crop top. Her desperate attempt to hold on to some false modesty is cute.

"Oh my fuckin god, get out!" she screeches. *Could be me, or the parachute pants guy, or both.* I don't stop. He ducks into the nearest stall. *Must have been him.*

Her pussy squeezes my cock as she squirms around, trying to clothe herself. The pressure in my groin grows tight. I keep pounding the shit out of her, grunting with every thrust.

"Dude, for real?" she snaps.

I ignore her. My orgasm sharpens and crests, spilling me over the edge. Wrapping my arm around her waist, she rocks back on her black platform boots as my cock slips in one last time and explodes like a defective pressure cooker. Waves of bliss wash over me so intensely, my teeth sink into my bottom lip. I brace us against the vanity as my knees threaten to give out.

I moan into her hair, and my cock throbs and twitches as surges of pleasure steal over my mind. Her fuckhole wrings every last drop of cum from my balls. As I pull out, the condom sags with my hot spunk.

"Are you fuckin kidding me?" Wednesday yells. When she twists around, her nails come in contact with my face; fire burns across my cheek. I stumble back, panting from my orgasm and chuckling. My heart beats heavily as I enjoy the afterglow of a solid squirt. *I'll give it to her—fucking on the sink was hot.*

Blood smears on my fingers as I wipe the scratch on my face. As I prop my back against a peeling blue stall, my dick kicks a few more times as I pull off the condom. A line of cum drips from my tip and plops onto the dirty floor. *Oops.*

"Why didn't you fucking stop?" she says, yanking her clothes back into place.

"You're the one who wanted to fuck in a busy public bathroom." Mimicking her high-pitched voice, I mock, "I love the thrill. Come on, baby, let's do something risky." Settling my pants back on my hips, I tuck in my cock and zip. Remnants of my climax cause my muscles to twitch. Thirst dominates my dry mouth, and I scan the dirty bathroom for the beer I had earlier. "At least I offered the back seat of my car."

I spy the dark amber bottle; a frothy puddle has formed underneath the tipped-over beer. *Dammit.* I swipe it up and chug the contents. A square, hard box in my pocket stabs my thigh. *Hell, yes, come to Daddy.* I drag out the pack of smokes and light one up. Inhaling deeply, I glance across the space between us. "You want one?"

She makes a disgusted sound. "You're a fucking pig." Wadding up white paper napkins from the dispenser, she shoves them up her skirt and between her legs.

"Well, Wednesday, say oink oink 'cause you're the one who wanted to get stabbed by my pork sword. I don't do buyer's remorse. Here's my info, in case you ever want a second helping." Reaching into my pants, I toss my business card at her. It lands at her feet.

Damp napkins pelt me and tumble to the floor, bright red smears across a few of them. A pang of remorse rolls through me. *She did say harder, though.*

"You're disgusting," she seethes. "I would rather die than let you fuck me again."

"I'm confused. So, you do or don't want to fuck again, 'cause I know you're into that slit-my-wrist shit, anyway."

"You'll regret this." A smile that's all teeth flares my way. Her middle finger curls up as she storms past me, purple lowlights flashing. Yanking the door open, she vanishes into a sea of black-clad people—green and yellow neon lasers beam over the throng like sunlight streaking through black clouds. The heavy door thuds behind her, barely silencing the demonic-sounding metal thumping in the other room.

Well, that's a bummer. I shrug off the pang of disappointment and remind myself that where there is one crazy woman, there are bound to be others. Musical screams cover the sound of my footsteps as I step over the pearl of cum and approach the sink. Gunk sticks to the silver hot-water knob. My nose crinkles. When I turn the handle, it sprays sideways and is an unwelcoming cold. My dick shrivels. I don't love the prospect of cleaning my cock in glacier water, but it might calm my aching balls. Before I can give my love gun a good wash and polish, one of the blue stall doors creaks open behind me, revealing the spike-headed dipshit.

"That was intense, man. Thought she was gonna eat your face off."

Eyeing dipshit in the mirror, I talk around my cig. "You don't have much experience with angry women, do you?"

Hot ash drops off the cherry, landing on the sink's rim.

"I'm gay."

I pause for a moment, contemplating. "How does being a gay man fare in this scene?"

He eyes me back. "It's okay, just have to stay away from the skinheads. You into men as well?"

Shocked laughter tumbles from my lips, my cig too. It lands in the wet sink, hissing as it goes out. If I were into men, the guy behind me wouldn't cut it. "I'll explain this in your language, spike head. I'm only into stabbing the gash."

Dipshit nods, but still checks out my ass. Rolling my eyes, I re-zip. He's seen enough of my cock for one evening. I abandon the shitty bathroom.

Gutted concrete floors and walls rise up all around me, and a lofty ceiling of exposed industrial bones arches overhead. Music—loud enough to please the dark metal gods—assails me the second I leave the bathroom.

Neon strobes flare, causing my eyes to dilate. Once I adjust to the flashing, I see a mass of stringy black hair whipping around to the music, like some kind of possessed hair monster. *Cousin Itt has joined the party*. Scantily clad women, all sporting some version of strappy black clothing, mill around, much to my delight. *The night is still young.*

Rings of glowing blue, pink, green, and yellow wrap around necks and wrists, dotting the crowd. Directly across the mosh pit of hair is Wednesday. Tears mixed with black eyeliner streak down her pale face. Hands flapping in irritation, she gestures toward the bathroom and back to the dudes in dark clothing that stand in front of her. Brows furrowed in a tight glare, one guy cracks his knuckles and nudges the other to follow him. *Shit.*

Slinking into the crowd, I bop along as they make their way over. Knowing I stand out with my slacks and a button-down, a spot of soft summer blue in a sea of black, I keep my eyes on the guys as I make my way to the stairs.

One guy in particular, the leader of the other two, is muscular. Prison thick, my mind supplies. As big guy turns to speak to his buddy, I catch a glimpse of a skull tattooed on his neck. Above it sits another tattoo, dead on the back of his shaved head—a swastika.

Yeah, it's time to go. Not that I'm afraid of a fight, just an unfair one. With a bunch of Nazis in a heavy metal club. Found in the depths of an old meat processing plant. *It just sounds like a bad idea, and it's probably best if I turn in, anyway.*

Industrial grated steps loom up and out of the darkened dance floor, their nonslip yellow and black safety tape peeling off in chunks. What remains reads, "Watch your step." I take them two at a time, heading for the parking lot.

Strips of plastic sheeting part and flap around me. Old sheetrock dust crunches under my feet as I exit through a battered hallway covered in graffiti. Cigarette smoke, cooking plastic, and stank, fishy air from the harbor assail my nose as I step outside. A few people mill around close to the entrance, if you can call it that. Without proper overhead lamps, the parking lot is pitch black except for the far-off lights from the smokestacks of the industrial yard.

A hand lands on my shoulder.

Fuck.

"Hey, man, you got a smoke?"

I fully expect to be in the grasp of two skinheads when I turn around. Instead, it's a rail-thin, tweaked-out scruffy guy who sways in the breeze, looking at me all hopeful-like. But behind him, the big nazi from the dance floor stalks down the hallway, joined by a couple of men. Unfortunately, we make eye contact, and my future battered face reflects in his vision. *Fuck.*

Running makes me look guilty; not running could make me dead.

I make like lightning and bolt into the darkened parking lot. Ramming my hand into my pants pocket, I rip out my keys. Footfalls slap against the pavement close behind me. The hair stands on the back of my neck. Their lack of threats or insults adds to my sense of panic. Average Joes around here usually do some kind of chest-bumping before the blows start. These fucking guys, with their quiet seriousness and deliberate purpose, are fucking unnerving.

Shoving my keys into the door, I manage to get it open and throw myself in, only to be dragged back by a set of hands.

"Motherfucker!" My back rakes across the seat buckle as I roll over and kick out, my tan loafers connecting. A grunt later and I'm free. I slam the door shut, pressing down on the manual lock. Glass cracks next to my face as a fist smashes into it. *Holy fuck, my car. My fucking baby!* Voices and terse cursing come from a couple of the guys—nothing I can make out. I shove the keys in the ignition. Someone punches the window again, the crack spiderwebbing out. "Fucking hell, who are these guys?" I grind out from between my teeth.

The engine roars to life, and I tear out of the parking lot. The big guy slams his hands down on the hood of my car as he tucks and rolls, narrowly missing being splattered on my grill. Glancing in the mirror, I see his dark silhouette join his buddies. I can feel their eyes watching me drive away. They shrink in the fading red taillights of my Trans Am.

Nervous laughter bubbles up from my chest. *God damn. Too close. Maybe a bit too spicy for a Tuesday night.*

Smoke curls around my fingers as I light up again and inhale deeply. A cloud of smoke rolls out as I expel some of my nervous energy. Exiting the industrial parkway, I wind the Trans Am through back streets, making sure I'm not being followed. After several minutes of empty highway, I relax. Music pours through the stereo, and my favorite song, "Sex, Drugs, Etc." by Beach Weather, pops up in my playlist.

Singing along, I take the scenic route home. My favorite highway back into town is a curving road down a dark and, hopefully, empty coastline. Nighttime beach drives have always refreshed my spirit ever since I jacked my first car at thirteen and took it careening down this very highway. A smile rolls across my lips at the memory of my youthful wildness.

I roll down my cracked window, and a cool, salty ocean breeze kisses my face and pushes back my hair. The wind catches the ash as I flick it off my cig, making the cherry grow bright. I inhale deeply, letting the melody and movement of the car wash away the night. Neon signs streak by like the tails of falling stars. Their light glints off the waxy shine of the hood.

Sailing along sandy beaches, I can hear the waves crash against the shore. Endless water and endless night sky stretch out alongside me—a black chasm of a mouth ready to swallow me. If not for the moon and the stars, I wouldn't be able to tell which is which, and a part of me loves that. A part of me wants to be swallowed. To get lost in the riptides. My eyes narrow at the ocean and the night. *Bring me the chaos. Double dog dare you.*

Sad Boy in a Used Furniture Store

LUKE

The bright-yellow neon sign of *Luke's Used Furniture and Mattress Emporium* beckons in the dark. Lightning flickers off in the distance as I roll into the parking lot. Music blaring, I drive down the one-car lane that runs the store length and park next to the back entrance. The large, square red-brick store is lined with white square exterior flood lights that jut off the building. An assortment of insects flutters around, desperate to stay in the light and away from predators that hunt at night.

Since Luke's doesn't exactly sit on the safe side of town, I try to keep it well-lit and scan my surroundings before getting out. Sometimes, I'm like those bugs sticking to the lights. I know what the darkness holds; I used to thrive in it. Live for it. Now, I enjoy taking a stroll through the shadows before scurrying back. It's taken me years and several torn wings to flutter my own way out. *Well, not all the way out.*

Standing with my car door propped open, I quietly study the building next to my store. My workshop, a long, narrow white concrete building, sits on the other side of the lane. I check it for signs of forced entry. Under the floodlights, the silver lock and chain appear untouched. *Good.*

Thunder rumbles overhead; the Southern humidity momentarily dissipates as the smell of salt water and rain lightly fills the air. My hair ruffles in the cooling storm winds as I cross the empty back lot.

I double-bolt the entry and lower the metal bar into its bracket. Keys clatter and scrape sharply in the dark as I toss them onto the table in what was once an employee break room.

A cracking, sticky sound followed by the rattle of glass condiments tucked into the fridge door fills the quiet space as I snag two beers. Watery warm light spills into the inadequate kitchen, overlapping the light from the hallway and illuminating the sparsity of food and decor. The old, grayish-flecked floor tile clashes against the simple black cabinets and white laminate countertops. Every time I'm in here, it reminds me to find some fucking motivation to remodel the depressing space.

Knocking out beer number one, I belch and lean against the wall. In the trash, the dead soldier goes, crashing down on all the others. I wince at the harsh sound—while unwelcome and grating, the noise is preferable to the hush that follows. Stillness and silence rush in to greet me in the semidarkness.

The clock in the hallway ticks.

The fridge next to me hums.

Rolling my shoulder blades and neck, I stomp out onto the open show floor and connect my phone to the store's Bluetooth speakers. "Little Deaths" by Sir Sly serenades into the hollow space under my tall commercial ceilings, soothing my jagged edges. The smell of furniture polish, cleaner, and old wood brings familiarity and comfort.

Setting down my phone, I let my feet carry me across the worn, blue-carpeted pathway that meanders through the sets of used living room furniture; each set is from a different decade, designed in dissimilar fashion and covered in murky shadows, muting their fabric color. There is no cohesiveness.

Used washers, dryers, and other appliances I've bolted back together sit crisp and white toward the front of Luke's. A yellow, murky hue from the lot filters through the floor-to-ceiling glass and mixes with luminescent blue lines that square off the windows on either side of the storefront. It's too *still* in here. I miss the hum of customers and, not for the first time, consider staying open twenty-four seven. If not for my need to empty my balls regularly, I'd give it the good old college try.

As I walk the narrow pathways, my eyes snag on the fake showroom kitchens that loom in the dimness. They no longer look warm or inviting, and a kitchen should be both. A hoppy, malty flavor lingers in my mouth, turning twangy and overpowering. I toss back some of the warming beer, refreshing the taste. *If I had a girlfriend, going out wouldn't be an issue, nor would the silence. Too bad things went the way they did with Wednesday.* I stop before the large windows.

Vacated storefronts face and flank me across a dead corner parking lot. Mist dampens the asphalt and blurs the black wording on the sign, filtering the world in a grainy haze. Droplets form and slide down the large windows, distorting the colors and lights of the occasional car that zooms down the street. My finger presses against the cool glass and follows the trek of one. Empty seconds tick by.

Fuck this. I'll just go to sleep.

The blue-neon strip lighting flickers, catching my eye. It pops and falters for a moment before flashing to life. My brows pull down, and my mood darkens; I should have checked it better before I ushered the repairman out.

Fucking asshole didn't even fix it all the way. My lungs expand in a deep sigh as I rub my hand down my face. That's what I get, hiring people from internet classifieds for cheap. Irritation crawls over my skin and gnaws at my insides, causing me to twitch. He had been sketchy from the beginning, and I know sketchy. I will have to retrieve a refund, plus a little extra for wasting my time.

With the flip of a switch, Luke's descends into deeper shadows as the glowing blue lines shut off. Navigating toward the back of the store, I stew over the money and energy it will take to resolve this lighting issue. I love my neon. Polishing off the beer, I elbow open my previous office—now bedroom—door.

The small practical room doesn't bring much joy. Shoved against the wall, a rumpled, full-sized bed with tannish sheets sits unmade. My charcoal comforter sags, half off the bed and pooling onto the floor. I leave it there. Overhead, the fan clicks and circulates stale air.

Kicking my classic loafers off, I throw my suit jacket onto the roller racks, where what's left of my clothing hangs. As I set it down, the empty beer bottle thumps on the small brown desk beside the bed. I don't undress fully, like most nights. Instead, I flop down and roll over. Lumpy pillows crook my neck at an awkward angle; I punch and elbow them into place.

An annoying itch flares to life on my ball sack. *Shit, I forgot to wash junior.* I stare at the ceiling fan, contemplating. Music from my phone plays gently in the background, lulling me to relax. I give my nutsack a quick pinch and the itch fades. *I'm already comfortable. I'll do it in the morning.*

The pitter-patter of gentle rain, soft music, and the clicking of my fan all meld together in a symphony of noise loud enough to block out the straying lonely thoughts. Finally, my body relaxes as I slip off into sweet dreams.

Meet Cute? Meet Not So Cute, Actually

LUKE

A n out-of-place squeak pricks at my unconsciousness.

Another bump and the soft rattling of glass shoots awareness, sharp like electricity, along my skin. Adrenaline dumps into my bloodstream. My mind jerks, fully awake now.

In one fluid movement, I'm up off the unkempt bed. My desk drawer glides open on smooth rollers, and I grasp my handgun, pulling it from the dark recesses. Trying to peer down the dark hallway and reach for my phone simultaneously, my hand slaps down on an empty desk corner where my phone should be. The untethered charging cable slips from the desk. *Fuck me.* My phone is on the show floor, and the music isn't playing. *Definitely dead.* I snag my burner phone from in between the mattresses.

My ears strain for any sound coming from the darkness beyond my bedroom. Rain hammers the pavement outside.

It's the skinheads from the bar. They're the only ones I've pissed off. Recently. *And my stupid ass left a business card behind.* My heart hammers against my ribcage. Forcing a quiet breath into my lungs, I extend the hefty

Glock out in front of me. Silently, I step out of the room. The hallway's typical cream-colored walls appear gray in the shadows, creating a darkness I hope conceals me.

A heavy, wet slap freezes me in the hallway entry, gun at the ready. A shaky breath escapes my lips as my adrenaline spikes, constricting my chest.

Rumbling fills the air as thunderbolts flash outside, temporarily illuminating the space. The strikes create a strobe effect, distorting my vision; I wish I hadn't turned off all the lights last night.

A loud whack and the jarring noise of wood furniture scraping against tile sounds off in the kitchen section, the only part of the show floor with tile. *How the hell did they get in?* Bolted and reinforced, the back door is inaccessible. The front dings when anyone enters. *Who are these fucking guys? SEAL Team Six? For fuck's sake.*

A string of curses in a soft feminine voice followed by, "Ouch. Ouch. Stupid table," leaves me less concerned but more curious. I listen for a response and am surprised when no one shushes the woman. Footsteps pad across the fake kitchen floors and again, the sound of table legs scraping fills the air.

"There. Now, you won't trip me anymore." Her voice carries on the high ceilings. My brows pull down.

Motionless, I squint into the darkness, as if narrowing my eyes will heighten my hearing. *Is she really alone?*

The sounds of a zipper and the unmistakable thud of shoes hitting the floor reach my ears. The woman hums. Loudly.

Whoever she is, she doesn't make a habit of breaking and entering. The adrenaline pumping through my body slows; I suspect the situation is less problematic than I initially thought. *Still, she's trespassing, and Luke's is all I have left.* Gun drawn, I step out into the hallway and flick on the lights, pointing it toward the noise.

My gun slowly lowers as I take in the unexpected sight before me.

The woman freezes in place as she sits on one of my blue paisley-printed mattresses for sale, her eyes wide with fear.

And not just a regular woman, but a half-naked woman. A half-naked, soaking wet woman who has perfect tits kissed with dark nipples. *Ohhhh. I'm gonna call her tits.*

She lets loose a shocked scream so blood-curdling, all the hairs stand up on my neck. My eyebrows fly into my hairline. An overwhelming primal need to turn around skitters down my body; I spin and check if anything worse than me is back there. When nothing jumps out, I swivel back just in time to catch a glimpse of her wet blonde hair disappearing into the mock kitchen layouts. I snort. *Hmmm, someone wants to play hide and get fucked.*

I stay alert, my bare feet slipping silently across the carpeted mattress section. An upended, wet black duffle sits at the foot of the blue paisley bed next to a dainty, soiled, baby-blue handbag with a silver chain—a black trash bag sags on the floor, holes gaping in the plastic. I'm amazed it still holds anything. I take in the contents—balled-up, wrinkled clothes, makeup with labels half rubbed off, pens, a torn notebook, loose change, a hair curler thing, a mixture of feminine basics—all of it makes me stop short. I've seen this before.

Images surface of my black duffle bag and skimpy trash bags filled with clothes too small for my growing body. All of it being forced into the trunk of yet another social worker's car. It's an experience and memory I deeply loathe—one that sharply reminds me of my childhood struggles. Unfortunately, for some people, life begins with a black bag and ends with one, too. And the places they visit in between aren't much better: street corners, truck stops, their dealer's house, and, in this case, a used-furniture store.

Eyeing the sopping wet shirt and bra on the tiled floor, I mentally shake myself and shove down all that bullshit. Not every day a man wakes up to a half-naked woman just getting undressed in his place of business. *I mean, maybe if he owned a lingerie shop. Hey, that's an idea.*

Chuckling to myself, I call out into the quiet, "C'mon out, tits. I'm armed, and *clearly,* you're not. What are you going to do, huh? Flash me to death?" My laughter carries out onto the show floor.

Steady rain falls on my roof, punctuated by the occasional clap of thunder. My gaze sweeps the hushed store, and I hunt for movement. The little lady tucked herself out of sight nicely. Those full coconuts come to mind, along with a delicious idea that makes a smile creep across my face. I adjust the half-mast red flag in my pants.

"Listen, tits. If you make me chase you, tonight will be harder on you than it already is".

"I didn't mean to." Her hoarse voice floats from somewhere ahead.

My eyes roll to the ceiling in disbelief as I let out a derisive snort. *Yeah, okay. Sure, she broke in accidentally.* As I tap the barrel of the Glock against my thigh, her words loop in my head; underneath the rasp of fear is a breathy youthfulness. That lines up with the perfect tits. Perhaps honey's better than vinegar, especially if she's younger. *Bring out the beating stick too soon, they never forget you have it.*

"Now, we both know that's a lie. But it's okay; I'm not mad. You startled me. Are you hurt? I can help."

Tits doesn't answer me.

Impatience makes me abandon the advantage of surveying the entire store. My feet pad softly across the chilled white tiles in the mock kitchens. Elevated cabinets and right-angle displays create a disorienting atmosphere; thankfully, Luke's isn't large enough to accommodate many of them. She is here, somewhere.

Quietly, I nudge open a sink cabinet large enough for a woman with my foot. Nothing. *Damn it.* Letting the door fall shut on soft-close hinges, I straighten. "If you're not hurt, why did you break in? I deposit all the money at the end of the night, so there isn't any cash here." That's a lie. I keep a lot of money here, although most of it isn't mine. I round the corner of one of the kitchens, glancing both ways. "Unless you were planning to drag a couch out the front door or steal a microwave, I can't imagine your plans."

"I just wanted to sleep inside. Maybe find something to eat. I'm sorry. Please, I'll leave." Tits' small soft voice carries to me, twisting up parts of me I'd rather she not. She does actually sound apologetic. *Fuck, I really wish she hadn't answered like that; it makes me feel bad for pointing a gun at her face.* A strong urge to put the gun away runs over me, but past experiences have taught me better.

Moving toward her voice, I ask, "How did you get in?"

She sighs faintly. "The window in one of the bathrooms was propped open. Please don't call the police. I'm sorry. You'll never see me again."

I'm a fucking idiot. Mentally, I kick myself for propping it open after a hurried joint in the bathroom before I hit the club. I step into a squared-off display space; four kitchens face each other. Rich colors and ornate trim styles brush up against lighter and simpler options. She is sitting behind a turquoise-washed wooden kitchen island. The legs of the table frame part of her slim, naked back. Her ribs protrude gently under tanned skin with each breath, giving her a slightly underfed look.

Stepping up to the table, I lean forward and tap the barrel of my gun on the countertop. Tits flinches at the sound, hunching in on herself. Slowly, her face turns and tips up toward me as she tucks a damp curl behind her ear.

Eyes the color of the coast during a hurricane search my face in fear. Her curls hang limp and frizzy down to her collarbones and share the same grayish-tan color that sand gets when wet. *She's a dirty blonde. My favorite type.* Her skin has a slight caramel color, enough that I can see the outline of bikini straps from a previous tan.

My cock twitches.

"Anyone ever told you that you look like the beach?"

I love the beach.

She shakes her head, eyes brimming with alarm. "No?"

I smirk.

If the sea had been given legs and an ass, she'd be the temptress before me. My hands itch to glide over her shoulders. I would pay good money to brush my fingers over the delicate skin on her face and wrap her curls around my fingertips. An obsessive desire hits me; it ripples deeply and sinks into my core. *Damn, it's been a while since I felt greedy over a woman.*

"Please, I'll leave." she offers.

My brows draw down at the thought that she wants to leave. *Maybe she has people?*

No, if she did, she wouldn't be here. No one is looking for her, and no one had better be.

I drag the gun across the countertop. "Stand up."

"Can I have my shirt, please?" There is an unexpected desperation to her tone, causing me to catch what I didn't before; fear, exhaustion, and anger all war across her features. It makes my musings recede. *Gentle. Remember the honey.*

I let the Glock point to the floor, and a panty-dropping smile flows across my lips. With a flick of my empty hand, I motion toward the mattress section. "Of course."

She stares at me expectantly. "Will you turn around?"

My eyes snap down to where her arms cup her voluptuous coconuts. "Definitely not."

A spark of anger alights in her eyes as she watches me check her out. When she's scowling up at me, an agitated breath huffs from her lips as she rises. Her arms band tighter around her ample breasts, squishing them together; soft roundness peeks above and below her forearms as she brushes past me, aiming toward the beds.

I can't help but admire the courage it takes to walk past me. She isn't giving in to hysteria despite being half-naked and alone with an armed stranger—*tough lady.*

Curious as to how long this bravado will hold out, I snag her elbow, closing the distance between us. Alarm floods her face as I trail my fingers across soft, vulnerable skin. My cock hardens in my baby-blue slacks.

Her face tilts away from me. Wary eyes clash with mine. "What are you doing?"

"Don't worry, sugar. I'm not going to fuck you unless you want me to." A smile plays on my lips and I wink. A snarl replaces the alarm on her face—*she's definitely a fighter.*

Thunder booms across the night sky, and the overhead lights flicker before steadying. "It's a rough night, no place for a thing like you," I observe out the front windows. My fingers skirt up to her shoulder, tracing delicate collarbones. She shrugs me off and takes a step backward, rage burning in her eyes. *Well, flirting isn't working. It might have something to do with the Glock; I should've put it up.*

Sighing, I know a lost cause when I see one—*a different approach then.* I relent, letting her go. I tuck the gun under the belt of my slacks and step away, holding up my empty hands. "Okay, sugar, this is how it is. You broke into my shop, interrupted my night, and then dared to ask me not to call the police. For all that hassle, I need a picture of you so I don't forget your face."

A delicate frown dents her forehead. "You have cameras; I saw them outside."

"And yet you still broke in? Baby, I'll have to teach you how to be a better burglar," I say, deflecting away from the fact that I do have cameras both in and outside of Luke's. Which I plan to use later to watch her get undressed. But, for now, that obsessive desire is demanding pictures.

She eyes the carpet and shrugs defensively. "I covered my face. I'm not a complete idiot. You're the idiot touching some strange girl you don't know. I might be diseased." She stares me down.

Laughter bursts out of my chest. "Honey, don't call the man with a gun an idiot; that's how you get shot."

Her eyes narrow, and she glances around for a way out. I can't tell if she is dumb for arguing with me while she's half-naked or brilliant. Between the lack of sleep and her sexy form, I'm having issues focusing on being angry. I shake my head. *Fuck, if I'm not a sucker for a hot mess.*

"The cameras aren't working. C'mon, a picture is such a small price to keep you out of trouble, don't you think?" I argue.

Pulling my burner from my pocket, I wave it in her direction and swipe to the camera.

"Right now? Can't I put on a shirt first?" she snaps, edging toward the mattresses.

We lock eyes and she freezes. "It's such a small price, one quick photo. Barely a second of your time."

She heaves a sigh and shoots me a pissed-off look. Ballsy, given her predicament, but I'll let it stand. She turns to face me as one of her middle fingers uncurls from her folded arms and flips me the bird.

I bite back laughter. *Oh, she's going to love this next part.* I swipe past photo to video.

Reaching between us, I tap her arm and push down, repeating, "It really is such a small price."

Her jaw drops as she catches my meaning. "Seriously?"

I shrug and toss her a playful grin with a flash of teeth. "For a cop-free evening, one picture won't hurt. Plus, I've already seen them. It's not like I'm asking to see anything else." *For now.*

Her guarded eyes rake over me, and an energetic thrill slips into my skin flute when she shakes her head and drops her arms. A muttered, "Whatever," falls from her lips; at the same time, those beautiful bouncers fall away from each other. She refuses to look at me, choosing to stare off across the store. "Let's just hurry up."

I don't hurry up. Instead, I take my time and drink her in, letting the camera roam over her body. Fuck, I was right. Her tits are beautiful. Perfectly bottom-heavy with tight nipples that would look best in my mouth. My dick swells in my pants.

When I brush my knuckle over her satin nipple, the warmth of her soft skin makes my cock throb painfully. Her head whips back to me, an incredulous look of rage widening her eyes.

I narrowly avoid the open-handed slap.

The force of that hit would have hurt.

"You didn't say touching, you douche!" She swats at my dodging frame and sprints away from me toward her clothes. Chuckling, I shove my phone into my back pocket and follow. *She gets feisty when cornered. It's cute.*

Tits yanks a navy-blue tank top down over her lovely skin, grabs the black duffel bag, and shovels in items haphazardly. Parking my ass on the bed opposite her, I pitch an offer. "Listen, why don't you stay awhile? I own this place. We can cut a deal. No need to run off. Plus, it's raining cats and dogs out there."

Her notebook and makeup tumble out of the half-full bag she throws on the bed. She pins me with a glare. *Boy, if looks could kill, I'd be pushing up daisies.* Her mouth opens, shuts, and opens again. Each time the words fail, she grows increasingly agitated. Finally, she pops off, "Why the fuck would I agree to that after you felt me up?"

Good point. Offering a reassuring smile, I barter, "Here me out. I won't touch you again unless you agree to it. You have my word."

Folding her arms across her chest, she snorts and shoots daggers at me.

"Think about it before your temper gets in the way of money and a safe place to sleep," I coax, nodding to her meager belongings. "Looks like you could use a break and some luck. That's what I'm offering. At least have a midnight snack with me." I gesture to all the beds on display. "Then, if you want, you can sleep in any bed out here. *Alone.* And, in the morning, you can start working for me."

"I'm not going to fuck you for a bed."

I half sigh, half laugh and rub my hand down my face. "Now, didn't I just say I wasn't going to fuck you without your permission? I'm talking cash. Cash for your hours worked and any extra jobs you do for me."

Her eyes narrow. "Real cash?"

"As opposed to fake cash? Yes, real cash. You got a driver's license on you?"

Pursing her lips, she shakes her head.

"Any ID at all?"

"No."

I sigh and glance around. "Okay, well, it will be contract labor. I'll figure it out. "

"Are you seriously offering me a job after I broke in? You pointed a gun at me and touched..." I raise my eyebrows as she trails off, a faint blush staining her face.

I hold up a hand. "Hey, you came into my space, fucked with my shit, and helped yourself to things that weren't yours. I just did the same. We're even steven now." I pause, giving that one time to marinate. "Plus, why wouldn't I offer you a job? You're in a tough spot; you need money. I need a worker, and I have money. It's a win-win."

She considers quietly, her pert mouth twisting. "I guess that's fair. I did plan on taking some things." She flushes and unfolds her arms. "And all that... earlier *business* is done?" She arches one eyebrow my way. "No cops? No more gun waving?"

"Of course, sugar. A fresh start." Offering her my best grin, I motion for her to follow me to the back. "Let's talk about it over some food while I put this up." I wave the Glock around cheerily now that tits seems somewhat convinced to stay.

She hesitates, probably still determining if she should follow some random gun-waving man into the back of his store, and truth be told, she shouldn't. But the almighty dollar is a strong hook for most people, especially a down-on-their-luck drifter.

I don't judge her desperation as her feet whisper across the floor and follow me down the hallway.

Lukewarm Noodles

LUKE

Fluorescent overhead lights flood the functional kitchen. The Glock thuds against the countertop as I set it down and root around in the cabinets, snagging a pack of ramen and some crackers. Tits fills the black metal-framed doorway and pauses. The space between my shoulders itches, and I'm unsure if she is assessing me or the gun. I usually don't mind a voyeur, but the night's events have me on edge.

Forcing a deep breath, I let the tension seep from my body. I lace my tone with faux familiarity and charm. "What's your name, sugar? Bet it's something nice to match that pretty face. Can I guess? How about Diamond? Cherry? Oh, I know, Blossom? Candy?"

"Those are stripper names," she retorts flatly.

I toss her an unwrapped cup of ramen, and she snatches it from the air. I motion toward the sink. "Well, now, that's unfair to every genuine Cherry or Barbie I've ever met. But I suppose I have known a few strippers in my time."

"Apparently, not very well if all you know are their stage names."

Snarky ass woman.

My lips purse as I smother my laughter. She crosses the gray-flecked tile and turns on the arching silver tap. Tipping my head to the side, I check her out from behind as she waits for the water to get hot. Even in her slender state, my new girl is curvy. *If I can get about twenty pounds on her, she will have an ass that can't quit.*

"Microwave is over there." I nod once she turns the tap off.

Her head follows the motion. "I saw it. You're not supposed to microwave Styrofoam."

Tipping my head back, I narrow my eyes at her. "Says who?"

She rolls the cup in her hands and points to the words "Do Not Microwave" printed in bold letters down the side. Sucking my teeth, I snort. "Never seen that before. Must be new."

She glances around before walking over to the table. "You don't have much going on in here." A soft clicking fills the air, and I glance down. Muddy colors stain her wet Converse and flared-bottom jeans. With each step, the soggy shoestrings dance on the tiles, the worn fabric pulling away from the soles, revealing a pinky toe tipped in chipped blue polish.

"Yeah, well, I don't need much. I'll be back."

Crossing the blue-carpeted hallway, I refuse to think of her shoes or the wads of clothes in the other room. I swallow deeply. Placing the Glock's heavy weight into the wooden desk drawer, I let out a sigh. Post-adrenaline fatigue washes over me, as well as gratitude that I didn't find a show floor full of neo-Nazis. *We all have to go sometime, but damn, not like that. Not over a quick fuck in a bathroom.*

My eyes snag on my reflection in the mirror and cringe. My dark hair flips in different directions, its natural waves begging to take over. What's truly tragic is how my mustache isn't lying right and the heavy five o'clock shadow visible beneath the dark circles that grace my eyes. The shirt and pants I passed out in are incredibly wrinkled. *I probably smell like booze and*

Wednesday's pussy, too. Fuck, it's no wonder she screamed.

"Are you going to microwave those noodles or not?" I call from the bedroom office. Slipping into a pair of black men's lounge pants, I toss around the idea of going without a shirt. I've seen her topless. Nipple for nipple is fair, but it might be over the top for tonight. I opt for a light-blue shirt, drag a brush through my hair, and fix my mustache. Much better.

"Thanks, but no thanks. I'd rather not get cancer."

"You're not getting cancer from a single cup of noodles, for fuck's sake." I grab a few smaller shirts from the back of the cheap plastic roller racks, a couple of pairs of socks, and a pair of stretchy gym shorts. A fresh pack of smokes crinkles as I shove it into my pocket.

"Why does it matter if the noodles are hot or not? You're not the one eating them," she calls back across the hallway.

My eyes lift to the ceiling as I shake my head. "Fine, have it your way. Lukewarm noodles it is." *I can give her my lukewarm noodle if she is going to insist.* Chuckling, I cross the hallway back into the kitchen.

She sits at the white plastic folding table, stirring the contents of the Styrofoam cup, the package of crackers already open. Her guarded eyes meet mine. "What's so funny?"

"Hmmm? Oh, nothing. Here." I lay down the clothing, patting the top of the pile. "Something for you to sleep in. These should be long on you. It gets cold on the show floor."

She looks at the clothes suspiciously before reaching out and fingering the fabric. "They're very soft."

"Yeah, I'm not into cheap fabrics. Too scratchy."

Her gaze dips to the noodles as her hands fall into her lap. "Thank you for not shooting me. Also, for not calling the police and for the food." Her head tips a little as she looks at the solid-colored Ts. "The clothes, too. Sorry I was a bitch earlier. You didn't... uh... catch me at my best." She offers me a lopsided smile in what I'm assuming to be a feeble attempt at a joke. But I'll be damned if it isn't the saddest half-smile I've ever seen.

My finger taps on the table. "One, I don't care for the word bitch. So don't call yourself that. Two, no need to apologize. No one is at their best at two am or when they're breaking in. Or when they're sneaking around the place with a gun. Three, are you ever going to tell me your name?"

"Why don't you like 'bitch'?"

A prickling sensation rushes along my body as she skips over my question, and my lungs expand as I dig deep for patience. I release the tension. Again. *Boy, we aren't getting anywhere fast.* "I've met bitches, and you don't strike me as one." *Yet.* "Don't get distracted. What. Is. Your. Name?"

She squirms in her chair, rocking side to side. "Carmella."

I snort. "Who has a stripper name now? Come on, tell me your real name."

"Carmella is not a stripper's name. It's my name."

"Carmella. Caramel. It's basically a step or two above Candy."

"It means garden or growth," she bites back, wrapping her hands around the noodles. "Not candy."

I lift my finger accusatorially. "You know, you're an argumentative little shit."

Her mouth drops open as her eyes narrow. "Me? You're the one insisting my name isn't my name."

I drop the topic, not willing to go 'round with her. My hopes for a cooperative and eager-to-please sales associate dwindle. Emotions roil in her narrowed, stormy eyes. Resting my forearms on the table, I spread my fingers across the chilly, gritty surface. Cool air from the overhead vent flows across my skin; I take a moment to let it soothe my heated annoyance.

"Okay." My lips curl up as I give her one of my most charming smiles. "How old are you?"

Carmella bites the inside of her cheek, eyes cutting to the door behind me. "Twenty-one."

"Yeah, if I were going to lie about my age, I'd be twenty-one, too," I quip.

Ashy-blonde brows pull down into a hostile glare. Arching an eyebrow, I wait. Carmella's jaw flexes as her arms fold across her chest, resulting in pronounced boobage. I do the polite thing and look without glancing down since we are business associates now.

"I'm twenty-one," she says steadily, holding my gaze.

"I see. You're really going to stick with that."

One small, sharp nod is all she gives me.

Sighing, I lean back in my chair and regard her, still without looking down.

My survey doesn't produce any clear answers. Carmella could be twenty-one. Youthful without being a young teen. Stubborn and temperamental. It could stem from being experienced enough not to be intimated. She could naturally be a hardheaded ass. It's difficult to tell with drifters. What she may have seen or know of the world could translate into this confidence, or she could be stupidly naïve. I need more information. It's unfortunate that she doesn't like to be questioned. We have that in common.

Silence fills the room, and a fresh cig calls my name.

The pack rustles as I dig it out of my pocket. Grabbing the plastic tab, I spin it around the small box, unwrapping the clear covering and crumpling it in my fist. The crinkling is violent in the quiet that sits between us.

Flipping the box upside down, I thump it against the table several times, packing the smokes. Carmella's eyes slip around the room, landing on anything that isn't me. Her noodles must be cold by now, as the water in the sink doesn't get that hot. Brows lowered, I scoot to the edge of the plastic chair, lean into the table, and let my stare bear down on her. I stare hard, scrutinizing every detail. This time, I don't try to hide my visual exploration of her tits, noting how her navy tank top lays over her hardened nipples or how she breathes a little heavier under my gaze. Her back stiffens, and I smirk.

Darkened by the sun, her skin is a lovely light-golden caramel color. *I'm really starting to have a new appreciation for caramel.* Paler lines of skin hide under the navy straps of her shirt. Her full lips twist as she shakes her head, refusing to rise to my baiting. Her wavy, dingey-blonde baby hairs flutter with the movement before settling to frame her face. A dainty nose sits above her full lips, and with those gray-blue eyes, she reminds me of a beachy, trashy Marilyn Monroe. *Trailer-park hot.*

An overwhelming urge to have her stick out her tongue hits me. I want to see it. Hot, pink, and wet. Fuck, she's got a mouth made for licking porn theatre floors while some lame weirdo shoves his cock in her from behind. *Hopefully, I'm that lame weirdo. I'd watch her take it. Fuck, I'd record it. The noises I'd get her to make. Oh, the fucking noises.*

And yet, she ignores me.

Reaching between my legs, I adjust my raging hard on, staring her in the face. She doesn't even flinch. *Fucking nothing. God damn, I should teach her how to play poker. We could really clean house.*

Carmella openly studies the black rubber runner around the base of the wall. *Bet if I flashed her my joystick, that would get her attention.* Tap-tap-tap, my foot rapidly fires against the floor, vibrating the table and making the noodles slosh in her cup.

I'm a charming guy, and a good-looking one, too. It's why I have four ex-wives, but still, I'm not all charm. You'd think being six foot and having just pulled a gun on her not more than twenty minutes ago, she would be... sweeter. But here she sits, forcing us into silence.

I fucking hate silence.

Minutes tick by. The hum of the fridge fills the air. I'm counting the rise and fall of her chest. Every tick of that fucking clock in the other fucking room makes me feel as though I'm slowly being eaten alive by tiny fire ants. I bite the inside of my mouth, ripping off chunks of flesh, joining in on my internal destruction.

Carmella studies her chipped blue nail polish, scratching at the patches still clinging to pink beds. A tiny pile of sapphire-colored flakes stands out against the white table. When I cross my legs to slow down the vibrations, an itch forms in the middle of my back.

I'm slouched over, trying to itch the space in the middle of my back against the corner of the chair, when I notice Carmella frowning at my struggles. Her nose crinkles. *Oh, now she wants to pay attention to me.* She arches an unimpressed, golden, ashy brow. Rightening myself, I scowl at her.

Slapping my hands onto the pack of smokes, I scoop them up, flip open the lid, and push back the foil. Carmella's drying wavy hair slips down over her shoulders as she sighs at the cold noodles. Rolling the white and orange stick between my fingers, I place it between my lips. *Serves her right. She should have microwaved them instead of arguing.*

Dragging my trusty Zippo from my pocket, I rub my thumb over the familiar raised metal lettering that reads, "You want to flickel my pickle?" The worn image of a curved pickle graces the top of the metal lighter. I smile to myself. The damn thing has never ceased to make me laugh since I stole it from a gas station when I was sixteen. The old gal takes a couple of tries to start up, but I don't mind, and she finally catches.

Hopefully, a few comforting draws and a dose of nicotine will help calm down the tent I've been making in my pants. The flame dances from the air conditioning, and I cup my hand to steady it. The cig catches, burns, and I take a long pull.

Leaning forward, I blow secondhand smoke directly into her face.

She shoots me a murderous look and waves her hand, swirling the smoke away. A dreamy haze permeates the air around us.

"Was that really necessary?" she snaps.

"I'm tired of this Mexican standoff. Go microwave your fucking noodles."

She doesn't answer but instead picks up her spork and stabs at the ramen. Silence begins to leak back in, and minutes pass as we watch her savagely chop the flesh-colored cold noodles into little bits. Alarm and concern deflate my hard-on.

I'm still determining how I ended up in a deadlock with her when my mind flicks back to our earlier conversation. *Oh yeah, her age. Fuck it. Old enough.*

I fold. "Fine, have it your way. Your name is Carmella, and you are twenty-one. Are you happy?"

She shrugs. The little shit shrugs at me.

"Finish your noodles, damn," I snap. She grins into her soup before looking up at me.

"So, what's your name?"

I consider for a half second while hitting my cig. "I told you, it's Luke."

Her hair slips across her shoulder as she tips her head to the side, and a sweet mocking tone coats her words. "Is it really, though?"

We lock eyes over the noodles, her steely grays to my dark browns. *I don't know if I should choke her or kiss her.*

"Yes. It's. Luke." And while it might actually be Lucas, I prefer Luke. Lucas has a public record and several active lawsuits, and the internet makes hiding shit so complicated these days. *I don't want my new store pet looking me up, at least not before we get comfortable.*

"How old are you, Luke?"

"I'm thirty-four."

"Yeah, I would say that, too, if I looked as old as you."

We're fucking fighting now. "Well, you must want me to go ahead and call the police, huh?" Stabbing my cigarette into the black ashtray that sits on the corner of the table closest to the wall, I stand.

"No! It's just really annoying when people don't believe you, isn't it?" Angry eyes flash up at me.

"Yeah. Well, I apologize for not believing the stranger who talked around my questions. And broke into my business in the middle of the night."

Her face flushes, redness creeping down her cheeks and neck. "This isn't working. I'm going." She stands.

Grabbing her wrist, I drag us both back down into our seats and shake my head. She twists and yanks out of my grasp, coiling her arms up against her chest. Eyes narrowed, she pins me with yet another glare. I hold up my hands. *This is getting to be exhausting.*

"It's late, and we've established that neither of us is at our best," I say. "You can crash out on the show floor as long as all your things are put away before the customers come in. I don't need people knowing I'm letting drifters sleep on the beds they want to purchase. This isn't a shelter. Okay?"

Her slight wince cuts off my tirade. Gentling my voice, I ask, "Do you have any more questions for me?"

She scoops up the circular noodle cup paper lid, rolling it up like a burrito. *Apparently, I'm not the only one who fidgets.*

"If I don't like it, you'll pay me what I'm owed and I can leave tomorrow?"

"Yes."

"And if I do like it, what about tomorrow night?" Her voice is soft and breathy. She has to feel small for asking. Her eyes flick around the practical kitchen, landing on anything but me as she waits for my answer.

The greedy part of me is delighted that she doesn't seem to have anywhere else to go, but in that same breath, out crawls the desire to burn down every fucking home that ever made me and her feel unwanted and alone. Homes that became places I couldn't run to. I wonder if she has anywhere like that.

Carmella pulls in on herself, making her skinny form even more delicate. *Fuck, she reminds me of awful and beautiful things.* I shake off the thoughts that threaten to derail me, skipping over mental black holes. *This woman brings up too much emotion.* I would've thought her caving in on herself was blatant manipulation if it wasn't for the reluctance in her voice. That stubborn backbone she displayed earlier clearly demands she not show vulnerability, but needs sometimes outweigh pride. I'm too familiar with that as well. I take a drag and blow out the grief. *Fuck.*

It's alright if she doesn't have anywhere to go. She can find a home on this dick.

"You ever hear the saying cash, grass, or ass?" I ask. She nods, warily peeking up at me from her hunched frame. "Well, you already said no ass, and I'm not interested in whatever cheap grass you're carrying. So, I suggest making me some cash and earning a little for yourself. We'll see about tomorrow night."

"That's fair." Carmella tosses her hair back as the tension leaves her body. Her chest expands with a deep sigh, and she shoves the last two crackers into her mouth.

If she can show a little vulnerability, then so can I. "Please go microwave your noodles. Don't eat them cold. There's no reason you have to. There're mugs you can pour the soup into in the cabinet."

We are quiet for longer than I'm comfortable with. Carmella's eyes flick over my face, and it's my turn to study the practical kitchen as a knot settles in my chest. *I've got to do something about the decor in here.* I fiddle with my pack of smokes.

The knot becomes a lump in my throat; I swallow it painfully. *Fuck, Luke, get it together. You see worst shit than this all the time, for fuck's sake.* It's got to be the booze and crash from the adrenaline. I've been partying too much the past couple of nights... weeks... months. Not enough fucking sleep. It's never enough fucking sleep.

Carmella gets up, grabs a mug, and fills it before popping the cup into the microwave. The knot in my chest loosens, and I blow out a shaky breath.

My eyes wander over to the nearly empty cabinets she left standing open. I'll get us some food after the store closes tomorrow. The microwave beeps, and she drags the hot cup out, scraping the glass plate.

She glances over at me. "Thanks." I nod.

Carmella bundles the empty cracker and noodle cup together before tossing them basketball-style into the trash. They sink home.

"Not bad," I say coolly.

"I used to play in high school, mostly for fun."

"I was going to say, you're not tall."

She gives me a feisty smile. "Nope, but I was fast."

The mental image of her vanishing half-naked into the mock kitchens flashes through my mind. Rubbing my forehead, I chuckle. "Yeah, I guess you are."

"Comes in handy when I'm running from a seventies movie star with a loaded gun."

My brow furrows. "What?"

"You look like the guy with the fast car, the one with the bird on the front? He picks up the runaway bride and loves beer or alcohol or something." She takes a big gulp of the chopped, soggy noodle soup.

Delighted laughter bursts out of me. "You mean Bert Reynolds? From

Smokey and the Bandit?"

"Mmhmm," she mumbles with a full mouth. "That's the guy. You look like him, but with shorter hair."

"Well, that just tickles my pickle, sweetheart. But I'm better looking. Less round in the face, stronger jaw. A more modern Bert Reynolds. Did you like that movie? They were bootleggers. That's where the alcohol plot comes from."

"Yeah, I saw it once. He had a cool car."

"Yeah?!" My eyebrows raise in mischievous glee. "Honey, you are in for a treat, then, c'mon."

When I motion for her to follow me to the back entrance, she drains the rest of the noodles. I check the outside camera monitors mounted on the wall just inside the hallway—too many close calls over the years. All clear.

Carmella's voice lashes from behind me. "I thought you said your cameras didn't work." Oops.

I grin over my shoulder at her. Hopefully, she'll forgive me once she sees the car. I swing the back door open, and humidity rushes in. The rain has slowed to a soft drizzle, and wet asphalt and salt water tinge the air. The back lot shimmers, grainy and dark from the floodlight. And there, next to the door, sits my baby.

Carmella squeezes between me and the door, more curious than hesitant, and pops her head out. "Holy shit, you have the car! You are just like him." The delight in her voice is unmistakable. "You ever avoid the cops in that? Probably not. It's flashy."

Technically yes, I have outrun a few five-Os in my day, but this eager beaver doesn't need to know that. No joy rides in my baby. My running around days are behind me... Well, not really.

"Nah, no cops. I'm a good boy, and that isn't the exact replica. His was black. Mine is red and a sixty-eight. His was from the seventies. What do you think?"

"It's very cool. Can we go for a drive?"

I can't see her face, smushed in the doorframe like we are, but she continues to stare at my baby.

"I'll tell you what." She looks back at me over her shoulder. Her hair is nearly dry now, and frizzy, dishwater blonde waves tumble down her back. "If tomorrow goes well, we can probably take her for a drive. Would you like that?"

I actually get a genuinely excited smile and it's infectious. My lips perk up as well.

I don't know why I'm being so damn nice, especially after how riled up she got with me. But Carmella looks so tiny and sweet right now, like a little caramel drop in the trail mix I sometimes buy. She mostly seems adrift and hostile. *I'm not much better, but it would be nice to have some company at home. She has no one, and I want to put my dick in her, so there is that. Didn't think I'd be getting another girlfriend so soon after the divorce.*

Carmella pulls away, probably due to my intense staring and the way I'm pressed against her in the doorway. She puts a couple of steps between us. I accept her retreat, knowing I'm not making her any more comfortable. The rain picks up, hammering the pavement, and another peal of thunder rolls across the sky.

I watch it sheet down over the back lot and let the door swing close, sealing out the rain slanting into my hallway.

She folds her arms across her braless chest. "That could be fun. But I'm feeling pretty tired, and if it's cool, I want to go to bed now."

Stepping into the hallway, I give her my most charming smile and gesture to the open bedroom door. "Sure, we can go to bed now."

She follows the motion of my hand and jumps away from the bedroom office as if it bit her. "You live here?" Carmella's voice holds a note of alarm as she squeaks, "Also, I meant sleep. Like sleep, sleep. As in, me out on the floor, and you... I guess in here."

"What, you don't mean sleep, sleep, sleep?" My eyebrows wiggle. "Like the sleep that makes you sleepy?" A deep laugh rolls around my chest.

She glares at me again, but this one doesn't land as harshly, not with her cheeks flushing pink.

I drop another stellar smile on her, the one I use to open wallets and get nuns to flash me their naughties. Carmella pauses awkwardly, her eyes flicking up and down my body. "Goodnight." She pivots and all but runs down the hallway to the show floor.

Well, it was worth a try. She didn't even take the clothes.

Following her, I stop at the end of the hallway and peek around the corner.

"Goodnight," I call after her. She turns, giving me hard eyes. That really just makes me want to bust out laughing, but I contain myself. Flipping off the showroom floor lights, I return to my bedroom.

WAKEY WAKEY

CARMELLA

"Good morning," a low, rich male voice says, breath tickling my ear. My eyes snap open as the bed shifts, and a presence looms over me. A pair of dark eyes bore into mine far too close for comfort.

I don't think. Lashing out, my fist connects with the stranger's forehead. A booming, "What the fuck!" sends me scrambling backward. The stranger clutches his face. My hand hits a pocket of air where a bed should be. Yelping, I go down. Tumbling legs overhead, I end up in a heap, staring at fan blades hanging from an industrial ceiling. They circle lazily in the air.

As my heart rate slowly calms, memories from the previous night return and I internally groan. I just punched Luke in the forehead. *Good job, Carmella. Fantastic.* My shin throbs from the fall and from ramming it into the coffee table last night.

The usual wet concrete, urine, and saltwater smell that greets me with the sunrise has been replaced with clean, shampooed fabrics, musty cardboard, and orange furniture polish. I inhale deeply. Smooth carpet glides under my hands as I lie in a small aisle that runs between two beds. Maybe if I stay down here, he will forget I exist and I can go back to sleep.

"Fucking shit, woman, did you break your neck?" A handsome face pops over the edge of the mattress. A red patch of skin blossoms between Luke's dark eyes. "Are you alive?" he barks.

I heave a sigh and stare past him to the circling fans. "Unfortunately, yes. Also, why were you in my bed?" Irritation spikes in my chest.

Luke coyly smiles down at me, a mischievous twist written into his dark eyes. Propping his head up, he stretches out on his side. "Technically, you're in my bed. In fact, all these beds are my beds. How did you sleep... in my bed."

I roll my eyes.

He snorts. "Really, no appreciation for my joke? Fine, it's almost ten. I tried yelling, even threw a pillow at you, but you kept snoring. A more hands-on wakey wakey was needed." He makes a squeezing gesture that I can only take as him honking my boobs.

I know disapproval is plastered all over my face when that charming grin grows broader and his eyes crinkle with glee. "I don't snore, nor do I need a wakey wakey."

Luke must live to torment the poor souls around him.

Slightly alarmed, and a little skeeved out about how hands-on he may have gotten, I check my clothes and relax after seeing they are all in place. It couldn't have been much touching, if any at all. This dude is just a bullshit-talking, antagonistic a-hole.

Luke rises off the bed and stands between the two mattresses, towering over me. Propping myself up on my elbows, I shoo a frizzy, wavy lock out of my face and gaze up at him. Dressed in soft cream linen pants and a tropical green-leaf pattern button-down, he looks ready for a lunch date on a yacht, not selling used furniture.

My gaze flicks from the warm brown loafers and matching belt to the heavy gold jewelry on his fingers. His shirt is unbuttoned at the top, in what I bet he believes to be a tasteful vee, showing off dark chest hair and gold chains. Forget the famous actor. He's reminding me of those porn stars in those old grainy movies that Gloria's ex used to watch in the living room when he thought I was asleep.

He's giving me hardcore I'm-the-eldest-son-of-an-Italian-mob-boss-who-day-drinks-mai-tais-at-a-beach-resort vibes. Someone who shouts at the employees because his towels aren't soft enough. Someone who has lived a better life than I have.

He's also younger than I thought. And he's just standing there grinning like a moron, eyes all crinkled up. Although, I kind of like it. It makes him appear warm, inviting, and less like the raging lunatic who felt me up while wielding a gun. With his sun-kissed skin, dark slicked-back wavy hair, and perfectly brushed mustache, I'm embarrassed to acknowledge how good-looking he is.

"I know I look good, but it's impolite to stare." He chuckles, cocking an eyebrow.

I flush, heat rising to my cheeks. Awkwardness swims through the moment, and I'm suddenly painfully aware of the worn, drab yoga pants and oversized shirt with holes in the back that drapes my body. My mouth twists. *Why didn't I wear one of the shirts he gave me?*

Even if they were given out of pity. Even if it felt like a weird type of intimacy. Like something I'd share with an old friend, not the man whose store I broke into. At least then, I wouldn't be lying on the floor at his feet, dressed like this and dying of shame.

Luke would never be caught dead in what I've had to pass as clothes.

I take a deep breath and exhale, trying to recover from my own runaway thoughts and actually get myself together. He mistakes my sigh as a response.

"Chop chop," he says when I don't rise to his baiting. "I got us breakfast. We have forty-five minutes until the door opens, and I need to show you some things before the day starts. C'mon, shit, shower, shave, and then let's eat." With that, Luke spins with a flourish and walks toward the hallway leading to the kitchen.

My mouth falls open in disgust. *Never mind! I take back every nice thing I nearly thought about this man.*

I felt differently in the soft shadows of the night about my decision to stay. The thunder and patter of rain lulled me into being trusting. The late hour and haze he cast from his smoke clouded my judgment. I was afraid and wanted not to be scared, wet, or uncomfortable. So, I stayed. But in the harsh light of the day, with Luke's sleazy rudeness at level ten, I feel like it's time to move on. But move on to what?

After a few minutes of picking up my meager belongings and sniff-testing a few pieces of semi-clean clothing, a delicious scent of food wafts down the hall and onto the show floor. A loud gurgle sounds from my stomach. I gaze in the direction of the hallway and consider.

Breakfast with Luke and earning some cash is better than my pointless wanderings and police evasions, even if I have to endure his vulgarity.

Slinging my bags over my shoulder, I trudge across the show floor and push into the ladies' bathroom, eyeing the clean white tiles, gray stalls, and white countertop on a dark-gray cabinet which I'm sure holds the standard under-the-sink objects. I drop my stuff and open it to check. Stacked to one side sits extra toilet paper, paper towels, and a few cleaning supplies, with most of the space left unoccupied.

My personal effects smack the wall and sides of the cabinet as I toss them in and kick the door closed, keeping out a pair of plain blue jeans, underwear, a red spaghetti-strap tank top, and a few toiletries. The tank puts a lot of skin on display, but it's the cleanest thing I own. *Which is super unfortunate... considering Luke.* The white countertop becomes my personal vanity as I slather on deodorant and rinse out my mouth. I dig around for my toothbrush, growing angry when I can't find it. *Great, one more thing I now need to buy.*

No one tells you how easily things go missing when you live out of bags or how expensive it is to have nothing.

I pump the hand soap container several times and sniff the bubbles' clean scent. "It'll do." I shrug. Lathering the frothy white foam onto my face, I scrub hard, rather enjoying the tight, squeaky feeling it leaves on my skin.

A pink bottle of cheap cucumber-and-mint body spray sits next to the mango-punch lotion I five-finger discounted from the drugstore the other day. I squirt a white glob into my hand from the lotion bottle, and the greasy texture isn't appealing, but it smells divine. I rub until it absorbs into my arms and face. Fine mist falls around me as I spritz myself with the perfume and pop off the top of my deodorant.

Crumbling chunks of antiperspirant skitter across the countertop as the plastic anchor falls out and hits the floor. I grab the anchor and smear what's still left into my armpits. My eyes catch on myself in the mirror. "One day, this won't be your life anymore," I promise.

As I yank a brush through my blonde waves and curls, they frizz with static and shock me a few times before I finally get fed up and wet down the brush, the water smoothing my waves. Gathering all my locks, I twist and shove them into my favorite matte purple claw clip, teasing out a few loose strands. I evaluate the look in the mirror. The tips that jut up from the clip are a little spiky, but the little wavy pieces I left down prettily frame my face. I pick at the spikes.

They weren't always so rough or dry. I mourn the time when I had toothbrushes and real perfume. When my waves lay softly and my mom brushed them for me. A time with full refrigerators, when being skinny was just something the girls in grade school talked about but didn't really understand.

I didn't realize you could be too skinny. I didn't know many things back then, but I do now.

And life's little lessons were all hard-earned.

Little pieces of ripped-out dry hair decorate the counter when I snap out of my morbid thoughts. *Get it together, girl; breakfast and money are waiting.*

I smear some concealer over the dark circles on my eyes and cover a few red splotches before pulling out the only pink lipstick I have, using it as lip color, blush, and eyeshadow all-in-one. It doesn't do my skin tone justice, making me look more like beach Barbie than a no-nonsense business babe, especially with all my boobage on display. I would kill for a hoodie and debate putting on something dirty.

My prized possessions are my gold hoop earrings. They glimmer, catching the overhead lights as they dangle from my ears. All my tanned skin is a bit too sexy for breakfast, and I don't mean it to be, but there is nothing to be done for it until I can wash some clothes. Slipping on my shitty Converse, I take a look at the final product. I put my hands on my hips and admire the outfit before tucking the tank top into my jeans. *That should do it. I'm ready to spend the day with the dude who saw me half-naked and pinched my nipples,* I think.

Fuck my life.

A low whistle and appraising eyes greet me as soon as I enter the functional kitchen. Luke sits in the chair I occupied last night, facing me at the little white folding table we had noodles at. An empty to-go box covered in crumbs and gravy sits before him. My face turns crimson at his appreciative eyebrow wiggles, but I cover it with a dismissive shake of my head and roll my eyes. The smell of coffee and food is divine. I spy the full dark pot and make my way over as steam rises from the brew.

Luke's voice wraps around me as I pour a cup. "What's cooking, hot stuff? Nothing because this man already got you breakfast. Come sit down and eat. Actually, wait, keep standing there." I hear the shutter of a camera.

Spinning around, I lock on the image of Luke kicked back in his chair, his phone aimed at my ass, and seeing him snapping photos immediately ignites my temper. I haven't even been in the room a full minute yet. "I will throw this hot coffee on you! Watch me."

Luke busts out in a belly laugh and slips his phone back into his pocket before holding up his hands. "Alright. Alright, peace. I was only commemorating your first day on the job, caramel drop."

I swear to God. If he does that again, I'll dump this whole pot in his lap and shatter his phone. Also, caramel drop? Eww.

Never in my life has a man just taken photos of me so casually. I'm not inexperienced with men. I even have a kind-of boyfriend, Tommy. But they've never been so blunt or aggressive about their intentions. Luke is just a whole new level of I don't even know.

How do I interact with a stranger who I know would bend me over the kitchen table and fuck me senseless if I so much as hinted at it? I avoid men like Luke, troublemakers, flashy smooth talkers, fuck-boy arrogant types, for good reason. "You make me feel like I need full body armor and a shield," I snap at him and walk over to the table where a white Styrofoam food box sits.

He offers me a megawatt grin. "All you had to do was say you're into roleplay, baby. I got some wigs."

My eyes lock with Luke's. His dance with delight and mischief, and mine are probably calling for blood. He rolls his to the ceiling. "C'mon, Carmella, crack a smile already. You're too serious for such a beautiful woman."

Bitterness gentled by sweet creamer runs over my tastebuds as I drink the coffee. I will not be flattered by this man. "I can be both beautiful and serious."

He just smirks at me, eyes all crinkly.

I pop open the to-go container in front of me, expecting something cheap, like a breakfast burrito or eggs. Instead, I find a massive chicken fried steak smothered with sausage gravy, a large scoop of skillet-fried hash browns, a biscuit with a packet of jam, and another container of more gravy.

My lips open in surprise. Mouth watering, I look up at Luke, and he eyes me with wolfish delight. "Thought you'd like something more substantial than noodles, and I don't have shit here. Gran's has the best breakfast in White Cove. If you like her cooking, we can eat there again. Try the biscuit."

I nod, bite into the crumbly bread, and nearly moan. It's lightly sweet and warm inside with a layer of salty crunch on the outside. He's right. The biscuit is fantastic. "So good," I mumble with a full mouth. He watches me eat, looking extremely self-satisfied, but I don't care. I dig in, unable to help the sinful moan that comes naturally at the explosive state of savory fried coating soaked in steak juices. *Fuck me, that's good.*

I inhale my plate in the most unladylike manner, but I'm not trying to impress Luke. We eat in silence. Well, mostly silence. I can't help but express how good the food is with a series of orgasmic eye rolls and moans.

I sigh—better slow down. *I don't want to puke on his nice shoes.* I consider my companion while weighing my choices.

Luke gives off chaotic energy and stranger-danger vibes, but he could've called the cops last night. Could've raped me. He could've killed me.

Instead, he tried to give me nice clothes, brought me this feast, and was excited to share his favorite biscuit with me. *Which is fair because it's a damn good biscuit.*

But I'm still slightly salty about being caught and felt up. It was embarrassing and stupid. Worse, it could have been the end of everything, but Luke let me sleep in a bed instead. He's feeding me, promising me money, and, for the most part, treating me decently. Things could be a lot worse than some handsome pervy guy with money wanting to dick me down. A lot worse.

I don't want to go back to sleeping on the streets, constantly being vigilant and worrying about my safety. It's exhausting and depressing. Not every drifter is your kindly drunk grandpa type; some of them are downright crazy violent. I hate being hungry all the time. It makes me grumpy. The cold and the rain suck as well, especially when the sky is dumping on me and I know I can't go to a shelter or women's home. Not that I would want to. Those places make it easy to be found. I can't legally get or keep a job either. No ID, driver's license, or birth certificate.

Sometimes, I wonder what's the point of trying when it gets you backed into an even tighter corner. I've fallen through the cracks of life, and when I vanish altogether, they will just roll my body into the morgue as a Jane Doe. A cold shiver of fear runs the length of my frame.

"Will that hold you over until dinner?"

Luke's voice dislodges the image of me laid out on an autopsy table alone, without anyone to grieve me except maybe Tommy, but that's only if they can identify me. My aunt Gloria probably wouldn't even tell him.

Luke looks at me expectantly, phone in one hand and cigarette in the other, smoke swirling up and around him. He's been fixed onto his screen for the last few minutes.

"Huh?" I ask.

"Will that keep you full until dinner? Then we can go get some groceries after work."

"Oh, yeah. Yes, I'm good." I scrape the last couple of bites into my mouth, enjoying the crunchy, salty potatoes.

I'm better than good. I'm stuffed, but I no longer care—better to be uncomfortably full. The cold loneliness that had settled in my chest warms unexpectedly at Luke's inclusion and thoughtfulness. *We. We will grab dinner and groceries later.*

When I lean back in the chair, my stomach pouches out with a giant food baby and I giggle.

Luke gives me a warm smile. *Dude smiles a lot.*

"I'm glad you enjoyed it," he says, setting down his phone and taking a drag from his cigarette.

"So much. Thank you."

He nods. "Good. C'mon, let's open the doors. I've got a few things to tell you about."

I groan but rise with him from the table. He passes me a bottle of cold water that he snags from the fridge and takes one for himself. The coolness in my hands makes me want to chug it greedily, but I don't. Exercising self-restraint, I sip it normally, grab my cup of coffee, and follow Luke onto the show floor.

My First Day at a Real Job... I Think

CARMELLA

"First things first," Luke says, stopping at the gray and blue horseshoe-shaped desk. "You got to cover your tits, but not too much. You can't sell furniture looking like a slut. You need to be sexy, but not too sexy."

My jaw drops at his words. "Excuse me, I don't look like a slut! It's Florida, in the middle of the summer, and it's freakin' hot out. I'm wearing a tank top, not running around naked."

He raises his eyebrows at my last statement, and I roll my eyes. "I'm not running around naked right now," I huff out.

"Caramel drop, it might be hot outside, but it's cold in here, and I can see you nipping." His eyes dip, and I follow his gaze, seeing little bumps from my nipples jut out from my flimsy shirt. Slapping my arms across my chest, I can't help but feel a bit of déjà vu as, once again, I'm hiding my tits from Luke. *I swear I will never know a moment of peace with this man.* A piece of fabric smacks my face and wraps itself around my head like a python.

"Put it on, Carmella," Luke says, amusement in his voice.

Snarling, I yank the cloth off my face and look at the standard black polo. Roughly pulling it over my head, I shove it down into my jeans and tuck it in. An embroidered yellow logo that reads Luke's sits on the right, above my breast.

"Mmm, you look good with my name on you," Luke notes. I can feel his eyes wander over my body.

I might actually stab this guy. "Do you always have something to say?"

He drops the grin that's always attached to his face, and his gaze narrows on me. "It's not my words you have to watch out for. It's my silence."

Turning, he strolls toward the front of the store.

Well, that was fucking ominous. I hurry to catch up.

He walks us between the used couches, headed toward the appliances, gesturing at the displays. "So, if a customer comes in and wants something new, but I don't have it on the floor or in the back, then we can order it. But I don't like messing with orders. It's a pain in the ass. Sometimes, the customer changes their mind and wants a refund, or we have to exchange the item," he explains. "Orders for new products keep me involved with the customers for too long, and the money stays in the air until they get their shit figured out. I prefer we hook them, get them to open their wallets, make that money rain, and get them out. Fuck all the other nonsense."

"So, customer satisfaction isn't really your thing," I observe dryly as we approach the front of the store decorated with rows of gleaming appliances. "Why even have newer products if you don't want to sell them?"

We reach the front of the store and he pauses, resting his hand on a pristine white dishwasher. "With any good con, you need a flashy hook to reel them in. That's why the nice-looking shit's upfront." He gestures to the clean, shiny appliances and fake kitchens. "Brings in people with money to spend."

"So, this is how it works." He clasps his hands with a little clap. Gone are his mischievous looks, replaced by something more complex and severe. "A customer comes in and you greet them happily. Make small talk and compliment their clothes, purse, or haircut. I don't give a shit what you say, just make them think you give a damn. If you can get them to laugh, even better. A shared laugh establishes a sense of trust among idiots."

I nod, following along. None of this seems complicated. Just be nice and say the right things at the right time. I can do that.

"Listen to me. You're not just selling furniture. You're selling yourself as someone customers want to buy from. This is true no matter where you are in life. Selling yourself as someone or even multiple someones to different people will get you through so many doors in life. Repeat to me what I just told you."

I do, verbatim.

He nods. "Good. Once they are comfortable, you'll want to find out what they are looking for and their budget. Remind them you are here to help save them money. Everyone likes a bargain, especially if they think working with you is in their interest. You want them to believe that you are the only person who can resolve their problems."

Luke continues down the list of dos, don'ts, and tips. Sweat dampens my lower back as anxiety grows in my stomach. My lip aches as I bite into it and try to remember everything he says. I want to be good at this, my first real job, which is ridiculous. It's just a job, but my head is divided. Working here means something to me, and I'm excited to tell Tommy about it later, if I can get him to answer the phone. Tommy is great, but inconsistent, but this experience would mean even more if I had someone to share the news with, like a friend, a roommate, or even a parent. Someone to tell me congrats and how proud they are. That I earned this, even though I didn't. I hate myself for wanting things like that, makes me hate the people around me who have that type of support. And hating is exhausting.

I'm reaching another significant milestone in my life and I still feel alone. Congrats, girl.

My would-have-been happy occasion is marred by my own desperate situation and Luke's pervy kindness. A sorrowful cloud of depression brews and darkens my mood. I remind myself that this arrangement won't last and I won't always have a source of income. And since I'm not sticking around, it doesn't matter what Luke thinks of my selling skills. *None of this really matters. Even though I wish it could.*

I'm always torn between the wish and reality.

I sigh. At the very least, I want to sleep in a bed again, have some money, and go grocery shopping with Luke. It would be nice to take a drive in his cool car, too. It's the closest thing to real living I've had in a long time. So, for that, I'll try.

For a second, I imagine a different ending for myself, one with a handsome guy with a cool car and we're cruising along the coast. We'd play music really loud, eat at all the restaurants I've never been to, and at night, we would stay in and watch movies. No cops, no Gloria, no courts, and no shitty judges. I could get into my college classes again. My guy would hang out on campus with me. I'd have lots of friends, and when he and I graduated together, he'd propose.

We would move into a beach house, and he'd only ever have eyes for me. At night, he'd hold me, and we would talk about our day, and he'd care. He'd do anything for me. He'd never leave or turn cold, and he would move mountains if needed to be with me. He'd just love me.

Fingers snap twice an inch away from my face and bring me back to the present. "Hey, fucking pay attention. I already know this information. You don't," Luke barks, ruining the fantasy.

"Sorry," I mutter. Embarrassment flames my face, and I avoid Luke's gaze. If my mystery man just so happened to look slightly like the well-dressed asshole in front of me, it's because Luke is handsome when he isn't talking. That's all. He's a shady skeeze, not a beach house hero.

It's weak, wanting to pretend that we are other than we are. Pretending never did anything but disappoint me.

Luke gives me an annoyed glance before continuing, "The goal is to steer the customer clear of the newer products and guide them to the used ones. If they are looking for a matching dining set, I have six of them. Get them to buy used."

"Why?" I ask, definitely not staring at his mouth as he licks his lips and smooths down his mustache.

"Because the used stuff is all profit. I pay next to nothing for those pieces. Any used item sold comes with an as-is, no-return policy, and that makes my life easier."

Outside, a car pulls into the drive and rolls to a stop at the front of the store. A couple sits in the front of the red four-door.

Luke notices my attention on the incoming customers. "If you do get a sale for a new product instead of used, wave me down. I will teach you how to mark up prices and include hidden fees. That way, we at least get something out of it."

See, girl, shady Luke, very shady Luke. "So, we are scamming people?" I ask. The couple gets out of the car and heads to the door.

He grins. "Consider it a challenge, not a scam. You're learning to be smarter than everyone else, stacking the deck in your favor, hustling before you get hustled." He boops me on the nose. My head pulls back in horror. *Dude did not just boop me like I'm a child.* He gives me an ornery smirk before continuing, "Be leaner, meaner, and wiser. Watch and learn, caramel drop." My brows pull down as I snarl at him and rub the spot where he touched me.

Plastering on a big, welcoming smile, he heads for the couple and holds the door open for them before they reach it. I roll my eyes at his back but follow his lead, trailing behind him.

After shaking their hands and casually commenting on the brand of the man's boots with approval, Luke dives into what brings them to his store. He seems genuinely intrigued by the couple's search for a used dishwasher that would fit the dimensions of their older model, which has fallen apart beyond repair.

He nods along with their explanation and "hmmms" in sympathy when they lament how many other places they have checked and their lack of funds to pay for the fancy imported ones small enough to fit into the designated space in their apartment.

"Well, I'm not going to have anything that fits those dimensions out on the floor, but I might have one in the shop. Please feel free to browse around while I check. C'mon, Carmella," Luke says.

My head snaps up at the mention of my name, and I give the couple a polite smile as I step around them. As we head to the back door, I ask in a hushed tone, "Is it cool to just leave them in there?"

He shrugs. "They're on camera. And, anyway, what are they going to do? Shove a toaster down their pants? Pry my safe out of the wall... steal my empty cash register?"

"To be fair, that was kind of my plan," I remind him.

Luke's face scrunches up as he snorts. "Yeah, and if I remember correctly, it's been pointed out how terrible of a burglar you are."

Humid heat hits me in the face as the back door swings open, and the familiar background noise of seagulls and traffic swirl around me. Sweat immediately slicks my body. The smell of hot blacktop and fishy salt water reaches my nose. We walk across the cracked and crumbling pale asphalt of the back lot and approach a long, narrow, white building that runs the length of Luke's store. "Wait, this is yours, too?" I ask him.

"It's extra storage and my workshop." Keys clink together as he retrieves them from a pocket.

Green shrubbery grows up the sides of the walls, ivy creeps along the corners, nestling into every crevice it can find, and the grass hasn't been cut in some time. An air of abandonment clings to the place as paint flakes off in patches, revealing wooden side paneling. The only thing that doesn't look like it's about to fall off this place are the wrought-iron security bars that fit snugly against windows painted so that not even the casual passerby can see what's inside. *Hmmmm. Definitely crack-shack vibes.*

Glancing over my shoulder, I notice some of the outside cameras aren't just pointed at the store lot. Nine of them are nestled up high on the store and storage building like perched birds. The cameras don't just take in the store parking lots; they cover the streets, the alleyway, this side building, and probably a good portion of the other storefronts across the street as well. *That's not alarming at all. How did I miss all of those last night? I really am a bad burglar.*

Another question pops into my mind. Why so many cameras both inside and out? Alarm creeps through my body as we stop in front of a weathered door. A thick industrial-looking lock dangles from a latch clasp. Below that sits two deadbolts and a door handle that requires a key. A two-car garage entrance that doesn't look like it's been opened for years is rusted next to the door and also padlocked from the outside. *Okay. What the fuck?*

Luke systematically unlocks the door, going down the line of security measures, and pushes it open, waving me to step ahead of him. "Ladies first."

"You're not going to lock it behind me, are you?"

"If I were planning on it, I wouldn't tell you." His pearly white teeth shine at me, as that stupid grin he always wears spreads across his face. Muttering about how much bullshit this is, I step inside the dark building.

I can make out a free-standing shelf littered with dusty grime-covered mechanical parts in various stages of rust. The smell of old motor oil, citrusy oranges, and wet concrete hangs heavy in the air. "I don't hear any screams from chained-up women, so that's good," I call out.

Luke barks a laugh from right behind me. "I keep them drugged and gagged. That's why it's quiet." He flips on a switch.

I blink as light suddenly fills the space. *Huh, it really is a workshop.*

Spare parts to an assortment of mechanical equipment lay strewn everywhere. Empty refrigerators, washers, and dryers are disassembled or tipped on their sides. Some are gutted, and others look brand new and are still in their cardboard boxes. Tools line shelves and are hung up along the wall. Snaking cables run under my feet and off into the maze of items. Bedroom furniture, microwaves, tables, and large mirrors are stacked along one wall. The shop is strangely cool, and the sound of a running air conditioner comes from deep within the building. Mismatched lawn furniture and a gray back seat of an SUV sit in front of the garage door in a half circle like some long-forgotten hang-out pad.

I nod toward the front part of the shop, where I can just barely see the outline of pallets, spare tires, and a big dolly for moving them. "What's back there?"

Luke is crouched next to a compact dishwasher, tape measure stretched out. Eyebrows raised, he glances in the direction of the front of the shop and shrugs. The tape makes a metallic wobbling rustle sound as it rushes back into itself with a click. "More product for the show floor."

"Where do you get all this stuff?"

"Some is delivered. Some I find. Some I buy."

"Find. Like, you actually find some of the furniture you sell? Like, set out next to the curb type of find? Is it the new stuff that gets delivered?"

Luke runs a hand across his face and sighs. "Someone is curious. You know what they say about curiosity. I'm sure the ladies tied up in the other room can answer all your questions about what I keep over there. Now, grab that two-wheeler dolly behind you."

"Har har, you're not funny." It's my turn to sigh as I grab the green dolly and wheel it over to Luke. "Will this one fit in their space?"

"Yeah, let's load it up."

"That's good, then." Luke tips the dishwater up slightly so I can slide the dolly under it.

"Good for us, not so much for them. It mostly works. I wasn't willing to pay for the replacement part."

I scrunch up my nose. "So what now?"

He looks up at me from his squatted position. "Better a half-working dishwasher that only needs one part than no dishwasher at all."

"Are you going to discount it for them?"

He frowns at me. "It's like you haven't been listening at all today."

We get the dishwasher rolled back into the main showroom, and Luke places it in front of the couple. Reassuring them that it does work, he plugs it in and all the lights come on. It makes the right engaging noises, which satisfies the couple, and they ask for the price. "Well, I like you two, and I know you've had a rough time, but this isn't an easy-to-find piece. I'll let it go for two hundred."

The couple and Luke haggle good-naturedly for a minute. I shake my head as he sells it to them for one-fifty, half broken and only sometimes working. He does give them the website where they can buy repair parts just in case they need it. I'm half impressed by how fast he made a sale and half guilty knowing they are going to need that website sooner rather than later.

And so the day goes—an endless stream of people looking for all kinds of household items, furniture, and appliances. I'm so busy welcoming people and practicing selling my personality that the hours fly by. It's impressive that Luke manages all this by himself, especially since it isn't the most honest work.

I quickly notice that Luke doesn't put the price on anything, forcing me to go look everything up. They are priced ridiculously high and I question him about it, and he whispers that this is on purpose so we can artificially slash them to sweeten the sales. Which makes sense.

We win some customers, and we lose some. Three of those wins come directly from me, and I'm proud of myself. Luke's a good teacher and is surprisingly honest about his "techniques," allowing me to duplicate them.

Luke's hustle is more like a performance than a job, and everyone shows up for the show. He thrives under the attention and thrill of winning over customers. The ladies love his flirting, and the men laugh at most of his jokes. *I bet he was super popular in high school.*

It's five pm before I know it, and my first official day is done. I feel a little guilty about the price markups, but that diminishes when Luke tells me that for every sale I finalize, he'll give me a ten percent commission on top of my pay. *I'm going to sell broken furniture all day.*

The bolts slide in place as Luke locks the front door and turns the neon closed sign on. The sun is beginning its leisurely descent, and all I want to do is lie down. I lean back in the black spinning chair behind the front-counter desk.

Luke steps around the counter. "Hey, doll, why don't you run the vacuum and tidy this place up while I do this paperwork? We will get food and groceries after."

"Do you mind if I make a call real quick?" I ask.

He pauses before taking his seat and gives me a look. "Who're you calling?"

Telling him about my sort-of-boyfriend is on the tip of my tongue when I bite it back. It's shitty, but Luke likes me and is giving me things I'm in need of. I'd love a shower and a chance to replace some of the essentials I'm running low on. The last thing I want to do is provide him with a reason to not give me my money.

I shrug, casual like. "Just a friend I check in with regularly, so they know I'm not dead."

His face scrunches up like somehow my answer put a bad taste in his mouth. He spins around to his computer, brows still furrowed. "A friend, huh? Sure, okay."

Pushing the rolly chair over to the corded phone, I snag it out of the cradle and punch in the numbers I know by heart. A bubble of nerves rises in my chest. I hope Tommy answers this time. Loud ringing trills in my ear once, twice, three times. My lip stings as I bite and tear at the dried skin, and after the sixth ring, I've resigned myself to this being the third missed call in as many weeks when Tommy picks up the phone.

"Who's this?" he demands.

"It's me. Carmella. Hey, how are you?" I cringe, my voice is a little too happy and high-pitched.

"Oh, hey, baby. Now isn't a great time."

I can hear masculine chatter in the background and a round of laughter, probably several of Tommy's buddies hanging out at his place. Imagining them all sitting around, making plans on where to best sell their newest batch of street drugs, which girl they are going to fuck, or what house would be the easiest to rob, makes me roll my eyes. Those are the typical topics, and their conversations tend to eat up evenings and early mornings as they sit around getting higher, drunker, and spewing more bullshit. But according to Tommy, this is his business. Personally, I think his friends are all dumb as fuck and he could do better.

"It's been a minute since I've heard from you and I have some news," I say, trying to brush off the sting of his dismissal.

"Yeah? That's cool, babe. Hey, Judo, is Bax still coming through tonight?" Tommy asks his buddy.

I don't think I've ever met a Judo. "I found some work. First real..." A round of laughter detonates in my ear as a bunch of men all start talking over each other.

"Hey, babe, call me later, yeah?"

Before I can say, "Sure, no problem," he's hung up, leaving me still holding the phone. *Love you too, dickhead.*

Sighing, I rise from the chair. I'm exhausted, my feet hurt, I'm hungry, and my conversation with Tommy has left me wanting. No, not just wanting, rather craving connection. There is no joy in cleaning, especially not now. At this point, I don't even want to go for a ride. All I want is a shower and to sleep for a hundred years. I fight back the looming cloud of depression that is never too far off.

A dusty chemical smell greets me from the closet when I pull out the vacuum and dust spray to wipe down some of the dirtier tables I noticed. I don't know if it's my conversation with Tommy or the smell that teases a memory to the surface of my mind, one I haven't thought about in a long time.

"Go on, it's through there," my new foster mother tells me. She seems nice, but bored, like I'm taking up her time. Wishing she would look at me, I open the door to my new temporary bedroom; the bottles of cleaning solution rattle in the mop bucket I hold. The room is wooden and brown. A twin bed and a lamp on a small bedside table sit off to one side. The only other furniture is a dresser set and chair, also brown and wooden. It's not the ugliest room I've ever seen, and it's all mine. I don't have to share. I smile at my new temporary mom, hoping she will know that I'm not disappointed.

But she isn't looking at me. She stares at her phone, and realizing that the door is open, walks past me, dropping the trash bags of my clothes and other items on the floor just inside the room. "I didn't get the chance to clean in here, so you'll have to. Dinner won't be for a couple more hours, so you have time. I'll get you some blankets. Just stay up here until I come to get you. We have mice and roaches, so don't leave any food in your room." With that, she walks out, firmly shutting the door behind her. She didn't look at me once.

Staring into the supply closet, I try to shake off the coldness of the memory. That room was miserable, and I was miserable in it, sweltering in the summer and frozen in the winter. It wasn't the temperature that haunted me, though.

It was the loneliness of the place. I cried for my real mom and dad in that room until dinner was ready. I would've loved it if someone had held me, pushed back my hair, and promised me it'd all be okay. But the image of that wooden door shutting on me so resolutely after my parents died taught me things about life and my own importance that I wasn't ready to know at eight years old. I just wanted my new mom to like me.

That house wasn't the worst place I've ever stayed, but the isolation nearly killed me. No matter how much I cleaned that room, the smell of dust and chemicals lingered. I couldn't go to any of the family events or play with her other kids' toys. The siblings I could've had barely spoke to me, forcing school and that room to become my entire life. That was the second time I considered suicide as a reasonable option, even at eight years old.

Every damn day, that woman and her kids made me feel invisible.

Bile turns in my stomach, and I quickly grab anything else I need and slam the door. More memories start to flicker in my mind from that year: coming home with a broken arm and no one caring for days until it was purple, getting into my first fight and being expelled. Faster, the unwanted thoughts are slammed to the forefront of my mind—the first time I cut because I couldn't stand the feelings in my body and having to explain to my elementary teacher that my new cat scratched me. Her unbelieving eyes followed me all that year.

I feel hot and shaky. The need to panic and run thrashes through me. To do anything other than stand there while the memories flood me. My mouth begins to salivate from the nausea gripping me. Invisible pressure squeezes my chest, and I try to breathe through the mounting panic attack. Anxiety ripples through my body, making my legs shake.

My panicked breaths are loud, and I'm terrified of Luke finding me like this. The store is so open, he could see how broken I am. Vulnerability washes over me. "Hey, Luke," I shout, forcing a laugh into my voice, hoping it hides the strain. "Can we listen to some music?"

"Sure thing, buttercup, give me a second." His voice floats to me from the desk.

Hurrying, I begin spraying down any surface I can find and wiping them in long, slow strokes, up and down, ensuring I get every inch. I throw myself into the work with a desperation only the broken know. The knot in my stomach starts to loosen with the cleaning rhythm and my controlled breathing.

"Neon Signs" by Suki Waterhouse begins to play overhead, and I'm more than a little surprised by the choice. The sultry, moody melody is soothing, easing the tension in me little by little as I commit the lyrics to memory.

I expected Luke to listen to old-school rock, rap, or even aggressive modern rock, but this alternative sound is a pleasant surprise. My breathing slowly returns to normal as I bop along with his playlist and let the music carry away all those horrible memories.

Watch Me. I Dare You

LUKE

Today was a good day.

Rerunning the numbers on the computer, I admire how quickly they rack up. I scribble down a few notes in the margins of the black book I keep for the other side of my "business." While I may be able to hide thousands of dollars in upcharge used sales, the new products are always more difficult, with too many fucking paper trails and receipts. I had to deal with a few new orders today, but thankfully, those had been pricey, making it a little easier to slip in some hidden fees and a few more bucks my way.

Too bad it's not enough to move all of Sasha's money. That thought is enough to remind me that I need to call my pseudo brother, Avtoritet of the local Russian mafia, and update him on the figures. My hand hovers over the burner phone before I decide differently. The amount of money I'm able to launder for Sasha out of the store is a drop in the bucket compared to what I could eight months ago.

There was a time when Sasha didn't make a dollar that didn't get cleaned by me, and now all that's left is the furniture store. My pet project. I rub my hand over my face. No, a phone call isn't going to erase the frustration and impatience in Sasha's voice every time we talk. It isn't going to make up for all the ways I fucked up.

I've spent the last eight months trying to drink and fuck the grief, embarrassment, guilt, and shame out of myself, but low and behold, there is always more.

What happens when you get hit with several lawsuits by victims of your old cons gone bad and suddenly things are looking pretty bleak according to the lawyers? You think it's a good idea to sign all your cash businesses and shell companies over to your partner in crime, your supposed other half. Your lovely wife. But, ironically enough, that bitch is already fucking some other dick, divorces you, and takes all your assets with her before disappearing into the wind. I snort.

At least I choose to believe she is in the wind. It's the most logical choice. If the Bratva catches up to her, I'll have my businesses back before she's "disposed of." I stare down at my hands folded in my lap. *Tracey was always overly ambitious.*

A fuckup on the scale of which I've fucked up usually ends in a lot of death. Bloody, painful examples being made of everyone involved. If I didn't already owe Sasha my life from when we were kids, I definitely owe him now. I don't know what he did—what deal he cut with our boss, the Pakhan—but I know his power and influence is how I'm still breathing and walking around a free man.

That makes the fact that I haven't gotten my shit together eight months later even harder to bear. An appreciative man would have been out there busting his ass all day, coming up with schemes, cons, anything he could to pay back the brother whose authority protects him. But my ex-wife did more than just take away my home and business. She did more than just deliberately leave me for dead at the hands of the Bratva. She took away my enthusiasm to keep living this life. She left my desire to be the Avtoritet's "man" at an all-time low. She stole my mojo.

That isn't a reflection on Sasha—which I've told him hundreds of times. I just don't know if I can recover from how badly Tracey leveled my world. *I really did love her, that fucking bitch.*

Rubbing my temple, I take a deep breath and wait for the rage that never comes. Even after Tracey's lover held a gun to my head, the restraining orders, the courts, the promises to return my companies and business before she took off... I couldn't find the anger. There is only heartache and ugly emotions to keep me company.

Grabbing the black money bag, I push back from the table. My gaze sweeps the floor for Carmella. The vacuum cleaner hums in the background as the refreshing scent of citrus wafts around me, creating a pleasant atmosphere. Her jean-clad ass sways to the beat of the overhead music and the push-pull motion of the vacuum cleaner as she moves across the floor. *Fucking adorable.* Consumed by her task, she won't miss me.

Stepping out from behind the front counter, I quickly head to the back door and out into the evening. The air has settled from scorching hot into a muggy, humid mess that feels akin to breathing hot soup. I'm dressed to impress, not to go swimming through the air, and suddenly wish I was wearing less clothing. Unlocking the shop once more, I step inside the moldy old building. Damp earthiness, metal, and old crayons make up the original scent of this place. Jugs full of uncapped furniture polish and wood stain are my addition to the overwhelming odor of the shop. New-car smell pine trees decorate the space—my buddy Daniel's attempt to make it smell less... workshop.

Shutting the door behind me, I walk into the shop's darkest spot, unzipping the empty black money bag. Grabbing a flashlight off the top of a rusted shelf and flicking the button, I follow a beam of warm light that shoots off into the darkness. Locating the stack of tires, I twist off the false rim. Ten-thousand-dollar stacks of hundreds are wrapped in plastic and line the inside.

Scooping up one wrapped stack, I drop it into the bag, zip it tight, and tuck it under my arm. The flashlight pans across the room as I leave, catching the ceiling-high stack of tires and crates of boxed microwaves that have false backs, all flush with cash I can no longer move the way I used to. *Fucking Tracey.*

Retracing my steps, I slip back inside and behind my desk. Carmella didn't miss me at all. In fact, I bet she didn't even know I was gone. *Good, the less my caramel drop knows, the better off she is.*

Carmella is a welcome distraction from the day to day of barely being able to live with myself.

She brought with her a streak of luck tucked neatly into a shapely package, which I appreciate greatly. If Carmella hadn't been a quick study, I would have lost out today. After watching me go a couple of rounds with customers, she stepped in, chatting and laughing. She seemed eager to work after that little bit of attitude this morning, which was a welcome surprise.

Fixing the numbers in my online spreadsheet to match my paper trail, I rebalance the black book. I mix the stack of cash in with the store's income from today.

When she watched me rip that couple off earlier, I didn't find much condemnation in her gaze. Instead, curiosity and wariness dominated her cute face. Little Miss Beach Barbie is bright, ballsy, and smoking hot. If I'm judging correctly by the crazy/hot matrix, and taking into account God only knows what kind of behavioral/mental issues she has that led her to be homeless, it's only a matter of time until that side of her raises its ugly head. I'm probably more excited about her being a little unhinged than I should be, *but hey, I like a little thrill in my life.*

Most people would have balked or argued the ethics and morality of my actions, but not my sexy little trespasser. She barely blinked. Everyone has a price, and I suspect Carmella's may be pretty cheap. If she is willing to bargain her ethics away for ten percent of every sale she makes, I'd like to know what else she'll let me buy from her.

A little money, food, a warm place to sleep, affection, and some security could seal the deal. And all those things are within my power to provide. I have a hope she's loyal, too, but time will tell. Keeping a cute, young something to pester and look at in the store definitely makes the time move quicker.

After a full day like today, I am more desperate for help than I realized. As much as I hate to admit it, running the deliveries on Monday, the store on Tuesday thru Friday, shopping for new inventory on the weekends, rebuilding broken furniture three nights a week, and partying on the other four have been taking their toll.

I finish the paperwork and calculate what I'm paying caramel drop, slipping it into an envelope. Hopefully, an envelope full of cash at the end of the next two weeks is incentive enough to keep her here. It'll give her time to adjust, take stock of her situation, and come to the natural conclusion that she is better off with me. *Better off on my dick than fucking on the streets.*

The song changes to one of my favorites, "Wet Dreams" by Wet Leg, and my foot taps to the beat. I'm not the only one who notices the bright rhythm. Carmella has stripped off the polo I gave her this morning, revealing that scrumptious red tank top and her pushed-up tits. She walks toward me and flashes me a smile before running the vacuum around the front counter.

I'm suddenly thankful I had the foresight to hide some of her best assets today. My mind wouldn't have been on making money. Right now, especially as she dances around, vacuuming the floor, her tits and body are all I can see. Desire rushes through me, and the trouser snake in my pants comes alive at the mental image of her tits bouncing in my face as she rides my cock.

My caramel drop turns away from me, and I nearly curse as I'm blocked from seeing those melons shake as she continues her cleaning. *Hello, I was watching that.* My eyes snag on her ass at the same time the phrase "love to watch you leave" flashes in my mind. Smoothing down my mustache, I pull out my phone and scroll to the video from last night. Holding the phone at eye level and next to the actual dancing Carmella, I open the clip of her half-naked and watch myself push her arm down and reach out to touch her nipple.

The scandalized look on her face on the tiny screen makes me chuckle. It won't be the last time she gives me that look. In fact, I can barely wait for the next opportunity to elicit such a response. *Get that woman all worked up.*

My cock swells in my pants as the clip plays over in a loop. In the background, Carmella sways her hips to the rhythm, unaware of my voyeurism. She's so fucking hot, and I still want to see her tongue. Her cute little updo has shaken loose over the course of the day and pretty little waves stick out this way and that, giving her a trashy sort of hot-mess look. The need to replace the hair clip with my fist as I drive my dick into her sassy mouth makes my hands twitch. A vivid fantasy of holding her pinned against the wall by her hair, forcing her to stick out that hot little pink tongue while I shoot ropey baby batter into her mouth, has me palming my erection.

Fuck it, she isn't paying attention to me, anyway. Popping the button on my pants, I unzip and lean back in my chair, tugging my cock and balls free. Stroking my dick from root to tip out in the open like this feels like a fucking high, especially with her less than twenty feet from me. If she glances this way, what I'm doing will be unmistakable. She'll be scandalized, no doubt, but also maybe curious. I'm packing some good-sized pipe after all. *I want her to look.*

I wish Carmella and I were in a place where I could just call her a good girl, bend her over, and stick it in long enough to dump my cum in that tight cunt. Then, I'd spend the rest of the evening making her orgasm over and over. The thought of doing just that makes my dick jump in my hand and sends me racing toward my orgasm.

My balls tighten as my fist pumps up and down the length of my cock. Spitting in my hand, I lube myself up and thrust into my tight grip. My breathing becomes erratic, and I'm thankful that the loud overhead music hides the sounds of me slapping my meat. *Fuck, this nut will be big.*

Grunting, I throw down the phone on the counter and stare at Carmella, daring her to turn around and watch me cum. She bends over to move the cord. The thought of her bent over one of the couches like that while I feed her my cock does the trick. Kneading my balls and squeezing my cock so hard I half wonder if it will bruise, I cum all over the plastic chair mats. Ropey squirts shoot out farther than I intended, smacking into the counter as my orgasm rocks me, making my balls kick hard. It feels so good that it hurts, and I get a little dizzy for a second.

Still jerking my softening cock while my heart rate slows, I take a steadying breath. *Holy shit, that one nearly did me in.*

Sliding my love stick back into my pants, I look up at Carmella, who has moved to a new spot next to the bed she slept in last night, still unaware. Shit, that was one of the hottest things I've done in a long time.

Surveying the mess, I decide a towel will be the easiest clean-up method. Carmella's mouth would be the best, though, but only if she were a very, very good girl.

I've cleaned up my spunk by the time I hear the vacuum switch off and her making her way to where I sit. My earlier orgasm has me feeling quite relaxed and more than a bit hungry.

"Are you ready to get something to eat, caramel drop? We can stop by the store afterward," I ask.

She nods eagerly, and a bottle of cleaning spray thumps on the counter as she sets it down. A dirty, damp rag joins it. "Fuck yeah. I'm starved and want to sit down."

"Good, let's fucking go then." The button clicks as I switch off the computer and grab the safety deposit bag. "I got to drop this by the bank."

"What's that?" she questions.

"Just the day's earnings." I scoot back in the rolling chair and stand.

"No, I know what that is. I'm talking about that."

I glance at what she is pointing at: a wet, whitish blob sits drying on the counter. Half of it has slimed its way off the edge and started a downward descent to the floor.

I freeze, actually mortified for a second. "Um, I have no idea."

"Did you eat a cinnamon roll or something? Looks like frosting or spoiled milk." She crinkles her nose in disgust.

I bite my lip. Part of me wants to die laughing, another part has wicked ideas, and a tiny bit of me is ashamed. A very tiny part. I know immediately which one will win.

"I don't know, babe. Why don't you taste it and find out," I suggest.

She gives me the same scandalized look I just jerked off to. "Eww, no, you weirdo."

Tipping my head back, I bust out laughing. She has no idea how accurate that is. She leans over and sprays the cum with the cleaning spray before wiping it up.

"There, all clean." She nods at her handiwork.

I snicker, earning myself a suspicious glance from her.

"Come on, caramel drop. Let's go get some grub."

THE SMOKED CRAB

LUKE

Warm saltwater air rolls off the coast and tickles the hair on my forearm as it hangs out the window of my cherry-red Trans Am. The sky is a pretty magenta and dark blue this evening, and the roar of the coast crashes into the beach as I tap to the rhythm of "Summer Vibe" by Forrest Nolan against the steering wheel. Seagulls and blackbirds fly overhead in the evening glow. Carmella and I sit at a red light.

"There is a place off the water called The Smoked Crab. It's a bar. They make killer tacos. You ever been?" I look over at my dinner date.

Carmella's hair lies loose and curly as the wind gently ruffles it, and despite my earlier orgasm, the desire to smooth her wild waves still bothers me. Her locks match the soft tannish color of the beaches behind her. She's been unusually quiet since climbing in the car. "No, never been. Will they card me, 'cause I don't have my ID, remember?"

"Nah, no worries, sugar. We'll eat in the restaurant section, but you've got to get that resolved, and soon. What happened to it?"

She shrugs, rotating her body away from me and staring glumly out the window. "Probably vanished when I was moving from place to place. You lose all kinds of things when they get thrown into bags. Sometimes shit gets left behind if you're in a hurry or it gets stolen. I've had my purse stolen twice now. Jokes on them, though. There wasn't any money, anyway."

Well, shit.

A few people still linger at the shore, taking an evening swim. Kids romp around, kicking sand at each other while their mom waves at them to stop. We watch them for a few seconds. "Lucky kids," she comments. My eyes flick to her profile again. The light turns green, and I pull away with the other traffic. I hate to ask her because my gut tells me I already know the answers to my questions, but I need to double-check. *Maybe I'm wrong. I've been wrong about a woman before.*

Observing her, I announce, "This week, we will go get your ID."

She stiffens and keeps her eyes on the waves as we zip by. "No birth certificate. Sorry."

"Proof of residency. Where do you get your mail?"

The silence is loud.

Checking the surrounding traffic, I lean forward, getting a glimpse of her side profile. She worries her bottom lip with her teeth and scrapes her thumbnails against each other in a nervous fidget.

"Social security card?" I prod.

Carmella shakes her head, and I sigh. "Alright, shoot it to me straight. Who are we running from? Boyfriend? Dad? Daddy? It's Daddy, isn't it?"

"Who says I'm running?" Her tone is biting.

"C'mon, you're telling me you prefer living out of bags? Clearly, you have someone you check in with. Can't they help you get your ID?"

When she speaks, her voice is soft. "No, they can't, and maybe bags and drifting are better than where I was before. Maybe those people are just as glad that I'm gone as I am to be gone."

Other questions die on the tip of my tongue, as my digging is burying the entire mood of the drive. I pull up to another stoplight. Empty parking spots line the beach boardwalk, and I consider whipping in one and dragging her down to the beach. We could dip our feet in. Anything to liven up the morose mood I've caused. Carmella rests her head against the seat and stares out across the waves.

I'm slightly scared to ask more questions. The pain she is suppressing pulls at the makeshift stitches I've sewn over my own heart. It's been years since I've been without a place to call home, but I still remember the fear and uncertainty of it. It makes me wonder what her past was like if the life she has now is the better option. I shake my head. *How the fuck do I end up being the better option?*

What brought her to this point? Where has she been sleeping? Fuck. Hopefully, a shelter. The beaches are sketchy at night.

We move on with the flow of traffic. *So much for a joyride with my new girl.* Turning up the music, I let Carmella have her moment of beach watching and leave her in peace.

The Smoked Crab parking lot is moderately full by the time we pull in. The restaurant sits upon pier pilings and juts over the water on the commercial side of the harbor. Smoke billows from the back of the eatery and hides the fishy smell, instead filling the air with the aroma of cooking meats. Carmella's brows pull down when I hold the door open for her. "Ladies first." She shakes her head as she steps inside.

Fake birds, plastic crabs, and little tiki totem salt and pepper shakers are just the beginning of the campy luau-themed decorations that coat every inch of the place. "Pineapple Sunrise" by Beach Weather, a happy beachy tune that compliments the decor, thumps out from the speakers hiding in the faux tropical plants.

"Can we get a table out there?" Carmella points out onto the dock overlooking the water, and I nod to the waitress to lead the way. Sitting down in the metal chair warmed by the sun, I'm thankful for the evening breeze off the water.

Carmella's head whips around as she takes in the other diners and the decorations. Soft sloshing sounds fill the air as the waves lick and slap against the wooden pillars of the dock. Carmella's smile damn near splits her face when she spies the bucket of crayons. "Do they have paper?" She glances around for the waitress.

My forehead pinches as I survey her tourist-like behavior. I tap the gray piece of paper rolled across the top of the table, and a pink flush stains her cheeks as she laughs a little. "Oh."

Reaching for the bucket, she pulls it over and roots around in the container, the crayons clinking against the metal sides. She looks up at me with her big blue eyes as blonde, frizzy waves fall around her face, and the air is punched out of my lungs by how young and lovely she really is. "You want some crayons?" she asks.

I take a deep breath and hold it for a minute, willing the arousal away from my dick. "No, sweetheart. I'm good. Do you like to draw?" I'm glad the moodiness she showed in the car seems to have passed.

"Sometimes, I draw. I'm no artist, but it's enjoyable. One of those adult coloring books with cool designs in it would be fun." I nod along with her comment, formulating my next question. I assume her hostile, distrustful, and frustratingly tight-lipped behavior has probably kept her safe and alive on the streets. Or at least, I hope it kept her safe. I have no idea what lurks in her past, but I think I've earned a little trust.

Now, how to get my fucking questions answered without triggering a bad mood from this spicy little firecracker?

A red crayon zooms across the expanse of the paper, guided by her hand. Two zigzag lines appear. She discards the red to dig through the pail for the white, biting her lip as she eyes the sketch. She abandons the white crayon for the black one and gets back to work, bringing whatever vision she has in her head to life.

My attention alternates between the menu and Carmella as she crafts her masterpiece. The waiter comes along to take our orders, and of course, my caramel drop hasn't even looked at the menu. I order for us both. Seagulls cry out gently along the shore, and decorative overhead lantern lights turn on, illuminating the docks in a warm romantic glow. And just like the old men who sit at the end of the boardwalk catching fish, I, too, am hoping for bites.

"So, did your parents bring you to places like this when you were a kid?" I sip my soda innocently.

The crayon stops moving. Carmella stares down at the paper. "Maybe. I don't remember."

"What happened?" I leave the question open-ended, letting her fill in the blank and answer however she sees fit.

She's quiet for what feels like forever, and I control my anxious fidgeting during the silence. *Which I deserve a fucking medal for.* The red crayon in her hand is really getting a workout as she wheedles it down. Several giant red blobs take shape on the paper. I sigh. It figures we're headed back into a nonverbal standoff.

Folding my arms over my chest, I consider her. *Maybe if I give a little, I'll get a little.* I dislike delving into my past. One, I don't owe a goddamned explanation to anyone. And two, I hate the pitying looks I get afterward when I do. That shit pisses me off enough to want to slug somebody in the jaw.

As I twist the empty straw wrapper around my finger, anxiety eats at my chest. "I grew up an orphan. A legitimate safe surrender baby Moses. I had a couple of foster families, or so I was told, until I was six. My recollection of that time isn't great, and what I know I've mostly pieced together by social workers."

Carmella stares at me with those big, liquid blue eyes. Turning away, I scan the rocky blue waters and wish the waves could wash away all the bullshit.

"Apparently, I cried a lot as a baby. And as I got older, I could never sit still, didn't listen, and was destructive. I'm sure these days, they probably have a shit ton of diagnoses for whatever was wrong with me back then." I chuckle humorlessly. "Probably was a meth baby or something." Carmella doesn't laugh.

Reaching into my pants, I pull out my cigarettes and lighter. "When I think back on those families, all that's left is just a general sense of anxiousness, confusion, and..." I struggle for a minute. "... loss. I was a little shit as a kid and not too book smart. Caseworkers tried to keep me in school, but I'd just fuck off. And one day, in high school, I got bored with the whole group home bullshit, packed up the few things I cared about, pretended I was going to class, and never went back to either."

I light my cig and take a long draw, letting the taste of burning paper and tobacco swirl across my tongue. Blowing it out, I give caramel drop a panty-stealing smile and continue my pathetic story. "So naturally, I got in trouble. Fourteen with no money, attitude for days, and an inability to chill out made me a textbook time bomb. And eventually, I went off. Ended up aging out of the system while serving a juvenile sentence for theft. The only good thing about juvie was I met my best friend and brother there. His name is Sasha."

There. A summary of my sad and fast childhood. I cringe when I realize that my tangent was more than just a "little share" and suddenly wish I could suck the words back into my mouth.

Carmella looks me in the eye. There is no pity or judgment. In fact, her smooth face gives nothing away, and for a moment, I would rather receive pitying looks than this blank apathy. I realize it's her eyes and those quick frowns that make her look older than she did while discovering the coloring. *C'mon, girl, say something.*

She opens her mouth, but instead of an apology or a well-meaning platitude, all she says is, "My parents died when I was seven."

Well, fuck, so much for avoiding triggering shit. A sharp stab of pain aches in my chest for her. The idea of no one wanting her, just as no one wanted me, makes my hand ache to punch the table or a wall. My throat burns, and I grind my teeth. *Deep breaths, man. Calm down. That shit was a long time ago. I am past that now.*

"And after that?" I say around the lump in my throat. I take a draw on the cigarette and flick off some of the ash.

She doesn't look at me, instead hyperfocusing on the artwork growing under her careful hands. "I bounced around a couple of foster families here and there. They gave me to my aunt when I was twelve."

An aunt? Why didn't she end up with the aunt when she was seven? My brow furrows as I stare at the paper covering our table.

She sees the confusion on my face because she continues, "Gloria had a drug problem. Still has one. She and my abuela didn't get along."

Abuela?

My smoke is halfway to my mouth when I pause. "Wait, you're Hispanic?"

She looks at me like that should be obvious. "My name is Carmella Maria Herrera." Her tongue rolls the r's in her last name, dragging them out perfectly. She looks down at her chest and arms. "I'm fucking tan, Luke. Like *naturally.*" Her tone is grossly offended.

Well, fuck me, how was I supposed to know?!

This date is going great.

Just fucking fantastic.

Childhood trauma.

Dead parents.

Mistaken ethnicity.

Maybe next, we will talk about school shootings.

I suddenly wish I had ordered a margarita.

It Takes Two to Play For Pay

LUKE

Mouth agape, I stare at her in disbelief. A sharp burning sensation flames in my hand as the cigarette cherry sears the flesh between my fingers. "Ow, fuck!" Flinging the ciggy over the dock railing, I rise, bumping my hip into the table, making it rock, and knocking over our drinks. Soda and water sheet off the top and drip everywhere.

Carmella gasps and shoves away from the mess. My chair tips back, and the metal clangs loudly against the wooden floor. Cursing and dusting ash from my pants, I glance up. A sea of faces looks on at the commotion I'm causing. Nosey assholes. "What are you all staring at? I burnt my hand. I'm not going to shoot up the place. Fucking calm down," I announce to the dock full of people.

"Seriously?" Carmella hisses, trying to shield her beet-red face with her hands, her eyes the size of dinner plates. "Sit down, Luke!" Her tone holds all the threats of a mother who can't scold an unruly child in public.

Righting my chair, I whisper-yell back at her, "Okay... Okay, fine."

We clean up as the wait staff rushes over. The waitress wipes down the table and refills our drinks, rolling out some new paper. "Thank you, I appreciate it, and sorry about the mess," Carmella tells her for the third time.

As soon as the waitress leaves, I bite into her. "One, you never told me your full name and you have no ID. Two, you have tan lines... so I assumed the tan was from... ya know, the beach." I hold up my hands when she looks ready to murder me. "Granted, Hispanic people can have tan lines as well, so my mistake. Three, you've never spoken a word of Spanish. Again, granted, I've also only known you for twenty-four hours, so also my mistake. And four, you are blonde and look..."

"So help me God, if you say white, Luke..." Carmella warns.

"European. I was going to say European."

"I'm Mexican, and skin color isn't always an indicator of race or ethnicity," she snaps.

"I know that. I know that!" I snap back.

Carmella's eyes roll to the sky. We sit quietly for a minute as awkwardness settles in, and my stomach growls. Shit, the food is taking forever.

Rubbing my neck, I try to coax her back into conversation.

"So Gloria, your aunt, has a drug problem, and she didn't get along with your grandma," I say, hoping she will pick back up with her story.

Carmella shrugs. "Gloria cut ties and took off long before I was even born. No one knew where she was. No contact information. Nothing. One day, she pops up after being gone for fifteen years and is searching for her brother, my papa, and my abuela. Of course, they were dead by that time, but she didn't know. So she contacts my family's lawyer and... yeah. The next thing I know, my caseworker shows up at my foster family's house and tells me to pack. I'm going to go live with family."

Family lawyer? Interesting.

I nod. "I take it she wasn't a great guardian?"

Carmella snorts. "Understatement." She picks up a black crayon and begins her drawing again on the fresh piece of paper. She's aggressive this time with the marks and ends up snapping the crayon in half. "What my caseworker and the family lawyer don't know is my aunt is a raging, pill-popping bitch who made my life hell the moment she laid eyes on me. Fuck being treated like that, so I took off," she says.

My eyebrows raise into my hairline at the viciousness in her tone. "So, no love lost there?"

She glares at me from across the table. "Not at all. Fuck her."

My mouth opens to ask her another question, but the arrival of our food cuts off the conversation, and I decide to drop it. Plus, with how Carmella stuffs her mouth, I don't want her to choke trying to explain something emotional with huge bites of taco filling her cheeks.

"What's this?" Carmella gestures to the two metal funnels, each held in a bracket and fixed over the top of an empty plate.

Dragging my funnel to me, I say, "This is the reason I brought you here, of all places. This is us living in the year twenty-ninety." Opening the red tortilla warmer, I slide one of the soft round corn shells under the funnel. Grabbing one of the overly stuffed beef tacos from my plate, I take a bite over the contraption and watch as goodies fall out the other end. The taco mix slides down the funnel and ends up on the fresh tortilla. "Ta-da! All your taco goodies stay in a taco."

Carmella eyes me while shaking her head. "I can't tell if this is brilliant or ridiculous."

"It's brilliant; now stop sassing me and eat."

We dig in, and eventually, I change the conversation to better topics. Movies first, which is short-lived as she has barely seen anything made in the past decade. Mentally, I take notes to get my girl some movies.

We talk about music, and I'm intrigued that Carmella has a narrow taste for indie alternative, which tracks with how moody she is. Introducing her to some of my favorite tunes is a priority. We talk about bands, interesting facts about rock stars, famous suicides, and overdoses. It's nice, a little dark, but really nice. I can't remember the last time I shared a meal and conversation where I wasn't immediately planning to get my date into my bed. Although, truth is, I'm still planning it.

Getting my caramel drop into bed is a long con, a challenge, but I'm feeling up to it. She's too suspicious and stubborn. We are being friendly now, sharing a laugh. Building trust. But it's tentative and fragile. Trying to cash in all the way now would be a disaster.

If she's as smart as I think, she will remember that I'm always selling myself; if she isn't, then I guess I will be fucking her sooner rather than later. I wear my most charming smile, and she breaks into a grin as she recounts the evening she almost gave herself alcohol poisoning at a bonfire. Chuckling, I can't deny that it's not manipulation every single time. I am enjoying the company.

"Let's take a walk down on the beach," I say.

"Yeah, that sounds nice."

After paying for the meal, we head to the front door. "Wait!" she says, heading back to the table.

I see her tear off a piece of the gray paper tablecloth and jog back to me. "I almost forgot this."

"Let me see it." I reach for the rolled-up picture and pluck it from her fingers. Lowering my voice, I whisper in her ear, "Go put the tip money back on the table or I'm going to spank you."

She at least has the decency to look chastised, then alarmed, before scowling up at me and stomping back to replace the cash she swiped. Little petty thief.

It's my turn to shake my head as Carmella glares, cuts me off at the door, and then heads to the beach with me trailing behind her. Laughter bubbles up in me. I kick off my shoes, and the cooling sand is rough against my feet. I glance around for a place to keep the picture dry and balance it on top of my brown loafers before rolling up my pants and walking down to the surf.

Closing my eyes, I breathe in the smell of salty minerals as the damp air rushes over me. Water laps at my feet, and the roar of the waves crashes over all other thoughts in my mind. People think the sound of the ocean is tranquil. Personally, I've always found it loud. Blessedly loud. Enough to block out all the other bullshit that rattles around my mind and give me a chance to exist in peace.

A presence close to me draws my attention. Carmella has abandoned her shoes and stands next to me in the water. Most of the beachgoers have left, and aside from a few people way down the line, we are alone under the darkening purple and navy sky.

I slip a fifty from my money clip and hold it up for her to see. "Do you want to earn that tip you tried to swipe from the table?"

She eyes the folded piece of paper like it's going to sprout fangs and attack her. "Maybe. What do you want me to do for it?"

A relaxed smile curls my lips. "Strip down to your underwear and play in the water. I want some pictures."

"Hell no, I remember the last time you wanted to take some pictures." She used air quotes around the word pictures, and I burst out laughing.

Turning my attention back to the ocean, I tell her, "I love the beach. It's my favorite place in the entire world. I come here at least twice a week. One day, if you are still around, I'll show you my favorite secret spot."

"What's so great about this spot?"

"If I told you that, then it wouldn't be a secret anymore, would it?"

Carmella hmphs, unimpressed, as she folds her arms over her chest.

My eyes trace the line of the ocean as my hands rest in my pockets. "You remind me of the beach. That's the first thing I thought about when I saw you yesterday. Your dark-blue eyes are like a storm over the ocean, and your hair matches the color of wet sand. With your golden skin, I couldn't help but think here is the prettiest summer girl I've ever laid eyes on."

When I glance over at her, she doesn't say anything, but a light blush covers her cheeks. I give her an appreciative slow, long look down her body, which takes her blush to an all-out flush as she avoids my gaze, even as a smile curls her mouth. She bites her bottom lip and glances back at me hesitantly.

"It's just such a fucking shame that my perfect summer girl is such a loud burglar, obvious thief, and now... Now, she's just a chicken shit who will swipe money off a table but won't take it from my hand when it's offered."

Her mouth drops open as she sputters, "I'm not a chickenshit."

I extend the fifty back to her. "Prove it. You don't have anything you need to buy at the store tonight?" Not that I would let her. Carmella is going to need every cent if she plans on moving on or starting over.

Sighing, she looks around. The beach has darkened into night, and the few lingering people have drifted toward the city lights. The fifty is yanked from my hand and she points at me. "No touching, pictures only."

Holding my hand up in surrender, I promise. Pictures only. Excitement courses through my veins as I watch her peel off the tight jeans, exposing a pair of blue panties with lace trim. My dick hardens in my pants at the sight of the flimsy piece of fabric, and my fingers twitch with the desire to slip along her slit and delve into her hot, wet pussy. Not much between you and me, caramel drop. And there will be less and less every day.

Taking out my phone, I switch to night mode and begin snapping pictures. The photos are a little dark, with only the residual lighting from the boardwalk creeping down on the beach, but I don't care.

She pauses her strip. "What's wrong?" I ask.

"My tank top has a built-in bra."

"So."

"So, if I leave it on, it will get wet. If I take it off, I'll be topless."

I grin. "Better take it off since we're going to get groceries after this."

"Better pay me more money."

Eh, fair enough. "Shit, okay, just take it off."

I keep snapping pictures as the expanse of her slim stomach comes into view, and I nearly groan when she pulls it over her tits. They bounce back against her body once free. Her nipples tighten in the evening air. Now, that's what I'm talking about.

She glances around nervously, cupping her chest.

"Don't worry. No one is going to see you but me."

She rolls her eyes and laughs.

"What's so funny?" I ask.

"I've literally been trying to keep you away from my tits since we've met, and here I am naked, so I can go buy a fucking toothbrush. It's either laugh or scream."

A dirty, biting aggression creeps along my arousal. "Don't worry, baby. I'm going to buy you all the toothbrushes you need."

"Oh. My. Fucking. God." She stares up at the sky. "Okay, let's just get this over with."

She steps into the surf, and I record her walking into the water. She trails her fingertips across the surface of the dark water as the misty air pushes back her curls. She is lovely in the twilight as she glances over her shoulder and gives me a shy smile. I nearly groan out loud.

Carmella's voice holds an edge of hysteria. "I've only ever been skinny dipping once, and I don't know what you mean by play in the water." She dips down to where her shoulders and head are uncovered.

"Come back up here. I want you to pose."

She frowns at me. "I don't know how to pose."

"C'mon, Carmella, work with me. Think sexy time."

Her laugh is strained, and I'm struck by the sound. I don't think she has had a carefree laugh once since I met her. Such a serious woman.

She walks back up to the shore, and I switch on the flash, snapping shot after shot. We won't be able to do this for much longer with the flash going off. Carmella kneels in the surf and looks every bit like the cover model of Sports Illustrated Magazine: Swimsuit Edition. My erection presses against my pants and demands attention. I ignore it, but arousal dominates my mind at the sight of her wet panties glued to soft pussy lips.

"Lie on your back with your head toward the shore," I say.

Stepping into the water, I stand in front of her. Looking past the screen at the naked women lying beneath me, I palm my cock through my pants. "Spread your legs for me, caramel drop."

She gasps a little at my words, and flushes crimson, throwing an arm over her face. Her legs fall apart, and the material of her panties suctions perfectly to her cunt. My mouth dries as I fantasize about dropping down and crawling between her legs to taste her and the salty water. But I know it's out of the question.

"Fuck, you make my cock so hard," I growl out as I snap more pictures of her glorious body. "I want to jerk off to you like you are right now. What do you think about that?"

She bites her bottom lip and shrugs. Her tits are so perfect. I taunt her, wanting more of a reaction than a shrug. "Where is my brave, little sassy shit that wasn't scared when I had a gun on her? Huh? Where is that ballsy woman? I think that Carmella would like to know how much I want to fuck her."

Her arm flops away as she glares at me for a moment. "Uh, different circumstances, asshole."

I laugh as I rub my dick over my pants. "There she is. Now, pull your panties aside and show me your pussy."

I watch as she slides her hand down her body, deliberately seductive, her thumb brushing against her pebbled nipple. Flicking it, she moans.

"Oh, shit yeah, like that. Good girl." I pant.

"Do you like that?" she asks.

"Fuck yes, you take my breath away." She damn near has me panting as my cock strains for more friction. My eyes flick to hers before I glance back down and follow her hand's descent past her breasts. Sliding her fingers down her wet stomach, she spreads her legs wider and trails her finger along her wet slit before hooking the material and pulling it to the side. "Like that, Luke?"

My dick jumps at the sight of her damp curls and nestled clit. "Fuck, that's so hot. Touch yourself for me, baby." I turn on the video, unzip my fly, and start to pull out my cock.

She cackles. "Oh, no. We're done. You wanted me sassy, and now you got it."

My head snaps up like her words are like a bucket of ice water. "What!"

Carmella is up off the ground and headed into the water to rinse off the sand before I can untangle my hand from my pants. "Wait."

"No," she says. "You paid for pictures. You got pictures. You're a businessman, Luke. Do business. It's simple."

I'm speechless. She left me holding my cock in my hand. That little seduction act at the end was just the cherry on top before she took the whole sundae away. That's ruthless. I'm impressed.

She strides past me, giving me a curt nod and a tight smile as she goes to pick up her clothes and get dressed.

Fucking hell. Well, at least I got pictures. Dark pictures.

Zipping up my pants, I stomp back up the beach to my shoes and scoop up the drawing.

Unrolling the paper, I see a giant red crab with a mustache, my mustache, come into view. In its claw is a pinched lit cigarette and a line of smoke trailing upwards. Above its head float some ridiculously suggestive eyebrows, and in the background is my sweet cherry-red ride. A text bubble made to look like smoke rolling out of the crab's mouth reads, "Hey, baby, you ever ride a smoked crab?"

I'm offended.

Holding up the grotesque, sleazy caricature of me, I pivot in the sand and glare at her accusatively. "Is this supposed to be me?"

Carmella grins.

"My eyebrows are not that suggestive."

She loses it and doubles over, laughing. It's the first genuine laugh I've heard from her. "I don't know. I think it's an accurate representation. When you flirt, your eyebrows get wiggly." As she says this, she gives me an arm wave like my eyebrows are on some stupid ass roller coaster.

Making a disgusted noise, I roll up the picture and pop her on the head with it. "They do not."

Carmella chuckles. "I would know better than you. Those caterpillars were dancing all over your face a few minutes ago. What was that little lesson you taught me today...? 'Always be selling yourself, Carmella.'" She mimics me. "And you bought in, Luke; now pay up." She holds out her hand for her money.

My mouth works to form words, but nothing comes out. This is harassment.

Reaching into my pocket, I slap another fifty into her outstretched palm.

I stew as we walk back to the car. I don't know if I should date her or leave her ass here.

Carmella cuts in front of me once we reach the steps that take you from the beach to the boardwalk. She blocks my path as she stands on the step above me, giving me hard eyes. "For the record, while I might not be the quietest burglar or the sneakiest thief, there's one thing I'm pretty certain I am good at."

Okay, I'll bite.

Tipping my face up, I ask, "Oh, and what's that?"

She leans down, and her lips hover a bit too close to mine. "Bothering you. And tonight is the last time you say an inch, but take a mile with me."

With that, she turns and sashays up the steps as I stare at her ass.

Touché, Carmella. Touché.

Margaritas in Paradise

CARMELLA

A WEEK LATER

My elbows dig into the U-shaped front desk as I lean forward and fiddle one-handed with some of Luke's junk mail, ripping an envelope into little pieces. Nervousness bursts in my chest like fireworks as the phone rings for the fifth time with no answer. "C'mon, Tommy, pick up," I say.

Familiar rap music blares out of the speaker as Tommy's signature voice greeting switches on. "Fuuccckkk, man, it's Tommy. I'm busy. Shoot me a DM and stop callin'." Instead of the normal beep that comes before leaving a message, a woman's voice speaks and informs me that the voicemail of the person I'm trying to reach is full. The line disconnects.

The phone clicks back into its cradle and I check for any missed calls, like Luke taught me. Nothing.

Sitting back in the swivel chair, I twist in my seat and stare out over the empty show floor. Light trickles in from the windows. The evening sky has settled into hues of soft yellow, purple, and pink over the buildings across the street. *I bet it's beautiful at the beach right now.*

The familiar pang of loneliness and uncertainty rolls around in my chest. It's been over a week since my last check-in with Tommy and the interactions with Luke keep ramping up. Guilt eats at me.

After leaving Gloria's and bouncing around, Tommy and I worked out a loose agreement. Whenever I move to a new place, I check in... somehow... some way, even if it's an email from a local library. I hated being at home, but with no type of tether, I feel cut off. Isolated. I shiver at the thought of truly being on my own. The image of me as a Jane Doe intrudes on my mind again. And I'm starting to think maybe Tommy doesn't want to hear from me anymore.

Luke's cherry-red Trans Am whips into view, sails down the lane, and, I'm assuming, into the back parking lot. *I guess, in the most technical sense, I haven't been alone much at all.* The only time I've had any quiet in the past week is when Luke steps out to have conversations with an ever-revolving door of people, most of them being of the scary thug-looking variety, or when he goes to make bank deposits. And that one time he got a shipment to the storage building, he threw an absolute fit about how many tires they unloaded. He spent the whole day either on his phone or talking to the men in the black SUVs that pulled into the back lot.

And while I may be curious about why there are so many tires, when Luke doesn't even sell tires, and who exactly all of these men are, I'm not dumb enough to eavesdrop. Some things are his business and some things are mine. We may share a space, but that doesn't mean I have to get involved. Especially with a bunch of men who look like actual gangsters instead of Tommy's stupid petty-criminal friends.

I'd like to say that Luke and I are weird roommates with unspoken agreements now, except that every time I turn around, he's there with a smile and an offer.

The unintended consequence of getting in Luke's face the night at the beach is now he believes I'm made for rougher games. If he were any other dude my age, he would have backed off some, taken my warning, or even ghosted me. But no... not Luke. He doubled down.

I thought I'd be able to ward off most of his advances and only participate in "safe activities." The things that I could do to earn an easy buck yet keep Luke at a distance. But I'm learning there are no safe activities or easy dollars. Occasionally, his propositions come packaged as help or even kindness. *I think Luke might be a con man. I also think I might be out of my depth here.*

It was sweet when he offered to paint my toenails for me. We were relaxing and listening to one of his playlists. He had ordered pizza and had some cheesy action movie playing on the TV he dragged over to the sofa. It was like a slumber party, all the way down to the toenail polish.

No one had ever offered to do that for me before, so I let him. It wasn't until his warm hands brushed against the arch of my foot and lightning bolts of arousal shot straight into my clit that I realized this was a mistake.

And when he bent down to blow on the drying paint, I froze, afraid he'd know that every lingering touch was making my head spin and my heart race. In hindsight, I'm convinced all his touches were deliberate as he instigated an intimate tickling match not much later, which left me breathless and giggling as my body tingled all over from his touch. His wandering hands were a bit... overly friendly.

Shaking my head, I stare at the blue countertop. Out of the corner of my eye, a beam of light sweeps the hallway as the back door opens. *He's baaaaack.*

The morning after he touched every inch of me that he could get his hands on, he wanted to take pictures of me eating an ice cream cone. I figured it'd be weird, but nothing like the beach night or the... tickle fight.

And I was wrong. It wasn't weird to eat ice cream in front of Luke. It was the opposite of weird. *Flattering, maybe?* Seated in his lap, the heat from his body radiated into mine. Strong hands rested on my lower back and high on my thigh while he watched me lick a vanilla and pineapple swirl cone. It was alarmingly sexy.

Between his intense, heated looks at my mouth, my ass tucked against the length of his erection, and the way the smooth, melty ice cream slid across my tongue, I couldn't help but move against him.

Just a tiny grind, enough to make his nostrils flare as he closed his eyes and tipped his head back.

It wasn't until he gently fisted his hands in my hair and tipped my head that my mind supplied me with the vision of his lips on mine. My legs clenched at the thought of our tongues mingling.

His mustache tickled against my ear as he whispered he had something else for me to lick and suck.

I abandoned his lap after that, but the ache between my legs didn't lessen until later—when I had a moment of privacy and came violently to the fantasy of taking Luke into my mouth and running my tongue over the hard ridge of his cock.

Guilt and shame take center stage.

I drum my fingernails against the counter.

Neither will ever happen again because I have a boyfriend. Sort of. I was adjusting myself for a better picture angle. Really.

Groaning, I shake my head. *Money makes people do crazy things, right? Except now, I sound like a whore.*

Keys jingle and scrape against the countertop as Luke moves around in the kitchen. Cabinet doors bang open and shut. I bite my lip as anxiousness floods me.

The money started appearing on my nightstand that next morning:

fives, tens, and twenties. Sometimes, I know what he's paying me for, and sometimes, I'm not really sure, and it makes me fucking nervous. Luke has a talent for painting the most innocent daily interactions as dirty by slipping me cash.

Desperation claws at me, and I snatch up the phone, calling Tommy for the fifth time today. *Please, for the love of God, Tommy, answer the phone.*

Luke's voice calls from the other room, "Hey, Carmella, where are you, my sexy little caramel drop?"

My eyebrows do the best impression of trying to climb off my face as I blow out a breath. *Fuck, if Tommy picks up and hears Luke...* I slam the phone into the receiver like it's burning me.

"In here," I say, smoothing down my frizzy curls.

Luke appears in the hallway looking every inch an old-school sex icon. His black button-down has a sprayed-on neon sunset with the word paradise laid over it. It's unbuttoned at the top, displaying a collection of gold chains and dark chest hair over his golden tan. He stares at me from behind a set of brown aviator glasses and low whistles, like I'm not wearing a polo shirt and jeans. He smooths his mustache. "Go get that dress you liked so much. We're having a fucking party tonight." He sways to some unheard rhythm and dances in place.

I arch my eyebrows. "For real? What for?"

"Fuck yeah, for real. It's been a long ass week, and we made fucking bank. I think that merits a celebration."

Luke calls the shots around here schedule-wise, and mostly, I'm pretty cool with that. *It's like Wednesday night, but it's his store after all.* I shrug. "Okay."

He grins. "Perfect, you won't be disappointed. After you get changed, come to the kitchen." Luke dance shuffles backward before spinning and boogying down the hallway, lightly singing. Leaning forward, I watch him do a sliding sidestep into the kitchen.

As my brows pull down into a frown, my head tips to the side and I consider him. *Man has got some moves, though.*

"Dreamin" by Skynny Dyck pumps through the overhead speaker system, probably streaming from Luke's phone, and chases away the silence. Bopping along with the music, I duck out of sight of the large glass windows and put on a floral, boho mini dress. We did end up going grocery shopping after the beach incident, but Luke said that I was such a good girl that he was also taking me to a boutique and letting me pick out several new outfits that he ended up paying for.

Rummaging around for a clean pair of underwear, I curse when all I have is a thong. Thongs and breezy, billowy dresses do not mix. It's asking for trouble, especially with Luke.

Shit, he could probably smell a thong from five miles away. The image of Luke's head popping up at the mention of a thong, much like a Golden Retriever who heard the mailman, is hilarious. Giggling, I scan the drawer again, praying I overlooked a fresh pair. No such luck. *I'll just have to be extra careful.*

I've been neglecting laundry since several pairs of panties went missing. They suspiciously got "lost" while Luke was washing clothes in the shop.

Either he has them and will lie or he has them and will tell me why. My desire for that conversation, or to even have them back, is zero. It's too embarrassing.

When I enter the kitchen, Luke's thumb is swiping across the screen of his phone, and the music changes to "Juice" by the New Beat Fund.

"You look stunning, baby," Luke says when he sees me, his mischievous eyes roaming down the dress. "Great legs... what time do they open? I'm up twenty-four seven." My face heats a little. You'd think by now I'd be immune to this. His lips curl up into a heart-stopping smile that borders on being lecherous.

The phone clicks as he sets it on the counter, and he sings along to the song while pouring ice into a blender. Cut up limes and oranges sit next to a couple bottles of hard liquor. Winking at me, he turns on the blender and loud, icy grinding fills the air.

"Margaritas?" I ask. He nods.

"There are tamales and hot wings on the table. Eat something," he says over the noise.

"You're always telling me to eat something."

"Yes, and you should always listen to me."

I snort as he grins. Switching the blender off, he fills two margarita glasses. The chair legs scrape against the floor as I pull it out. Folding my arms, I lean against the table and say, "Oh yeah?"

"Well, yeah. I am older, wiser and more experienced in the ways of the world. If you let me, I can share some of that experience with you." He stands over me, and as he runs the chilly drink up my exposed arm, cold shivers pebble my skin. My nipples tighten as I snatch the drink from his hand and set it on the table.

His laughter wraps around me as he walks back to the makeshift bar, and I fill my plate with goodies. Luke returns a second later with a shot glass full of tequila, a cut-up lime, a saltshaker, and a folded twenty.

There's a dangerous glint in his eyes as he says, "Hey, caramel drop, you ever done a body shot before?"

Broken Tables, Broken Hearts

Carmella

Sweat slicks my lower back and my pussy throbs. The entire world is soft and dreamy as the alcohol swims in my bloodstream. Grabbing my hand, Luke pulls me down the hallway.

I'm giggling uncontrollably and the more I try to stop laughing, the funnier it is. I'm not looking where I'm walking, so my shoulder slams into his, knocking him forward. The hallway seems like such a long walk tonight, and Luke's voice is warm and slurry. "Fuck, Carmella, you're such a lightweight."

Laughing hysterically, I can't keep my feet under me and end up sliding down Luke's body and puddling on the floor in a heap. Luke's booming laugh fills the air. He bends over me, chuckling with a big smile plastered to his stupidly handsome face. "For future reference, caramel drop, you're a three-drink girl. Not a six-drinks-and-three-shots girl," he says.

Catching my breath, I choke out, "It's your weed. It's too strong." Wooziness washes over me, and for a second, I'm weightless. It feels like I'm floating. Luke hauls me to my feet and brushes me off. "Nah, that's just how you know it's good. C'mon, hold this." He passes me the bottle of tequila.

Holding it in both hands, I stare at the label, half expecting it to say, "This shit will fuck you up." An arm slips around my back, and I'm hoisted into the air as Luke cradles me in his arms. "You're blushing," he notes.

"Gah, why do you always got to say something?" A warm sensation that I chalk up to the tequila spreads across my body and settles into my pussy as he holds me and strides across the show floor.

"You're strong," I say.

He smirks down at me as we weave around appliances. "You think so?"

"Well, yeah, and handsome... I mean, I'm sure women tell you that all the time."

This time, the smirk is arrogant. "They do, actually."

"Ugh, conceited much?"

"You know, I think I like drunk Carmella," he says.

He deposits me at the end of an oval dining-room table that seats six. I don't want to leave his arms. The tequila works its wicked games on me, reminding me of how little I've been touched and how much I miss it. Taking the bottle from my arms, he unscrews the top and takes three giant swings. "Woah, slow down," I say. Luke steps up in the chair and onto the tabletop of the dining-room set. My mouth drops open as he stands over me.

"What are you doing?"

"Dancing."

"Not on that table. You'll fall." I reach for him and the table wobbles. He steps back and counterbalances the weight on one end. "Luke, get down." My voice is a little slurry, even to my ears.

He snorts. "No, you get up here." He takes out his phone and changes the song to "Swoon" by Beach Weather while taking another swig straight from the tequila bottle.

I stare at him. "You're such a brat."

He chokes on the clear liquid, a line of it running down his chin as he struggles to swallow. Nodding in agreement, he winks at me. I shake my head in disapproval, which brings on another round of laughter from him.

"Smile, caramel drop. You're too young to be this serious." He snaps his fingers and shifts his weight from foot to foot. Setting down the bottle, he rolls his hips and dances to the song, putting some of those earlier moves on full display. Biting the inside of my lip, I watch as Luke closes his eyes and comes alive in the shadows and the flickering glow of the blue neon. *Holy shit, I'm in trouble.*

I'm transfixed. The lights from the back of the store cast across him softly as he shakes his ass on the table, completely uninhibited. Not an ounce of shame or embarrassment crosses his full smile. *When I grow up, I want to have as much fun as Luke does.*

His fancy loafers, oiled belt, and necklace gleam in the light as he moves across the table, maintaining his balance. He offers me a heated grin, and his fingers inch up his stomach and pop the top button on his beachy shirt. As his hips sway to the rhythm, he sings along with each verse, his eyes glued to me.

Light-headedness hits me, but not from the party favors. It's Luke. His magnetism. Being with him in the darkness is like being consumed by the ocean. He is the waves and riptides, stealing control of your body and sucking you into murky, ceaseless waters. I don't know what's out there underneath his current, but I am curious.

Part of me wants to be submerged, drowned out, but I want to breathe, too. I bite my lip harder as the air seems to be in limited supply. Full body tingles race along me as Luke undoes another button. There aren't many left, and the thought that I've never seen Luke without his shirt on punches what little oxygen I had out of me.

My gaze flicks down to the gap in his shirt, and my nails dig into the palm of my hands as his abs roll and flex. The tequila and weed have doubled my libido, making my face flame. Taking a deep breath, I shift in my seat and squeeze my thighs together.

Luke unbuttons the rest of the shirt before pulling it from his black linen slacks, revealing a solid chest and just a hint of a six-pack. There is an ornery darkness in his gaze that wasn't there a second ago. An edge of a challenge lingers in the shadows of his face. "Do you want me to take more off? I bet you do," he purrs into the darkness.

A black-and-white cresting wave is tattooed on his upper pec and my finger aches to touch it. Even with my untrained eyes, the work is top-notch. Luke only ever puts quality on his body, and I love that. My gaze drinks him in, along with those perfect crotch-hugging pants.

He tsks. "Really? No response? Well, I clearly must not be naked enough." The jingle of his belt catches my attention. *Surely, he wouldn't.* I glance at the large storefront windows that look out into the night, checking to make sure we are alone. My attention snaps back to him as his belt sails across my line of vision and slaps the carpeted floor.

Grinning, Luke steps wrong, and the table wobbles, tipping on one end. I yank it back down as he steps forward. It stabilizes, but he laughs like a madman.

"Luke, get down. You're drunk," I say.

"No, you're drunk. You get up here."

"I'm not getting up there."

The challenge is back on his face. Creaking from the wood intensifies as he takes a step back and the table rises. I push it back down with my body. An edge of angry, hysterical energy creeps into my buzz. He is fucking with me, but I'm not going to let him flip this table and hurt himself. *Fucker, I am too wasted for this.*

The nervous energy has to go somewhere, so I laugh.

"There, now she is having a good time." The smile in his voice settles across me. Looking up at him, I watch as he pops the top button of his pants.

Thoughts rapidly fire through my mind and it lands on Luke standing on the table naked and me sucking him off. I squeeze my eyes shut and shake my head, trying to dislodge the image.

The song moves on to "Maraschino Love" by EZI and the lyrics swell in my head.

The slow zip of his zipper makes my clit tingle and nipples tighten, and I curse the day Luke was ever born. "KEEP YOUR PANTS ON, SIR!" I shout and scramble onto the table before he is totally naked.

Which puts me within reach of a horny, half-naked Luke, who, as soon as I'm on the table, wraps his arms around me like an octopus.

Satisfied that we are standing in the middle of the table, I relax. "This is probably the jankiest table you have on the floor, Luke."

His dark, lust-filled eyes roam up my arm as his fingers trail along my skin. "Hmm, don't worry about it. Dance with me." He smooths my curls out of my face, his mustache brushing my skin as he kisses me on the forehead and cheek. A soothing warmth tingles where his lips were. At least for now, he has lost interest in taking off his pants.

The smell of smoke and tequila, mixed with his cologne, fills my lungs. It's a pleasant scent, with a note of what I imagine a seedy bar after a long night smells like. I would almost consider it bad if it didn't go straight to my pussy and make me want to fuck him on this table. My mind tries to come up with words for the scent: dirty, nasty, naughty. All things very Luke.

Pulling me against him, Luke dances us to the rhythm. "You're blushing again." He chuckles in my ear.

"Well, you are half naked and..." My mind goes blank as he grabs my ass, wedges his thigh between my legs, and grinds against my cunt. I gasp and bite my lip.

Leaning down, his velvet voice whispers in my ear, "I want some more pictures, Carmella. I've already jerked off on the other ones. You need to stop fighting this and let me between your legs." I swallow thickly as adrenaline pumps through my body, and my pussy pulses at his words. Whimpering as he presses my hips down on his thigh, I want to say yes, rip the Band-Aid off, and let him pin me to this table with his hips and fuck me into oblivion.

It's not like I didn't know what he was doing with the photos, but it's different when he says it in such a low voice and squeezes my ass. My face falls forward onto his collarbone. Giving into temptation, I press my lips onto his hot, salty skin and lick a line up his neck. He cups my head and sucks in a breath as I press kisses along his jawline.

"Be a good girl and lift your dress for me," he says, his voice thick with arousal. The familiar cocktail of shame, embarrassment, and desire that's unique to Luke's propositions rockets through me. I feel the folded money slip into my hand and I groan in defeat. "Atta girl, lift your dress like a dirty slut. Let me see you," Luke growls in my ear.

He grinds his thigh between my legs once more, and I can feel his erection pressing into me. The warmth and power of his body vanishes as he kneels in front of me, pulling his phone from his back pocket.

Morally speaking, I only struggle for a moment before inching the dress up my thighs and staring down at his hungry face. The flash of Luke's camera momentarily disrupts the surrounding darkness, making me feel exposed. I lift the dress higher. Luke squeezes his erection over his pants as his breathing kicks up. The pooling desire in his eyes as he scans my face nearly floors me. I've never had a man look at me like that before, not with so much raw hunger. Glancing away, I take a shaky breath as the nervous energy returns.

Luke's warm hand runs up my exposed thigh, over my hip, and pushes my dress higher as he sucks in a breath, taking all of me in. He stares at my thong, then up at me, not even paying attention to where the camera is pointed as he snaps off photos. "I slipped you a hundred, so don't be mad."

Breathless, I ask, "Mad about what?"

"This." Luke drops his phone and his arm bands across my ass, dragging me forward as his face dips towards the V between my thighs. My hands sink into his hair as I balance myself. His nose brushes against my clit and my body turns into an inferno. A soft, slippery tongue slides along my panty-covered slit. Teeth nip at my pussy lips through the flimsy scrap of fabric.

"Oh, shit. Oh, fuck." I gasp.

He pushes his face against me harder as his tongue laps against the fabric and my clit. I see stars and grind myself shamelessly against his face. His voice is rough when he pulls away. "Yes, give it to me, baby girl. Fucking ride my face." Moaning, I do as I'm told, wishing he would remove the fabric between us.

He moves under me, stretching his out legs between mine and forcing me to straddle his face as his hand slips up between my thighs, leaving fire in its wake. He yanks my underwear to the side, and cold air swirls across my swollen, exposed clit.

Luke's tongue slides between my wet folds, and he moans. His breath tickles my skin and sends lightning bolts dancing throughout my whole body. A hot mouth closes over my clit and my hips jerk as he sucks the bundle of nerves into his mouth. "Oooh, shit." I don't even recognize the sounds my voice makes.

A growl rolls from between his lips as his teeth scrape across the sensitive numb. "That's fucking right, Carmella. Let me taste you. Fuck, I'm so hard."

Luke lies back on the table, pulling me with him. I end up straddling his face, and he disappears under my dress as his tongue snakes inside of me before returning to torment my swollen clit with long, slow licks. Hands squeeze my tits before diving under the fabric and flicking my nipples. I close my eyes and chase my orgasm as lust singes my body to a fiery crisp.

"I'm going to cum," I tell him, greedy for more. I want his fingers inside me, fucking me until I scream and drip all over his hands and face. A pinch of pain as his teeth scrape across my sensitive nub nearly undoes me. "Oh, fuck, that feels so good," I groan out. His hot tongue swirls between my pussy lips and I pant.

Glancing to my side, I can see myself in a dresser mirror, riding Luke's face while he strokes an impressive-sized cock from root to tip. His hips rise and pump into his hand. His pants are pushed down below his hips, and my mouth dries at the sight. A clear drop of pre-cum leaks from his cock. Luke moans from between my legs. "Ahh, yeah, caramel drop, scoot down and take this dick. I want to fuck you."

His words, in combination with our reflection, roughly act as a bucket of ice water on my consciousness, cutting through the spirits, weed, and arousal. *What the fuck am I doing?*

Guilt and shame open up on me like my own personal thunderstorm. *Tommy. Ugh, I am a horrible person.* I drop the money.

Making a sound of self-loathing, I push up and roll off the table, sliding out of Luke's arms. "Hey, where are you going? We aren't done yet. You still need to cum."

Ignoring his words, I don't look at him as I fix my panties and right my dress.

"Carmella." His tone is sharper now.

"I have a boyfriend," I say with my back to him.

I hear him blow out a breath as he moves around. "No, you don't." He laughs. "Now come back here and let's finish this."

"Didn't you hear me? I said no. I have a boyfriend and this shouldn't have happened," I snap back, turning to face him.

Luke has pulled his pants back up to his hips and sits balanced in the middle of the oval table, legs dangling off the edge. The amused smile on his lips melts away as anger kindles in his eyes. "Oh. We're being serious."

He nods as he mulls over my words with a sour twist to his lips. "Okay. I heard your bullshit excuse alright, but I'm calling it like I see it, and this..." He motions to me. "... is bullshit. You don't have a boyfriend."

"I do too. His name is Tommy."

"The fuck you do, Carmella." His tone slices through the air.

He hops off the table and reaches for his pants. I take a step backwards and he notices the movement. A humorless laugh escapes his lips as he fastens and zips them up. A cruel smile I've never seen before smears across his face. "Hey, I have an idea. Let's list all the fucking things you don't do when you have a boyfriend. I'll start, feel free to chime in."

Anger and hurt pulsate across my body. I shake my head and try to block him out.

Luke snatches his shirt and slides it back on. "You don't work for the man who pinched your nipples and saw you half naked the first time you met him because a boyfriend wouldn't be down with that. You don't take another man's money for sexual favors, and you don't go on dinner dates with him." I flinch as he lists my sins by ticking them off on his fingers. "You don't get naked and flash your cunt at the beach, and you don't sit on another man's lap or grind your ass into his cock. You don't let another man get you into his bed and feel you up as he tickles you. And you CERTAINLY DON'T RIDE ANOTHER MAN'S FUCKING FACE ON A DINNER TABLE IN FULL VIEW OF CAMERAS." His arm cuts angrily toward the cameras perched in the store's corner. "ESPECIALLY WHEN THE OTHER MAN YOU'RE FUCKING AROUND WITH IS RUTHLESS ENOUGH TO SHOW THAT CAMERA FOOTAGE TO WHATEVER DUMBASS BOYFRIEND YOU CLAIM TO HAVE."

My mouth works wordlessly as his words lash me, and I swallow down the lump in my throat. Squeezing my eyes tight, I wish to be anywhere else but here right now. "Luke, please... ," I beg, terrified he is going to kick me out, terrified he won't and I'll keep messing up, and terrified he will show Tommy and he will never speak to me again. I don't have anywhere else to go. That thought kills me, and a heavy helplessness rises in me.

His voice is less harsh when he speaks next. "I'm not done, Carmella." My eyes flick up to meet his icy gaze. "I need you to think long and hard about what I'm going to say next because if you have a boyfriend, then he either doesn't give a shit about you or he's too much of a fucking limp-dick chump to keep you safe, fed, and off the streets. He's useless either way, but I'm not. I'm not going to fucking play these stupid, childish games with you and whatever boy toy you're stringing along. Get your shit together." With that, he scoops up the remaining tequila.

He stands there and looks at me expectantly, but I don't know what to say. All the words get bungled and caught in my throat. The unspoken emotions suffocate and drag me under in the worst way, but nothing comes out. I look at the floor as the song changes to "Come Here" by Dominic Fike.

His clipped and final tone forces leagues of distance between us. "Fine, thanks for the evening. Keep the money."

With that, he turns and walks to the back.

Standing alone in the darkness, the tears come, and I quickly wipe them away. A war between hating Luke and hating myself is short-lived as the sound of jingling keys and the back door opening cuts through my thoughts.

He wouldn't just leave like that, would he?

Running to the back, I notice Luke's phone on the counter and snatch it up. I quickly push open the back exit and freeze in the store's doorway as Luke heads toward his car.

"Where are you going?" I hate the petulant neediness in my voice. He doesn't stop walking.

"Out," he says.

"Wait."

Opening his car door, he turns back to me and waits. The shadows seem to suck at him, and the only reason I can see his face is the motion sensor floodlight. His eyes are flat, and I can't stand the apathetic look on his face, as if he suddenly doesn't care anymore.

"What do you want, Carmella?" he demands.

That's a loaded question, one I'm scared I'll shoot myself with. The motion sensor light shuts off, and he's plunged into darkness. Shadows eat up his face and I shiver at the sight of this dark, new stranger staring across the lot at me.

I look down at the phone in my hand and back at him. "You don't have to leave," I say. "Come back inside."

His voice is ominous. "No. You get in the car."

Fear slithers down my spine as lust pools in my groin.

"Where will you take me?"

He doesn't answer me. Luke stands there, unmoving in the darkness, as the song behind me cuts off and silence wraps between us.

"Get. In. The. Car." He grinds out each word between clenched teeth.

The light clicks back on as he stalks toward me, illuminating the determined fury etched into his face. I know without a doubt that if I climb into that car right now, I'm getting fucked, somewhere dirty, and it won't be on my terms and he won't be nice about it. He'll fuck me cruelly for fucking with him, and he will probably make me beg for it.

Stepping back, I slam the door closed between us. Fleeing down the hallway, I stop short at the counter and wait as my heart pounds. The back door never opens. Instead, the engine of Luke's car roars to life and the tires peel out as he flies by the store windows and out onto the road, whipping the Trans Am out of sight.

Misery and confusion make my chest ache as I slide down the counter and onto the floor. *Dumbass didn't even take his cell.* I glance down at the smart phone cradled in my lap and realize it's the wrong color. Luke's phone is blue, with a stupid dolphin sticker on the back that always makes me smile. This one is matte black on black.

Curiosity gets the better of me and I click the side button. The screen glows. It's unlocked. There are no apps aside from the basics. I click on the gallery icon. Only two images are there: the picture of me from the first night we met and the video he took. Opening the call log, I see line after line of numbers listed across the screen. I frown. *Why are these all unsaved?*

The messages leave me even more confused. Two conversation bubbles to unknown numbers are all that are available. Luke sent them about a meeting for brunch on the docks and as a reminder to the receiver to not forget the donuts. I have a creeping suspicion that donuts and brunch are code words.

Sighing, I click the phone shut. *How well do I even know Luke, really?* I wrack my mind. *I thought I did, at least a little. There are things we don't talk about, and I'm holding one in my hands right now. Fuck me, I've basically had sex with him, cheated on Tommy, and he has it recorded.* Tears streak down my face as I give into the sorrow and confusion dragging me down. I'll try to assemble some kind of plan for what I'm going to do when Luke comes back later.

Dragging myself to the bed, I cry until exhaustion carries me away.

More Red Flags than Green Ones

Luke

I'm an asshole.

I wasn't mad at Carmella so much as I was mad at myself for knowing it was too soon and pushing the issue. It blew up in my face and ruined last night for both of us.

The empty bed hugs my ass as I sit across from Carmella's sleeping form and watch her catch her breath before settling. It doesn't go unnoticed that her face is still puffy from crying. I checked the camera footage, fully intending to make a copy of our tryst. Instead, I deleted the video after watching her cry.

A pang of guilt and remorse washes over me. The metal cap on the glass bottle makes a swirly sound as I unscrew it from the vodka. Alcohol burns my throat as I suck it down, and the vapors work up my sinuses and into my eyes. *Fuck me.*

Although I'm pretty heated about that boyfriend horseshit, I'm sorry I left things like that. I'm sorry that, sometimes, I'm a rough man. If I knew a better way... or could be other than I am... then I would. The skunky smell of the giggle stick between my fingers wafts around me, and I take a drag, letting the flower do its job and ease the grief in my chest. *This shit feels like Tracey all over again.* For a moment, I spiral.

I'm back in the house I built, sitting at my kitchen table. My wife sits across from me. Her short blonde hair is still damp from the shower, a shower she didn't take with me, and the pink silk robe I gave her as a birthday present wraps around her body, molding to her athletic figure. I squeeze the pen in my hand so hard I wish it would snap and ruin all the forms and documents spread across the table we had breakfast at earlier that day. The barrel of the gun presses against my temple as my wife's lover shoves it into my face.

"*Don't do this, Trace,*" *I beg.*

She laughs, and it's the coldest sound I've ever heard. "*Already done. Sign it.*"

"*They'll come after you. Sasha won't work with you, knowing that you betrayed me.*"

She's flippant. "*No, they'll come after you. If Sasha won't work with me, maybe someone else will.*"

I shake my head, knowing we all might be dead soon.

"You were always too ambitious, Trace," I whisper to the darkness.

I polish off the bottle of vodka, knowing it's a bad idea. My stomach is already revolting.

Carmella looks so young and sad; it twists something up inside me. I don't really blame her for being caught between desires. It doesn't take a leap of imagination to know that what Carmella really needs are the things I'm offering. Yet another man holds the title of being hers, even if he isn't offering her shit. *Is that what I want? To be her... boyfriend?*

I snort at the idea. It seems ludicrous. *I'm thirty-four years old. Can I still be someone's boyfriend?* Yet the thought of another man calling Carmella his girl, touching her, putting his dick in her... Well, he's dead already and just doesn't know it. *Fuck it. He's dead for leaving her on the streets. I'll wring the life from his pathetic neck myself if he ever bothers to show up.*

I can't tell if this aggression is because of Carmella or Tracey's lover. Maybe both.

Getting up, I lay down another crumpled hundred next to her. *For the trouble I caused.* Stumbling toward the kitchen, I groan as the early-morning light trickles through the windows. It's going to be a horribly long day.

Stopping to puke up all the vodka in the bathroom, I decide it's probably time to switch to water and wonder, not for the first time, if I'm an alcoholic.

Snagging a bottle of water from the fridge, I chug it, and it, too, comes right back up. *I'm a fucking idiot. I'm not going to make it today.*

A smell catches my attention and I sniff myself. Sex and alcohol cling to my clothes. *I didn't even wash my face last night after eating Carmella out. It's definitely a shower day, but a quick rinse wouldn't hurt.*

I'm standing on a stool, splashing cold water from the kitchen faucet onto my dick, when a sleepy Carmella rounds the corner, startling us both.

"What the fuck!" she yells, slapping her hands over her eyes. Backpedaling out of the room, she ducks behind the wall. "Are you jerking off in the sink!?"

My heart sinks. *Well, fuck. This was not how I wanted this morning to go.* Shaking my head, I ask, "Why would I do that?"

"I don't know, because it's easier to wash down the drain or something?"

Technically, she isn't wrong. Chuckling, I reach for a washcloth to dry my cock. "Sorry, thing's got to get washed. Speaking of that, when was the last time you cleaned those tits and lips?"

"Oh. My. God. Luke. What does that matter? I wouldn't do it in the kitchen sink when I have a... guest who could walk in on me!"

I snort and step down from the stool. "Well, I don't remember you being so modest last night. Don't know why you're so shocked at seeing my dick now. You nearly rode it a couple hours ago. But I apologize. It's an old habit."

"It's a habit to wash your dick in the sink?" Her incredulous voice floats back to me.

Stopping in the doorway, I stare at a freshly scandalized Carmella. "Hey, you saw my cock. What did you think? It's big, right?"

A blush creeps over her shocked face as her jaw drops open. Her lips make a perfect O. Shit, there is her tongue, hot and wet, a deep red instead of pink. I haven't even had time to kiss those plump lips yet. It reminds me of the deep rose color of her pussy, and while a stab of lust shoots through me, my dick remains flaccid. *Fucking whiskey-dicked myself.*

"That's what you ask me after last night? Oh my God, you're still drunk. Did you drink all night? Luke, what about the store? We need to talk." Pain flicks across her face.

That's too many problems and questions for me to process right now. "You know, the last woman who tried to hold me this accountable was my ex-wife. You looking to get wed, sugar?"

Carmella says nothing. Hurt just stares out at me from her eyes.

Waving all that away, I say, "Okay, fine, chill, sweetheart. I got us. I'll make some coffee, eat some toast, pound a Red Bull, and we'll be fine."

Her eyes cast down to the floor as she nods her head. I can see the disappointment flaring across her face as she tries to hide the quiver in her lower lip. *Christ, she is so fucking emotional and I am not currently equipped for this.* Grabbing her shoulders, I pull her against me hard and wrap my arms around her in a bear hug.

My head rests perfectly on top of her curls until she relaxes and buries her face into my shirt. Tropical fruits and a soft floral smell wrap around my senses. Tentatively, she places her hands on my hips before wrapping them around my back and giving into the snuggle. We stay like that for a long moment. An ache in my chest that I didn't even know was there eases, while she holds me back.

I only want good things for Carmella, things I couldn't give myself: safety, peace of mind, and, occasionally, my dick if she'd stop running from me. I don't have to know all of her past to know she got the raw end of the deal, and I'm not looking to make it worse. Nuzzling my face into her messy curls, I breathe deeply, filling my lungs with her scent.

Her muffled voice floats up to me. "Why are you still drunk?"

My mind flickers back to me leaving, enraged that she had the gall to tell me she had a boyfriend mid-sex, then chase me down, only to tell me no again by slamming a door in my face.

I could tell her I'm still drunk because I'm a loser that had every intention of fucking another woman last night, couldn't get my cock to work, left the bar, and pulled over at the beach so I could puke my guts up. And I stayed there, sitting pathetically in the sand, until I could drive. *Honestly, I don't even know how I'm standing right now.* I'm saturated with so much liquor that the hangover shakes have kicked in and my whole body quivers. But that story has more red flags than green ones, and I am pretty sure that it won't make her feel better.

Telling her I get drunk because I'm lonely, traumatized by a shitty childhood, a slew of shitty marriages, and trying to move hundreds of thousands of drug and blood money through a used furniture store, and I'm low-key losing it, isn't going to be reassuring either. Especially when I tack on the fact that the Bratva is breathing down Sasha's neck, and he, in turn, is breathing down mine because both of our asses are on the line... *Where was I going with this? Oh. Yeah, that doesn't seem like a suitable answer either. She probably thinks I'm an alcoholic.*

I have nothing, so I just hug her tighter.

"Is it because of last night? If I'm making you miserable..." She pauses and tries to pull away, but I don't let her. The tears in her voice are thick. "I can leave. I won't bother you again." Her voice is soft and small.

Fuck, I need to sober up. "No, it's not you. I drink 'cause of my own bullshit. Nothing to do with you, caramel drop."

"Promise?" she asks.

I squeeze her as tight as I can, molding her to me. "Promise. Why would you think that my drinking has anything to do with you? You being here is the highlight of my day. If I could, I would spend all my time with you. You are the only good thing I have going in my life, and I don't want you to leave." The confession is out of my mouth before I can shut the fuck up.

Good job, Luke. She rejects you, and here you are pouring out your heart and soul like a sad sack of shit. Might as well give her a knife and show her where to carve out what Tracey left of you.

"A foster dad I had used to blame his drinking on me. He told me I made the home rotten, and the only way he could be happy is if he drank around me. And all my aunt's boyfriends are drunks because she is also a drunk, and I just..." She trails off and shrugs.

I close my eyes against the battering rage that surges in me, threatening to drown out all common sense. I tuck Carmella closer. "What was his name?"

"Who?"

I look down at her. "The foster dad. Do you remember where he lives?"

Whatever promise of violence is written in my face causes her to still under my hands. She pales as her lips squish together and she shakes her head. "I don't remember."

We both know that's a lie. Sharp, angry pain slashes across my chest, and I breathe through the discomfort. It's probably for the best. Getting myself tossed in jail for beating up some stranger does nothing to help my girl.

I rub soothing circles on her back as I tuck her into my arms. Those little motions seem to ease both of us.

I control my voice when I speak. "He was an asshole. I'm an asshole, and you aren't rotten. His drinking started long before you. Only fucking scum of the earth blame their adult problems on a kid. Gutless. Dickless sack of shit. He wasn't even a real man, and all you got to do is say the word. I'll find him and remind him of that."

She squeezes me and rubs a little circle on my lower back, mirroring my attempts at comfort. That's sweet, but I'm not the one who deserves it. I smile to myself, and as much as I am loath to stop touching her, I need to. She has earned some space from me this morning.

Stepping back, I keep my hands on her shoulders. "Okay, I am sorry about last night. Can we have a do-over this morning?" I ask. She nods.

"Great. Good morning, Carmella. Did you sleep well?"

Her mouth twists into a sad, tearful smile, and she wipes at her face with her sleeve. "Good morning, Luke. I did a little. How about you?"

"I haven't actually been to sleep yet, but that's alright because caffeine, food, and beautiful ladies like yourself exist. If a rough day with little sleep is the price I have to pay to enjoy those things, so be it."

She gives me a genuine smile, and it makes her entire face brighten. My hands have a mind of their own as they brush her sandy-colored curls behind her ear. Twisty locks smooth between my fingers and I admire the thick, silky texture. I make a mental note to get her a stylist, a good one that knows how to cut curls.

"I can make you coffee and grab the bleach," she offers.

"Planning to poison me already?"

Cocking her hip out, she folds her arms over her chest with a renewed attitude. "Planning to disinfect the sink."

"Ahhh, I will do that. It's my custard launcher, after all."

Her eyes widen in horror as her face slips into that familiar scandalized look. "Custard launcher! Luke, that's disgusting. Who says shit like that?"

I burst out laughing, which sets off a migraine that's akin to having my skull fucked by a garden trowel. *If she only knew how much custard having her around produced.* Gasping for air, I turn and wander back into the kitchen as my stomach clenches and threatens another round of vomiting. "I need ice and cold water."

"You need a drink?" she asks, following me. Stoppering the sink, I dump a fresh bag of ice into it and turn on the cold water.

"No, it's for my face," I say before plunging headfirst into the icy water.

Making the executive decision to wait until noon to open the store was the best thing I've done all day. Not my finest moment, to be sure, or my most responsible, but at least the hangover shakes have passed.

I can hear the TV playing from the front of the store, and empty microwavable mac 'n' cheese packages sit on the countertop in the kitchen. Grabbing a pot of cold coffee, I pour a cup and stick it in the microwave.

A berry-flavored Gatorade sits chilling in the fridge, and I unscrew the lid, gulping down half the beverage before rooting around in the drawers for ibuprofen. The microwave beeps just as soon as I find the pill bottle. Swiping a sleeve of crackers, I stumble to the microwave and take out my coffee. Burnt orange pills tumble into my hand and then my mouth as I chug down the cup of go-juice, praying both the pills and caffeine kick in at the same time.

It's time for a shower. I can feel it. Been a couple days since Carmella and I went to the truck stop showers, and marinating in my tequila-vodka sweats probably isn't getting me any points in the hygiene department.

Carmella probably needs one as well after the sticky mess I made of her. I chuckle at the memory of how she sounded riding my face. Shit, I've had multiple pussies on me in the last twenty-four hours and a sink rinse off only goes so far. A flash of disappointment on the face of the blonde barfly as she learned I couldn't get it up flicks across my mind. My nose crinkles up in disgust at myself as I try to dislodge the memory of trying to stuff my limp dick in her and it folding up like some sad, broken accordion. *The self-loathing is real.*

Grabbing the hangover cures, I head toward the show floor. Hopefully, caramel drop is dressed and ready to start the day.

Carmella's giggle and perky voice bring me up short before I step out onto the floor. My eyes narrow on her. Sitting at the desk with the phone to her ear, she spins in a circle, tangling and untangling herself in the landline wire. "No, it's all good." She laughs. "I just hadn't heard from you and was worried."

Steam rolls out of the cup of java as I wait in the hallway and eavesdrop.

"I'm so sorry about all that. I feel like it's my fault." She pauses. "Well… yeah, I know. And yeah, she is. It doesn't make me feel any better, though." She blows out a breath and spins again. "So, like I was saying last time, I'm fine, and I found a place to stay. I also got a job now." She hesitates, biting her lip. "Umm, yeah, it's going great. It's that used furniture place off Seadrive Blvd in White Cove." Another pause. "Mmm hmm, that one. The owner gave me an advance to buy some stuff, but I have to pay him back."

Never in my life have I asked for a single penny back from her.

She leans forward in the chair. "Of course, he's been kind to me, so I'm going to stick around and work off my bill." She picks up a pencil and rolls it in her fingers.

"Where am I staying? Um, it's with this girl from school. You don't know her. She moves in different circles. Real nice. Her name is Lucy."

I snort and realize she is probably talking to the "boyfriend." *It's not a stretch of the imagination to know who Lucy is. She lies to me and to him. Liar liar, pants on fire.*

I don't like her tone. It's too perky. *Flirty even?* Leaning against the wall, I watch her twist the phone cable in her fingers and laugh. She uncaps a tube of ChapStick and runs it along her lips before rubbing them together and grinning. *Damned woman looks like she just got invited to a fucking ball and the glass slipper fits. Or some stupid fairy-tale bullshit.* She grins ear to ear and giggles in a way that makes me want to snip the landline running to the phone. *Can't fucking flirt if the phone doesn't work.*

It's got to be the boyfriend. *He must be who she's been calling to check in with. What fucking excuse could he possibly have that earns him a giggle and an easy pass while I'm over here arguing with this little firecracker on the daily? Where he's fucking been while she's sleeping on the streets, breaking into places, all skin and bones?*

I'm going to grind this chump ass motherfucker's skull into dust. Fucking sack of shit. Useless cuck. And he still has the balls to sniff around Carmella. The only silver lining I can figure is that if he hasn't come around yet, then he probably isn't going to start now. That eases the angry wasp zipping around in my chest somewhat until she says, "Yeah, I'm available tonight."

The. Fuck. You. Are. Maybe you're not banging me... yet... but you sure as fuck aren't going to bang this guy, either.

I startle for a moment. *So... I guess I have my answer about what I want from Carmella.*

Stomping around the corner, I beeline it to where she sits. "Carmella, get off the phone. We have to open the store."

She spins, looking like a deer caught in headlights, and nods, acknowledging my order. She leans forward, rising out of the seat to hang up. "Oh, hey, my boss just walked in the door. We have to open now. Yeah, I'll talk to you later."

The. Fuck. You. Will.

She hangs up the phone and I pass her the keys, ordering her to unlock the doors and turn on the open sign.

When she returns to the counter, the keys make a scratching noise as she slides them back to me. "How are you feeling?"

"Like death warmed over. I need a shower. You need a shower. We will do that tonight after dinner. How about you bust out that new Crock-Pot and throw in a roast?"

She shifts her weight and fidgets with some papers. "Sure, that sounds great. Um, what time will we be back?"

"Why, you got plans smelling like that?" Her eyes snap open and she sniffs herself.

"Is it bad?"

I want to be mean, but seeing her so alarmed gentles my tone. "No, it's not bad. You never smell bad, but we should wash up and do laundry."

She considers this a moment. "Yeah, that's fair. I could use a hot shower. Plus, my curls are getting dry again and I want to use that deep conditioner you got me. We won't be out late, right?"

If I have my way, you'll be busy the whole night. I give her a noncommittal nod. I bought her a whole slew of essentials during our last grocery trip, plus food and a few cooking tools. There were other things, too, that she didn't notice I picked up, like a fresh box of condoms.

I follow the logic of wrap it before you tap it, especially when I pick up strays. The reality is, I don't know what Carmella brought in with her. My caramel drop might not even have all her shots, or worse, based on that phone conversation. I never considered that she might be currently fucking someone. She could have some pussy of the wild between her legs. *And I nearly raw dogged her on the table.* I drag the palm of my hand down my face and groan. *The "boyfriend" complicates issues.*

As Carmella wanders around the store, busying herself, my curiosity gets the better of me. Rolling my chair over to the phone, I punch the redial button and the call goes through. I wait a couple seconds and check to see where Carmella is. A deep male voice answers the phone. "Hey, beautiful, miss me already?"

"I got the wrong number. Was trying to call a business associate of mine." I drop the phone in its cradle, more pissed off than ever. *Whoever he is, I already don't like him.*

The next couple of hours pass by painfully slowly. However busy last week was, today is dead. I go over a few things with Carmella and help her bring in a couple of new pieces from the shop onto the show floor.

"Thank fuck it's five," I say, locking the doors and turning off the open neon sign. The nighttime blue neon flickers unhappily. *Dammit, I forgot to call that light repairman. Carmella is turning into a huge distraction.* Scowling, I open my phone and scroll down to the messages between the technician and me. Punching the call option, it rings a couple times before going to voicemail.

"Hey, it's Luke from Luke's Furniture, the job you supposedly did a week and a half ago. You said the neon was fixed, and it wasn't. I'm none too happy about it. I paid you and have nothing to show for it. Call me back when you get this." I hang up. Dude has till tomorrow before I go knocking on doors.

I'm in a sour ass mood and the idea of waiting in line at the truck stop for a used shower room irritates my sensibilities. I want some privacy, and I want to relax. Preferably with Carmella. Weighing our options, a wonderful dirty seedling of an idea takes root in my mind before blossoming into a full evening of events for my girl. *I can work with this.* I chuckle. *She's going to hate it, though.*

It's Not Love, Just Lust

LUKE

"That Crock-Pot was a great idea," Carmella says as we head out of the store. Turning to lock up after her, I nod my agreement.

"I should have bought one sooner, saving me money, and that roast was freaking delicious. Good job, sugar. Didn't know you could cook."

She grins at me as we approach my other baby. It's a perfect summer day. The type where the winds are strong enough to push cool air from the coast onto land and chase away the muggy Florida heat.

"You got all your stuff?" I ask, watching as she swings the duffle bag off her shoulder and into the back of the car, followed by her beat-up baby-blue purse. *That's something else I need to replace for her.*

"Yep, we will be back before nine, right? It's already six."

"I don't see why we wouldn't," I lie. "Hey, you never got that drive I promised you. Want to take the top off?"

"Hell yes!" A smile splits her face.

"Alright, help me." Pulling off the hard panels on the top of the Trans Am isn't difficult, and I show her how. As Carmella slips the panel in her hands into the trunk, her hair falls over her shoulder and I'm hit by a tenderness I didn't expect. Not for sex or obsession, but just for her company. Her time. The ability to touch her and hold her. To comfort her.

Squeezing my eyes against the familiar emotion, I rub my fingers across my mustache. I've been around the block enough times to know when I'm romantically fucked. Us working together, the closeness it fosters, and my rare need for nonsexual intimacy have once again plotted to ruin my life. *Sex is just so much easier. I must be the world's biggest fucking idiot. Sasha is going to kill me.*

My stomach actually hurts at the thought of being in love again. Bending over, I brace myself on my knees and inhale slowly, hoping it keeps the spiking panic hidden. *The alcohol and five-ish hours of sleep are making me an emotional pussy; that's what this is.*

"You're not going to puke again, are you?" Carmella says.

"No."

"Okay. You, uh, need help?"

"No."

"Are you dying?"

"Carmella, get in the car."

"Okay."

The trunk slams while I practice learning how to breathe normally again. *I can't be in love. I mean, we barely know each other. It's infatuation and loneliness. My need for a distraction from self-hate. That's all.*

Getting a straight answer from Carmella is like asking a hooker for her real name or trying to nail water to a wall. *I didn't even know she had a boyfriend until I was two seconds away from telling her I'm her boyfriend.*

Deciding it's not love and just an obsession with a healthy dose of lust and affection doesn't loosen the death grip on my lungs. *Oh shit, I'm having an actual panic attack.*

It's been months since one made an appearance. They came nearly every day after Tracey left. Between the grief, loss of money, and threats, the nose candy, beer, and panic were my constant companions.

A ride out of town will air me out and help get my head on straight.

After righting myself, my lungs expand, and the slightly brackish air grounds me. My legs wobble as I walk to the car door and slide into the driver's seat. Carmella gives me worried eyes but says nothing. Warmth from her skin soaks into my hand as I pat her thigh, a well-practiced smile firmly fixed on my lips.

Static blares from the radio as I connect my phone to the Bluetooth FM transmitter. Flipping to my favorite playlist, I turn on "Dead Inside" by Younger Hunger.

Seagulls launch themselves into the bright blue sky as we pull out of the parking lot.

Taking my normal route, we pull onto Seadrive Blvd. The wind whips through Carmella's hair, the yellowing sky making it more golden than ashy. She closes her eyes and gives a satisfied sigh into the wind. This is where she belongs, next to the surf and under the sun, her natural element cleansing us both.

"This is nice." Her voice floats to me.

I nod, fighting back the deep desire to lean over and kiss her. To bury all my aches and pains as I bury my cock in her. Instead, I light up a cigarette and smoke.

Shops line the main strip. Tourist traps decorated with surfboards and sandals pop up on every other street. Murals of sea turtles and sea creatures stain concrete in public places. The people are even more interesting, in various stages of being undressed or overdressed depending on the activities. Fancy diners in their long summer dresses head into reservation-only restaurants. Beach bums walk about in bikinis with and without unbuttoned jean shorts, and occasionally, an overly cautious tourist sits under an umbrella wearing a hat, full-sleeved swim gear, and bathes the few spots of uncovered skin with sunscreen.

As we drive out of town, the road opens up along the coast. I take the curves easy, soaking up the sunshine, the beach, the music, and Carmella. Feeling much more like myself, I can't help but be in love with the moment.

The song changes, landing on another favorite, "Mol y Sol" by Brijs.

We drive a while more before Carmella speaks up, shouting over the wind, "Can I ride up there?"

She points to the leg part of the T of the Trans am top. Shaking my head, I give her a "fuck no" look.

"Please, for one second!" She laces her fingers and gives me a cartoonish pout that has me rolling my eyes.

She flops back in her seat, defeated, and stares out at the scenery. Her brow furrows. Leaning forward, she looks around curiously. "Hey, where are we? I thought we were going to the truck stop."

Yeah, about that . . .

"You know what? I changed my mind. Just be safe and hold on." My foot gently pumps the brake, and the car slows down to a more manageable speed.

Carmella requires no coaxing, and she scrambles to stand up in her seat. Watching her try to spider monkey on top of the car in two seconds flat while we hurdle down the highway gives me a heart attack, and I pull over.

Once she's as secure as one can be while straddling a T-top, I look both ways and slowly pull out again onto the deserted highway.

"Go faster, Luke," she yells.

Absolutely not. There is a rule I have about driving. I try to only break one vehicular law at a time. If I'm going to drive drunk, I wear a seatbelt. If I'm sober but refuse to wear a seatbelt, then I can't have any substances, illegal firearms, or wanted felons with me. Also, I mind my turn signals and never speed. Breaking multiple laws at one time increases the likelihood of being arrested.

We are currently breaking several. *But for caramel drop... eh, we're rolling the dice.*

Her tanned calf rests against my upper chest, and the crook of her knee is at eye level. I glance up when she whoops into the sky, causing me to drop the faux smile for a more natural one. The wind roars in our ears and rushes around her, tangling her curls and whipping them back into her face. With a smile brighter than the sun, she holds onto the T, tips back her head, and laughs freely.

The moment feels suspended in time. My seaside, summertime girl finally lets go and experiences the type of carefree fun she needs. This is where Carmella is meant to be: on adventures—experiencing life to its fullest. Untroubled and delighted. I want that for her.

Pressing a kiss at the point where the back of her knee attaches to her thigh, I smirk when she doesn't pull away and give her skin a little flick of my tongue. I let the little daredevil stay up there another couple of miles before pulling over and making her get down.

The music shuffles to "Too Late" by the Happy Fits and I sing along. She settles back into her seat as we pull out again. "That was awesome. Thanks, I've never done that before. Also, why did you lick my leg?"

"You're welcome." Maybe it's the mood I'm in, or maybe it's because I'm back on my bullshit, but part of me gloats that I'm giving Carmella some of her first.

We drive a while more before, out of the corner of my eye, Carmella's smile falters. She squints around before turning to face me. Suspicion blankets her face.

"Hey, Luke, this is the opposite direction of the YMCA or the truck stop. Where are we going?"

"Alright, Magellan. You caught me. I wanted to do something nice to apologize for last night, so I'm taking us to a... spa. It's about forty minutes outside of the city."

Her face wrinkles as she glares at me so deeply that I pull away from her in the car. My head snaps back and forth between her and the road. *What the fuck?*

"What aren't you telling me?" she asks.

"Nothing! It's a spa with private rooms and big hot tubs. It's a bathing house."

"Hmmmm..." She pulls back, settling into her seat again.

"It's nice. I promise!" Carmella takes her time studying me before replying, "I've never been to a spa before."

I grin. "Baby, at this place, they'll treat you like the guest of honor."

But that's only because women aren't exactly common at men's spas, unless you count the lot lizards and whores. I chuckle to myself.

"What's so funny?" she asks.

Shaking my head, I answer, "Nothing, caramel drop. Nothing at all." Wary eyes rake over me before she goes back to watching the scenery.

Never been to a spa before. I smile, glancing over at her. *What a sweet girl.*

Carmella gets her first hint that Oasis Men's Spa isn't the type of spa she had in mind when I take the off ramp with the big *XXX Adult Store and Men's Spa* sign flashing in neon blue and the shape of a woman bent over in yellow neon.

Her eyes grow wide and her mouth flops open as she stares at me in horror. "No."

I draw out the o in, "Oh, yes."

"But I... We... I can't... I've never," she sputters before falling silent.

A smile curls my lips, and I fail to keep the edge of naughtiness out of it. *I knew she was going to hate it.* "Of course you've never, caramel drop. I'd be surprised if you had. And yes, you can. Sweetheart, you're with me. No one is going to bother you." *Except me.*

We drive by the ladies loitering under Oasis's turn here sign. Their tight, dark clothing, heels, and come-hither body language mark them for what they are. The steering wheel spins under my hands as I turn into the lot. Oasis itself glows green from the aesthetic lighting and the tropical plants up front. At the top of the building, yellow and orange neon lights flicker and grow into firework bursts, making it hard to miss from the highway. A sign flashes beneath the light display: *Mega XXX Adult Store. Theater. Private Rooms Available. Trucker Lounge. Semi Parking in Back.*

Oasis has always reminded me of a flashy Vegas casino. It's also a damn eyesore and a collecting place for the unwanted. Hence why the local city council threw a fucking fit and forced it to move forty minutes outside of town to the highway.

Carmella twists in her seat, eyeing the whores near the sign. "Can we please go to a truck stop?"

"When you think about it, this is kind of like a truck stop," I say, pointing to the big rigs packed into the gravel parking lot off the side of the building and the sign on the roof.

I continue, "Plus, we are already here, and this place is great. All the sex toys I own I bought from here. C'mon, you'll love it. They have a pool and a steam room." Carmella stares at me like she's never seen me a day before in her life. She doesn't move.

Sighing, I grab our bags from the back and get out of the car. Walking around to her side, I open the door and offer her my arm. "Let's go. Neither of us is getting any younger."

"You're not getting any younger, you mean," she snaps.

"Don't make me pull you from this car and spank you like a naughty girl. I'll enjoy it too much and so will the men who can see us through the windows," I say, eyeing the two-way glass that covers the entire front of Oasis. Carmella nervously checks the windows as if she can see the dirty old bastards. "You wouldn't."

"Yes, I most certainly would, caramel drop, and I'd want you to suck my cock afterwards. We agreed to shower. Here we are. Get out."

She turns her face up to me, big pleading eyes with long blondish lashes that flutter in my direction. "What if we make a deal, Luke? You love making deals."

That's true. "What's your offer?"

She bites her lip and looks around the car. "I'll... I don't know." She slaps her thighs with a pop and sighs, exasperated. "What do you want? No sex."

Tipping back my head, I bark out a laugh. "What I want is for you to come inside and see that it isn't as bad as you think."

She makes a sound like my request is killing her and grumbles in my general direction. My eyebrows inch into my hairline at her tiny tantrum.

"Fine, let's just go inside, and quickly. The faster we do this, the faster I get home." She pulls on a hoodie from the back seat, tucks the curls inside, ducks her head as she shuts the car door, and straight lines it inside. My brow pulls down as I follow behind her. Her behavior makes no damn sense sometimes. Taking one last look at the hookers who wave to me, I follow her inside.

Oasis is a smut heaven for the dirty-minded. The front doors open directly into a sex shop filled to the brim with sex toys and porn. Swings dangle from the ceiling (I *miss having one of those*), and monster-inspired shaped cocks as thick as my forearm are displayed proudly on the wall. Double dicked dildos shine happily in their packages. I catch Carmella staring at one and wink at her. She rolls her eyes. *That woman has no appreciation for my humor.*

Enemas and flavored lubricants sit side by side on the shelves. Anal plugs and self-thrusting vibrators buzz wildly in the hands of customers at the sample table. Adorning the walls at the back of the store are the more serious playthings: whips, handcuffs, leather harnesses, needles, and, last, scalpels for those interested in blood play.

The things the owner, Ollie, keeps on the shelves for the public are pretty tame to what he sells in the back rooms. I know for a fact that his sexual tastes run more toward torture than porn. *Not my kink and I try not to shame, but the dude is weird even by my standards.* One good thing about him is he knows how to keep a secret and forgets a face as soon as he meets them.

As we approach the counter, Ollie looks up from the dirty mag he was browsing. Light reflects off his bald head. He's a skinny dude, not bad in the looks department. The hookers seem to think he's harmless. "Hey, Ollie, how's it hanging?"

"To the right and halfway down my thigh," Ollie chirps back. We share a familiar laugh and shake hands.

"Been a minute since I've seen you, Luke. How the hell've you been?"

I glance around, looking for Carmella. The sample table has caught her attention. She studies a self-thrusting vibrator as it inches its way across the tabletop.

"I've been good, man, busy all day and all night. Just how I like it. You?"

"Can't complain. Free facilities, women outside, discounts on any porn I want? Life could be worse. Do you want your usual? I could send some company your way for an extra fee. Unless you brought your own." He eyes Carmella. "She's new. Young too. Not your usual."

"She kind of fell into my lap and was in a tight spot. I'm taking it as divine intervention." I laugh. "Although for who, I'm not sure. The jury is still out."

"Well, she's about to be in an even tighter spot, I'd imagine, before the night is out."

I snort. "You know it."

The doorbell goes off behind me as a trio of road workers walks in. I can tell the moment the shortest one spots Carmella standing alone. He nudges his companions and tips his head her way. They check her out. My eyes narrow on their thick heads.

"I'm not gonna have any problems with you, am I, Luke?" Ollie assesses me out of the corner of his eyes as he rings me up.

I offer him a whole good-ol-boy-can-you-blame-me-they-were-checking-out-my-girl smirk. "Of course not, Ollie. Let me get a private room with a private spa. I want it for about... six hours." My credit card slaps on the counter. That should put us getting back to the shop at one and we have work tomorrow. *No going out with the telephone mystery man tonight, caramel drop. In fact, I may just block that number.*

Old school motel keys jingle as he passes them and the credit card back over the counter to me. Carmella's eyes snag on mine, and I nod my head to the hallway behind me. She takes a deep breath, pushes her shoulders back, and marches past me like she's headed to the hangman or some shit. *This woman needs a relaxing soak even more than I do. Fucking hell.*

Chuckling, I let her get halfway down the hall before I flag her attention. "Where are you going?"

She stops and glares back at me.

Humor laces my voice. "Well, if you insist on marching off into the unknown all hot and bothered, pick a door."

"No."

"Pick a door."

There are only four options. One, I imagine, is a supply closet or office. One lets out onto the public bathing area, if that is your scene. One leads to a theater that shows porn twenty-four seven, and one goes to the private rooms.

She lets out a heavy sigh and motions to the one in front of her.

She picks the porn theater. Grabbing the handle, I prop open the door with my shoulder. The cinematic surround sound of an orgy washes over us. Carmella peeks inside and is met with nothing but shadows.

She looks back at me. "This one?"

I shrug. "Sure."

"What's in here?"

Her skepticism cracks me up. "Go check for yourself."

"It sounds like porn."

"Then it's probably porn."

Carmella is calmer now as hostility gives over to curiosity. "Why don't you just answer me?" she asks.

"Why don't you go look for yourself?"

She huffs and steps inside.

Curiosity killed the cat, baby girl. The moment she's firmly in the dark hallway, I let the door thud behind us, crowding her with my body.

Carmella plasters herself against me in an attempt to backpedal. "Luke, you fucking dick, why did you close the door? I was just going to peek." I bite my lip to keep from losing it as laughter bubbles up. Her body is ramrod straight and full of tension, as if someone shoved rebar up her ass. I smother a laugh in her curls and push us forward.

A high-definition close-up of a triple penetration bukkake party slaps us in the face the moment the screen comes into view. Glancing down at

Carmella, I see her stare slack-jawed at the three men trying to stuff their summer sausages into the same hole.

"I didn't know places like this existed," she says, her eyes still glued to the screen.

Bending down to whisper in her ear, I say, "Yes, but normally, they aren't as nice. Ollie has some financial backing that I've never asked about, and you probably shouldn't either. "

Speaking of sausages... Stepping wide, I give my growing erection a little more room. Taking a quick glance around the room, I note the couple in the back trying to sneaky fuck. The woman wears a dress and sits in her man's lap like we all are blind and can't see what they're doing. A couple of lone dudes split their attention between the couple and the screen.

Pulling Carmella's ass against my cock is divine, and I wonder if I could get her to come here again wearing that dress from last night. She might be too embarrassed with all the attention.

Carmella shoots me a glare as my cock digs into her, but doesn't pull out of my arms. *Hmmm, I've gained more ground than I thought I had.*

Carmella must have noticed some of the guys not looking at the screen because her head swivels to the back, toward the couple, and suddenly snaps to the ground. Crimson creeps into her cheeks as her eyes round even more than they were already. One of the lone guys groans, bringing her attention back to him as he rubs his erection through his jeans and stares at the couple in the back.

She watches him, the screen, the couple, stares over her shoulder at me, and then back to him. Her face doesn't change, but her breathing does. The rise and fall of her chest gets faster as the stranger unzips his pants and buries his hand inside.

Watching her watching them surprises the shit out of me and heats my blood to a boiling point. The soft material of her hoodie glides under my hand as I slip it down her stomach. Her warm hand wraps around my forearm but doesn't make any move to stop my descent.

The stranger works his cock vigorously inside his pants.

My lips brush against the shell of her ear, sending tingles racing down my chest. My dick jerks and swells. Her fingers glide up my arm as I shove my hand between her legs and press my fingers against her pussy, rubbing roughly. Her breath catches.

"Do you want to cum?" My other hand snakes under her hair and wraps around her throat, tipping her chin back against my chest. The need on her face sends me spiraling. There is no mistaking the lust burning in her eyes. "Let me touch you, Carmella. No one can see us." I unzip the front of her jeans and slip my thumb in between the parting material, running it over heated skin.

Carmella bites her red bottom lip. My eyes track the motion as the desire to replace her teeth with my own haunts me. My mouth hovers over her as her hot breaths fans against my face. I whisper the words, "Let me," softly over her and slip more fingers through the parted material. Her tongue flicks out and licks her lips in invitation, and I know I'm lost. Our lips brush. It's not enough. It's never going to be enough. I need to drink her in, to drag the air from her lungs and replace it with my own. Consume her. Pulling her hair back gently, I slant my mouth over hers, but she's gone, having turned her face away at the last minute.

I was so sure she was saying yes. She shakes her head and untangles us, skipping out on all I'm offering. She abandons me in the hallway.

Running my hand through my hair, I take a deep breath and lean against the wall. *I know she wanted it. It was written on her face. What the hell am I doing wrong?*

Temptation in Oasis

Carmella

Luke snags the soft material of my hoodie out in the hall. *Damn, nearly made it to the door.*

"You're going the wrong way."

"Do you bring all your girls here?" I hiss, trying to pick a fight.

His eyes burn as he barks a laugh. "Jealous?"

Clenching my jaw, I squeeze my arms across my chest and stare him down.

Cocking an eyebrow, he roughly yanks me into his arms and pushes us against the hotel quality beige walls. "I planned on making tonight fun, but if you insist on fighting as foreplay..." His breath fans across my face.

My body roars to life as my pussy picks now to replay how the soft brush of his lips against mine felt. His hip bites into mine as he grinds us together. Luke's voice contains an edge of malice as he whispers in my ear, "So what if I did? I'm single. I'll do as I please with whom I please, and right now, that's you. Honestly, I'm not the one with 'a boyfriend.' Where do you get off asking about my body count?"

I whimper as lust dampens my common sense. His hands roam over my body as he crushes me. The pain and intensity of his frustration ignite a yearning that slicks the place between my legs. My head falls back against the textured wallpaper.

I meet his gaze and try to hold on to my resolve. *I'm supposed to meet Tommy tonight.* "Why did you bring us here?"

He stares down at me severely, the previous lighthearted humor and sly, quick smiles gone now. "You know why, no more running." His words are like lead in my stomach.

Luke flags Ollie's attention, the bald man's regard sliding across us, and I shiver as nothing untoward registers, even as I'm pinned to the wall.

Luke motions to the door off to my left. "Buzz us in." Ollie gives him a thumbs-up.

The door releases with a click, followed by a long beep. Swallowing thickly, I say "You're right. It's none of my business what you do with whom. I have a boyfriend."

An unpleasant smile twists Luke's lips as he shakes his head. "You don't have a boyfriend, Carmella, at least not one you get hot for, because if you did, you wouldn't want to fuck me so bad. So let's not talk about him anymore."

Whiplash swamps me as I'm stretched out by a thousand emotions, each one pulling me in a different direction. His words render me speechless, and my thoughts spiral out.

You're wrong.

Fuck off.

How dare you say that out loud?

It's not true.

Fuck, why am I horny?

I should find the tallest building and jump from it because I'm a cheating whore.

Might as well join the other ladies at the corner. Cause I'm probably getting paid for tonight.

If I just fuck him, then the itch will be scratched and I can move on.

The fucking audacity of this man.

Shock still ripples through me as Luke hauls me across the threshold. The clicking lock of the door behind me feels final. Cries of pleasure from behind closed doors mixes with ambient elevator music in the hallway where we now stand.

Luke laces our fingers together and pulls me along. He stops at a door. It's teal and a brassy number eight sits in the middle. Unlocking it, he reaches in and turns on the lights before pushing the door open.

My panicked thoughts pause for a minute as I take in the room in front of me. *Wow. Okay, so that's cool.*

"Holy shit," I say out loud.

"I thought you might like it," Luke says.

The smell of water, bleach, and freshly laundered linens hangs in the slightly humid air. Water condenses on cloudy blue privacy glass that is wrapped around an octagon-shaped Jacuzzi. It dominates the space to my left. Stepping inside, I open the double doors. The tub is set into the floor and tiled dark teal. It's deep, needing several steps to get down into. Lights around the edge hold a steady blue color, making the panels glow.

There are places for drinks and a submerged bench. Along the edge of the Jacuzzi, is room to sit if someone only wants to dip their toes in or dry off. It holds candles, rolled towels, and even some flowers on several floating shelves.

Directly in front of me, up on a platform, sits a square glass shower with a waterfall showerhead coming down from the ceiling. I walk around, noticing how the bed is angled to see the shower. *Oh. I get it. That's why it's on a platform and see-through.*

The king-size bed and couch take up the rest of the space. Large mirrors dominate the room, creating the illusion of openness... but I'm certain the mirrors are for other purposes, especially the one on the ceiling. The entire room glows soft lavender from the wall fixtures and the neon in the pocket ceiling. It gives the room a relaxing, almost spa-like vibe.

More rolled towels, hooks for hanging clothes, another private bathroom, overhead speakers, a massive TV, dresser, closet, a couple of chairs, and one bowl of complementary condoms make up the rest of the room.

"This is... probably the coolest and skeeziest hotel room I've been in," I say.

Luke, who's been quietly hovering by the door while I explore the room, nods. "And I plan on utilizing every inch of it."

"It's definitely not what I was expecting. That hot tub is huge."

Luke chuckles. "See, you got to trust me, caramel drop. I've been around. I know what's good."

It grows warm in my hoodie, but taking it off might start something, so I suffer. Luke unzips the small, insulated cooler he packed and pulls out two hard lemonades, offering me one.

My eyebrows arch into a question. "Drinks again? Aren't you dehydrated?"

"Chronically," he says. "Ollie doesn't let alcohol in the place, so this is our secret, yeah?"

I nod, accepting the cold drink. The tangy fizziness on my tongue is cool and refreshing. I can barely taste the alcohol.

Luke unbuttons his shirt, and the seashell wall art suddenly becomes very interesting while the temperature ratchets up another notch. *Why did I wear this damn thing? It's summer outside.*

His leather belt whispers as it slips around his waist. The metal buckle jingles in a way that makes my mouth go dry. Shoes thud against the floor. Trained on the sounds from behind me, I'm no longer staring at the painting as much as I'm painting a mental picture. "You've seen my cock, Carmella. No reason to be shy now."

His zipper is loud in the silence, but I feel the noise in my clit. As I squint my eyes shut, my chest expands in a deep breath. Releasing it, I steal a peek.

Dressed only in gold necklaces and a smirk, he tosses his pants onto the table, and my eyes drink him in. My pussy throbs as I take in his strong shoulders. They run along the lines of his collarbones, dipping to his pecs and stomach. He doesn't have the body of a Greek god, but denying the strength in him would get your teeth knocked out.

My voyeuristic peek travels lower, landing on his half erect cock that bobs and swells under my gaze. All the blood rushes to my head and tingles develop in my fingers at the thought of caressing that silken hardness. A knowing chuckle drags my vision up. We lock eyes as my face flushes.

Luke picks up his phone and drinks, then he gives me a wink and heads into the Jacuzzi, flashing an adorable butt with little dimples on his lower back. Biting my bottom lip, I smother a giggle as he vanishes inside the privacy screens.

His groan of satisfaction from the water does wicked things to my body. "Fuck yes, this water is amazing," he says.

Sitting down, I debate what I'm going to do. *I could lock myself in the private bathroom and wait it out, but I don't want to.*

Luke decides for me.

Lapping water fills the quiet that's settled over us. His voice floats to me. "Caramel drop, I've got some money with your name on it."

The familiar drug of shame, arousal, and wrongness works through my veins and tightens my nipples. Squeezing the spiked lemonade bottle to distract myself from the excited shiver that runs through my body, I sigh. "What do you want now?"

"I want to finish what we started in the theater. I still need more pictures, and I want you to kiss me."

"You and the fucking pictures," I whisper to myself, blowing out a breath as I look up at the ceiling. *Always fucking taking pictures.*

The water smacks as he moves around behind the screen. I imagine the way it licks at his skin. Luke continues, "Strip and come relax with me."

I chug the lemonade. "Maybe," I say.

Luke's voice deepens. "I already know what one pair of your lips taste like. I'm curious about the other, and I'll make it worth your while."

"One kiss?" *It's never just one kiss with Luke. Girl, you know this.*

"Hmmm. One kiss, but you've got to sell me on it. Make me believe that I'm the only man you think about. The only man you want to be kissing."

I can't do that. "No."

"No? You're telling me you don't need any cash on hand? Every penny counts when you're trying to get your feet under you. Or do you think you're not woman enough to convince me? I think you could."

He isn't wrong, but I know this ploy. Luke's used it more than once to bullshit me. I am no longer a stranger to Luke's maneuvers. *Maybe if I make the price too high, he will back off for a minute.*

"Fine, I want a grand."

A soft, sucking, sputtering sound emits from the glowing blue panels before a round of rough coughing rips through the air, followed by a wheezing breath. *I think I might have killed him.*

"Caramel drop. Baby. I can walk outside and pay one of those nice whores two fifty to let me fuck them in the ass bareback. I'm not giving you a grand for a kiss and some pictures."

Standing, I saunter over to the open doors. A pissed-off Luke clears his throat as he leans against the edge at the back of the pool. The exasperated irritation on his face is worth more money than he could offer me.

"Well, I guess you'll go ask one of them, won't you?" I snip, rolling up the legs on my jeans. I kick off my shoes and ease into the hot water, sitting on the edge.

He growls at me and dunks himself under the blue water with a splash. Emerging, he slicks the liquid from his face. The heat in his voice is biting. "My counter: five hundred. But if I pay five hundred fucking dollars, you better put on the best fucking show of your life. I want full length video, not just clips or pictures. I want to finger bang you until you squirt all over my hand. And then I want to jerk off on your face and tits. Plus the kiss and a dance. And... and... I want to watch you shower."

My mouth drops open. Floodgates of desire break open and slam into me. The images that flick through my mind wash away all logical thought and my desire to be offended.

He points at me. "It had better be a fucking wonderful kiss. I mean it. Deal?"

I say nothing.

His eyes root me to the spot. "Deal, caramel drop?"

Say no. Just say no.

I lick my lips.

Say noooo.

"Okay, deal."

Anxiety lances through me. *Shit. Why did I agree to that? I've never seduced anyone before.* "Um." The words die in my throat.

Luke smirks and approaches, looking every inch like one of those scenes where the sexy movie star walks out of the surf and tosses his hair. But instead of a toss, he runs his wet hands through damp waves, smoothing them back, highlighting his jawline and dark, lust-ridden eyes.

I swallow hard.

The water dips below his navel and glistens on the subtle V right above his cock. The liquid laps at his happy trail and dips even farther with his movements, revealing his rock-hard erection. It's like someone punches me in the diaphragm. *Sometimes, Luke is too much man. Not because his dick is big—I mean it is—but because he, in his entirety, is too much.*

No wonder he's so... cocky.

He places a hand on either side of me and leans in as his eyes search my face. "So..." he says.

"So... I'm a little nervous," I admit.

He pushes back, rolls his eyes, and snorts. "You weren't nervous last night. Or on the beach, or while you were trying to take me for a grand!"

That gets my back up. "I was drunk last night, and I was very nervous those other times. Anyway, I didn't expect you to agree." *Or expect me to initiate.*

He leans down. My lips tingle, and for a moment, I think he is going to kiss me. Running at a full gallop, my heart slams into my chest. His words make me quiver. "You underestimated how much I want you."

I'm disappointed when he moves away and steps out of the water. "Be right back."

I check out his ass again and sigh.

Why does he have to be hot in that trashy yet kind-of-sexy, kind-of-scary daddy way with his stupid, handsome face? I hate it.

The lines between boss, pursuer, and sort-of-friend are so blurred, I can't tell where one ends and the other begins.

He's back in literally two seconds. Luke stands over me, putting his erection at eye level, and grins down with dark mischief. I stare at his face and shake my head at his brattiness. His rings clink against the glass vodka bottle as he holds it right next to his dick. "Liquid courage will perk you right up. Go on, take it."

I glare at him. My hand brushes against his cock as I grasp the bottle. It's heavy as I accept it. "You have no intention of getting us back before nine, do you?"

He shrugs. "My intention is to relax, have a little party, and if you were so inclined, which you aren't, ram this fat, hairy canary into your cute little fuckhole until you scream."

I stare at him with my mouth agape. "Fat, hairy canary?! Who says that? What does that even mean?! I'm not sure how to take that."

A wicked smile turns his lips, and his eyes flash. "Hard. You take it hard."

Now is the time to drink, Carmella. Less talking to Luke and more drinking.

He sits beside me, and I lift the bottle to my lips; the vodka is smooth. A hint of nutty floral rolls around on my tongue. *Maybe almonds and honeysuckle?* I take another pull and lower the bottle. Sure enough, the image of almonds and honeysuckle is on the front. "That's good."

"What did I say about trusting me?" Luke says. His normally pristine hair kinks in the humidity, and a bead of water drips from a lone curl, cutting down his nude body. The vodka heats my blood as I follow its journey. *Fuck it.* I ditch the hoodie and breathe a sigh of relief.

Taking another big swig of the clear liquid, I reach out. Cool, wet hair slides along my fingers as I push it away from his face and let my touch linger on the cuff of his ear. Blood roars in my ears as my heart tries to beat out of my chest.

Suddenly, this place doesn't feel real. The moment is too much like a fantasy. *Real life doesn't happen like this. Strange older men don't just take in burdens like me. They certainly don't want their problems the way Luke seems to be curious about mine.*

Maybe this can be a thing that only happens here, a moment encapsulated within the walls of this Jacuzzi. When I look back, I'll remember this as a dream, a touch of sex magic in real life. I know I'm being whimsical, but it makes me feel better. Confident.

I curl my fingers and brush my knuckles along his jawline. His pulse jumps under the skin, inviting me to touch it, while the cords flex in his neck. My hands skirt lower, along his collarbones. I trace the black-and-white cresting wave tattoo. Luke blows out a long breath, closes his eyes, and leans back, bracing his hands on the tiles, giving me access. "Yes, touch me like that," he says.

This moment is mine. And for once, I'm in control. A shiver of power races down my spine, emboldening me. I take another swig and set the bottle down.

Angling my body more toward Luke, I lean in and kiss that fluttering pulse, feeling his warm skin under my lips. He groans as my tongue licks over the sensitive spot. Skin bunches under my teeth as I bite him. "Fuck, Carmella, keep doing that."

Water softly splashes and ripples outwards across the surface as I pull out my feet and sit on my knees beside him. Ghosting my fingers across soft chest hair and outlining hard pectoral muscles, I sprinkle bites and kisses on his neck. Nipples harden under my palms, begging me to flick them. My tongue slides over one pebbled nub. Luke's hips jerk and flex at the sensation.

My hand wraps around that rigid member, and I admire how hard and hot he feels in my hand. Slowly, I swirl my tongue over his nipple and tease his cock with gentle strokes. A breathy "fuck yeah" tumbles from his lips.

My mouth explores him, and I take extra time dusting kisses around his belly button, enjoying the way his muscles jump and tense under my whispered touches.

Lust vibrates through me. Passion and power. If I stop right now, he would beg. The heady thought makes me moan and I bite down on him again. Luke groans. "Baby, who taught you this shit? I'm going to send them a fruit basket. Jerk me harder."

A devilish giggle rises in me. I tighten my grip and am awarded several more colorful curse words from Luke. Maybe I'm drunk on control, or maybe I'm just finally giving into this annoying goddamn need to touch and be touched. The loneliness and fear that's haunted me for months is unbearable.

Luke's cock stands straight up, a bead of clear pre-cum begging for attention at the tip. I'd be a liar if I said I didn't want him in my mouth. As I bite my lip, my breath catches as my fingers slip over hot, velvety skin. Dragging my hand from base to the tip, I swirl the clear liquid, marveling at the slippery feel, before sliding down the other side.

My mouth waters at the desire to feel him sliding between my lips.

Luke's breath is erratic. "Stop teasing me. Put it in your mouth," his husky voice orders. "Suck me off."

Just a taste. One taste.

"Where is your phone?" I ask.

He pulls it from a towel behind us, staring at me with heavy lust-ridden eyes as he opens the camera and the familiar shuttering starts.

Bending down, I blow hot breath over the tip and lick him, just enough that I'd imagine the desire for more friction must be maddening. *I want him panting and moaning.* The slick arousal between my legs drips into my underwear as my clit demands release.

Sliding Luke's firm cock between my lips is better than I imagined for both of us, and I moan. He curses and his length presses at the back of my throat. My gag reflex lets itself be known, so I hollow my cheeks and suck as I slide him back out. Luke gathers my hair into his hand, holding it as I work up and down his shaft, gagging myself.

"Oh, fuck yes, don't stop. Suck me like that, baby. Such a good girl." Luke grunts as a constant light from his phone follows my actions. *Video.*

"Look up at the camera while you gag yourself on my cock," Luke says.

Doing as he says, I stare through the blurriness of my watering eyes at the phone. Luke's hips curl and he thrusts up into my mouth, making a wet, smacking sound that echoes around the walled tub. He tightens the fist in my hair, holding me in place as he pumps in and out. My body goes limp as I relax into the rhythm, and a fire fans between my legs every time he slides over my tongue. Slapping, gagging noises fill the air as he fucks my mouth, mixing with the grunts and sharp inhales from Luke. "God damn, you take it like a pro."

He thrusts once more, forcing my head down, and I can feel him slip past my gag limit, blocking my ability to breathe. I go without oxygen as long as I can while he fucks my throat. He moans and uses my mouth like a toy to get off. *Fuck, that's so hot.*

The need for air claws at me, forcing me to pull away, gasping. Stringy spit slicks my lips and chin, a line of it still connected to his dick. I suck in air. My lips, puffy and numb from the beating, feel delicious. Blinking away the tears, I'm delighted to see I'm not the only one completely un-done.

Luke's chest heaves as he stares at me, his eyes dark as pitch and feral. The hand that never left my hair fists painfully as he drags me back against his body. "Again, slut," he says, pulling me back down.

I groan. "Yes, use my mouth." I don't recognize my voice.

He's rougher the second time, and I don't last long until I'm spent, gagging, coughing, and sucking in air as I hold myself up over him. Molten desire courses thickly through my body. I have no thoughts besides the need to cum and do everything I've ever wanted to with Luke.

Regretfully, I pull away and wipe my chin. My head spins a little and I rub my hand down my body, loving the way he tracks the movement. A husky laugh rolls from my mouth as Luke drinks me in. "Where has this minx come from, huh? I need to see more of her."

"You will. Now put on some music, something I can dance a little to, and go over there." I point to the back side of the pool.

He arches an eyebrow. "Yes, ma'am. No lie, caramel drop, this bossy side of you is hot," he says, slipping down into the water and making his way across the pool. "Want You So Bad" by The Vaccines pumps into the room. Wispy blue steam rolls off the water as I stand up.

"Ready?"

He points to his cock. "Been ready."

The silk, cream-colored camisole that was under my hoodie glows a soft baby blue in the lights. Slipping my hands underneath the fine fabric, I unsnap my bra. A stab of lust goes straight to my clit when I hear the shutter on his phone.

"Take the straps off slowly, like you're trying to hide from me, like you don't want me to see. Don't look directly at the camera. Just peek at me and bite your lip," Luke says.

Dude is so kinky. I'm getting the idea that Luke might be into a lot of different things. Hell, maybe I am too.

His voice twists my desire as I slip the straps down my arms slowly, marveling at how my skin looks in the lights. My hair falls forward, hiding part of my face until I look up at Luke. He studies me through his phone, the camera shuttering repeatedly in his left hand while the other is between his legs, stroking his cock. Wishfulness washes over me. The cobalt water could stand to be more transparent.

The knowledge that he is just as turned on as I am right now makes me desperately want to abandon the no sex rule I've been clinging to. I slide the bra out and drop it on the floor. My nipples press against the lustrous material and the hypnotic beat calls me to follow its rhythm.

Shutting my eyes, I trail my hands down my body as the moment and the music seduce me. "Fuck, I don't have the words for how much I want you," Luke whispers.

A smile curls my lips, but I ignore him. This is as much for me as it is for him. Turning around, I undo the top of my jeans and deliberately work them down slowly, baring my ass and a pink G-string.

The fabric is damp and a deep magenta color with my arousal. I push the jeans farther down, they catch at my knees, and I can tell Luke spotted the evidence of my arousal by the muttered, "Oh, shit, fuck yes." The shutter goes crazy.

His enjoyment makes me feel brazen. I peel the jeans off my wet legs and toss them to the side, making eye contact with Luke over my shoulder. He seems to have some trouble keeping me in frame while he jerks off. *I'm flattered.* I pull the silk camisole from my body and toss it on my jeans.

As I hook my thumbs under the thong, I lock eyes with him, wanting the connection as I leisurely work the fabric down and bare my pussy to him. Luke's eyes drift away from my face and a dark feminine energy pulses within me at seeing him struggle. Where the butterflies once were is now occupied by aggressive excitement. "Sharp as a Knife" by Danny Ayer twists through the humid mist coming off the water. *Maybe there is something to this seduction that I hadn't considered before. Power. Control. I've spent my life having little of both. But here, now, I've got plenty.*

I let the music wash over me and sway to the rhythm, running my hands down my nude body. Hot water licks my hotter flesh and laps against the curls between my legs, tightening my nipples. I imagine Luke dancing on the table last night and close my eyes, enjoying the sensation of being in my own skin even more than knowing Luke's eyes wander over my body.

Luke's breathing is so loud in the space, I'm surprised he hasn't cum. I'm more surprised by the fact that I don't want him to yet. Not unless I'm the one making him cum.

Fixing a come-hither smile on my face, I slowly sashay down into the water where Luke stands. The phone is all but forgotten in his hand as my thighs brush against his. His erection presses against my stomach. Luke stares down at me, concentration and so many questions in his eyes. I won't be answering any of them.

I slide my hand up to the center of his chest, pushing him backwards until his heels hit the underwater bench, and he sits. Heated water licks the underside of my breasts as I straddle him. Luke's eyes widen as he asks breathlessly, "Who are you right now?"

I'm not sure, but I love her.

The song rotates to "Bathroom" by Montell Fish. Whether it's the liquor, the ambiance, or my desire fueling the mood that's stolen over me, I'm channeling sacred power that comes from having your partner completely wrapped around your touch. I know at this moment, Luke would let me do nearly anything to him and I'm drunk on it.

My lips whisper over his, "Touch me."

Luke needs no encouragement. His hands circle around and grab my ass, squeezing as he kneads and pulls me to him. I press my nipple against his lips in a wordless order. He hums deeply as he sucks and flicks the tight bud between his teeth with his tongue. Whirlwinds of sensation swamp my body. Slipping my hand between us, I stroke his cock and slide it against my clit, teasing us both.

The camera is back and Luke records himself squeezing and biting my nipples until I'm breathless. He sucks one into his mouth so hard I cry out and my hips jerk. His lips unseal with a pop, and a perfect imprint of his bite mark rests in my skin.

Fisting my hands in his dark hair, I snap his head back. "That was naughty," I say.

"Oh, baby, there are so many naughty things I want to show you. We are only getting started. Now pull harder."

Luke moans as I increase my grip in his hair, watching with fascination as pain flicks across his face and his cock hardens in my hand.

Face tipped up to me, supplication in his gaze, I accept the offering of sweet lips against mine. Skimming the edges of his mouth with mine, I nip at his pink bottom lip. I deepen the kiss and seal our mouths together, letting the moment carry us away. My tongue sweeps into his mouth and he meets me greedily. Luke tastes of lemons as our tongues clash and we explore each other.

His hand snakes down between us, brushing over my swollen clit. I grind my mouth against his painfully. His teeth are neat and sharp. I imagine them biting the tender flesh of my sex and moan.

Gasping, he pulls back. "That's it."

Looping an arm across my waist, Luke pulls us from the water and tosses me on the narrow strip of tile alongside the tub. His heavy body crawls on top and presses me into the floor as his hand delves between us and he roughly shoves two fingers between my swollen pussy lips. I cry out in ecstasy as he pumps his fingers inside me. The sounds of my slick eagerness fill the room. Lips and teeth ravage my tits while he finger fucks me into oblivion. My eyes flutter close. A thumb slides between my folds and presses down on my sensitive numb, strumming me toward euphoria.

Warm, humid air swirls against my body as his weight rises off me and he stands on the submerged bench. A bright light illuminates me as he turns the video on. "Spread your legs for me, slut." Another finger slips inside me, stretching my walls and making me writhe. "That's it, take it all. Show me how much you want it, yeah? I know you've been wanting to show me. That's a good girl. Fuck yourself on my hand." His voice is harsher, demanding and rough. Unhinged. *Dirty.*

My fingers grip the rough tile and I roll my hips, sliding his hand in and out of my slick cunt. He adds another finger, and it's too much, pain so sharp and burning, but it feels delicious. I'm so close. Luke flicks my clit, rubbing little circles. Each pass of his thumb takes me higher and higher. I imagine him taking me against the tiles and coming on his cock.

"Please."

"Please what?"

"Please, harder."

He props the phone up on the cloudy panel, grabs my jaw, and squeezes. "Open your mouth and stick out your tongue like a good slut."

I do as he says, desperate for him to supply a little more friction. I'm about to lose my mind.

Luke leans over me and spits in my mouth, shocking me. A hand shoves my lips closed in tandem with his fingers hitting my G-spot and flicking my clit. "Swallow it, slut," he growls out. With his spit sliding down my throat, his order snaps me like a stretched-out rubber band.

My orgasm floods through me, glorious and dazzling, blinding me. My muffled scream echoes into his hand and around the pool. I lose control of the rhythm of my hips, wiggling down on the four fingers ramming inside me, begging for more. More pain, more pleasure. Luke presses me onto the floor as my body jerks under his grip. Wave after wave of delicious convulsions consume me while Luke finger bangs me through the best orgasm of my life, leaving me a panting, sweaty mess. I've never cum so hard or hurt so much.

Dark, satisfied laughter falls from his lips as he grins down at me like a cat who just got all the cream. He continues to play with my oversensitive clit, dragging out the pleasure. I grasp for his arm, a silent plea to stop torturing me.

His hand releases my jaw and fists in my hair. "Look." He holds my head where I can see his hand slip from my cunt. My fluids coat him as he wraps it around his cock and fucks it, using my cum as lube.

His breaths come hard and fast as his hips lose rhythm.

"Close your eyes, slut, and open your mouth," he commands. I do as I'm told, my body giving a lusty jerk. *I want to make him feel as good as he did for me.*

I can hear the pants and wet sounds of him stroking his cock. "Fuck yes, caramel drop." He groans and a hot spray of cum shoots across my tits and face. "Suck me," he demands, pulling my head toward him. I peek at this still throbbing cock and take him into my mouth, sucking every drop from his shaft. Licking, I clean him up until he releases my hair. He grabs the phone, and the shuttering sounds start again. He slides his dick from my mouth. A drop of cum runs down my cheek. He rubs it into my skin and across my lips, working it into my skin, even sliding it down over my swollen pussy.

His voice is aggressive and satisfied when he speaks next. "Well, I don't know about you, caramel drop, but I feel better about my five hundred dollars. I learned a lot of new things today about you. Worth every penny." He shoves his fingers back inside me and flicks my nipple, making me whimper.

Laughing, he scoops me into his arms and carries me across the pool. "We're getting out?" I ask.

"You need a shower, although I rather like you wearing my jewelry."

"I'm not wearing any jewelry."

"That pearl necklace I gave you says otherwise."

Glancing down at the whitish glaze that covers my chest, I roll my eyes. "Ha, ha, hilarious."

A dark smirk lights up his face, but it's off. He watches me and I'm more aware of it now than ever in the new quiet that steals over us.

He sets me down next to the shower and turns it on for me. The shower rains down. I fidget. *Where's all your dark sexual energy now, Carmella?*

Luke pets me, smoothing down my hair, and drops little kisses on my ears, cheeks, and lips. "Are you showering with me?" I ask.

"No, I'm going to watch, but you did great tonight. Such a natural," he murmurs into my neck. He unlocks the phone and shows me some of the pictures. I do look super hot in them, but the feminine power of the moment is gone now and I feel more than a little embarrassed that Luke has some seriously explicit, pornographic material of me. Especially the pictures of me sucking his cock and the ones of us in an intimate embrace as he bites my nipples.

"Wonder what your *boyfriend* would think of these. I bet he'd be jealous. I doubt he even knows where you are right now or how greedy your cunt is. Maybe we should send him these. What's his number?" He doesn't wait for me to respond before slapping my ass and ushering me into the shower, closing the door behind me.

Anxiety and arousal double-time me now that scary Luke is back. *You knew this. It's never just one thing with him.*

I try to not think about Luke calling me a slut, spitting in my mouth, or how much I liked it. Or that jab about Tommy, but it's there, rolling around in my mind. *He's mad and jealous, and I have no idea what to do about it.*

The hot water runs through my curls and beats down my back as I lather my hair and body with soap. Cries of pleasure leak from the room next to us, mixing with deep grunts as a bed bounces against the wall. Goosebumps break out along my body at the feel of Luke's eyes on me.

Tension, anger, and desire arch between us when I meet his gaze. The desire to go to him, to apologize for what I can't even comprehend, roots me to the spot.

He counts out five hundred. As each bill he lands on the table, it lashes my soul with punishment and a promise that breathes a second life of desire in my clit. Shame, guilt, and a desperate need to fuck Luke are beginning to be my drug of choice. When he's done, that bullshit smirk is back. He sprawls naked on the bed, twirls his finger in a silent order for me to continue, and rubs his relaxed cock.

I try to not notice how he watches my every move through the glass door. Pretend that his eyes aren't off, that they don't make me fucking uncomfortable and breathless with how covetous and possessive they are. Embarrassment and arousal swirl inside me, slicking my pussy again as Luke strokes his cock and I slide my hand between my legs.

The camera light from his phone comes on again, and I abandon myself to his desires and pray I never have to look at myself again.

Honesty Carries More Weight Than Lies

CARMELLA

The kitchen is empty, much to my relief, when I shuffle in at eight thirty am. My early morning ritual of dragging my stuff off the show floor and getting ready for the day is chipping into my nine am beauty sleep. I just want to pass out for a small eternity and give my body the rest it's demanding. The longer I'm with Luke, the more relaxed I become, and the more exhausted I am.

A soreness between my legs reminds me I'm not recovered from being so... stretched or the hours of orgasms after my shower. My face flushes at the memories of Luke's complete hand nearly disappearing inside of my greedy pussy. *I need a mental holiday before I see him.*

A conversation with my elementary school counselor floats at the edges of my mind. *What did she say again? It's been so long. Something about resting and being kind to myself... Seems like weird advice to give to a young kid.* But she wasn't wrong. School and bouncing between homes took their toll. She talked about how always being in a survival state can cause depression and exhaustion. Stress can make you take risky choices, act out, do things outside of your character. I stare ruefully into my coffee. *How right she was.*

I don't regret last night, but there are "concerns." Chief among them are Luke's expectations now and what I'm going to tell Tommy. Fresh, hot coffee steams from the pot. The mug I use every morning sits clean and ready for me at the little coffee station. Pouring myself a cup, I try to think back to when I drank from it last. *I definitely didn't wash this.*

"Good morning, hot stuff," Luke's sultry voice says behind me, and my head snaps up.

Knots tie in my stomach while things down low get a little heated. Quickly bringing the black coffee to my lips, I take a huge gulp and choke. Bitter acid blasts across my tastebuds and I nearly gag. I rip open a pink packet of sugar and the granules fly everywhere.

"Having problems?" He chuckles. "I had fun last night with you. We could have a lot of fun, don't you think? I got ideas."

I swear I can feel his eyes on my ass. I've got to get out of this kitchen. Taking a deep breath, I brace myself and turn around.

"Good morning, Luk…"

Nope. I'm not prepared. Luke leans in the doorway, shirtless, wearing loose burgundy sleep pants slung low on his hips and the smuggest grin. His gaze roams over my body before landing on my tits. Glancing down, I can see just a hint of my nipples through my black work polo. *Why don't I own any padded bras? I'm going to need a fucking parka to work around this man today.* My immediate reaction is to cross my arms, but he's already seen everything.

"I'm gonna go get ready for the day. Just… got to do my makeup," I say. He doesn't move to let me pass as I approach the door, nor does that shit-eating grin he's wearing falter.

"Um. Can I get by?" I ask.

"Sure." He steps slightly to the side, giving me just enough room to get by him.

I attempt to slip past, but he crowds me in the doorway. Slapping my hand out to block him, I feel the hair on his naked chest tickle my palm, sending blistering heat into my pussy. I jerk back and slam my elbow into the doorframe. The force of it rocks me and hot coffee splashes out all over my hand.

"Ow, shit. Double shit."

"Carmella!" Luke feigns astonishment. "Such a dirty mouth. Come here and let me clean it up." A dark light sparks in his eyes. He spins me, yanking my ass into his hard dick. More coffee splashes. "I'm going to have fucking burns, Luke."

He murmurs a satisfied sound into my curls and I'm fairly certain he didn't hear me at all as he grinds himself into my ass. Fingers brush the bare skin of my stomach and scorch a path to my clit as Luke's hands shove into my pants and cup my pussy. *Oh fuck.*

Abandoning all pretense that he and I are cool, I untangle myself from his arms that seem to have tripled. I don't know how he did it, but my pants are around my thighs and my bra is unclasped. Yanking up my jeans, I race down the hallway to the bathroom. Only a few sips of my morning brew are left in the bottom of my cup.

Once inside the bathroom, I lean against the door, button my pants, and heave a breath. My heart races and a sharp ache lingers between my legs. Bent over, I hang my head and squeeze my pussy through the jean material in a silent plea for us to get our shit together. *So much for last night only existing inside Oasis.*

I yelp as the door pushes open an inch and thuds closed with my weight against it. A rapid banging makes me flinch as Luke hammers on the other side.

It stops.

"You can't run from me forever, caramel drop. And you certainly can't hide all day. Come out and I'll behave myself." Luke's tone is a bit too charming for my peace of mind.

"I've got to do my makeup and you have to get dressed!" I sing-song back to him like I'm not currently barring his entrance.

He huffs on the other side of the door. "Fine, but this isn't over, Carmella."

Wavy blonde hair lies gently around me and stands out against the black work polo. I wrap a few strands around my fingers, enjoying the silkiness courtesy of the shampoo that Luke bought me.

After applying some lipstick and a few finishing touches to my makeup, I'm ready to talk. Luke will have to understand that this thing between us can't happen. I'm leaving eventually. Never did I have the intention of making the city of White Cove a home. It was always a pit stop I got stuck at. I'm going to tell him that while last night was fun, it was a one-time thing, and then pray he doesn't kick me out.

And what if he does? I stare at myself in the mirror. Tired eyes look back at me. My face is flushed and fuller than it was a month ago. *Then, I guess I take the money I earned and leave.*

The bathroom door creaks loudly and swings open, startling me. My heart jackhammers when Luke walks in—wearing full black with silver chains and rings—not a drop of good humor on his face. We stare at each other in the mirror. Those uncomfortable intense eyes of his are back and make my skin crawl.

"This is the ladies' restroom, you know," I snip.

"This is my fucking business, you know. I don't appreciate your personal affairs taking up work hours."

My brows pull down. "I was just coming out there to help you open. What is your deal?"

"There are multiple missed calls and voicemails from some guy named Tommy. He keeps calling. For you. He's tying up my landline during business hours. That is my deal."

I flush. "Oh."

The grin he gives me is twisted, like he wants to rip off my head, but is also enjoying watching me squirm in this fucked-up game of my own design. His smile is all clenched teeth. "He seems nice. We chatted. He's waiting for you on the phone. I told him I'd get you," Luke spits out.

My lungs stutter and stop working. "I see, and what did this chat consist of?"

His smile is unpleasant as he holds the door open for me and waves for me to go ahead of him. After tucking my stuff away under the bathroom sink, I head to the open floor, Luke trailing behind me.

Luke settles down beside me in the black rolly chair as I pick up the phone and press the flashing button. "Hello."

"You stood me up last night." Tommy's annoyed voice cuts out of the speaker. He's annoyed but not angry.

"I know. I'm sorry... Something came up."

Luke snorts beside me while he clicks around on the computer. He notices me staring and raises his eyebrows, as if daring me to contradict the fact that something had, in fact, come up.

"You couldn't have called? I waited like an hour," Tommy says. *So, he can be annoyed over being made to wait an hour, yet can ignore my calls for weeks. Now I'm annoyed.*

I sigh, wracking my brain for a good excuse. "You know I don't have a phone, Tommy. And I wasn't exactly in a position to call you last night." I glance around, hoping a good excuse is hidden amongst the furniture. "An opportunity to take care of a few things came up, so I had to jump on it," I say and immediately regret my word choice.

"You were in a position to have jumped on it. But you just weren't brave enough. I could have made you scream." Luke's voice is a whisper next to my ear, and his hand slips between my legs.

Fire ants eat up my chest as anger seizes me. *Motherfucker.* I feel positively possessed as my head slowly swivels and I pin him with my best red, fiery glare. My mouth forms the word "stop."

That twisted smile is back, and I want nothing more than to wipe it from his face. He may have paid for me last night, as fucking cringe as it is, but he doesn't own me. And Luke isn't going to ruin five years of friendship with the one person I have left from my old life because he feels threatened.

"Is that your boss?" Tommy asks.

"Sorry, we are trying to open the store. Give me a second."

Putting my hand over the receiver end, I cradle it to my chest. "Don't you have a door to open?" I hiss lowly.

"Don't you have a boyfriend whose heart you have to break when you tell him you found a bigger, more useful dick?" he hisses back.

My nails dig into the palms of my hands. I suck in a breath. Rage eats at my common sense. Luke folds his arms over his chest, sits down, leans back into the rolly chair, and props his legs on the counter, crossing them at the ankles. "It's my door. I'll open it when I'm good and ready."

"What about the business hours you were so worried about?"

He says nothing and continues to stare. Exasperated, I give up. Putting the phone back to my ear, I apologize to Tommy.

"Hey, I get it. Shit is bad for you right now. I just wish I'd known you weren't coming."

Warm shame splashes me. I could have called him before we left yesterday. Luke and the demands of the shop make me feel so insulated sometimes, it's like a different life. My whole life, actually. In my defense, I was told I'd be home in time. My eyes cut to Luke in a glare and an idea strikes me. "Hey, how about you let me make it up to you? I'm free this evening."

"Yeah, that sounds good. You want me to pick you up?"

I nearly agree when common sense kicks in. Tommy could easily be followed.

"How about I meet you at that Chinese place off Jay Street?" I say.

"You sure you don't want a ride?"

"I'll be fine." *And if there is a cop car anywhere near there, I will split before they even know.*

Carefully choosing my next words, I ask, "Hey, I've been meaning to ask: has my aunt or any of her partners been by since we talked last?"

My eyes cut to Luke once again, who hasn't moved an inch and glares at my head. Guilt lashes me harder, not because I messed up but because I don't regret playing prostitute and sucking Luke's dick. *I am trash.*

Tommy is saying something, and I startle, guilty for tuning him out. He sighs. "Yeah, but I didn't talk. But I'll give you the full deets later."

"Okay, yeah, sure. I'll see you tonight at seven. Be careful driving over. You never know who is on the road. Crazy drivers." My laugh is a bit forced.

"I'm always careful, babe. I'll see you at seven."

"Bye."

He hangs up, and I set the phone down.

Luke's expression is sour. His nose wrinkles as he squints at me. "What, no 'I love you, honey'? Not even a miss you? Aww, he called you babe. How fucking cute! I can't wait to meet him."

Hurt flashes through me, but I accept the verbal dragging. I've earned it. Whatever minor victory I had getting Luke to back off is gone along with his playful banter and quick smiles. "Where's your grand confessions of feelings and apologies, Carmella? Thought you were going to crack and confess how you found a bigger, better, more useful dick to suck."

Okay, snide, bitter Luke is definitely not my favorite. Part of me wants to reassure him, but of what, I'm not sure. Tommy is the only person who knows what the hell is going on with Gloria and won't immediately rat me out to her. If I'm going to stay two steps ahead of her, then I need to talk with Tommy, find out what—if anything—has been going on. So, I'm definitely going tonight. No more distractions.

Luke has been wonderful, but it doesn't change the fact that my aunt hates me, wants me home, and the cops have probably been looking for me. Maybe.

Anxiety coils around me about meeting Tommy. *Someone could definitely follow him. I refuse to go back to Gloria. I'd rather die.*

"That was the least spicy conversation between a couple I've ever heard. What is he, eighteen? Twenty? Can he even get you into a bar without getting carded himself? He sounds like a dumbass kid." Luke's rantings finally break through my thoughts.

"Luke, honestly, I just can't deal with this right now. Whatever this is," I point between the two of us, "is not the center of everything in my life. Okay? I have to talk to Tommy at some point."

Luke's jaw snaps shut with an audible clack of his teeth. He levels a glare at me so severe, it makes me wither on the spot before he turns back to his computer screen, clicking around.

The store keys lie on the desk between us. Sighing, I scoop them up and walk to the front door. I don't understand why he's so upset, anyway.

He knows I'm not staying. A navy-blue SUV drives by the store slowly, probably seeing if we are open yet. I click on the neon open sign, and the blue flickering strip lighting that I'm scared to remind Luke is still broken, crackles to life. *It's going to be a long day.*

A good, steady flow of customers keeps me from worrying too much about my aunt, or Tommy, for that matter. What downtime I have is taken up by an extremely disgruntled Luke.

In fact, the closer it gets to closing time, the grumpier he is. I'm torn between wanting to smooth things over in order to guarantee I still have a bed here at the end of the night and letting him suck it so he knows I'm not cool with him acting like a crazy, jealous boyfriend. Another piece, a much smaller piece, is thrilled he is acting like this, and that my going out has wrecked his whole day. *Maybe I'm a little petty.*

And then I have to remind myself that I'm not staying and the entire process starts all over again.

I assess the Tommy/Luke/housing situation from a thousand different angles before getting exhausted and settling on one. Truthfully, I don't want to deal with this at all. It would be so much easier to just slip out and deal with the ramifications later. Dust billows up as I run a feather duster over one table.

I know I've been tight-lipped with Luke about a lot of things, choosing to live in the moment with him and avoid the unavoidable. Just for a little while. All I wanted was an opportunity to relax and feel free. And because Luke has given me all that, he's also probably earned some honesty from me.

Putting the duster down, I decide it has to be now or I'm sneaking out. He's doing paperwork at the desk—like every evening. Walking around the large U-shaped counter, I heft myself up onto the work surface next to him.

"Hey, can we talk for a minute?"

He pauses in his paperwork, looks up at me, and quirks one eyebrow.

I fidget with my hands. Anxiety spikes, turning my stomach. "My aunt probably has the cops looking for me. I'm not sure, but probably," I say.

Luke's other eyebrow joins the first as they attempt to climb into his hairline. I pick my words carefully. Luke just needs to get the gist, not the fine details, of how fucked my life really is.

"Gloria is fucking insane, Luke. She called the police when I left and filed me as a missing person. I'm not missing. I just don't want to be found, not by her. She has ruled my life since I was a kid, and she fucking hates me and wants me gone. But she also wants to have control over me. When I left, I had to leave behind my ID and... well, if I'm being honest, I didn't leave behind much because I couldn't keep anything with Gloria. Either she'd trash it or use it to manipulate me. I learned not to keep things so they didn't become weapons against me." Exhaustion swamps my body as I think about getting through this conversation.

I push through. "Gloria has chased off most of the people in my life by turning them against me or just being so fucking malicious they don't want to hang out with me because they have to deal with her. But Tommy has always been there in his own dysfunctional way. He's the only person left from my old life, and if I'm going to avoid Gloria, I have to know what she is doing."

Luke pops his neck and stares back at the computer screen. Keys click and clack as he types. "I can't stay here forever; it's too close to home." I finish.

His hand clenches and flexes open. From his side profile, I can see his mouth twist. "I don't understand. You're old enough that even if the police find you, they can't make you go home. Right?" he snaps.

"That's true. Legally, my age isn't a factor." *But this is where it gets complicated, and this is the exact line of questioning I don't want to deal with.*

His eyebrows draw down, and he quietly assesses me. "I don't get it then."

"She wants control over my whole life and always has. And if that means she has to put me in jail to achieve it, then so be it."

"She sounds like a fucking bitch," Luke says. *You don't even know half of it.*

"She is. I could never make her happy. In fact, I've never been able to make anyone happy with my company. I'm either fucking things up or being too combative." I sigh. *This conversation is a mess, and I don't even feel like I'm making sense.*

I make eye contact with him but quickly turn away. "I spent years trying to be the perfect kid so I could fit into someone else's family in hopes they would want to keep me. Tiptoeing around people, always trying to read the room, say the right thing. As you would put it, I was always selling myself as a perfect little girl some pleasant couple would want to keep, and I buried all my rage and grief. Smothered by the disappointment and the unfairness of it all with smiles and being helpful. But it never happened. No one ever bought in. I could never pretend enough to convince someone to want me.

"And then Gloria came into the picture and I thought, here is family, someone who has to love me. And that was the biggest joke of my life. Gloria enjoys playing games and hurting me. The only person who stuck around through all of it is Tommy. I owe him something more than just dumping him over the phone, and he also lives by Gloria. She dropped by his place a bunch of times after I took off. He's the only one who understands my past with her."

Luke's chest expands sharply, and he shuffles his papers unnecessarily before straightening his shirt. He clears his throat, and I accept this as a sign that maybe he is actually hearing me.

I continue, "I have a life outside of here. It's not much, but there is at least one person in it, and I need to see them. You're unhappy with me going out and that's understandable, given what I've been allowing to happen between us. You've been great and kinder to me than anyone in your position probably would've been. I'm not dumb. You give me opportunities for my own money, you pay for everything, and you've never hurt me more than I ask for. I'm thankful for all of it, even if I don't always act like it."

Quiet, Luke stares at the computer screen and the documents under his hand. The warning he offered me on the first day on the job about how to be wary of him when he is silent surfaces in my mind and my spirits plummet.

Defeated, I ask what's really bothering me. "If I leave tonight, do I need to pack my stuff and take it with me?"

Luke's jaw tics and clenches as his head swivels around. Dark eyes pin me to the counter. His mouth works like he is trying to hold back a massive round of word vomit. "Why would you do that?" he grinds out.

"I know we hooked up, or you paid me for my company, or whatever that was. It happened, but I'm still my own person. And you're not saying anything. That makes me think that if I leave, I won't be welcome anymore." I mumble the last part, and embarrassment trickles through me over how needy I sound.

If he kicks me out now, I'll die, especially after spilling more of my sob story.

Roughly sticking his hand into his pocket, he yanks out the door keys. They jingle as he flips through them and slides one off the key ring, tossing it to me. "It opens the back, but be careful walking around out there at night. I've been jumped before, and it's dark back there. Check the cameras before you leave."

I stare at the key in my hand. It's silly how much I want to cry over a stupid hunk of metal. Swallowing back the lump in my throat, I bend down to kiss him on the cheek. Luke turns his head slightly and presses his lips against mine. He bands his arm around my waist, pulling me into his lap. Heat licks up my body as gravity presses us together and fireworks blossom under his touch.

Nails scrap my scalp as he snaps my head back, angling me for a deeper kiss. As his tongue sweeps into my mouth, relief courses through my body. *He still wants me, and I can come back tonight.* Reassurance and desire make a heady cocktail on my tongue as Luke devours my mouth. Goosebumps break out along my body as he sucks at my neck. I groan at how good it feels. His hand tightens on my ass, and I can feel his cock growing harder through his pants. Pulling back, I give him a sly smile. "I should have known."

He's breathless, but answers me with his typically charming smile, one I'm starting to look forward to seeing. "You really should have. If there is an opening, I'm going to stick my dick in it."

Closing my eyes, I nod. "Charming as ever, Luke."

He gives me his flirty eyebrows and quirks up his lips, making that mustache move with them. I shake my head, but when I hop off his lap, that charming smile fades. "Barring all the other bullshit I think about this guy, he can't really be your boyfriend unless he's willing to follow you; you know that, right? Leaving you to the streets, not stepping up or stepping in... If he isn't willing to help, then it's over. It's been over. Because you deserve better and you shouldn't accept a half-assed love."

I swallow thickly. "He's my only friend."

He nods quietly. "I see." That tic in his jaw is back, and he swivels around to his computer.

Awkwardly, I drift away from Luke, stealing one last look before leaving him to his paperwork.

No Good People Here

CARMELLA

The kisses Luke pressed so passionately to my lips aren't even four hours old before gagging noises fill the quiet space of Tommy's car while his cock hits the back of my throat. His hands fist in my hair as he pushes my head down and holds me in place. He flexes his hips and his shaft slides in and out of my mouth as he face fucks me.

My eyes instantly water. I sniff back my runny nose, the smell of rusty car and Tommys' balls filling my nostrils only resulting in worse gagging. Trying to relax, I breathe through my mouth, but being face down, ass up in the front seat of Tommy's cramped and rusted out 1995 Toyota Celica GT isn't exactly Oasis-level relaxation.

My lungs burn as I try to catch a breath, but each thrust from him shuts my windpipe off. My stomach threatens to empty itself as I gag again. *Fucking hell, get off me.* Yanking my head back, I try to not lose the dinner I paid for. Anger simmers in my chest.

Tommy's impatience leaks into his words as he pants, "I was nearly done."

I nod and try to summon some of that dark feminine power from the night before to put myself in the mood. I stroke his shaft and run my tongue over the flared tip, flicking extra hard in the spots he likes.

"Oh, shit yes, fuck, baby, just like that. You're gonna make me cum."

Fucking finally.

Grabbing my hair again, he shoves me back down and rams his cock against the back of my throat. "Fuck yeah, take that dick." He moans loudly and thrusts a few more times before blowing his load. I wince at the salty flavor and tamp down on the desire to bite his dick.

I'm not sure what's wrong with me tonight. Normally, Tommy swinging by and us finding a place to park is the highlight of my week. The thrill of getting caught, the fresh air, and a bit of naughty freedom bent over the hood of his car is just what I need.

Like the moon controlling the tides, impatience rules me tonight. Instead of getting down to the actual issues, I was forced to listen to Tommy regale me of tales from his "business" adventures and the drama his buddies get into as they fuck around. The real question is why Tommy thinks I'd give a shit about seventy percent of our dinner conversation. Especially when my situation's unsettled.

It doesn't help that I wasn't horny when Tommy pulled out his cock. Or that I suspect my reason for not being interested is due to a certain mustached bullshitter that gets off on harassing me.

A wave of nausea rolls through me as my stomach settles into a more natural position as I fold back into my seat.

"Damn, babe, that was so good. I totally needed that," Tommy says.

Tommy tucks his softening dick away by pulling up his gray sweatpants. His black studded earrings flash in the reflection of the streetlamp. Trash tumbles across the empty parking lot of the abandoned fast-food joint we parked behind. Reaching into his pocket, he pulls out a pack of smokes and lights one up. My brows pull down as I watch him. Light flares from the cigarette and the cherry glows brightly in the car. Normally by now, it's my turn to cum, or he works up another hard-on and we go fuck.

Tommy's slim, angular face turns toward me. He's buzzed his pale blond hair down to the scalp. It makes the jutting cheekbones, jawline, and nose that dominate his features stand out. It's a harsh look for him and if I'm being honest, it makes his head look small.

Tommy props his arm up in the window, letting the smoke curl around his fingers before the wind carries it away. "So, you gonna get yourself off or what?" Tommy asks around his cigarette.

I stare at him, unsure if I heard him right. "That's normally something we do together," I say.

"We don't have to do it together all the time. I mean, I can watch."

What's his problem tonight? I should have bitten his dick. "No, that's okay. Another time. I wouldn't mind a baggie, though, if it isn't too much trouble." It's a miracle that I'm able to keep the sarcasm out of my voice.

He flashes me a smile before reaching into the back and pulling forward his livelihood, a portable pharmacy of illegal substances. He unzips the pack and rifles through it before tossing me a rolled-up Ziplock bag of weed. "That's gonna be forty."

My head swivels up, and this time, I know my face reflects the frustration brewing in me. Tommy's eyes widen. "Damn, I'm kidding. I don't expect you to pay. Shit, maybe you should smoke some of that now. You've been so serious and on edge tonight." He takes a drag off his cigarette before tucking away his pharmacy.

"Tommy, my crazy fucking aunt is looking for me and lives only thirty minutes away. Yeah, I'm stressed out."

He nods. "That's true. When you said you were taking off, I figured you meant, like, leave the state, not skip to the next town over."

I fold my hands over my chest. "Can't get far with no money. Plus, you think I'd just cut out on you like that?"

Tommy snorts a laugh. "I'm not anyone to get arrested for, which could happen. To you."

His words sting as they bring more merit to what Luke said to me before I left. But to be fair, I didn't stick around for Tommy. I literally had no place to go and no money to get me there. Crashing on mutual friends' couches only goes so far, and once the cops started asking around and bothering the few acquaintances I had, they made it clear I'd overstayed my welcome. Luke was more than right. The streets aren't kind and most people aren't either. *Which brings me back to Gloria.*

"How has Gloria been?" I ask.

He low whistles. "That woman is a ripe cunt. I'm still fixing the shit she broke the first time she swung by after you left. I can't get over how she just walked into my place and started tearing things up. Opening doors, screaming she knew you were there. Fucking crazy bitch."

My face is hot with shame as I imagine the position Gloria put him in. It's not like he could call the police without incriminating himself. Guilt gnaws at me.

"She drops by every now and then, asking if I've heard from you. Which I always give her and the cops the same answer. No, and fuck off."

"So the cops are still looking?"

He shrugs. "Yeah, I assume so, considering the felony you got slapped with."

My eyes round. "What?!"

"C'mon, Carmella, you don't gotta lie to me. I know about the money." Shaking his head, he puts the cigarette out in the already full ashtray of the car.

My brow pulls down. "What does that mean?"

"Gloria told me about the stolen two grand."

"What?" I ask, flabbergasted.

"Yeah, she found the money missing and went back to the police. Told the cops she lied about how you were just missing and that you had attacked her and while she was locked in the bathroom, scared for her life, you stole two thousand dollars and took some kitchen knives."

My mouth gapes open and I squint my eyes at him, trying to tell if he is joking or not. My brain doesn't compute what he is saying. The night I left my aunt's replays through my mind. Gloria was high off her ass and had some guy over. They had forced me to listen to them fuck on the couch, with my aunt's fake porno moans permeating through the headphones I used to help drown them out. I figured after a couple hours of quiet, it was safe for me to slip out. That was a mistake. The resulting argument ended up with her punching me in the face repeatedly as we fought down the hall. Gloria's guest hit the road while we tussled, and it ended with me locking myself in my bedroom, stuffing as much as I could into a couple bags, and scrambling out a window.

"No, there was no money, Tommy. No kitchen knives. She attacked me. How can she just go back and change her story like that?" I stare in horror out the window. "When did this happen?"

He shrugs and glances out the window. "Maybe a month ago. I don't really remember. I've been busy."

"What the fuck, Tommy? Why didn't you say anything?!"

"Whoa, whoa, I figured you already knew, hence why you lit out of town like feds were after your ass."

"They will try me as an adult, Tommy. I can't afford a lawyer on top of all the other legal shit she has put me through."

"So, there was no money?"

"If there was money, I wouldn't be here, now would I?"

He shrugs again. "I don't know why women do half the shit they do."

Oh my fucking God, he's an idiot.

He sighs. "Well, if you are worried about it, there is one lawyer you might be able to afford. His name is Daniel Tunnell, but he goes by Dan. He enjoys helping pretty, single women, but only as long as they will let him help himself to what's between their legs. He's a youngish guy, so at least it won't be Grandpa." He looks at me. "You know, if it gets that bad."

I'm too shocked to be offended that Tommy just told me to whore myself out for legal counsel. My eyes skate across the desolate parking lot. Its crumbling emptiness reflects the emotions that swirl cold and ugly in my chest. It's moments like these I don't know why I try anymore. Better off just to end it.

The desire to lash out at anyone, even for a moment, is overpowering. I'm so angry and cornered. The sharp feeling turns inward and not for the first time, I wish I had a razor.

If self-harm hadn't landed me up in a psych ward twice in my younger years, I'd probably still be cutting. My fingers curl into a fist, nails biting into the palm of my hand. Cutting had only made my situation worse, so I promised myself never again, but fuck, I need an outlet. Something to release myself into. Any way to check out for a moment.

Eyeing the baggie of weed in my lap, I'm about to ask Tommy for some paper when I freeze. Tommy knew I was a wanted felon. He knew and didn't even care enough to ask me about it or have a conversation with me. He knew I was struggling, he knew how bad it was, and I didn't hear from him for three weeks. He rarely answers the phone anymore and... I replay our whole night together. The hours wasted hearing about parties I won't go to. The money I spent on our dinner. The unreciprocated sex.

Hurt crushes me, finishing what's left of my fight. Sadness wells up in me and floods my entire being. Luke was right. Tommy doesn't give a shit about me. Things have been done with Tommy for a long time and I'm the fool that kept holding on. *Tommy's using me, and I'm the pathetic fucking homeless girl that jumps on the first flimsy excuse he gives me.*

"So, what are you going to do?" Tommy asks.

I can't even bring myself to answer him. A white paper bag dances across the parking lot as I fold my arms across my chest. Swallowing down the lump in my throat, I shake my head.

"Well, White Cove is bigger than Dotteville, and you don't know anyone here. I'm sure it will be fine until you can get some cash from your job. Don't worry." He pats me on the shoulder, triggering a desire to rip out his eyes. *Fuck him.*

Tommy thumbs the steering wheel in my silence. "This conversation sucked. Do you want me to drop you off at your friend's place? That way, I know where to pick you up next time?"

"No." *There won't be a next time.*

"You sure?"

"Yeah, just drop me off at 32nd Street."

We pull out and drive for a bit before turning. My skin itches as the rage builds every time Tommy glances at me. We pull alongside the curb half a block away from the stop. "Hey, before you go, I wanted to let you know there is a big party tomorrow night here in town at the abandoned storage facility. I'm gonna go, and I sorta told Sarah I would take her."

His words process in my brain like a bomb going off. "Sarah who?"

He rubs his shaved head and puts the car in park, sighing. "Sarah Longcryer."

"Sarah the whore? The whore Sarah? That Sarah?" I snap, no longer able to control myself. *Wow, that didn't take long. Who does he think he is? Must be so nice to just move onto the next, most convenient, piece of ass.*

"It ain't like that. We haven't even fucked. She definitely isn't blowing me in the front seat like you do." *How nice.*

"Oh, poor you, she isn't blowing you in the front seat. Well, that's just fucking sad, isn't it?"

He snaps, "I'm just taking her as a friend. Plus, you have problems. You can't go to a party, and it's not like we are official, anyway. I can take someone else."

"And it just so happens to be the girl who has been instant messaging you for months, whose primary goal in life is to steal boyfriends and men. Okay, well, you know what... you and the whore have fun together. I wish you all the best, jackass."

Swiveling in the seat, I pop the door and kick it open. It lashes out, bouncing against a sign pole, clanging loudly. I get a little thrill knowing I put another dent in his rust bucket. Tommy grabs my arm and yanks me down into the seat. "Hey, I'm putting up with your crazy bitch aunt and lying to the cops for you. I almost got busted because of you and her. I think you could stand to be a little nicer to me."

My hand flies at his face before I can stop, slapping the snarl from his lips. I'm so livid I could kill him. Tommy has never been like this to me before. Ripping my arm from his grasp, I scramble out of the car and slam the door. Bending down to where he can see my face, so he can read the anger in my gaze, I go off. "Your weed fucking sucks. This car is a piece of shit, and I'm not going to be responsible for my orgasm. Wash your fucking balls. They smell like asshole and nearly made me vomit in your lap. You're a loser, Tommy." I flip him the bird, turn, and stomp all the way to the bus stop.

The engine of his piece-of-shit car revs and the screech of tires rips through the air as he tears off down the road. *What a massive asshole. I hope he gets a ticket and an STD and a boil on his dick from Sarah's stank pussy. And his engine falls out. Yeah, all of those.*

I'm still fuming when the bus pulls up. It's a Friday night and every drunken tourist and pickpocket is out on the town. From my seat next to the window, I stare out at White Cove and the neon of the main drive comes alive. The bright colors of restaurants and nightclubs reflect off the glass and blur past.

In the back of the bus, some idiot thinks we all want to hear his taste in music and starts playing his phone loudly. Just what the crowded space needs more of: noise. Between the ruckus of drunken friends barhopping and the ramblings of the headcase up front, who has spent the last twenty minutes talking to his invisible friends, I'm surprised I can hear anything.

The bus stops close enough to Luke's that I disembark, feeling on the edge of a mental breakdown. A sobbing girl in a dark hoodie on a public bus brings too much attention. I shuffle home, and as the store comes into view, I'm thankful the place looks dead. Aside from the broken, flashing neon blue that outlines the windows, I'm pretty certain all the lights are off. *He must be out. Thank God.*

In the shadows outside of Luke's, the tears finally come. I can't hold them back anymore. It's just too much for one person. Sliding down the red brick, I let grief wash away all the walls between my pain and me.

In the Thick of It

CARMELLA

I don't know how long I'm outside—probably not long—when the back security door clangs against the concrete wall and hurried foot-steps approach where I am curled up. The overhead flood light comes on and the brightness makes me feel physically and emotionally exposed. I scrub at my face, wiping away the tears, as Luke appears around the corner.

His voice cuts through the air. "What's wrong?"

Standing quickly, I make a show of brushing off my pants. "Nothing. I thought you were gone."

Frown lines deepen on his handsome face as he stares down at me. "Oh, so you're just curled up in a ball outside the store for fun? Fuck, Carmella, I thought you were dead or something. Are you hurt?"

He's changed into a white button-down with little cacti all over it and tan pants. His hair is slicked back and curls slightly at the ends. The gold jewelry is back. Relief that he's still here and disappointment that he's leaving flood me. *It's fine. I don't want him to see how much of an idiot I am, anyway.*

"No. I'm fine."

Ducking my head so he doesn't see my shame, I skirt around him. "I'm tired. I'm going to go inside and lie down. Have a good evening."

Pulling open the back door, I head down the hallway and out onto the darkened show floor. Zigzagging my way amongst the many beds, I come to the one I call my own. It sits bare and white, similar to all the others except for the blue comforter rolled up and tucked away. *I'm living in a furniture store and there isn't a single person who gives a shit.* The thought knocks loose and lands in the middle of my mind. A mockery of a home surrounds me. Fake kitchens and living rooms. Complete pieces that belong somewhere, but have nowhere, so they pretend to belong, just like me.

Somehow, comparing myself to standalone pieces of furniture is probably the saddest thing I've ever thought about next to being a Jane Doe on a cold metal slab. Also, a potentiality for my life. Wrapping myself up in the comforter, I flop face-first into the pillows I tossed on the mattress and drag the blanket over my head.

I'm a failure. A sharp stabbing pain eats away at my chest, making it feel as though it's caving in. The tears come hot and quick as I give myself over to the grief.

Sobs muffled by the pillows consume me as the silence of the show floor settles around me. The bed shifts and squeaks. Freezing, I suck in a breath and hold it. Luke's presence falls over me as the bed dips under his body weight. Releasing the deep gulp of air, I try to quiet the fit that grips me, but the pillow is smothering. Gasping, I turn my face to the side and curl into a ball.

"Talk to me." His voice is soft, but not gentle.

Crying about Tommy to Luke after making such a fuss about having a boyfriend and needing my freedom or venting my thoughts about how I am a failure for living in a furniture store when it is, in fact, Luke's home seems really shitty and ungrateful. The words bottle and stick in my throat.

Slowly, the blanket inches down. I don't fight him as he pulls it from me. The look on Luke's face is the darkest and calmest I've ever seen, and it's not because of the shadows we sit in. The promise of violence and blood stirs in his expression. It chases away all his handsome charm and brightness. He looks every inch his thirty-four years, if not older. And meaner. Luke looks like someone I wouldn't want showing up on my porch at night. The soft blue comforter slips lower, revealing my upper torso, before he drops it.

For the first time, I think back to what he said about being fifteen and on the streets, what those early years must have been like alone for him. I wonder if he felt much like I do now. Sometimes, the things he says resonate with me so intensely, like he understands even without me explaining. *He must know then.* I take in a shaky breath and pull myself up into a sitting position, wiping my face.

"I'm just an idiot. Okay?" I say. *An idiot that might be in some real trouble here soon if the cops find me.*

He raises an eyebrow. "No, not okay. You're not explaining anything."

I sigh, wrapping my arms around my chest and squishing myself, attempting to relieve the raw ache in my heart. "You're right. Tommy doesn't care about me."

Sighing, Luke runs his hands through his hair. "Tell me what happened. Did he hurt you?"

"No."

"Then what's that?" He points to my arm.

There, under the maroon-colored straps of my shirt, purple bruises stain my skin. One is clearly the size of a fingerprint.

"Oh. We were fighting, and he grabbed me, but honestly, Luke, I've got bigger problems than Tommy right now, and I don't think I can talk about all this."

Frustration bubbles up and hot tears track down my face. The police are looking for me. Gloria. I'm going to end up in jail or back on the streets and no one can stop it. The desire to scream works itself up my chest. And behind that scream are all the things that I have left unsaid.

His eyes flash in the darkness as he shakes his head. "Why were you fighting? I need you to explain why you are so upset, caramel drop. I'm not going to let it go this time because I'll make myself crazy wondering. Why did he grab you?" A box of tissues appears in my lap and for the life of me, I have no idea where Luke materialized it from.

I'm a shit person. The knowledge that I shouldn't tell Luke about Tommy because it's unfair is thick on my tongue, but also, he's the only one I have to talk to now. I don't want to carry all this shit alone. The world grows bleak when you survive without anyone who cares.

I word vomit on Luke, and it isn't fucking pretty.

Starting at dinner, I bitch and moan over Tommy's crap behavior and about how I had to listen to his utterly irrelevant bullshit when he knows my situation, and then how he made me pay. I skip the blow job portion—pretty certain Luke doesn't want to hear that. I know I'm being a bitch, but the rage simmers again.

Tossing back the comforter, I wear a path in the carpet from pacing in front of Luke as the words spew from my lips about my aunt and her hatred for me. The lies she told the cops about the money and how I made her scared for her life. *Fucking ha!* All my fear and pain come hurtling toward the surface.

The only thing I could think to do was leave or kill myself because I couldn't take being with her one more day, and now I'm going to go to jail for it. She has me cornered and I'm terrified.

I even tell Luke Tommy is taking Sarah "the whore" to a party tomorrow and how I'm supposed to be cool with it because he lied for me and didn't tell the cops where I was. Well, guess what? I'm not fucking cool with any of this shit. It's not that I'm jealous. I'm just furious that I didn't catch on sooner. I finish by slapping my hands against my thighs. Tears coat my face and my chest heaves with the roller coaster of emotions. Just as quickly as the rage came on, it's sucked out of me and my head drops.

Somewhere in the middle of all this, I realize what a hot mess I am. *I must be the biggest red flag he's ever encountered.* For sure, he is going to kick me out now—*no one wants to deal with this much of a mess.* The sobbing starts back up again and I'm too kicked to pick up any of my pride as I stand before him. Desperation and insecurity rocket through me and my gaze searches for his. Dark eyes meet my blue ones. My nose runs and my lips are sticky and dry. "Am I really so awful that I'm this unlovable? What did I fucking do to deserve any of this?"

Luke's face crumples as he shakes his head. Rapid breathing mixes with my hiccupping sniffles in the silence of my tirade. Standing, he reaches for me and tucks me into his arms. Soft fingers weave into my hair as Luke presses me into his chest. "You didn't do anything to deserve this. You aren't unlovable. There are a lot of shitty people in your life, and that's not fair. I'm so very sorry."

We are quiet for a long time as we stay locked in each other's embrace, Luke's warmth thawing the coldness that's taken up residence in heart. I soak up every drop of his affection, letting it be a balm to my ragged emotions. His voice drags overhead. "Sooo, starting with the easiest problem. Your unofficial ex-boyfriend is a cheating drug dealer and you *don't* want me to hurt him? Because I want to hurt him. In fact, it'd make me happy."

I sniff and bury my face in his shirt, inhaling the scent of clean laundry, smoke, and lemon oil. "He sells weed and pills, so not like a real drug dealer, and no, it's not worth you getting in trouble."

Luke's chin rests on my head. "Caramel drop, if you're slinging pot and pills nowadays when everyone can get their cards or see a doctor, you're a fucking wannabe. How old is this idiot, anyway?"

"Twenty-three."

Luke sits down, coaxing me into his lap, where he once again wraps me in his arms. Tossing the blanket over us, he tips my face up to look at him. "Listen, you and me, we got the same problems. When you go so long without love, you believe bad things about yourself. The voices in your head tell you... all sorts of terrible shit. I battle those same demons. Neither one of us asked for it. Neither one of us deserved it when we were little. For what I've done with my life, I probably deserve it now, but you don't." I shake my head, wanting to argue with him.

"Shh, let me finish," he demands, laying a finger over my open mouth. "I may be a nasty shit for brains, but any woman of mine is always going to have a roof over her, food to eat, and a safe place to rest. And any person I call a friend, which includes you, if they ever get into a tight spot, they can call me and I'll come running. I made the choice to be a loyal friend, even when it sucks. If you won't even try for the people you claim to care about, then as a person, what good are you really? Caramel drop, don't go looking for stability in a good-time guy. You won't find it and it will leave you empty." He brushes his fingers across my cheek, wiping the escaping tear or two.

"You were a good-time guy, weren't you?" I ask.

His eyes narrow on me. "What makes you think that?"

I snag the box of tissues and clean up my face. "No offense, Luke, but you look like the type of guy who would hook up with my friends."

"No offense, sugar, but I might have fucked some of your shitty friends. You'll have to introduce me to be sure." His eyes crinkle as he winks at me. *Charming.* I lightly punch him in the stomach. His mouth curls up into one of his devastating smiles as he laughs. "You think I'm kidding, but I'm not. I used to get around."

"Eww."

Luke tips back his head in a full belly laugh. "You say eww now, but wait until you see how good my dick game is. You'll be singing a different song."

My face flushes with embarrassment and a dash of shame as my clit picks now to let herself be known with a warm tingle. I bite my lip and shake my head as laughter trickles from me, unbidden.

It's cut short when another thought forms and apprehension swirls in my stomach. "There is something else I need to tell you. You could get in trouble messing around with me."

He blows out a heavy breath. "I fucking knew it. You're underage, aren't you?"

"What? No. No, I wish. That would be easier to fix."

"Well, that's good. Except now I'm worried." He draws out the word as his brow knits in confusion. "If this is about being arrested, I know it's scary. But the best thing for you to do right now is make some money, get it put back, and lie low until you are ready to surrender. Then I'll bail you out. Just keep your head down and power through. It's your first offense as an adult, right?"

I nod.

He pats my leg and drops a light kiss on my lips, making them tingle to match my clit. "It will be alright," he says.

I feel a flush of guilt for not telling him everything sooner. The desire to word vomit again rolls up. I fear that once I do, he'll understand the overwhelming hopelessness of my situation and he'll wash his hands of me.

"I'm under a conservatorship. The court awarded it to my aunt after I turned eighteen."

There, I said it. The only thing worse than my aunt being a shitty person is the court-approved power she has over me. The reason I worry about being arrested, about her finding me, about not making it out of White Cove is because once I'm taken into custody, they will give me back to her if they don't ship me off to some mental facility or prison.

Luke frowns at me and tips his head as the confusion grows. "What exactly does that mean?"

"It means that my aunt has control over my life even after I became a legal adult. I can't work a job without her permission, and the money has to go to my care, a.k.a. her pocket. I can't date unless she approves it. Can't marry. Can't have kids. Can't live on my own, have my own bank account, or access to my own funds. No college. No future. She stole my life, and the court agreed with her."

With every passing sentence, Luke's face grows more horrified. "But how? She just holds you captive? How is that legal?"

I sigh. Exhaustion swamps me and my shoulders slump. "It's a long story. Just know I tried to fight her. I had a lawyer, and she wasn't even sure how we lost the case, but we did. My aunt had evidence proving I was mentally unstable, and they questioned my ability to care for myself."

"You are perfectly capable, Carmella, and if the court can't see that, then they are the mentally unstable ones. What in the actual fuck?" he snaps and squeezes my arm like he wants to strangle someone.

His outrage on my behalf is very sweet. My lips perk up in a halfhearted smile.

"Am I capable, though? Look at my life. I wound up here half because of Gloria and half because of my own stupid choices. My aunt's lawyer was exceptional at painting a picture of a broken, emotionally disturbed girl suffering from her dead parents and foster care trauma. It also didn't help that my aunt had all the police reports from every time we physically fought. She would pick a fight, but I would swing first. It took me a couple of times before I figured out her game."

Luke's eyes flash with the promise of murder and his body turns hard under me. "And that's all it took for the court to say you couldn't be responsible for your own life? If that's the case, where's my conservatorship?"

I flinch. "No." Heaving a sigh, I scoot off his lap. Crossing the show floor, I flip on the light and return to the bed, sitting criss-cross next to him. "When I realized I couldn't lash out, I started turning that pain inwards."

I gesture to my wrist, and the faint silvery scar lines are barely visible. He grabs my arms and peers at them. "I can barely see them."

"I know. I tan well and the cuts were never deep. I made sure I marked myself where people could see. I wanted someone to know I was hurting. Gloria found them and shipped me off for a week of inpatient care. She thought she was getting rid of me until they launched an investigation into my home life because of the things I told them. They couldn't prove anything, which made me look like a liar, and Gloria brought me home."

I hate this ugly bit of my history, how cringy and costly my childish emotion-fueled mistakes were. Picking at the blanket on the bed, I avoid Luke's gaze. "Gloria laid off me for a time, but it always got worse so I'd cut again, show it to anyone who would listen, and end up in more rounds of inpatient care. Therapy and medication were shoved down my throat. Some of those pills and the rage I felt had me ranting like a crazy person about all these abuses I'd suffered but couldn't prove. And this became the cycle for a while. That time in my life was dark. I went a little crazy for a couple years, being a kid still and trying to—I don't know—get help... find my way... find love... get away from Gloria."

Luke nods. "And I'm sure that police reports naming you the assailant when you and Gloria fought didn't help convince anyone of your story."

Humorless laughter falls from my lips. "It definitely made it easier to say

I was crazy and detain me. My aunt filed to take control of me on the day I turned eighteen. While I was out having drinks with Tommy at the beach and talking about college, she had already put months into building a case against me with evidence that I gave her. So yeah, sometimes I wonder if I am actually able to care for myself."

Fury burns in his eyes as he takes me in. "I got a lawyer friend. When you are ready to fight this, we can go see him."

Blonde curls slip across my shoulder as I shake my head. "I don't want to fight it. I already tried and lost. Luke, I can't even pay another lawyer to pick up the case. All I want is to slip away and become someone else. What she has done now—making me a wanted felon... I'll go to jail, and then some criminal ward for the mentally unstable. She's robbed me of all peace and is trying to take my freedom."

He nods. "You mentioned money. What money? Could you buy her off?"

I screw up my face, trying to remember. "Oh. Yeah. I have some inheritance that helped care for me after my parents died. My family's lawyer oversaw it. The rest was supposed to go to me when I turned eighteen. My other lawyer tried to argue it was a money grab, but Gloria had receipts showing bills paid, clothes bought, and blah blah blah... basic care covered. I don't even know how much is left, and it's not like I can even touch it now."

"Why not?"

"I was deemed unfit to care for myself. I'm not gonna get that money." A humorless laugh falls from my mouth as a light bulb clicks on. "Ah, I get it now."

Luke's brow furrows. "What?"

"Without me in Gloria's care, the payments from my inheritance should stop. No wonder she upgraded her report from missing person to missing money. Cops will stop looking for a missing person, but they never stop looking for a wanted felon."

I'm so fucked.

"What do you want to do then, caramel drop? It's your life." He smooths my hair back from my face and the warmth from his hand feels like the sun shining on me. I should've known Luke would never turn me away.

My lips tip up in a wry smirk. *What do I want to do?*

Burying all the hard things that I don't want to carry in Luke for a while seems like a nice thought. I'll crawl up inside his world and pretend nothing else exists until I have to go. Pretend that everything is fine for a bit and let him take care of me the way he has been offering to. I know it's running, but it's all I got and it won't be for long. Plus, Luke has been offering me a ticket to pound town since I broke in. *Pound town? Jeez, I think this guy is rubbing off on me.*

"I think I want to watch some TV or a movie. Is it okay if I watch in your room while you're gone?"

Luke simultaneously rolls his eyes and scoffs, "Like I'd actually leave you now. Come on, we will have a drink and watch something."

"I don't want to take over your entire night with my problems." I stand up, hugging the comforter around me.

Rising with me, he says, "Carmella, I don't do things I don't want to do." Strong arms snake around me as he kisses my lips firmly. This time, there are no roadblocks in me reciprocating. No need to run. I open my mouth and let him deepen the kiss. The motion of his mouth against mine fades away as I bask in the closeness and steady heartbeat under my palm. This isn't a kiss of grand passion or a prelude to sex, but it leaves me breathless. The message he delivers to me when we break apart is clear. I'm not alone.

T he body lies whitish blue and stiff on the table. Her eyes are milky and clouded. The mortician slices into her chest as her tits jiggle in an unnatural, dead way. The eerie silence of the scene has me totally weirded out and leaning away from the TV screen, especially when the mortician's fingers brush over the dead girl's nipples and he moans.

My mouth turns down and my stomach screams "ick" as his hands continue their exploration downwards to her pubic area and his breath hitches as he pants. *Ooohh, no. I'm going to have fucking nightmares.*

"What the fuck is the name of this movie again?" Alarm laces my voice as I tip my head toward Luke, but don't take my eyes off the screen as the man cups the space between the dead lady's legs.

Luke chuckles. "*The Lonely Mortician.*" My mouth drops open and my eyes bulge, snapping over to him in horror. "Why would you pick this?" I hiss.

Luke busts out laughing and shakes his head. A rueful smile plays across his lips. "Caramel drop, you have got to learn when I'm being sarcastic." A sudden clanging from the TV startles me. The dead woman has hold of the mortician's throat as she strangles him with her newly formed zombie strength. The clouded, milky eyes have been replaced with blood-red ones as she bites into the man's face. His screams of pain make me giddy—*serves him right.* "It's called *Revenge 3: Back for Blood,*" Luke says.

"But why did you pick it?"

He shrugs. "The zombie girl is the hero. She murders the people who stole her life and then eats them. And then she kills the other zombies. I thought it might speak to you. Scoot back here by me."

He smacks the pillows next to him. We piled them up against the wall so we could prop our backs up, but the start of the movie had me so stressed out, I ended up clinging to the edge of his bed. I scramble up to sit by him. He puts his arm behind me, and I accept the invitation to settle against his chest. Once comfortable, he passes me the one of the margaritas he made for us in the kitchen. The cold glass in my hand pulls my attention away from the TV, and I sip the frosty drink and the explosion of lime and sweet citrus hits my mouth along with a god-awful burn.

I choke a bit. "How much alcohol did you put in this?"

"Enough to hide the roofie flavor." This time, I know he is being a sarcastic ass. I elbow him. His drink sloshes and spills all over his nice tan slacks. *Whoops.*

Luke's eyes crinkle with mischief. "Oh no, looks like I have to take off my pants. This was all part of your devious plan, wasn't it, Carmella? To get me drunk and take advantage of me. Pantsless." He feigns a scandalized look by pressing a hand to his chest.

I stare at him, deadpan. He gives me wiggly, flirty eyebrows and a shit-eating grin. It's impossible to be serious when he acts like this. I laugh.

Setting down his margarita, he rolls off the bed and unbuttons his little cacti shirt. His dark eyes are all for me. Pretending modesty now when the dude has literally wiped his cum on my face would be a moot point, so I watch him undress.

My pulse can't help but speed up, and he gives me one of his charming dimple-inducing grins. Lately, I've grown fond of the mustache. Luke flaunts his own personal style. It's definitely not for every man, but on him, it's sexy. He pulls the shirt off and tosses it into the dirty laundry, revealing a nicely sculpted chest covered in dark hair.

Never thought I would be into chest hair, but here we are. I take a huge gulp of margarita, hoping it cools down my budding desire.

Unbuckling his pants. He unzips and drops them down his legs, humor on his face. I stick my tongue out at him. "I can make use of that," he says, eyes twinkling.

He flexes his abs and his dick bounces in the most obscene way. Startled, I nearly drop my margarita. "Put some pants on! Damn!" I scold him and close my eyes.

Luke lets loose the loudest belly laugh I've ever heard. "Carmella, you really are the most refreshing combination of prickly angst and false modesty."

I grin as the bed shifts. "Are your pants on?" I ask.

Warm breath swirls over my ear and cheek, causing shivers to race down my spine and tighten my nipples when he speaks. "Look for yourself."

Cracking my eyelid a smidgen, I peek at him. Luke sits back against the wall, his hands folded in his lap, looking the picture of innocence clad in soft black sleep pants. I'm convinced he could sell Christianity to the Antichrist with his disarming smiles and dirty humor.

He plucks the drink from my hand, setting it on the table. Moving closer, he leans in on me. My eyes flutter close as I tilt my lips up for his kiss.

The button on my jeans goes slack, and a hand shoves me back on the bed as my pants are yanked down my legs faster than I can protest. "You need to get more comfortable," Luke says, pulling my jeans over my bare feet. "There, so much better."

Alcohol and sleepiness steal away my retort, and I decide lying down is the best place for me, anyway. I do feel wrung out, like I ran an emotional marathon, and Luke's bed is so comfy. I wiggle out of my strappy, restrictive shirt. "Damn, baby, that's a lot of milk jugs on display. All that calcium makes me grow big and tall." He shifts the crotch of his pants. "Plus, I like my milk with cookies." He stares down at the V between my legs.

I snort and roll my eyes. "You worked really hard at that one."

He tsks. "I did, but the delivery was off, wasn't it?"

"Very off." A yawn makes my jaw crack, and my attention shifts back to the movie.

He shrugs and sprawls out beside me in the bed, propping up his head, "Well, you can't win them all. I'll have a better joke tomorrow. Tonight, we watch the full bush naked zombie woman murder people brutally. Now bring that ass over here and let's snuggle."

Giving him a sleepy smile, I do just that.

Insecurities and Secrets

Luke

A rock-hard woody urges me awake. A deep purplish sky is just begging to glow with pale yellow, and morning light streams through the window above my bed. Carmella's soft, warm body stretches out beside me, her breath even and deep. Naked, smooth legs tangle with mine. With the blanket kicked off, I can see the lithe lines of her body. As I admire how her hips flair, and how gentle she looks in her sleep, my hands itch to touch her. Until I also notice the pale lines on the insides of her thighs.

I don't know how I missed them earlier, other than to blame the lighting. The night of the table dance had us in shadows, and Oasis's moody colored lights didn't exactly reveal anything. I feel a bit like a jackass for not noticing sooner. *My poor caramel drop.*

Her tits rise and fall with a deep sigh. Tousled waves frame her face and spread up over my arm. I rub the ashy-blonde strands between my fingers, enjoying the fine silkiness.

The painful throb in my dick is killing me. Carefully, I slip my hand into my pants, squeezing my eyes at the overwhelming sensation of jerking myself next to her. It's nearly enough to make me blow my load. A thousand ideas slam to the forefront of my head, most of them revolving around waking her up by climbing on top of her and yanking those panties to the side so I can slide my dick in her tight fuckhole.

I settle on something less extreme because I know where I want our first time together to be and isn't a clumsy morning fuck after a rough night. But that doesn't mean we can't have fun.

Gently letting my fingers trail up her body, I nudge the cup of her bra to the side, revealing a handful of tawny skin and a dusky nipple. Leaning down, I flick my tongue across the pebbled surface and freeze as Carmella stirs slightly.

Shoving my sleep pants down past my hips, I work my cock up and down the shaft, squeezing the head, wishing it were her hand or mouth. *Hell, any part of her at this point. I'd settle for feet.* Her breathing evens out as I quietly fuck my hand and suck gently on the rosy bud. *God, she has me horny this morning.*

Letting go of her nipples, I roll back and slide my free hand down her stomach and slip under the band of her panties until I can feel the soft curls at the juncture of her legs. The pads of my fingers stroke along the line of her folds, making my dick jump as a drop of pre-cum rolls down the shaft, lubing my strokes. *Fuck it, I'm going for it. She can wake up.* Creeping my fingers between her pussy lips, I circle her clit. Her body jerks, and a slight frown forms on her forehead, making me want to kiss it away. Carmella isn't a morning person, but I'm about to change her mind. *Mornings can be very enjoyable.*

Her eyes flick under her eyelids, and I smile to myself as she stretches and opens her legs a little more. I don't know if it's intentional or not, but I'm taking it as an invitation, rolling onto my knees above her. Carmella is hot and beginning to dampen for me when I press inside her and curl my fingers to work her G-spot. I don't stop jerking myself.

Her blue eyes flutter open and she rolls her hips, making cute whimpering sounds that turn into a hot moan. This time, when she spreads her legs, I know she means it. "Fuck yes, baby, take these off," I say, pulling her panties down her legs.

Carmella's lips turn up into a smile as she undoes her bra. When she's completely naked, the need to feel her skin pressed against mine consumes me. Tossing the blanket off the bed, I spread her legs on either side of me, crushing myself against her. With my dick trapped between us, the friction curls my toes and I grunt. My lips find hers in a hungry kiss. I bite down on Carmella's lower lip, my tongue flicking the ripe fullness until she opens her mouth. Little whimpers and moans fill my ears as she squirms her hot pussy against my dick.

"You better stop before I cum." I chuckle.

Carmella's answering grin is full of mischief as she rubs her body along mine, creating delicious friction on the head of my cock. I bite down on one of her nipples in warning. She yelps and giggles, stormy eyes flashing at me, and I love the sound. *This should be how every morning starts.* "You're a brat," I mumble around a delicious, perky nipple.

I pull off her tit with a sucking pop and grab my cock, sliding it against her entrance. "Naughty girls don't get fucked, caramel drop." Teasing us both, I thrust lightly against her wet slit, refusing to let myself sink inside her and satisfy the burning arousal lashing my body. I spread the clear drop of cum from my dick as I thrust against her clit.

Carmella moans as her nails dig into my back. I could do it now; she would let me. She wants me too, but I want her to burn for it. Slut herself out for it. Not flinch when I spit on her and call her a slut. I want her to want every drop of filth, humiliation, and even pain I can offer. I want her to lick it off the floor and still want more. *Then I'll let her have it, even if the wait kills us both.*

Kissing and licking my way down her body, I seal my lips over her sensitive bud and flick my tongue. Her hips buck as she sucks in a deep breath. "Oooohh, yes, that feels so good."

With one hand holding her down and one hand jerking myself, I set to work on her, showing off nearly twenty years of fucking skills. The air fills with cries torn from her lips as I dance my wicked charm across her most sensitive skin. Her uninhibited moans make my blood sing as I push my finger inside and swirl around her clenching walls.

Carmella pulls my hair and rips the sheets from the corners of the bed as she thrashes in ecstasy. Gone is the hesitancy that's been plaguing her anytime we touch. *I like this dirty, unrestrained version of her so much better.* Sweat slicks her body and her legs shake by the time I'm ready to let us both cum. When I bite down on her pussy lips gently, she whines, "Please, let's fuck, Luke. I want to fuck."

"You don't know how long I've been waiting for you to say that." I chuckle. Getting off the bed, I open a drawer and grab a purple vibrator custom-made in the shape of my dick—made the mold myself—and a self-sucking pocket pussy. I turn the purple toy on and it buzzes around in my hand. "You ever use one before, caramel drop?"

She bites her swollen lower lip and shakes her head, dropping her legs further apart. I run the tip of the little monster over her lovely pussy, coating the silicone rod with her slickness, before sliding it into Carmella's dick holster. Watching her pink muscles stretch to accommodate the thick shaft has me spitting on the pussy-shaped silicone toy in my other hand and working it down my cock, enjoying the way it grips me tightly.

Turning it on, I feel the vibrations and tightness pull me as it seals and sucks my cock. Kneeling between Carmella's legs, I thrust my hips into the pocket pussy as I fuck Carmella's actual pussy with the vibrator. My balls pull up and tingles start in my groin as the little monster greedily suckles my dick. The curls between Carmella legs are wet from my licking and her own juices as I fuck her in tandem with the sucking toy. Watching her take my pseudo cock is the most arousing thing I've ever seen. Sweat trickles down my back and a moan escapes my mouth as I rock into the toy suctioned to my dick.

Ecstasy rises in me and freezes my breathing as my orgasm rockets its way across my body, leaving me shuddering and panting as I cum hard into the machine, which milks me until I'm so sensitive, I rip the damn thing off.

Aftershocks rock me as I lean down and lick Carmella's clit while the vibrations from the molded toy rock her world. Sharp nails dig into the back of my neck, pulling me closer as she goes rigid. I smile and lock my lips down on her, sucking the little nub into my mouth and licking while she comes apart against me. Her panting cries of, "Fuck yes," never sounded so good.

I slip the molded toy from her, and it thunks onto the floor next to the pocket pussy as I crawl back into bed next to her. Breathless, she laughs. "That was fucking amazing. I was dreaming about dragon-shaped fireworks and they were scampering all over my skin, making me horny with their bursts of energy. Then I woke up and realized it was you. Ten out of ten best ways to wake up ever. Better than coffee. Whoooo." She pumps a fist into the air and gives a victory yell before exhaling a huge breath and dropping her arm like a wet noodle.

She is glorious spread out like this. My personal buffet. My hands run all over her skin, and I gently pinch her nipples, relishing in the feel of being able to touch her unhindered. I doubt I'll ever get enough. *Mine, every piece of it. She crawled through my window. That's a cosmic decree in my book.*

Carmella's soft snore draws my eyes back to her face. I'd like nothing more than to want to sleep and fuck all day, but I can feel my senses coming online. The adrenaline from my orgasm floats in my bloodstream and pushes me to get out of bed. Orgasms have always been an upper for me—not as good as a line of cocaine, but just as addicting. Gently scooting out of bed, careful not to disturb her, I wander into the kitchen and start the coffee.

Heading to the storefront, I flip on the switch that brings the overhead lights on and sit down at the horseshoe desk to do my occasional routine of watching the playback of the security feed from the night before, just to make sure no one is fucking around with the shop.

I didn't see a car when I noticed Carmella crouched down outside from the back door monitors, but that doesn't mean one didn't drop her off. Then, I can make sure Tommy never comes around again. *Permanently if I have to.*

I click yesterday's date in the line of recordings and skip to the evening when she arrived home... somewhere around nine, but who knows how long she was outside. I watch the camera with a view of the lane between the store and the shop. This angle shows the main road that runs out front, so even if he dropped her off on the curb, I should be able to see something. Putting it on fast-forward, I wait as cars zip by at an accelerated rate. A few people are on foot. At eight-twenty, she rounds the corner, arms folded. I pause the screen and drop it down to normal speed.

Instead of watching Carmella curl up into a ball, I watch the road, waiting to see if a car appears from that direction.

Not a single one does. *Damn.*

Well, hopefully Tommy will be off dealing with whatever dick funk he contracts with his new girl and he won't even think of caramel drop. *Tommy. Just his name alone is a fucking joke...* Movement catches my eye on the screen.

A navy SUV drives by slowly. Too slowly. They crawl to a stop on the curb on the opposite side of the street, away from Carmella. Whoever is in the car kills their lights. I stare at the vehicle. There is no reason for them to be parked there. The business across the street—a tax filing office—closed up a year ago and has been vacant since.

Their windows are abnormally dark, and in the early shadows of the night, they look pitch black. The longer the SUV sits there, the more convinced I am they are watching her.

The hair stands up along my arms and my gut whispers, *Not right.*

Is it the boyfriend? Did he come by to check on her and didn't know what to say?

I watch myself walk outside on the screen; we talk. She goes inside and I check the locks on the shop before following her in.

The lights on the car flare to life and it slowly pulls back out onto the street.

I flick to the monitor for the main entrance and front parking. The dark-blue SUV crawls by before speeding up and vanishing outside the camera's view.

I flick back to the night before that while we are at the bathhouse, hoping I'm overreacting.

Starting around noon, I let the recording jump forward at quick speeds. Nothing abnormal before three. All good before five. And then bam, navy SUV at seven pm. It rolls down the street, driving just under the speed limit.

Blowing out a breath, I tip back in the chair and run my fingers through my hair, lacing them at the back of my head. Carmella and I pull out onto the street at the same time. The SUV does a lazy loop and turns to follow us.

My stomach knots and adrenaline dumps into my bloodstream. *It could still be the boyfriend. Maybe.* I stare out the storefront, suddenly wishing it were comprised of actual walls instead of durable glass. This wouldn't be the first time someone cased out my place to rob me. Or even the first time the feds have sniffed around.

My mind rushes through all the possibilities. Some have merit and some are flat-out insane. Are Carmella and Tommy pulling a long con on me, like my ex-wife and her lover? Did Sasha make a new enemy? An old one? Cops? Feds?

My leg shakes under the table. I've got three open lawsuits against me currently, but I didn't think any of them were worth this much trouble. Too many potential enemies on the table and not enough evidence to rule many of them out. *Maybe my life has been too spicy?*

Grabbing a pen and paper, I make a list of the days and times the navy vehicle shows up on camera and I notice a pattern. Wherever Carmella is, the vehicle isn't far behind. Only a few times does it follow me to do deposits at the end of the night. This scares me more than anything. Whoever is in that car knows I'm carrying money on me and I'm alone, but instead of jumping me, they choose to watch the store.

Emotions of betrayal and distrust swim to the surface. *I swear to God, if Carmella thinks she is going to rob me...* I spin to stare back down the darkened hallway where Carmella sleeps in my bed.

I sigh, letting go of some of the tension. *Carmella being a con artist doesn't fit. She isn't Tracey.*

For one, Carmella doesn't have to live here or sleep with me to have gained access to the store. She didn't ask; I offered. If she had walked in and asked for a regular job, I would have given her one on the off chance she would ride my face someday.

Two, I've left her alone for hours at a time. She had all the time in the world to clean me out. Carmella knows where my gun is and could have tried to hold me up while her friends stole from me.

Three, she didn't ask for a key; I gave it. She's never asked for the code to the safe or even if we have one. She's only ever taken what I've offered. I rub my hands over my face.

We are too close and too raw for me to be a mark.

I think.

I hope.

A New SUV and Twelve Fuck Faces

LUKE

Another horrible idea crawls into my mind. If they aren't here for the payday, then the SUV could be feds scoping out Carmella. She knows my comings and goings. She would make a great informant on the money side of Sasha's organization. But the feds would get her killed. Sasha would gut her. Stress hammers my body. The right people could leverage away her legal problems for ratting me out. *Would that be enough to make her do it?*

Joke would be on them, though. She knows nothing of substance. I think.

If it were the cops or a detective here for her because of her aunt, they would have already called it in. Boots would have been on the ground by now, and Carmella would be in cuffs.

"What are you doing?" her sleepy voice calls from the hallway. I look up just in time to see her walk out wearing one of my shirts. It drapes down to mid-thigh, making her look so snuggly. My gaze travels down to her wrists and forearms where the self-inflicted scars rest. Self-harm was never my thing, but rage certainly is, and I took it out on anyone I could when I was younger.

If someone were going to send in a woman to con me, they sent the right one—sad, broken, and beautiful, with enough of a temper to keep me interested. The creeping feeling of doubt clouds my mind as I watch her walk toward me.

"What kind of car does Tommy drive?" I ask.

She pauses a few feet from me, surprise coloring her face. "A beat-up teal-green Toyota. It's ugly as sin and rusted along the bottom. Trust me, you can't miss it. It screams, 'I'm a drug dealer,' or 'Hey, kid, come get some candy.'" She laughs at her own joke. "Why?"

She spots the monitors behind me and her eyebrows draw down. "He isn't outside, is he?"

I watch her body language. "No, does he drive another car?"

She snorts. "He can barely keep the one running, Luke. He doesn't have multiple cars."

She steps closer, and I lick my lips. "What does your aunt drive?"

She gives me a harassed look, but her next words come out mocking, high pitch, but somehow still dripping with venom. "A twenty-twenty silver Nissan. She got such a good deal on it." Carmella rolls her eyes and folds her hands over her chest in faux innocence.

She drops her arms as she takes me in, concern marring her features. "What's with the twenty questions, Luke?"

She stands close now, within the U-shaped desk. I rise and wander over to her. Pushing her against the desk with my body, I gently wrap my long fingers around the column of her throat and squeeze. Her eyes widen in surprise when I don't let up, those dark pupils dilating inside the oceans of her irises.

My lips whisper against hers, coaxing her mouth opening as I deepen the kiss. She makes an unsure sound, a mixture of surprise and arousal. It ends in a little moan when I break the seal between our lips. Hesitation plagues her face as she rubs her neck, but her eyes wander back to my mouth and I can't help but smirk. Seems caramel drop has developed a taste for me. "Are you okay?" she asks. Warmth seeps through the palm she places on my chest and into my skin, and I want her to touch me with that type of care for the rest of my life. It feels so nice. I could curl up into that touch.

I recognize this for what it is. Carmella is a new weakness.

Weaving my fingers through her hair, I enjoy the feel of it. *If she's fucking me over, I'm going to take what I want and make her regret ever knowing me.* My gaze scans her face, and I watch the uncertainty and confusion knit her brow. She bites her lip and stares at me, silently asking for answers I'm not going to give her.

If this is acting, she is going to be a star one day.

"What changed?" I ask.

"What do you mean?"

I untangle my fingers from her hair and wrap them back around her neck. The quick squeeze meant to intimidate backfires. My dick has other ideas about how Carmella's pulse feels under our hand and grows into a half chub. *Great.* "Are we doing one of your kinky games?" she says.

Cocking my eyebrow up, I repeat to her, "My kinky games?"

"Yeah, you know. First, you were kinda paying me, but we're not doing that anymore... So, are we doing something new now?" A pink tongue snakes out and licks over her lips. Our eyes meet. "Are we doing, like, rough stuff now... or what?"

I want to laugh and shake my head. At first, she was too cautious of me, and now that she's all in, she isn't cautious enough.

"Yesterday, you literally hid from me in the bathroom, and this morning you're moaning and letting me fuck you with my pseudo-cock. What changed?"

Her face turns crimson, and she tries to pull away. I tighten my grip and grind my body into hers, pinning her against the desk, my dick responding with glee. Her eyes flair open in shock when I don't back off. Her chest heaves rapidly in anger. I think I may have offended her. "What's your problem today? Let go of me," she spits.

"Not until you talk to me. You've been the chattiest I've ever seen you for the last twenty-four hours. Don't stop now. Tell me what changed."

"Nothing changed."

"Lies." I squeeze her face, making her look at me. "Tell me."

She squeezes her eyes shut as she tries to yank herself away. "Fine, you want to know what's different?" She mumbles a little from where I have her face smashed. I let go. Her eyes snap open, fires blazing. *Yeah, I definitely pissed her off.* "I'm scared of what will happen when the cops and my aunt find me this time. And I thought here, I was safe." She glances down at my hands. "Well, mostly safe. And I wanted to do things with you even before Tommy was out of the picture. I thought it was finally okay to act on this between us, but clearly not. I wanted to date you, or at least I did before you woke up this morning and decided to be a dickhead."

I know I'm being a jerk and ruining a good morning. I dip my head and suck her lower lip, offering her a bit of tenderness. Letting go of her throat, I fist my hands into her hair and consume her mouth, forcing her back until she bends and clings to me for support. I crush her lips against mine over and over until the noises she makes are half panicked, half desperate for more. I shove my hands under the shirt, finding her still hot and slick. Thrusting my fingers inside her tight pussy, I finger bang what's mine on the front desk in full view of the glass windows.

Later, after her legs stop shaking and her orgasm flushed skin cools, I watch as she sucks in a breath and steadies herself against the table, touching the redness spreading across the lower half of her face from my scruff and mustache. She looks at me with arousal and what I can only interpret as confused hurt. I was rough today, and I had been so nice.

My dick throbs, letting me know his interest and whining because I took nothing for myself. Draping my shirt back over her, I place a line of kisses from her throat to her ear. She eyes me cautiously. *I can't blame her for being leery of my hot-and-cold attitude.*

"I need to make some calls. Go pour us some coffee and make mine as sweet as you were when you spread your legs for me." I slap her ass—not hard—and she glares at me. When there is enough distance between us, she tosses a middle finger over her shoulder, making me chuckle despite the battle brewing inside me.

Walking back to my bedroom, I snag my burner and punch in the necessary numbers before walking back to the front of the store and observing the traffic out my windows as the phone rings.

"Finally. Been expecting a call from you for over a week now. Where are my reports?" Sasha's clipped voice comes over the phone.

Normally, I would make a snide remark or dance around the reason for my call just to push my brother's buttons, but not this morning.

"We have a problem."

Sasha is quiet, but I hear his chair squeak and can imagine him in his office, leaning forward onto his desk, preparing himself to deal with whatever issue I'm about to lay on him.

"What problem?" I can hear the lilt of his Russian accent slip into his speech, the first warning sign that I'm stressing him out.

"Someone is casing the shop. I don't know who, but I've caught them on camera watching the place several times. I'm gonna need some men over here for the foreseeable future."

A string of curse words come across the line. The accent is thicker now. "Who do you think they are?"

"I was hoping maybe you might be able to tell me?" I say, skirting around his question. The reality is, my potential enemies list is too long, and going over every possibility is not only going to piss Sasha off but also draw a lot of attention to Carmella. And to the fact that she could create real complications for my and Sasha's business if he finds out about her dirty laundry. He'll want me to get rid of her. *Hell, he is going to want me to get rid of her even if she didn't come wrapped up in legal red tape, and I can't hide her forever.*

I can hear Sasha in the background giving orders. "We will be there soon, Luke." With that, he hangs up.

"**P**lease, Carmella, just stay in here," I beg. I'm standing in the doorway of my bedroom, watching her pace the small space like a dog on a short leash. The smooth skin of her thighs flash under my shirt, still draped on her body.

Her blue eyes clash with mine. "Why should I?"

Because I don't really feel like hashing "us" out to Sasha and the men, especially when it will cause more problems than solve.

I open my mouth, but have no legitimate excuse as to why she needs to stay in here that doesn't expose the type of work I do. We've been going round and round about her staying out of sight once Sasha arrives and I've been able to avoid why in so many words until now.

"If you stay in here, I will buy you whatever you want, let you lie in bed all week. Whatever you want, but please, just stay here," I say.

"I'm not some child that you can just bribe, Luke!" She pushes past me and into the hallway, headed for the show floor.

"Why not? It's been working for sex since I've met you. Why not now?"

I mutter.

The daggers in her eyes tell me I'm treading on thin ice. She flips her hair and takes a seat at the horseshoe front desk, spinning away from me. Frustration makes me want to shake her, grab her by the arm, and lock her up in the closet.

Three black Escalades cruise down the street and pull up to the front of the store in uniform. Men pile out of the doors, some dressed in wife-beaters and others in suits, each one of them armed and serious looking. And just like that, it's too late. Carmella—still clad only in my shirt—whips her head around to look at me with rounded eyes before getting up and backing away from the desk.

"Luke, what's going on?" she asks, her voice an octave or two too high.

"Just get in the bathroom. Hurry. Go," I tell her, walking toward the front door to greet my brother and praying they haven't seen her yet.

I'm halfway to the front when I hear the bathroom door creak shut and the ringer on the front door open.

Sasha strolls in, dressed to the nines as usual, and pulls his leather driving gloves from his hands. *Why he insists on gloves in one-hundred-degree weather, I will never understand.* Sasha's long blonde hair is pulled up into a tight, smooth bun that sits atop his head, a style that accentuates his sharp cheekbones and steely gray-blue eyes. The motherfucker has always been runway model handsome and caused many people over the years to underestimate him. They're all dead now, but the ladies love him. Too bad he has ice where a heart should be when it comes to pussy. Actually, when it comes to most things.

Sasha's posture and movement speak to a man in control, not only of the men around him, but also of himself. A trait I've always admired and failed to imitate. Graceful and as sharp as a blade, he cuts a nod in my direction. There was a time when we would have greeted each other with a hug and he would've thumped me on the back. I swallow thickly.

"It is good to see you, brother. Been a while since you've been out to Lux. Why is that?" Sasha says pointedly.

His intense eyes bore into me, and I squash the flicker of guilt. I offer him my most charming grin. "Oh, you know, just scheming and dreaming."

Sasha pivots to check the store. "Business looks... dead. That's bad, Luke. Very bad." He slaps the driving gloves into the palm of his hand before circling back to me.

"Well, technically, I haven't opened yet due to the problem I mentioned on the phone." I'm getting a little exasperated with Sasha's behavior. I don't know what he expected to find, but twelve gun toting fuck faces rolling up on a store full of customers while they debate countertops isn't how I do business. I bite my tongue to keep from saying as much. How Sasha and I speak to each other privately is unacceptable around other members of the Bratva.

He "hmmms" a bit before saying, "Let's see this problem of yours," and brushes past me. I nearly roll my eyes at his dramatics but fall in line, letting him lead the way—in my store.

He takes my seat at the main desk while the men fan out around the place and Aleksi steps up behind us. We exchange handshakes and I try not to be resentful. Since my fall from grace, Aleksi has stepped into some of my roles as Sasha's right-hand man.

Sometimes, I think Aleksi is doing a better job than I did. Sometimes, I know he is.

Sometimes, I wonder if Sasha likes him better. Sometimes... I know he does.

I open the security software and go to the video logs, showing Sasha and Aleksi the preselected time frames. After the fifth video, Sasha asks, "How many times have you caught them on camera?"

"Nine so far."

"And they haven't rolled on you?" Aleksi asks this time.

I shake my head. "Not yet."

"Have they followed you anywhere else?" Sasha says, and I know what he really means. Have I been anywhere that anyone outside of the Bratva shouldn't be in the time frames that I've been followed?

"No, I've mostly just been here." Sasha nods, his face as cool and unruffled as always, even as he shares a look with Aleksi. Aleksi shrugs.

"Do you know who it is?" I ask, glancing between the two of them.

Aleksi laughs as I shift back his way. "Not a single damn idea, Luke."
Well, that's great.

Sasha cuts in. "It doesn't matter who it is. We will find and deal with them. They won't be a problem for long. There is a reason the Bratva are the only organization in these parts." He snaps his fingers and six men come forward. I'm thankful it's men I'm familiar with, who used to work under me laundering Sasha's cash when business was at its peak. I offer them a few greetings and smiles.

Unlike other Avtoritets of the Russian Mob, who would have picked a flashier city like Miami or Tampa to work out of, Sasha prefers the control the small town of White Cove offers. Close enough to a big city to get shit done, but far enough into the weeds that he can barricade himself in with local, loyal men. It's also far enough away that Sasha's boss, Konstantin the Pakhan, can't just fly in without some kind of notice coming our way.

"Luke." Sasha's voice pulls me back to him and our eyes lock. "Put them on a rotation and deal with this issue quickly and quietly. I want this resolved—no drama, no waves. Do I make myself clear?"

The unspoken meaning in his words eats at me. *Do what needs to be done. Be the man you once were. Don't disappoint me again. Come back into the fold. Don't get us caught or killed. Don't draw the attention of the Pakhan or the other Avtoritets.*

"I'll deal with it," I promise him.

Sasha rises from the desk and walks around to the front. *He's leaving already?* He takes another look around the empty store. "Maybe it's time to consider selling this place and putting your money into more lucrative ventures." I flinch as his proposal knocks the air out of me. It isn't the first time we have discussed it, and he knows my opinion about selling the place. I don't answer him.

"I expect you at Lux tonight, Luke. Now, the reports."

I sigh internally at the thought of the low numbers and spending the evening with Sasha after he gets a look at them, but I pull out the black ledger, anyway. Arm extended, I hold it out for him. Sasha slips the driving gloves over his long fingers, stretching the fabric with precise and practiced moves.

My brother looks at me once more, his face bored and maybe even a bit let down by my presence, nods, and steps away from the desk, making his way out the doors. He never looks back and fuck if it doesn't hurt. Aleksi removes the ledger from my hands.

"Thanks," Aleksi says as he unfurls his sunglasses, placing them on his face and follows our boss back to the vehicles.

Tucking away the feeling of being a colossal failure, I glance back at the monitor. Whoever is in that navy SUV is fucked. Whatever they want, whatever they are hoping to achieve, they will find out quickly enough that I don't play well and neither does Sasha. *I won't fuck it up this time.*

Organizing the shifts between the six men left in the store makes me feel better—there will always be two sets of eyes on the store and shop. I nearly breathe a sigh of relief then realize there will always be two sets of eyes on the store and shop. Eyes that report to Sasha... and I have to go retrieve Carmella from the bathroom.

I groan inwardly.

HOW MANY EX-WIVES?

LUKE

"Will you please come help me with this?" I snap. Irritation flares in my chest as Carmella blows a pink bubble and pops it with her mouth before continuing to chomp and ignore me. She's been salty all day and never did bring me any coffee.

Dressed in a solid teal spaghetti strap tank top and light blue jeans, she leans against the large furniture van with her Converse sneakers peeking out from the bottom hem and her hair pulled back in a perky ponytail. Her gaze is fixed on the red-brick wall that forms the back of an apartment complex. We're parked at the entrance of an alleyway close enough to the ocean that the seagulls have invaded the open dumpster next to the metal futon bed frame I spotted from the road.

Seagulls scream at me and each other as they pick apart the open trash bag for crumbs. Normally, they don't bother me, but today the fucking winged rats are everywhere.

The matching mattress sits in a puddle next to the futon frame. I thought about grabbing it but didn't want to spend the time shampooing it out. *Plus, it smells like the worst kind of dog piss and is covered by white circles of seagull shit.*

I drop the frame and stare at her. "Remind me why I'm paying you to stand there?"

Her teeth gnash into her gum as she turns on her heel and stomps back to the cab of the delivery van. Yanking open the door, she steps up and in, slamming it behind her. The noise sends the fucking seagulls shooting up all around me. Their shrill calls and squawks make me want to punch them as they launch into the sky.

Beads of sweat trickle down my neck, and I take a deep, calming breath and immediately regret it as I suck in lungfuls worth of ammonia and rotten vegetable stench. Scanning for the SUV for what feels like the fiftieth time today, I walk to her side of the vehicle, plastering a practiced smile on my face. The door opens with a metallic groan. "What's wrong, sugar? Not having fun with the seagulls?" My tone is sharper than I'd intended.

Her head does an imitation of that chick from *The Exorcist* as she swivels to spear me with her cold blue eyes. "You're just like every other guy, you fucking know that? I'm good enough to fuck, but immediately after, you all turn into raging dicks and I end up hiding in the bathroom. Fine, if that's how it's gotta be, then fucking pay me and I'll go help you with your fucking futon. Hey, why don't you pay me some more for this morning? You and Tommy should have an asshole party together." The venom in her voice is scathing and, for a minute, I'm shocked into silence. The handle wrenches out of my palm and the door snaps shut in my face.

Blinking, I stare at the fuming blonde. Trying to get a hold of my temper in this heat is like trying to hold on to sand in a windstorm. It's not my first rodeo with a hostile woman. Arguably, I'm an old pro, both at pissing off the ladies and getting back out of trouble. That being said, Carmella has a nasty way of not letting things go.

I grab the handle, popping the door open again, and she grabs it from the inside, holding it in place; the door hovers between us. "Let go, hun," I say through gritted teeth.

Carmella pulls hard, nearly closing the door, and her hand scrambles to hit the lock. As I yank it back, her body lunges forward with the force and she glares at me with renewed hostility. *Here we fucking go.*

"Let go of my fucking door, Luke!" She throws her body back, pulling my arm with it.

"You're being fucking ridiculous, Carmella. Stop!"

"You're fucking ridiculous! Leave me alone!" she hisses.

We end up in a childish battle of wills in the shape of tug-of-war with my delivery van door. It creaks and groans in protest as it swings between us, witnessing our meltdown.

"Women, your language gets worse every day. Now open the door."

"YOU'RE NOT MY DAD!" Carmella yells.

"I'm the closest thing you've had to a daddy since you were seven. Now let go of the goddamn door before I spank you!"

She sucks in a breath like I've slapped her. "Maybe a fucking trash daddy!"

"WHAT DOES THAT EVEN MEAN?!" I yell back, more confused than ever about how we got here and what I'm supposed to do now. Pulling the door, I watch her slide across the seat. *The woman must have super-glued herself to the door latch.* That thought pisses me off even more. *If she could just relent for one fucking minute.*

"LET GO OF THE FUCKING DOOR AND STOP. FUCKING. YELLING!" I roar, ripping the door open, determined to take her with it if that's the cost for this bullshit to be done.

And she lets go. It's just unfortunate that I had most of my weight pulling against it. As it swings loose, the lack of tension sends me backward to the ground, ass-first into a puddle of piss-warm alley water full of seagull shit.

"Fucking hell!" I yell, attempting to scramble up, which results in me splashing about as my hands land in more water. "Ahh, shit fuck!" It's too late to salvage my outfit. Out of the corner of my eye, I see a flash of blonde hair as Carmella flies down from her seat and runs past me.

I'm off the ground and bearing down on her as wet fabric clings to my ass cheeks and drips down my legs. My face is flushed with rage and embarrassment. *Never in my life . . .*

When I snatch the back of her hair, she howls like a banshee and lashes out, scratching my face. The marks burn like hellfire. Scooping her up, I toss her over my shoulder. She kicks and screams, cursing at me. Banding my arm across the back of her thighs, I reach up and slap her ass hard enough to sting my hand. At the back of the tall vehicle, I dump her unceremoniously onto its metal floor. *I was fucking right about that crazy/hot ratio.*

She crab walks back before standing up and pacing the van floor like a caged tiger. "You will not treat me like shit, Luke!"

"How have I treated you like shit?" I snap, waving my arms.

"You were nice this morning, and then when I got up—because I wanted to find you—you interrogated, intimated, choked me, and offered no explanation or apology once you calmed down from whatever the fuck was wrong with you, and then those men came and I had to hide in the bathroom, but now you want to pretend like everything is okey dokey. Guess what? It's not."

I put up a hand. "I feel like you might still be a little upset about Tommy."

She glares daggers at me. "Maybe so, but you're the one I'm most upset with right now. Also, fuck Tommy. Fuck you."

A pain starts between my eyebrows. Between the heat, Carmella, the water dribbling into my shoes, everything that happened this morning, and the screeching seagulls, I can feel a headache brewing. I'm caught between wanting to rub my temples and laughing hysterically. *Boy, she can really be a handful.*

She's right though. I've been an ass, but she's far too emotional to have a logical conversation about the threat that hangs over our heads. Right now, I worry she will flip out and run off once she learns about the SUV. *Clearly, we are already on edge.*

Infusing my smile with tranquility and levelheadedness, I try to defuse the situation by grinning at her. I open my mouth to tell her...

"What's your last name?"

I falter. "What?"

"What is your last name?" she asks again through gritted teeth.

Completely caught off guard, I answer, "Reeves."

"Don't you fucking smile at me, Luke Reeves! I'm onto your bullshit," Carmella snarls at me, arms folded as she paces the small space.

Okay. Well, fuck me. Never mind. Usually, we are further along in the relationship before they use my full name. I hold up my hands in surrender.

Pulling out a crushed box of cigarettes from my pocket, I pick through the remains and find one that is only slightly bent. Lighting up, I take a moment to have a long drag and breathe it out.

Carmella huffs while staring down at me. "Why were you mad this morning, Luke? I could tell. One minute, you were like, 'Oh, sexy time,' and the next, you were strangling me and looking all pissed off."

I sigh. My mind flicks through how I can spin this without offending her or freaking her out. The smell of my cigarette tinges the air around me. *There is no good spin. Just suck it up, Luke. She is going to flip.*

Pulling my wet pants out of my ass crack, I pick through my words carefully while studying her face. "There's an SUV watching the store. I thought maybe you knew who they were after everything we talked about last night."

Carmella stops pacing. All the color drains from her face as she bites her lip. "Who do you think they are?"

Isn't that the question of the hour?

She continues, "Why did that make you mad at me? Who are the men that came to the store? Why were some of them still there when we left? Be honest, Luke."

Be honest. Hell of a thing to ask from a used furniture salesman, mob employee, and con man. I made my way into the world being a professional liar. I take a longer drag from my cig.

My shoulders slump a bit. "I really don't know who is in the SUV, Carmella. I've spent the entire morning trying to piece it together." She bites her lower lip, worrying it as she stares down the alley. Lines crease her face, making her appear older. The last thing I want is Carmella freaking out, taking off, and making a mistake that lands her in jail.

"Look, I'm sorry about this morning. I'm a dick. I was reeling from the shock of finding someone watching us, and I didn't take it well. That's not your fault, nor is it a reason to mistreat you. I'm sorry and I want you to know that whoever they are, I'm not going to let them hurt you."

Her face softens, and she sits down, dangling her legs off the back of the van. "Do you think it could be a detective looking for me?"

"If it's a detective, I imagine the police would have already come." Flicking what's left of my ciggy into a puddle, I watch it snuff out.

"Shouldn't we be back at the store?" Carmella tugs at her pale ashen ponytail, the baby-hair curls coiling and uncoiling.

"I've got the cameras on and, as you noticed, there are men watching the place now. I doubt anyone is coming through the door in the middle of the day with malicious intent." *Especially since they've stuck to only watching you so far.*

She fidgets with her ponytail harder. "Who are the men watching the store?"

I stare down at the pavement and shake my head. I can't keep Carmella from noticing things, but I can sure as fuck spare her from knowing too much. "I'm not telling you that, and it's better if you don't ask."

That gets her back up. "What, you don't trust me? I told you everything about my shit."

"Goddammit, Carmella. Maybe I'm trying to help keep you safe. You ever think of that? Maybe it's better if you don't know certain things because once you do, you can't... unknow. And knowing can make you a target in something you didn't sign up for. Did you ever think that maybe concealing things from you is my way of helping protect you from more trouble? That if I didn't care about your well-being, I would toss you in the deep end and see if you drowned or not?"

She rocks back at my outburst and takes a deep breath. "Concealing things like why you have a shit ton of tires but don't sell them, or the extra phone in your room and the shipment that arrives like clockwork, or the scary-looking men that are parked outside Luke's currently?"

"Yes, Carmella. Things like that."

She stares past me, into the distance. "I don't consider lying to be a kindness. Are the men parked outside because of the SUV?"

"You don't have to worry about that. They shouldn't bother you, and if they do, tell me."

I feel a space open up between us and it fills with the things I'm not willing to tell her. The feds, rival criminal organizations, cops, all of it goes into the hole. None of them provide reassuring answers and all options lead to Carmella asking questions she is safer not asking. I settle on a less disturbing possibility to offer her. "The SUV could be one of my ex-wives."

"Wives? As in plural?" Her eyebrows arch into a question.

I flinch. "Yeah. Well. Actually, only one in particular I'd be concerned about."

She stares at me before shaking her head.

"How many wives?" she asks.

Pondering how much trouble it will create if I tell her it isn't any of her business, I motion to the metal bed frame.

"Help me get this loaded, and I'll tell you."

She narrows her eyes at me but hops down from the van and walks over to the frame, helping pull off the bags of trash as I wiggle the futon loose. "You know, when you said it was shop restock day, I pictured something more businesslike, not dumpster diving and garage sale shopping," Carmella says. The frame scrapes free from the pile of trash and I drag it toward the truck bed, checking it out as I go.

"I told you I get my inventory cheap."

"True. I guess now I understand why the used section of the store really is all profit. But this seems like a lot of legwork."

I nod, approving her assessment. We heft the frame into the back of the van. "It wasn't always like this, you know. I used to have a shit ton of employees and several thriving businesses. People called me successful. It looks like it's missing a few bolts and a rail is bent. Easy fix if I have the part." We shove the frame next to the dresser, table, and bed frame set we picked up at a liquidation sale. My mind races ahead to what I'll need to do to get these pieces showfloor ready. The wood needs to be refinished and oiled, maybe new hardware for the set.

Curiosity flashes across Carmella's face. "What happened to your other businesses?"

I wave her to follow me out of the back and help her down. The rolling door clamors as it slides closed, making a ruckus. "Get in and we will talk out of this fucking heat," I say, wiping my brow with the back of my hand.

Carmella nods and walks around to the front of the vehicle. Getting in on my side, I turn the engine on and crank up the air. "So...?" She draws out the O, nudging me into talking.

"The wives and the businesses kind of go hand in hand."

She looks at me with raised eyebrows. "So, how many?"

"Four," I say, staring out over the flow of traffic from our vantage point in the alleyway.

"Four ex-wives?" Her voice is incredulous.

I nod.

"You're thirty-four with four ex-wives?" she says louder.

I frown and shrug at her. "You asked, and it's not like I've kept it a secret that I'm into women."

She leans on the gray middle console that separates us and observes me. I scowl. Carmella blows another pink bubble and it pops loudly in the silence. When I reach to turn the radio on, she grabs my wrist and pulls it away.

"What happened to them?"

I sigh and sit back in my chair. "Is this really what you want to talk about?"

She agrees, her ponytail bouncing. "Since you won't talk about other things, the least you can do is tell me this. I told you my shady history. You can tell me some of yours," Carmella argues.

Letting the cold air wash over my face, I brace myself to bring up all this old shit again. "The first time, I was eighteen, and she was sixteen. Her name was Pearl. I thought I was in love and her parents agreed to let her marry me because they were dirt poor and wanted someone else to be responsible for feeding her. We got a small apartment. She worked in the evenings after high school and I worked…" I pause. Technically, by then, I had been working for Sasha and doing whatever odd job I could do to make money as a high school dropout with a rage problem.

I continue, "I worked full time. It didn't take long before things went south, as they often do with young couples. We were kids, and we both ended up fucking other people. She got pregnant with another man's baby. We got divorced two years later."

"Shit, Luke, I'm sorry. Did you raise the baby?" Carmella offers.

"Don't be. I was cheating too. Hell, I know for a fact I slept around first, and no. We separated when she got pregnant. It just took us two more years to finally get the divorce," I admit. She nods.

Carmella touches my wrist, her fingers trailing up my forearm. I look down at where our skin connects. That sweet, brief touch nearly makes me haul her into the back of the van so I can give her another round of leg-shaking orgasms.

I continue, "After the divorce, some buddies and I took off to Vegas. Picked up some girls and spent the whole week smashed and high."

A chuckle drags from my mouth over the hazy memories of rolling through the maze of casinos and bars. "I apparently got so drunk, I married one of those girls on a dare from my friends. But knowing my luck, I ended up marrying the craziest one I could find. Come the next morning, that girl fully thought that she was moving across the country and into my place with me and we were really going to be husband and wife. She even called her parents to tell them."

Carmella listens intently. I put the van in drive and slowly navigate through traffic. The ocean rises to my left and I stare at the sparking blue waters and gray, tan sand, lost in thought and pain from a long time ago.

"It was a fucking nightmare. On the weekend I was supposed to be celebrating my divorce, I fucking married another woman. Thankfully, the license wasn't filed, and I burned all the papers in the sink at my hotel. That woman was so pissed off at me when I told her our marriage was a sham, she threw a plant through my windshield."

Carmella blinks and her eyes widen. "Wait, a plant? Like a green one? How did you end up having a plant tossed into your windshield?"

"Yeah, like a big fucking terracotta potted plant. She was spitting mad and followed me into the parking lot after I broke it off. The hotel was doing landscaping and she just hefts this big motherfucking plant and throws it at me. But I'm sitting in the front seat of the rental car. So now I got this fucking tropical greenery growing out of the windshield, dirt all over me, roots dangling down across my steering wheel, and she is screaming like a hellcat, trying to yank the handle off the door. I won't lie. It scared me. She was going to kill me. Security came and then the cops. I flew back home the next day."

Carmella burst out laughing, making my lips quirk up on one side. It is pretty funny when you think about it. She gasps. "You were scared?!"

"Fuck yeah, this woman just chucked a hundred-pound projectile at me with a crazy level of strength and was threatening to tear the door off my car. She probably would have snapped my neck if she'd gotten in. Just because women are physically smaller than men doesn't make them less dangerous."

Carmella howls with laughter in the front seat. I shake my head, but it's good to see her laugh again after the tension of this morning. All thoughts of the shady SUV are gone for a moment. Her laughter is infectious and gets me chuckling along with her. She calms after a while, with sporadic bouts of giggles.

She grins at me. "The third wife. What about her?"

"Well, it took a long time to convince me to get married again after that."

"Naturally," Carmella agrees with a conspiratorial grin.

My tone changes with my third wife. It always does when I talk about her. "My next marriage was wasteful of me. We were the same age, twenty-six, and we got it right that time. I married a good woman. She was a wonderful, loving wife. Beautiful too. A wife any man should be proud to have. Her name was Jocelyn."

"Did she die?" Carmella's soft voice carries into the space between us.

I scan the road, refusing to look at her. "No. The problem was, she's a good person, and I wasn't."

At that time in my life, Sasha's business ideas and mob life absorbed every bit of me. I developed a coke habit and party lifestyle that Jocelyn could never be a part of, mainly because she wouldn't have approved of the hookers we partied with or the violence.

"You've been kind to me. Mostly," Carmella says.

I smirk. "Let's just say life has dropped me down a peg... or five. At some point, a man has to ask himself, 'Am I the problem?' and if the answer is yes, there's a defining moment where you have to decide if you're always going to be a shithead or not. I didn't want to be a shithead for the rest of my life. I'm not the best at it, but I... try."

Carmella gives me a tentative smile and nods. "So what happened with Jocelyn?"

"It became increasingly clear over our three-year marriage that I was the asshole who couldn't keep it in his pants or keep his nose out of the coke. I robbed our marriage of all trust and peace. Robbed her, as well, of many things, and stole away whatever affection or kindness she held for me. I lied to her. She'd catch me, and I'd pick a big fight." I shift my shoulder as the weight of the memories comes back. I have a lot of regrets over Jocelyn. I accepted what I lost a long time ago and moved on, but taking this box off the shelf, dusting it off, and sharing it with Carmella is harder than I thought it would be. It doesn't paint me in a flattering light.

"Anyway, I made her bitter and angry, and then I would push her away for not being the loving wife I first met. I called her a shrill bitch. Made her out to be this bait-and-switch villain that lied to me in order to get me to marry her. Accepting my own faults while using coke was impossible. It was easier to blame her, and I did. It's hard to love when you don't know what it looks or feels like. Harder to be a decent person when every day you are running around with a bunch of other dysfunctional assholes. Unimaginable to be a better version of yourself when drugs and women provide such a delightful distraction from your own pain. It took me years to own up to the fact that I ruined the marriage and broke her along the way."

It's dead silent at my confession, and the need to fill it urges me to take a lighter tone. "But you know, she went on and remarried a real stable guy; he makes good money. He gave her a couple of kids, which she always wanted, and she seems happy. I see her now and then around town with her family. We don't talk and that's fair. I'm the bad guy. But her kids are cute, and they look like her. She got a better ending." I blink back the tears that attempt to form in the corners of my eyes.

Carmella says nothing. Her hand pulls away from my arm, and the emptiness of her touch hurts me. I shift in my seat. "Sorry. I am not always the better man. I'm definitely no hero, which I think you already kind of knew or suspected."

I take an off-ramp to the highway and head back to the store, my desire to keep looking for furniture plummeting. The bay opens up alongside the road as more seagulls fly overhead. "If it makes you feel any better, Jocelyn was the last woman I ever cheated on. I made that choice, but the universe, or powers that be, decided that one right choice wasn't enough to undo all the bad, so they sent Tracey."

I glance at her. She stares out the window. "Tracey is the fourth wife?"

she asks.

"Yup. The fourth ex-wife, and the one I worry might be behind the SUV. You can only put so much nasty shit into the world before, eventually, it returns to you. And Tracey is a fantastic example of that."

Carmella looks at me curiously. "What did she do to you?"

I snort, unable to keep the anger from my voice. "What didn't she do? Why do you think we live in the back of the store? Bitch took me for everything I owned. My house, the bank accounts, my business, and our retirement—she got it all."

I chuckle humorlessly and shake my head at my stupidity. "When I met Tracey, I knew she wasn't a good woman in the same way that I wasn't a good man. But we worked well together, made a shit-ton of money, and the sex was amazing." Carmella tosses me a glare I catch out of the corner of my eye and it almost makes me laugh.

"I thought it was a partnership where neither of us had to pretend to be anything else. Being with her felt like a relief. Like I was off some moral or ethical hook. I no longer had to pay the price of acting like everyone else just to exist in this world because I was loved and accepted for who I was and what I did. And call me a sucker, but I fell for that. Blindly. And I was her long con."

We pull up to a red light. "Tracey was running around on me the entire time." Carmella opens her mouth, but I cut her off. "Before you say anything, I already know it's karma. I willingly married my worst traits personified. I'm sure there is some egotistical, narcissistic psychology in there somewhere about why I found a woman that was a more cutthroat version of me super attractive and I should have seen the writing on the wall, but I didn't."

Carmella winces and closes her mouth before settling back into her chair. The light turns green, and I follow along with the flow of traffic.

"Anyway, Tracey and her lover came up with a plan, so she gathered as much blackmail on me as she could. Not that I made that job hard for her. I was excited to be with her. It was new and refreshing and I told her everything about the cons, money, and my big wins. She was my business partner and my wife and was on all the paperwork. She knew everything, and that still makes me feel like an idiot. So when I got into some legal trouble, I signed everything over to her, thinking it was the best way to protect everything."

"She fucked you over bad, huh?" Carmella whispers as my fist clenches the steering wheel. I bark out a laugh.

"I get served the divorce papers out of the clear blue and when I get home, all her stuff was gone. Some of my stuff too. So, there I am, in the house I built for the woman I'm madly in love with, sobbing because, once again, I got it wrong and wondering what the point is, when I get hit over the head. I come to, tied up at my kitchen table, where Tracey and I'd had breakfast that morning, and she introduces me to her fucking lover like its teatime. Then, they laid it all out nice and simple. I could either sign over my portion of our estate and cooperate with the divorce proceedings and she would hand back over my businesses after it was all done or her lover was going to shoot me in the head. I agreed."

"Did you go to the police?" Carmella asks.

"Couldn't. She had blackmail: tax evasion, under reporting, and larceny and assault on a few people. Plus some other stuff." *Murder, transporting money, laundering, working for a criminal enterprise. Forgery. The list goes on.*

"I cooperate, she gets everything, and on the day she is supposed to sign my businesses back over to me, she's gone." Technically, Sasha tried to find her, but aside from our day at court, Tracey vanished into the wind. My chest burns with rage but extinguishes quickly as I remind myself I had it coming. "I had that lawyer friend liquidate everything she didn't know about, which wasn't much. Tracey didn't want the furniture business, so it was the only thing I kept. The liquidated funds went to the IRS to keep my ass out of prison and to pay off my lawyer's fees."

"I'm sorry, Luke."

We pull into the store parking lot. "Don't be. You didn't do it. These things are all on me. You were right. It's fair that you know some things if you're going to keep fucking around with me."

She nods and gives me a small, sad smile. "Thanks for telling me." She hops out of the van and walks around to open the shop's sliding door so we can unload.

Two of Sasha's men get out of the black Escalade parked at the front of the store and make to help Carmella and me unload the furniture van. I wave them off, watching them retake their positions. *The less they mingle with her, the better off things are.*

Lux

LUKE

I'm back on my bullshit before five o'clock rolls around. Standing in the doorway of my bedroom, I take in Carmella, lounging in my bed. "Who wants to go to a party?" I point at myself. "This guy."

When I flop on my bed, Carmella bounces. While being a little standoffish since our earlier conversation, she has still taken over my room, binge-watched TV, and eaten hot chips while I was putting together the futon and getting caught up with the men outside. The sides of her mouth are covered in flakey red flavoring, as well with the tips of her fingers. My bed is covered in crumbs. *She's definitely sleeping on that side.* She doesn't respond, eyes glued to the TV.

"And who wants to be my hot date?" I ask. Pointing at her, I answer my question. "You do, of course."

Sliding my hand up her jean-clad thigh, I squeeze. She doesn't acknowledge me. A few more inches up and my hand is between her legs. I pinch her pussy lips through the material. A rolled bag of chips slaps into my face. "Ow," I mutter into the aluminum bag as it crinkles against my lips.

Carmella pulls the bag back and shoots me a look. "Oh, please. I think you'll live."

Leaning down, I kiss her forearm. "You want to come with me, right?" *Don't make me go alone.* Nuzzling my head into her side boob, I turn my face and nip at her bicep. Traveling up to her neck, I shower down little kisses on her skin. She giggles and tries to stay focused on the TV, but her arms break out in adorable little goose bumps.

Sliding up to sit beside her, I snag the remote and shut it off. "Come with me to the party. Pretty please." I lift her spicy-flavored fingers and suck one into my mouth. Carmella flushes crimson.

"Shouldn't we stay in, you know, in case of the SUV?" She gives me big, dramatic eyes.

I shake my phone in front of her. "Cameras and men, baby, it's no big thing." Then, I pull open the drawer, showing her the Glock. "I'll be carrying. Plus, we both need a shower and you need a new dress to be my date to the club."

Carmella may think this party is optional, but it's not. I've been avoiding Sasha for too long and he's noticing. While he may not be my biggest fan and things are a little stained right now, if I don't show up for his birthday, he'll be offended and pissed.

I crawl over her to check my hair and mustache in the mirror.

Carmella sighs, flopping back on the bed. "Luke, I can't go. Warrants, cops, no identification. Any of this ringing any bells?"

"Carmella. Wigs, fake ID, and a dimly lit nightclub run by a trusted friend of mine. Do you honestly want to stay in this store twenty-four seven, living in fear?"

Hesitation washes over her face.

"Come on, be my date, caramel drop," I say. I give her a little, playful pout before dropping an award-winning smile on her.

She laughs, shaking her head. "A wig?"

Oh, she is going to love this. Opening up a drawer full of sex toys, I pull out a slick black wig with red highlights. Holding it up for her, I give it a little spin so she can see the bangs.

She narrows her eyes, bites her bottom lip, and considers. I'm struck by how cute she looks like that. Like she is going to scam the entire world. *My little, slutty blonde siren sent straight to me from the sea.*

Setting down the bag of chips, she grins up at me, a conspiratorial look on her face. "Okay, did you say fake ID?"

Carmella's heels click on the sidewalk as we approach the slick black building with shiny onyx-colored windows, the name LUX scribbled across the reflective glass in gold lettering, making it pop.

"I'm still in shock over how easy it was to get this." Carmella admires her new driver's license. Her face lights up. "Can I drive with this?"

I drop a bemused sideways glance at her as we walk across the parking lot. "One, it was not easy to get that. I had to convince a close friend you weren't a cop, and now I owe him a favor. Two, no, you can't drive with that. I mean, technically, nothing is stopping you from driving in general. Licensed or not. But it does limit you to only committing one crime at a time."

I scan the parking lot, looking for the navy SUV. Keeping my hand on my girl's lower back, I guide us toward the front doors. Carmella's brow pulls down as she stares at me, hustling to keep up with the pace I'm setting. "Is that like an official law? Why would they even have that?"

I scan the line out front. *No way in hell I'm waiting in that.* The crush of people is ridiculous as they all crowd around a single entranceway. "What?

No. Listen, what I'm saying is, if you are going to drive with a fake driver's license, then you wouldn't be able to skip wearing your seatbelt, drink a beer, smuggle money, have a felon in your car, or even get road head. Only one crime at a time. Ok, I'm going to give the bouncers our names. Take my hand."

The frown lines are so deep on her concerned face, I pause for a minute. "Luke, the things you say sometimes. Those ideas seem... not good."

I shrug. "Ah well, I suppose you don't have to commit any crimes. Wait, do you even know how to drive?" Her red flush matches the highlights in the wig as she shrugs. Coming to a dead stop, I'm smacked in the face with the truth. Carmella has never had a driver's license. *I should've known.*

"What the fuck, caramel drop? Unbelievable. Give me that."

Snatching her wrist, I pluck the license from her fingers and drag her along into the crowd. I tell the bouncers our names and they wave us through after checking our IDs. The neon fluorescent hand stamps flare to life as we step inside the foyer of LUX. Shiny black marble tile hugs the floor and muted cool blue lights skirt the edges of the ceiling and floors.

"Can I have it back now? I want to put it in my new clutch." She holds a sparkly silver sequined bag that reminds me of a disco ball and isn't at all Carmella's normal casual attire. "Isn't it so shiny? I love it."

A smile tugs at my lips. This little shit thinks I'm not on to her. I wrap an arm around her, chuckling at her excitement. "Caramel drop, how do you get a driver's license?"

She glances up at me, skepticism on her face. "You take a driver's test... duh."

Tucking her into my body, I pull us off to the side so we can chat. "And what do you have to know in order to pass your driver's test, to get your driver's license?"

Her eyes narrow. "How... to drive."

"Mmm hmmm, you said you lost your license. That's very different from *I never had one in the fucking first place because I didn't learn how to drive,* right? You remember that bullshit the night you crawled through the window?"

She grunts unhappily. "So what, I never learned to drive? What's the big deal?"

"The big deal is, you say you are twenty-one. You say age isn't a factor in your legal issues, but now finding out you never got a driver's license, its making me fucking nervous." I grit my teeth. Thankfully, the age of consent in Florida is sixteen. *Even so, Jesus fuck. She doesn't look sixteen.* My stomach clenches.

Her mouth twists like she sucked on something sour. Carmella sighs, insecurity flickering across her face. "I never got a driver's license because my aunt wouldn't let me and no one would teach me. I'll be nineteen in October," she sighs.

Eighteen. Old enough. Sorrow worms it was through me, but not for myself. It's not fair for her to have lived such a short, shitty life and then end up with a money-laundering boyfriend that's old enough to be her dad. I squash the emotion. *She crawled through my window. We share the same pains. Same background. She's mine.*

I stare down the dark hallway into LUX. Sasha will have a fit about her being underage. He likes his fronts to move smoothly. Underage drinking is a hiccup. "One crime at a time" rings in my head. "If anyone asks, you're twenty-one, okay?"

"Well, duh," she snaps.

I shake my head and slip the ID back into her hands. Carmella beams at me. I grab her and guide up deeper into the club.

"Galaxy" by Hensonn spills in the air as we step out onto the main floor of LUX. The space reflects its namesake and is a luxurious take on a nightclub. A customer won't find any cheap, plastic cups or beer bottles here. Everything from the floor to the ceiling is top of the line or very close. Blue neon lights up black-and-white marble, casting the bar and surrounding dance floor in a cool tone.

Heads turn our way and some of the faces I recognize. Jimmy waves over to me and I tip my head in return. Several of Sasha's men stop short to shake my hand, forcing Carmella closer to me as we draw a crowd.

"Well, looky at this shit. Haven't seen you in fuck ever, brother," Jimmy croons, leaning in and giving me a half hug. We thump on the back. "You ready to fuck this shit up? We got a hell of a party lined up for Sasha. Who's this?" He leers at Carmella.

"This is Carmella, and she's with me," I clarify, giving Jimmy a look that clearly says, *Try it and I'll kill you.*

Jimmy has the decency to shrug. I can't blame him exactly, as we've shared women before. I shake a couple more hands, exchanging a quick laugh and a little good-natured shit talking before I notice the look Carmella is giving me. Her brows are knitted tightly as she glances around the gathered crowd, all focused on us and then up at me.

A crackle goes through the air and the music fades as the DJ Denver's voice booms, "Hey, party people, my man Lucas Reeves is in the house! Let me hit you all with one of his favorites." He spins a few more rhythms before settling on one of my most requested: "Joe Doe" by Adam Jensen.

I flush and look over at Denver, who waves from the DJ booth. I acknowledge him with a head toss and point my finger at him, letting a tight smile slip across my face and into my eyes. *Thanks for the unwelcome fucking announcement, Denver. Now everyone knows I'm here.*

My gaze falls on a confused Carmella. "I come here often," I say, shrugging.

In the middle of the dance floor, a marble fountain sits raised with glowing blue arches of water. We skirt around it and make our way to the steps of the VIP section where Sasha's party is.

A bouncer with bulging muscles and a LUX logo plastered over his too tight tee shirt steps down to take our names. He unhooks the red rope and nods us through. Bringing Carmella's hand to my lips, I watch her step up and catch the attention of several men in the roped off area.

It's the dress. I knew it the moment she tried it on that it had to be hers. Blood-red and clinging to all the right places, the dress claims false modesty with full sleeves and a high neckline. But then it promises filthy things as the entire back is cut away, barely covering the top of her ass. The keyhole in front shows much of her full tits, and a peekaboo diamond shape showing her abdomen and belly button beckons attention. It's a short thing that ends just below her crotch. To be honest, it's less a dress and more of a skintight collection of holes. And matches the red-and-black wig I talked her into wearing.

Dan waves at us from the back of the VIP section. A mixed group of men and women sit on the three-long, black, minimal-looking couches nestled around a white table. I stumble when I see Starla and several of her friends sitting with Sasha. A bubble of nerves for Carmella worms its way inside my gut. *Nothing like your new girl meeting the prostitute you used to fuck.* I scratch my head and sigh. Wrapping my hand around Carmella's waist, I make a mental vow to keep her close.

"Fuck, you really are letting anyone in here now, aren't you, Sasha?" Dan complains as we get close enough to the table to hear him. He eyes me with a sarcastic smirk.

"Ahh yes, but look what the piece of shit brought with him. That one is new." Sasha raises his glass and points at Carmella. His Russian accent is thick on his tongue. He's been drinking. Aleksi stands behind him, the forever watchful guard dog.

Dan and Sasha share a chuckle together at my expense.

"Please, the fact that I am here is the only thing making this birthday party an event worth coming to. Sasha isn't good-looking enough, and you certainly aren't funny enough, Dan," I snap back.

That gets me a round of laughter as Dan rises to greet me with a hug. Sasha steps around the table and slings his arm over me. "You didn't tell me you were bringing a friend. I wouldn't have told Starla to come," he whispers in my ear. His mood is such a contrast from our earlier interaction; it gives me a bit of whiplash. He must be several cups into his celebration.

I glance over at Carmella, who is busy giving a polite smile, but I notice the tension around her eyes. *Might as well get this over with. He's going to find out sooner rather than later.* "Sasha, let me introduce you to Carmella." She turns to look at us as the proper introductions start. Anxiety spikes in my chest as Sasha kisses her hand. If Carmella only knew the company she was keeping tonight, she would tuck tail and run. Sasha flirts with her for a minute, causing her to laugh and give him a gorgeous smile. She wouldn't be smiling so much if she knew the man holding her hand currently is the leader of this branch of Russian mob and how many people the fucker has killed.

"She's pretty," Daniel says next to me.

I glance over at my friend. His slicked back hair and tight suit always make me wonder if he's trying to imitate Patrick Bateman. I eye the gray, small cylinder in his hands as he unconsciously shakes it. The contents rattle softly under the thump of the base. Daniel likes to collect the teeth of the people who have ended up on his shitlist. So, maybe he could give Bateman a run for his money. "She may need some legal help later," I whisper to him. Interest sparks in his eyes as he sips his whiskey.

Sasha laughs at something my girl says, and I realize he looks good tonight. His long blond hair is loose and perfectly framed around his face.

His silk, blue button-down shirt matches his eyes. Brown trim slacks encase his legs, and he looks almost normal except for the heavily inked forearms and neck that show. Carmella smiles at him again, and I've had just about enough of that.

"Sasha, don't be a fucking heathen. Let Carmella meet Daniel," I snap.

When Sasha turns, I'm shocked by the look he gives me. Etched into his face is the anger I didn't expect until later. The glare disappears into a smile as he steps aside so Daniel can greet her.

Sasha eyes Carmella once more before returning to his seat, shaking his head. Dan swings his arm around Carmella, "Hi, Carmella. I'm Dan. The only decent motherfucker in this place and best friend of your boy toy here."

I snort. Carmella's eyebrows attempt to climb into her hairline as she looks at me, then back to him. "Hi, Dan. It's, um... nice to meet you."

"No problem, sugar lips. Let's take a seat," he chirps back and motions for us to sit on the empty couch.

I try to catch Sasha's eye, but a bouncer bends down to talk in his ear while he observes his club like a high lord ruling over his kingdom.

"So, what do you do for fun?" Daniel asks Carmella. There is a twinkle in his eyes that makes my fist curl into a ball. *I said she might need legal help, not issue a blanket invitation to fuck her. Jeez Dan.*

"Hey, Lucas." Starla's sour greeting slices through Daniel's and Carmella's chatting. Carmella sends me a questioning look, and I shrug away the use of my full name. "You know I prefer Luke now, Starla. By the way, this is my girl, Carmella. Carmella. Starla. Starla works for Sasha as an escort."

Starla glares at me before turning to Carmella, her smile so saccharine, I'm surprised her teeth don't rot out. "Actually, I'm a girlfriend experience, something your man should be able to tell you about should you have questions."

Carmella turns to me. "You really have a payment kink, don't you? I should have taken you for more money when you asked for pictures." Daniel makes a choking noise as he inhales his whiskey, and Sasha's eyebrows vanish into his hairline as he chuckles quietly.

"How much did you get him for?" Sasha inquires.

"I don't know. It's probably at a grand now," she counters.

I grimace. *This conversation is not going in the direction I thought it would.*

"A grand just for photos?" Sasha says, and she nods. Sasha looks at me. "You got had. Starla is much cheaper." He gives me a look that says, *We will talk about this later.*

Carmella gives Starla a vicious grin before turning to me with a look that says, *We will talk about this later.*

I snatch up a bottle and one of the empty champagne glasses at the table and pour myself a drink. *I'm planning on being shit-faced drunk later.*

Daniel puts down his drink, and I notice he is still wearing his full suit. "Did you just come from work?" I ask him, desperate for a safe conversation.

Daniel grins. "Yeah, I had to meet a client late. It's a charity case I'm doing. She needs a divorce from her douchebag husband, and you know me." His eyes widen and a grin spreads across his face. "I have a tender heart for those recently separated mothers."

"Tender heart, huh?"

"So very tender," he agrees.

I catch a look of recognition on Carmella's face as she looks at Daniel. "You're the lawyer?"

"Sure am. I do a lot of family law, but some other stuff as well."

She nods. He smiles down at her. "So, tell us about yourself. What do you do for work? How'd you get stuck with this worthless jackass?"

Carmella hesitates. When she does finally speak, it's nothing but half-truths. Sneaking through my window at night becomes looking for a job application. Not having a place to live becomes when she broke up with her ex and I came to the rescue, letting her crash with me. I have to admit, Carmella is a skilled liar and paints me in a light I don't really deserve.

I can tell both Sasha and Daniel know it's bullshit, but they don't question the story. If it comforts her to lie to them, I won't stop her.

"Looks like we're both fucking where we work," Starla purrs. Her silver dress is even more illumined in the flash of black lights.

Sasha leans over and says something to her quietly. She sneers at him before waving to her friends to move out of her way. As she stomps from the table, the other ladies drift after her, probably unsure of their place without their dictator.

Sasha opens his arms, palms up, and addresses Carmella. "I apologize. Starla is aggressive. It's great for business, but she isn't good with... competition."

Carmella purses her lips. "I'm not a whore, if that's your meaning. Luke and I live and work together, as I just explained." Sasha observes her dress before folding his hands and leaning toward me, his accent thick. "Is that the case, Luke?"

Awkward silence descends, and I accept my fate. Sasha will soon learn that this is the case from the men outside the store. "Carmella is... She and I..." I lick my lips. "Yeah, we're together. Carmella is my lover."

"And I'm not a whore," she prompts me.

"And she isn't a whore," I add, holding Sasha's gaze.

"And we live together, right, Luke?" she asks. *I should've left her at home or at least given her a list of things to not say. But for the life of me, I didn't think she was going to gush about our relationship to strangers.* She nudges me with her elbow.

"And we live together," I say, defeated. Not because I don't want her, but because of the weight of Sasha's gaze.

I can see Daniel shake his head out of the corner of my eye and take a big gulp of whiskey. Aleksi gives me a look from behind Sasha that speaks volumes. Sasha would have definitely preferred it if she had been a whore. The tension is palpable.

"Hey, you know what? You don't have a drink. Let's go get you one." Daniel extends his hand to Carmella.

She glances at me and as loathe as I am to let her go off with him alone, I nod. "Go on, I want to talk with Sasha. Dan here will chat your ear off if you let him." I look up at my friend. "Daniel, I'll kill you if she isn't having fun."

Daniel scoffs at me as Carmella takes his hand and gives me an uneasy look. I smile reassuringly at her. I glare at Daniel, who throws his head back and laughs harder, his perfect white teeth gleaming. Anxiety trickles through me as I watch them exit the VIP section. *He better not try to fuck her without me.*

Lacing my fingers, I turn and face Sasha. He hasn't moved an inch. I'm pretty certain that whatever buzz he had going on is gone now. "So?"

He flicks two fingers, dismissing Aleksi, and we are left alone. He shakes his head. "It's no good, brother."

"What isn't?"

"Carmella. How old is she?"

"Twenty-one."

He shakes his head again, his accent rolling in thick. "No. I know this one is not twenty-one. I run a nightclub."

I twist in my seat, uncomfortable by the sudden direction of this conversation. Defensively, I add, "She's twenty-one."

His gaze bores a hole into my head. "You're lying to me."

"So, you're mad because maybe she isn't old enough to drink alcohol in your club?"

He stands and slides in next to me on the couch, throwing an arm around my shoulders good-naturedly. And I won't lie, it makes a chill skitter down my back. With his free hand, he makes a gentle and soothing flourish, as if not trying to frighten a flighty animal. "Anger makes you defensive. We will try a different way, yeah? I'll make you a deal. You leave your kitten here with me. Take Starla and some of her friends. Take a couple bottles, on the house. Go have a party. I'll clean up the mess when the kitten cries. Tomorrow, you get back to work."

I pause for a minute. "No offense, Sasha, but fuck you. If I were to leave her with you, in a couple months, I'd find her working with Starla."

"No." He shakes his hand, an affronted look on his face. "This one I put behind the scenes. She can bus tables and check in VIPs. In a couple months, she meets a nice boy on the dance floor and they go off together. Not your problem and not my problem anymore."

I stare at him. "You're serious right now."

We make eye contact. "Yes. I see the way you look at her. You're not right about this one. My friend, we are getting old, and we are not any good to one so young or so sweet. Please tell me she knows nothing about our business."

I don't answer.

His hand tightens painfully on my shoulder, his thumb biting into my skin. "Tell me she knows nothing."

I stare him down, letting the budding rage in my chest show on my face. "She doesn't know anything important, and the answer is fuck no."

Sasha sighs as his arm slips away from my back. "Listen to me, when you married Pearl, I said no, it's a bad idea. But I'm your friend. When you met your Jocelyn, I said no, it's an even worse idea, but you were so in love, I shut up and said a prayer for her. When you married Tracey, I considered kidnapping you from your own wedding, and then I refused to come. You remember."

"Yeah, I fucking remember. I also remember you were the one who dared me to get married in Vegas," I bite out.

His accent comes out rough as he slips back into the speech patterns of a younger Sasha. "When we were younger, it was funny. But this time, I tell you no! Just no! She is too young. She lies. You help her lie. You wanted to punch me for making her laugh. This is not good for you, not good for the money, and you will make it not good for her!"

I grind my teeth and suck in a breath through my nose. "Okay, so I'm getting old. Maybe I want something different."

Sasha tips his head and the ice in his eyes thaws, revealing the sorrow in his gaze, and finally, I feel like I'm actually talking to the friend I grew up with. He gives me sad eyes. "Maybe you do. Maybe I do too, but you can't put that on her. I saw the reports. It's worse every time you check in. You move less and less each time."

I shoot back what's left in the champagne glass, but it's not nearly enough to take the edge off this night. I pour another while Sasha eyes me. *I don't know what he wants me to say. I'll make it better?* I guzzle the second drink as the lines around his mouth tighten and the nerve in his temple pulses. When I look back at him, the anger I expected to find is there. "It's not good, Lucas."

"I go by Luke now," I say.

"You promised me you would get back on track. Tell me you have a plan."

I shake my head.

The argument we have had about a dozen times is brewing. "Listen, I know you want me back on top. I know you want me to be out there hustling, creating new lines of revenue we can wash the money in. But I can't do that without capital. I need cash. Or you need to find Tracey and break her arms until she puts the businesses back in my name. I can't create something out of nothing, Sasha."

Sasha's jaw twitches again. With the sobering nature of our conversation, his perfect, clipped English becomes more prevalent. "You did before. You loved the challenge."

"Yeah, and like you pointed out, we are getting older. I'm tired of rebuilding the wheel. Talk to your higher-ups. See if they will let me scrape some off the top. And if not, then..." I shrug, knowing he won't like what I have to say, "you have outsourced most of it to other people already. Yeah, they take a larger percentage than I would have, but they're able to handle the amount you're receiving, Sasha. You don't need me. So maybe it's time I step down entirely."

Sasha's hand snakes out and wraps around my neck, squeezing. "This is the mob. You don't get to just fuck up as massively as you did, then retire because you are too tired to try again." He scans my face. "How long have you been seeing that girl?"

"And why the fuck does that matter?" I snap.

"Because you're distracted. She is a distraction. You do this. You meet a new woman and she gets all your attention while you let things slide. I saw the neon in your front window is broken. The Lucus I knew would have had that fixed in one day."

I flush red hot.

He growls at me. "I am the only reason you are still breathing after your fuckup with Tracey." Each sentence is punctuated with more pressure on my jugular. "I put my neck out for you. I paid fines for you to the Pakhan. I'm still paying fines for you." He leans forward into my space. "You should be thanking me. I protect you anytime someone asks the question, 'Why do we still need Lucus?' Stop pissing me off, find me some new revenue streams, be my man." He shakes us as his body leans into mine, his voice low in my ear. "You don't have any choice. And stop fucking around with this child."

I'm pissed now. "Did you ever stop to consider I took her in because I am the better option for her? Am I not allowed to offer my companionship to someone while I fucking jump whenever you say jump?" My throat feels tight and raw. My eyes burn.

"You have felt this strongly about every woman you have ever broken. If you are Carmella's better option, then she is fucked." He shoves me away from him.

I stand. My knees knock into the table, sending champagne glasses toppling over and smashing onto the floor. The noise draws attention. Sasha rises alongside me, smiling at them. I turn to face him. "Out of long-term friendship and the fact that I don't want to undermine your authority in front of the other men, I'm not going to punch your pretty face in." I spit.

He looks at me for a second and shakes his head. "I have other guests to go greet. Please keep yourself from making a scene." He walks away, motioning to the bouncers, who have approached the VIP section, to leave me alone.

Turning on my heels, I leave to go find Carmella and Daniel. *I need to blow off some steam. Fuck Sasha.*

THERE'S NO PARTY LIKE A LUKE AND DANIEL PARTY

LUKE

I find Carmella and Daniel dancing next to the fountain.

She waves me over to her, and I cut through the crowd and slip in behind her. "We did shots!" she yells excitedly.

I dip my head down so she can hear me. "Wanna do some more? I need a drink."

She nods and makes the shot glass gesture to Daniel, who gives a thumbs-up as he bops along to the music. *Good ol' Daniel, probably the best wing man I've ever had. He's my good-time guy.*

The only thing Daniel has ever been serious about is the practice of law, and that's only so he can get paid the big bucks to tell people how to skirt around it. Family law practice is just a hobby. How else would he meet as many soon-to-be single ladies as he does?

I order us three more rounds. "Hey, your girl is fun and she can dance, too," he says next to me. I know what he's angling for, and I consider Carmella for a moment.

"Tell me about it. I got a couple videos I could show you." Dan widens his eyes and arches his eyebrows at Carmella.

She huffs. Her elbow connects with my ribs, and my drink sloshes down my arm. Daniel cackles. "She's a firecracker." He leans down to talk to her over the sound of "drowning" by Vague003. "Luke needs a firm hand from time to time. Just smack him around when he acts up."

Reaching around Carmella, I flick his perfectly cut and sculpted hair. It reminds me of one of those *GQ* slicked-back hairstyles. Daniel swivels on me. "I don't give a damn how close we are, touch my fucking hair and we're fighting."

Carmella spits out her drink as a fit of giggles hits her when I wink at her and laugh.

Daniel smooths back his hair as if a small flick would do anything to disturb all the hair gel and spray he's used to sculpt it. We finish our drinks and head back to the dance floor as a couple, as Daniel heads off to deposit his jacket back in the VIP.

Carmella's fingers lace with mine and she wraps herself in my arms, pressing her back to my chest as she grinds her ass into my lap. We sway to the rhythm, and her body against mine helps soothe the ache in my chest from my fight with Sasha. When Dan returns, his sleeves are rolled up. He settles in front of Carmella, matching our rhythm. He slips his thigh between her legs and begins to grind on her. She glances up at me, a question on her face, and my lips curl up as I shrug. *She can tell him no if she wants to. We can do this entirely at her pace.*

The world around us becomes a dark blur of flashing lights and a crush of people as "Haunted" by Isabel LaRosa thumps from the speaker, vibrating in our chests.

Carmella's face is hidden by her hair. I can't tell if she is tolerating Dan's closeness to humor me or if she just enjoys being caught between us. But then one lithe arm slinks around his neck, giving him more access to her.

Daniel arches a brow at me in question. I mouth, "Shoot your shot." *The worst she can do is tell him no and maybe kill me.* He grins and nods.

As the alcohol loosens my muscles, the music loosens my soul. I lose myself in the rhythm and feel of Carmella for a long time. The lights flash over her face, and she's grinding on Daniel with her eyes closed and a big smile on her face. My lips curl into a grin at seeing her having such a good time and being able to provide it.

Stepping into her, I pin her against Daniel and raise her chin up to capture her lips. They're soft and warm, parting gently. I can taste the tequila on her breath. My dick is instantly hard. Sliding my hand up, I wrap it around her throat and squeeze. She moans and rolls her hips against us both.

Holding her head tipped up, I break our kiss and Daniel takes my spot and kisses her soundly. Her eyes fly open in shock for a second as she searches my face out of the corner of her eyes. Running my hands up her body, I slip my fingers under the diamond keyhole and brush across her erect nipple. She moans in his mouth, her eyes fluttering closed. I watch as Daniel's hand creeps around to cup her breast through the dress.

She pulls away, glancing at the both of us and blushing as red as her dress. I grin at her and lower my head to whisper in her ear, "We're gonna have some fun with Daniel. I want to watch him touch you. Is that alright?"

"He's the lawyer, right?" she whispers softly back to me. "The one that accepts sex as payment?"

I frown. "That isn't what this is about. If it comes to that, I'll pay him in cash. This is for fun. He's a friend."

She bites her lip. I lean down again. "It doesn't change anything between us. I promise," I reassure her.

She grabs on me before I pull away. "You promise? Nothing changes?"

I slam my lips down on hers, bruising us both in a scorching kiss. Her mouth is rubbed red and swollen when I let her go. "I promise. It'll be you and me back at the store in a couple of hours."

She glances at Daniel who, while he's been right beside us, has been giving us mental privacy while dancing and watching the surrounding people. She nods and gives me a mischievous grin that makes me want to bend her over the fountain and fuck her stupid.

Snapping my fingers in Dan's face, I point to the back of LUX and navigate our way off the packed dance floor. We plop down on an arrangement of black couches tucked into a corner under the staircase that leads to the second floor. The beat changes to "Shot It Club Mix" by KVPV. After ordering a round of drinks, Daniel pulls Carmella into his lap and kisses her. She relaxes into him eventually and loses herself in the moment, reaching up to touch his face. Daniel's hand makes slow circles on the inside of her thigh.

Burning lust pumps through my veins as her legs spread apart just a hair and his hand slips higher. My chest expands as I take a deep breath. Our drink order arrives with a bottle of whiskey, courtesy of our host. The table girl explains that Sasha had to step away for a minute, and I nod and motion her away.

I move to sit in front of Daniel on the table, blocking most of the club from seeing us. Sliding my fingers to the back of the Carmella's wig, I fist her hair and my mouth captures hers, nipping at her bottom full lip with my teeth. Kissing my way down her neck and back up, I breathe into her ear, "Spread your legs, you dirty slut. Show Daniel how wet you are."

Wrapping my hand around her thigh, I tug it into my lap. Carmella blushes and I nibble her lips as Daniel's hand slips up and under her short red dress. We both watch her face as he rotates his hand and pushes his fingers into her. More of his arm disappears under the dress as Carmella tips her head back and moans in a way that has me wanting to shove my cock in her open mouth.

"Fuck yeah, baby girl, you are super wet," Daniel hisses.

She groans. "That feels so fucking good." Daniel tips her head back to his lips as he rocks his hand under her dress. I do a quick glance around to make sure no one is watching before I push her dress up and yank the black thong to the side, watching Daniel's fingers pump in and out of her pink, tight cunt. "That's it. Take it, baby girl. Spread yourself open for Daddy. Do you like it?" Dan all but purrs into her mouth.

Carmella sucks in a sharp breath and nods her head.

"What's my name?" Daniel asks.

"Um..." She looks at me and I want to snort. Dan has had a kink about being called Daddy since I met him. "Daddy?" Carmella asks hesitantly.

He smooths his hand down her wig. "Good girl," he coos, kissing her. "Good girl. Are you going to let Daddy fuck this little pussy? It's so tight. I'll make it feel so good. I promise."

She giggles as her face grows even more scarlet, but the embarrassment doesn't stop the moans as he shoves his fingers deeper inside her. Licking my thumb, I rub her clit in the little circles I know she likes. She digs her nails into my forearm and fists Daniel's shirt. She whines and pants as we play with her. I palm my cock with my other hand and fantasize about what she'll look like with my cock down her throat as Daniel fucks her.

Daniel's free hand wraps over her mouth to keep her noises down. He is jack-hammering her cunt so hard, I'm surprised he doesn't fist her. "That's a good girl. Take it all. Tell me you're going to let us fuck you."

Her voice is tight and muffled as it leaks around Daniel's fingers. "Yes, please fuck me."

Carmella's hips dance under our ministrations as she nears her orgasm. Wet, gushy sounds come from between her legs as Daniel slips a fourth finger in her. Kicking up the speed, I rub her clit vigorously and watch as her eyes flutter closed and her orgasm carries her away and breaks her apart in Daniel's arms.

Putting my forehead on hers, I whisper, "You are so fucking beautiful. I wish you could see what I do." I drop a kiss on her damp forehead while I push her hand against the bulge in my pants. She swallows thickly. Standing, I pull her into my arms and bite that pouty bottom lip, relishing the feel of her. Lust clouds my mind; every movement of her body against mine sends delicious friction rocketing against my cock.

"Let's go find somewhere private," I tell Daniel. He nods.

I lead Carmella by the hand to the back of the club that says staff only. Looking back at her, I can see the hesitant curiosity and heavy lust on her face in the flashing lights of the club. Green and red lights run across her smooth skin, and she gives me an anxious smile. Daniel appears behind her, carrying the bottle of whiskey, with a wider grin.

I tip my head to the staff only door. He slips his arm around Carmella's waistline, placing a kiss on her cheek before pushing her forward with his body. I push the door open and wave them through, smiling at her as I do so.

The pulsating music of "Intro" by The xx is muted as the door clicks shut behind us. The room is cast in blood-red lights and dark shadows.

Daniel stands with Carmella pulled into him and hands her the bottle. He whispers something in her ear and she laughs. His hand trails down to grab her ass, pushing her into his hard cock.

Her eyes snap to mine. My desire to watch her get fucked is bleeding out of every pore. I don't even care where we are right now. Walking up behind her, I pull her flush against my chest. Tipping her face up, I breathe in her fruity shampoo and wrap my hand around her throat, squeezing. I fuse her lips with mine, and my body burns as I grind against her ass.

Daniel pushes into her as well as he kisses and licks her neck, pinning her between us. He tugs the stretchy material that makes the diamond shaped keyhole in her dress to the sides, revealing her tits. His hands grip and squeeze them as I devour her mouth. Carmella sucks in a breath from between my lips, whimpering and wiggling between the two of us as Dan sucks a nipple into his mouth.

My cock is beyond hard and every rotation and bump of Daniel rubs her ass against me in delicious and maddening friction. If Carmella were a little sluttier, I'd fuck her ass while Daniel takes her pussy. *We'd really get her crying and panting that way.* But those hesitant looks, the way her hands cling to my face, and the desperate touch of her lips against mine tells me I'm pushing her.

She whimpers as I break our kiss. As I bite her earlobe, she moans. Daniel's mouth has sealed over her nipple as he pinches the other one. He grunts as he looks up at her, the sound of his wet tongue flicking her sensitive tips making it hard for me to breathe. The look of her half undressed, pinned to my lap, my hand at her throat, and Daniel pulling her thin black thong down her legs does some crazy shit to my head. *What a fucking slut. She needs to get on my dick.*

I suck in a shaky breath, trying to not blow my load. My body feels like a wire ready to snap. I grab the bottle of whiskey and take a long draw. Licking my lips, I ask, "What do you want to do here, caramel drop?"

Her eyes are heavily lidded and her mouth puffy between Daniel and me abusing her lips. A sweet blush decorates her cheeks. "I don't know," she whispers, biting her bottom lip, looking at me like she wants me to continue punishing her with hard kisses.

"Yes, you do. Tell us what you want. I want to hear you say it. Tell me how you want it," Dan says. My hand dips to squeeze her unoccupied tit before dropping lower and gripping the hem of her dress. I drag it up. Carmella whimpers and does this adorable little frustrated head shake, looking at me, her face full of desperation and lust.

"I'm horny. Please." She whines.

Daniel chuckles. "That wasn't a *fuck me, Daddy*, now was it, Luke?"

I laugh. "He's right. That wasn't a *fuck me, Daddy* at all."

She looks between the two of us, unsure.

"I got an idea that might loosen her lips. If she doesn't want to talk, she can suck," Daniel says, unzipping his slacks and pulling out his cock, stroking down the shaft. Carmella turns crimson and licks her lips as she stares down at him.

"Hey." I tip her head back so she can look at me. "Show Dan what the mouth does." Her jaw drops open with absolute scandal written into her features. "Atta girl, keep that mouth open." I pull the wig from her head and fist my hand around the blonde bun, forcing her to her knees.

Carmella moans as Daniel's dick brushes her lips, and she slides his cock in her mouth as I yank her head back so I can see him use her face like a Fleshlight. I hold her there, letting him ruin her cute little mouth with his cock. She gags and grabs onto his slacks and my hand as he hits the back of her throat.

"Breathe through your nose," he tells her, tipping his head back and forcing his length down her throat. His breath hitches as his hips settle into a thrusting rhythm. Carmella gives him a hot little moan and sucks in her cheeks, latching onto him like a fucking pro. Wet, gagging sounds fill the air as Daniel yanks her forward, pushing his cock down her throat again. He pulls away, and she gulps down air like she's run a marathon.

"He told you to breathe through your nose," I say, popping her on the cheek with a gentle slap. My cock is screaming for attention. I can feel the pre-cum soaking into my pants, making wet spots in the cream linen.

Her eyes water as she coughs. Daniel laughs. "So, what's the deal, butter-cup? You wanna keep getting fucked or not?" She nods. Leaning forward, she wraps her lips around his cock and sucks, bobbing up and down the length of him as he spreads his legs and palms the back of her head.

Pulling out my phone, I turn on the camera and crouch down to her level. I snap off a few pictures before turning on the video and watching her slurp down his length like he is a tall glass of water. She gags herself on his dick, and I don't think I've ever been so turned on as I am watching her blow him.

I rub myself through my pants and nearly cum at the friction. I've got to take the edge off.

"Take over." Daniel's eyes pop open as I pass the phone to him and grab Carmella by the hair, maneuvering her off Daniel's dick with a pop. She looks at me with smokey dark-blue eyes heavy with lust and tequila. I undo her bun, threading my fingers through her ashen locks. I unzip and free myself, putting my cock against her mouth. My dick jumps as her warm breath hits the tip of my sensitive skin. My voice, laced with desire, orders her to: "Suck me off, slut."

Her eyes flick up, and her fingers wrap around me. I shake her hair. "No, just your mouth. Jerk him off while you do it and look at me." She takes Daniel in her hand, rubbing up and down his shaft, and she leans forward and slides my cock into her mouth.

Her warm tongue flicks across the bottom of my shaft, and I have a moment of deep regret that we won't be able to do this long or I'm going to cum. She slides her hot mouth down the length of me, hits the base, and we both moan. *God damn, her mouth feels like heaven.*

Her tongues dance out, licking across the tip and swiveling in a circle, setting off all kinds of lightning bolts in my head. "Oh, fuck," I grunt out. I so badly want to face fuck her until she cries, but I'll nut. I let her set the pace even as my hands fist in her hair. It feels so good. Too good. I let go of her and run my hands through my hair, lacing my fingers behind my head.

It's glorious having her suck me. My balls tighten and muscles start to kick as my orgasm builds. I pull away from her wonderful mouth at the last minute.

She kneels on the floor between us, devastatingly beautiful. Her dress is bunched in the middle, her hair wild, lipstick smeared and mascara running. Drool and pre-cum has dripped onto her tits, making them glossy. *If she wasn't a slut before, she sure is one now.*

Daniel stands, jerking himself off and rubbing his pre-cum on her cheek. "What do you say, baby girl?"

She looks at me. The words are for him, but the intention... Oh, the intention is all for me. *"Fuck me, Daddy."*

Reaching down, I twist her arm behind her back and she yelps. Dragging her naked backside against my aching cock, I dig it into her. "I got her waist if you got her legs," I say to Dan.

Daniel has already shoved his pants down past his hips. Rolling a condom on, he grabs her thighs and lifts, exposing her pink, tight fuckhole to him. He whistles. "Going to be a snug fit."

"She can take it," I tell him.

Carmella gives us a sexy little pant. "Feels like you guys have done this before." Daniel and I grin at each other. He chuckles as he leans in, lines up, and thrusts deep inside her.

Her blonde curls part around him, and she moans, tipping her head back against my chest. "Oh, shit. Oh, my God." She bites her lip as she turns her head into my chest, grabbing onto my neck and arm for support.

He sets a quick pace, thrusting into her hard. The air fills with the sound of his balls slapping against her cunt and Carmella's cries of pleasure. With every thrust, Carmella's ass bounces against my cock till I'm dizzy with lust and near coming again. My balls ache.

"Fuck yeah, you take dick like a champ, don't you, baby girl? Take all of

Daddy's cock." He thrusts into her tight hole as I slip my hand down into her curls and flick her clit. She comes alive in my arms, wiggling down on his shaft and against my hand for more friction.

"What do you say?" Daniel says, pulling out of her.

"Fuck me, Daddy." She says it over and over again as Daniel nails her with his cock. "Fuck me, Daddy. Fuck me, Daddy." Her breath hitches as I circle her clit with my fingers. Picking up the pace, I watch as she comes apart. Her orgasm pulls a string of curse words and sweet cries from her lips and we continue to stimulate her. Tears slide down her cheeks and she jerks and moans on Daniel's dick as I punish her clit. He freezes as she twists on his cock. "Fuck yeah, I'm going to breed you." *He better fucking not.* His eyes close as he rocks into her, riding his own orgasm.

Our harsh breaths fill the air as they both come down from their orgasms. My dick screams for attention. Daniel drops her legs gently and stumbles back. Sliding the condom off, he plops it in the trash next to the door. He slips his dick back into his slacks and zips up. "Luke, I needed that. Thanks."

"Carmella." He finger guns at her. "I'll see you out there, babe."

With that, he turns on his heel, throws open the door, and disappears into the crowded dance floor. Carmella lies against my body, her fingers rubbing against my five o'clock shadow, and stares after Daniel before turning to look at me. "What the hell was that?" she asks breathlessly.

"That was Daniel."

"Oh," she says. I grind my cock into her ass, letting her know her work isn't done yet.

She looks back at me. "Do you want me to blow you again? You could cum in my mouth." The sweet little ask nearly does me in and my dick jumps, straining against her.

"I have a better idea." Leaning her against the table, I straddle her closed legs and slip my cock between her pussy lips. My dick glides against her clit and grazes her slick fuckhole.

Wrapping my hands around her throat, I tell her, "Take a deep one," and she obeys, sucking in air, and then I squeeze. Her face quickly turns red as I shut off most of her oxygen. "Grab my dick, slut, and tease yourself with it."

She wraps a warm hand around my shaft, and I thrust in and out of her grip, the tip of me rubbing against her clit. Putting my forehead against hers, I press our faces together. Caught in the feel of her life flickering under my fingertips and my cock in her hands, words come unbidden to my lips. "If you ever let another man who isn't me cum in you raw, I swear I'll fucking kill you both."

Carmella whimpers or laughs—I can't tell—and swallows against my hands. Pushing against my grip on her throat, she kisses me deeply and bites down on my bottom lip. Her hands tighten, squeezing me hard, and pain lances up my cock.

My hips lose their rhythm as my balls pull up. Pleasure mixes with pain and it pushes me over the edge. My orgasm hits, stealing away my breath. Carmella's nails dig into my shaft and my dick jumps, shooting ropey cum onto her clit, slit, and thighs. I moan and shudder against her, and the metallic coppery taste that fills my mouth as her teeth dig into my bottom lip. Blood.

She pulls her nails out of my softening shaft, making me flinch and moan in pain. There are bloody half-moon marks on my dick. Staring down at her, I see my blood on her smeared lipstick. Her stormy blue eyes are steady as she stares back at me. "And if you ever abandon me, I'll never forgive you."

I chuckle a bit and nod. "Okay, that's fair, just as long as we both understand the rules." I drop a kiss on her forehead. "Fix your dress and let's get the fuck out of here. I don't know about you, but I could go for a burger." *And to get away from Sasha. I also don't want her spending any more time with Daniel.*

Her steady eyes haven't left mine. She flinches a little and bites her lip, rolling my blood into her mouth. "We're crazy, aren't we?"

I stare at her with a little smile tugging at my lips. "Oh yeah. We definitely are, caramel drop."

Farewell, My Summer Love

CARMELLA

My mind rotates to the words of passion Luke and I said to each other.

Carmella, what have you done? Why did you say that? He owes me nothing, and I asked him to not abandon me. Shame flares in my chest and I toss an arm over my face.

Heat of the moment, it had to be. Luke was being weirdly possessive, and I was on a sex high. I rolled with it. *Yeah, that tracks.*

Things get said in the heat of the moment that people don't really mean. I confessed love to Grady Felton after giving my first blowjob at fifteen, and clearly, that didn't pan out.

I sigh. The white stucco ceiling stares down on me, judging my sluttier than normal behavior. The blankness of the canvas gives me a screen onto which I can replay last night's events over and over in increasing arousal and alarm.

Luke's soft, even breathing and the dead weight of his arm draped over my stomach let me know he is deep in sleep. His face presses into my shoulder, the rest of his body wrapped around me. Two nights in his bed have confirmed that Luke is a cuddler.

It strikes me as oddly sweet and vulnerable, especially in someone like Luke.

I like it. It makes me wonder what other types of softness lurk under the con artist. My hand lifts of its own accord to touch his deep brown hair. I can't date Luke and Luke can't date me for multiple reasons.

One, he is much older than I am and he probably doesn't have any long-term interest in a routine fuckup like me.

Two, I can't stay in White Cove. Staying here is a death sentence in the form of either going to prison, a mental institution, or back to my aunt.

Three, aside from strikingly similar pasts, complimenting interests in movies, music, and the beach, love of the same foods, and an agreement on the harsh realities of life—and barring the fact that the world never seemed to want either one of us—what could we even share?

My chest feels tight and my eyes burn with unshed tears. Nausea churns in my stomach. Pain and pressure pushes in on me like my heart might just cave in from the weight. *Then, I'll be this hideous thing with an empty chest and a crushed heart. Everyone will know how broken I am just by looking.*

Fuck. I run my fingers through my hair, pulling painfully at the roots. When that isn't enough to get the overwhelming emotions to subside, I dig my nails into my thighs and flinch at the burning sensation. Eventually, the pressure in my chest eases.

The cool, oily sensation on my fingertips has me gently sliding from the bed before I get blood on his sheets.

Padding into the kitchen, I rifle through the cupboards until I find the scattered remains of a first-aid kit and a few loose, floating Band-Aids.

I search around for some ibuprofen and antacids as well. Should have figured I am a little hungover by how emotional I am. Popping the pills out of their little silver packages, I scope them up and set about making coffee.

L uke finds me several hours later at the front desk.

"What are you doing out here?" His voice holds the edge of sleep and frustration.

I glance at him and hold up the piece of paper I'm doodling on. Little characters of Luke the crab decorate around the page. "I couldn't sleep anymore, so I made some coffee and came in here."

"Oh." He seems a little chastised. "I thought maybe you took off or something." He walks closer to inspect the little crabs. It makes his mouth curl up in a cute smile. I find myself looking for his smiles more often than not.

I frown. "Why would you think that I'd left?"

He sighs and puts the page down, staring out the front windows. "You were pretty drunk and cried a little before you passed out last night. I thought maybe you were upset about Daniel, but you wouldn't answer me."

Shame rolls up through me. *Great. That's great.*

"Sorry, I occasionally get upset when I get drunk. It just sort of shakes loose once I get too tired. At least I didn't puke on you. I puked on my best friend Trixie on her seventeenth birthday before crying on her shoulder. Not my best moment." I pause. "I didn't puke on you, did I?"

He chuckles. "No, it was a puke-free evening. So, you're not upset about Daniel?"

"I haven't given him a lot of thought. If I have to decide... I would say I was into it at that moment and I wanted to make you happy. I was also horny. Other than that..." I shrug.

He nods. "Okay, good."

A knock comes at the front of the store. Two men stand outside next to the black Escalade that was here when we left for Lux. The men are different from the ones hanging around yesterday. Luke looks at them and back at me. "Um, give me a second."

"Should I leave?" I ask.

He walks toward the front doors. "No. No reason to. Sasha knows now."

He opens the doors and lets them in. "Good morning, Lucas. Coffee?" I hear the larger of the two men say as he raises a thermos. He reminds me of Tommy with his close cropped hair, but only if Tommy was also over two hundred pounds of muscle and wore black sweats instead of gray. The man next to him is so unremarkable that he borders on boring. Neither good-looking nor ugly, he's dressed in a nondescript white tee shirt and jeans.

"You know the way, Rikki, in the back there. Anything happen last night?" Luke says, pointing them toward the kitchen, and the group makes its way toward the back.

The two men look at me seated at the desk and back at Luke. He comes to a stop near me and motions for them to continue. The man named Rikki answers him and jerks his thumb at the man next to him. "Casper here thought he saw a vehicle matching the pictures you gave us drive by at a distance early this morning, but it was still dark and the vehicle didn't linger or act out of the ordinary. Didn't get a look at the plates. And other than that, we didn't see anything."

"Thanks, fellas, I appreciate you hanging around," Luke says.

They nod and head into the kitchen, leaving us alone.

"Do you think seeing them out there was enough to discourage whoever it was?" I ask.

"Maybe. Probably." Luke shrugs. "Honestly, it makes me feel better that nothing happened because it could mean we were on high alert for nothing. Or maybe it was something, but nothing that had to do with us."

I sigh as some of the tension flows from me. "That would be a relief."

He smiles.

An awkward quiet settles between us.

Spinning the pen in my fingers, I search for something to say while I stare at the paper. I feel like the words we spoke to each other in the back room are what's causing the awkwardness between us, or at least on my end, they are.

He breaks the silence. "About last night... are you going to stick around? Cause I'd like you to."

My heart skips a beat before twisting horribly, and I chew the inside of my lip until it hurts before meeting his soft brown eyes and tousled hair. I don't know how I can stay, but a part of me wants to. "I'll stay as long as I can."

I can't tell how he feels about that answer. There's a flicker of something and then it's gone. Slapping his hand on the tall table, he straightens up with a full smile. "It's Sunday. You know what that means?"

My eyebrows rise into my hairline at his sudden shift in mood. I shake my head.

"That means it's beach day. "

"I thought last night was our fun day."

"What's wrong with another fun day? You seemed to have thoroughly enjoyed the last one. Especially as you were getting stuffed."

My cheeks heat at his words, and I glance to the back and shush him. He grins.

I know I shouldn't go out, shouldn't fuck around, and a thousand arguments rush to my lips, but I just nod. "Okay."

"Yeah, she wants to get stuffed again," Luke announces loudly.

I suck in a mortified breath at the idea of *that* happening again or the men in the back hearing him, even if my pussy clenches and I get a little warm. I swear, if I can blush all the way down to my toes, this man is going to cause it.

Luke laughs and bends over to drop a kiss on my head before heading into the back.

I watch him go. Embarrassment and arousal leach from me as sadness settles in. *I really am going to miss him.*

The beach is magnificent. It's a bright, hot day, and the teal-blue waters are refreshingly cool.

They lap around me as I float nearby. A rogue wave higher than the one I had been floating on raises me up before washing over my face. I sputter and spit, blowing salt water out of my mouth as my eyes burn. Another wave catches me unaware and makes me lose my balance. A familiar laugh sounds next to me and an arm slides around my waist, anchoring me.

"Jump," Luke says. We push up from the seat floor as one, riding the next wave as it flows around us. This time, I keep my head above water.

Blinking away the salt water from my eyes, I turn in Luke's arms and jump up, wrapping my legs around his waist. "You're lucky those shorts don't rip off in the water, *dirty Daddy.*" He snorts. "If your stringy triangles can hold up to the waves, then my dirty Daddy short-shorts definitely can."

"Excuse me. I risk a nipple slip every time there is a big wave. People will forgive a nipple slip. I doubt they'll forgive a cock slip. That's indecent exposure. "

"Double standards," he mutters.

We've done nothing but flirt and play all morning. It started out as a game of kicking sand—which I lost because he got sand up my butt crack—then Luke brought me a couple of small seashells to make up for it. I tucked them into my beach towel. *I want to keep them forever.*

When I ran into the waves to rinse the sand from my most intimate places before I got too itchy, Luke trailed after me. Since payback was in order, I tried my best to dunk him, but the man wouldn't go under.

So, the only natural solution was to tackle him and drown us both, which ended up with us in a tangled heap, both spitting out salt water and laughing hysterically.

I eye the shoreline as Luke carries me farther away from it, and the people shrink in size. The beach is packed today. Its tawny shores are laden with families, couples, and friends, all drawn to the azul waters and hours of memory-making fun. The water glimmers and licks at us as the warm sun beats down and heats my skin.

I look behind me, out into the blue expanse of water and sky. "How far out are we going?"

"Until we have some privacy, just us and the ocean. I want to show you my special place. Don't worry, it doesn't get too deep."

"You swim all the way out here by yourself?"

He nods.

I would be terrified of sharks or riptides this far out. I wrap my arms around him tighter as the darker blue water deepens to our necks. The rocks ahead come into view and the people on the shore look like tiny figures.

He was right, though. The water begins to drop away from my neck, and

I sigh in relief. He squeezes me back, his breath in my ear. "See, I told you."

I let my finger trail down his back and lay my head on his shoulder as he carries me to the blackish rocks. One, in particular, is an oblong gray oval washed smooth by the waves. It lies partially jutted up and out of the ocean at an angle, making it a prime place to sit or sunbathe. It's big and some parts of it sink in, becoming holes that the ocean washes in and out of. I love it. It's like a tiny rock island.

My fingers touch Luke's damp hair. I press my lips to his cheek, giving him a kiss and leaning into the feel of him under my hands. Heat rears up in my clit and I wish I could squeeze my legs together to ease it... or maybe I can convince Luke to ease it for me on the rocks.

Feeling brazen, I bring my mouth to his ear and give it a playful nip and tug, letting my tongue flick against the lobe. He grunts and laughs, pulling me closer. Taking the invitation, I drop kisses along his jawline before dipping down to lick and suck his neck, moving his golden chain out of the way. He stops walking and holds me to him. "Shit, you're making my dick hard, honey."

I open my mouth and suck onto the place over his collarbone, the chain settling against my mouth. As I bite down a little, he moans. "Harder." I do as I'm told, reveling in the feeling of him under my teeth. I flick my tongue against his skin as the heat between my legs becomes an inferno. The desire to bite down until he yelps and fucks me into oblivion washes over me and I let go. Panting, I admire the deep red-purple bruise I left on his shoulder.

He seizes the back of my hair, and his lips come down on mine, crushing and hot. Our teeth click as I open my mouth at the insistence of his tongue, and it dances with mine. He drops my bottom half into the water gently, and my hands roam his chest. I let my nails rake gently down the front of him, delighted by the response I get when he squeezes me.

I'm lightheaded by the time he breaks the kiss. His hard cock rubs against my pussy for a split second before ending up pushing into my stomach.

"I've never brought anyone here before. This is my place." His thumb brushes my cheek and rubs across my lower lip.

My swim top sags as purple strings suddenly dangle free, his nimble fingers working the next knot. He pulls my bikini top away, tossing it onto the rocks, and I'm topless in front of him and the endless sky and water.

"What about Tracey?" I ask.

"She wouldn't have appreciated it," he says, pushing my hair away from my face.

I swallow thickly as we look at one another. My mark sits proudly on his tan shoulder, bruised and deeply colored. The sea coats his body, making him look like some kind of dark, chaotic water god.

"I thought you didn't like the quiet." This far out, the only sounds around us are the waves hitting the rocks and the far off calls of seagulls.

He steps into me. "The ocean isn't quiet. It gives me privacy without silence."

His hands palm my ass, dragging me back against him. He squeezes and kneads my muscles, inches away from where I genuinely want his fingers. My heart soars at the meaning of his words. Butterflies dance inside me.

I pull his face down to me and kiss him soundly. My lips bruise from the force of it.

Cool, wet stone presses into my back and suddenly, I'm being lifted and placed down on a smooth, warm surface. Luke hefts himself out of the water and crawls up my body before settling his weight down on me.

My nipples tingle as he rolls one into his hot mouth and flicks the other. It sends sparks straight to my clit and I push my hips up and into him, seeking friction. His hands slip under the seam of my suit, parting my curls and rubbing against my clit. I moan and grab onto his arm as he plays my body, stringing me out.

He unties the bottom of my swimsuit and pushes it out of the way. The stroke of his fingers over the entrance to my pussy has me sizzling on the rocks. He dips a finger into me, and it's not enough. "More," I tell him, letting my fingers trail lazily down his body.

He bites my nipple, making me jump and whine against him. "Beg me and maybe I'll give you more."

"I need more. I want you. Please, I just... Finger me. I want to feel your hands on me."

He doesn't move, doesn't give me any friction.

I spread my legs wider, opening myself to him, and push his hand deeper into me as I ride it. "Please, Luke, touch me." My words are a sweet surrender.

Three fingers push into me, gloriously sweet and filling with a hint of pain as I stretch to accommodate the size. My head kicks back, and he feasts upon my tits, stimulating my nipples until I'm a panting, sweating mess.

His voice is thick as he withdraws and shoves his short-shorts down his legs, his cock springing free. The words escape from my lips. "Finally. Please fuck me, Luke. I want your cock in me."

He drops a glorious smile on me. It's magic, that smile. I want to purr and cum and crawl inside him all at once.

He stretches out on top of me, settling his weight as he kisses my neck, shooting little sparks of lust between my legs. I gently play with his nipples and earn myself another low moan from him as he slides his hand between us. Using his cock, he parts my slickness and thrusts against my clit. "Oh fuck, please, Luke. Please, fuck me this time."

"You want me to fuck you like a dirty slut?"

"Yes, please, oh God, yes." I stare between our bodies as he holds himself up to watch as he teases me.

He looks down at me and shakes his head. "Today, we are going to take it slow." On his last word, he dips into my opening, just a whisper of his size spreading me before he pulls away. I'm desperate and panting, and a moan of frustration is pulled out from me. He eases into me a little more, and I raise my hips greedily.

"Tsk, tsk. No, you don't." He pulls away, chuckling, his voice rough with desire. "Be good and be still." He gives me a little more. I try to pull him to me, kiss him, but he dodges me.

I slide one hand down between us and flick my clit, clenching around the tip of his cock nestled in me. I moan at the sensations. Luke pins my arms above my head and settles back down between my thighs, blocking the view. "Such a greedy girl. See, I knew you wanted to get stuffed." Flexing his hips, he slides into me all the way to the base and hisses.

The full sensation of him being inside me flutters my eyes closed. I roll my hips and my breath is stolen away by how good he feels. I roll them again, fucking myself on his cock. Luke pants as he rubs my nipples, cranking up my arousal. He drops little kisses on my neck, lips, face, and hairline before resting his forehead against mine.

The moment is perfect: our limbs entangled, him filling me, pressed against each other so closely. I feel seen and beautiful spread across the rocks under him in his favorite spot. This is a bittersweet gift and one I accept covetously. *No matter where I go in life, my memory will always exist here in his favorite place. A place he only shared with me.* My eyes sting and I blink back the tears.

He cages me inside his arms as he begins to rock himself inside of me. I come apart sharply and suddenly, a hot gush covering us both as I cry out. "Fuck, that's hot, caramel drop. I didn't know you could do that," he says and thrusts again, sliding into my body, hitting that perfect spot. I bite my lip. "You feel so fucking good," he praises.

He thrusts harder. "I knew the moment you reminded me of the beach, this was where I was going to fuck you." He thrusts again and I hold on to his back, locking my legs around his waist and rising to meet him. He stares down at me. "I want you to stay here. With me. I know there are problems, but stay." He rocks into my body, hitting my cervix with an arousing shock of pain before withdrawing.

"Fuck, you're so wet. Tell me you'll stay," he begs. I moan in frustration, as he continues to fuck me. "Tell me and I'll let you fuck yourself on my cock."

"Tell me." He pulls out, and I'm bereft.

"No, I'll stay. I'll stay. Please come back, Luke." I beg.

"Look at me."

It hurts me, but I look up at him.

"Tell me you'll stay."

"I'll stay."

He slides into me again. "Because you want me?"

"Yes." I whimper. He thrusts deeply against my G-spot and I see stars.

"You want to be my slut?"

"Fuck yes." His hand slips down and slaps my clit.

"Say it again." He rubs that bundle of nerves in a circle.

"I want to be your slut. I want to be with you. Please." I'm embarrassed but too far gone, and his restraint snaps. He crushes me into the rock. It bites into my back as he sets a brutal pace, fucking me deeply.

I cry out as the friction becomes too much and I clench around his cock. Hot juices coat the both of us, the wet slapping of his body against mine dominating the heavy, warm air around us.

"I'm going to cum in you. Tell me you want it, slut." His voice is dark with need.

The thought of him filling me up drives me mad. It's stupid and reckless, but the need is there. "Cum in me. Fuck yes, cum in me."

I don't recognize my own voice, but I don't care. His fingers are on my clit and his cock slides in and out of me while he kisses me into oblivion, and I'm lost.

My orgasm rips through me. It draws up my back like a string on a puppet, and a slew of curse words roll out of my mouth as wave after wave of ecstasy rolls through my body. My muscles squeeze Luke's dick, and the friction makes me cry out, "Oh, God, yes."

Luke groans and a sudden sense of heat, hotter than before, flares inside me. His hips lose their rhythm as he thrusts into me. I can feel his cum coating me inside and out as he continues to ride my pussy, rocking into me until his dick softens and he slides out.

Lying down next to me, he pulls me into his arms, and I feel a gush of fluid from between my legs. I've never let any of the guys cum in me before. It's sexy and scandalous and a primal part of my brain is so turned on, I could purr, knowing the slickness between my legs is from him.

His voice distracts my thoughts of how hot that felt. "We'll get you on birth control." He pats my arm.

"Probably best because I think I just discovered that I really love being... creampied." My cheeks heat at the phrasing.

Laughter bursts out of Luke. "See now, didn't I tell you that you wanted to get stuffed again?"

I smack his chest but truth be told, if I wasn't sore from last night's events and the rocks against my back, I'd probably try to ride him right now. Seeing him spread out and naked like this in the daylight is addictive.

"You are very handsome, in case I haven't told you." He props himself up to grin down at me.

"Sweet words from caramel drop? I must be dreaming." He chuckles as I roll my eyes. "You are beautiful too, but I've always thought so." I smile. He drops a kiss on my forehead. "How do you feel about getting some lunch?"

My stomach agrees. "Yeah, food would be great, and a Plan B? Have you noticed that you pair fucking and food together?"

He laughs. "I mean, it's a great combo. There is a pharmacy across the street and a place where we can get a bite."

I wash in the salt water, praying that it's enough to keep any of his little swimmers at bay, and tie my suit back on.

"Hey." He grabs my wrist, pulling me against him before we leave our little rock island. "I meant what I said. I want you to stay. I know you have problems, but I feel rather strongly about you. So, I hope you meant what you said as well."

I swallow back a load of sudden word vomit and nod. He searches my face. I smile at him and force a laugh. "Yes, I meant what I said. Come on, or I'm going to end up pregnant or starving."

He smiles and lets me go.

I've never wanted the ocean to drown me more than I do right now because I don't think I can bear leaving him.

Starfish

Carmella

I watch Luke walk up the stone steps that lead from the beach to the boardwalk. He disappears into the throng of tourists and locals all mingling about, enjoying a day of swimming and trinket shopping.

I wish I could have gone with him to pick up the Plan B and grab our food, but every day, the noose around my neck feels a little tighter. I probably stand the same chance of being arrested as I did two weeks ago, but now that I know how serious my lying bitch of an aunt has made the situation, it's become all the more stressful.

Yet here I sit, on the beach with a man I can't have, risking my foolish neck for something that can't happen. I sigh and cram a ball cap down over my curls, tucking them up and under.

We made our little resting spot under the pier to avoid too much of the midday sun. But now, with the wind cutting off the water and the cooling shade, I shiver and pull out my hoodie, yanking it over my head.

Ball cap and hoodie girl sulking in the sand, not conspicuous at all. I shiver again as the air nips against my damp skin.

Curling up, I watch the waves roll in and out. I never really got to spend a lot of time at the beach as a child. A couple of foster families brought me once or twice. It wasn't until I was a teenager and living with my aunt that I discovered that when she was drunk or high, I could walk out the front door. I could spend all day or night stomping around with my friends, hanging out on deserted playgrounds or in parking lots.

My aunt's drug problem gave me freedom, and I rediscovered the beach, especially in the wee hours of the night with a couple of friends, hiding in the tall grasses from the beach police. Hours were spent swimming, drinking cheap vodka, and horsing around. Chatting about how when we turned eighteen, everything would be different. I'd go to college and move out, be in charge of my own life finally.

But that was before the lawyers and courtroom verdicts. Before I was manipulated into losing everything. I close my eyes and let the misery overtake me like the waves do the beach. I don't know how long I lie there, but a gentle nudge wakes me up.

Luke sits next to me, unbagging our food and grinning down at me. "I got extra fries. You have to try them from this place. They're great."

I look from him to the fries and back. *I'm seriously going to miss him. Like really bad.* Once we devour every last crispy fry and I swallow my Plan B, we decide to swim a bit more before taking a nap. Luke brings a blanket from the car and lets me use his chest as a pillow while he scrolls on his smartphone. After that, we meander along the boardwalk before ducking into a little tourist trap.

The walls are white planking lined with glass shelves covered in beach-themed snow globes, picture frames, seashells, and big wooden words like *Beach* and *Summer Days.*

The lightly stained wooden floor holds woven baskets full of stuffed animals and pirate-themed children's toys. Metal racks with a bright assortment of tee shirts with annoying phrases like *I got my tan at White*

Cove are littered around the room.

Boogie boards, flip-flops, hats, and snorkeling gear are tucked in wherever it's most convenient.

"You've been staring at that stuffed starfish forever." Luke's voice startles me as he stands looking over my shoulder at the baby-blue-and-black-striped plush starfish I'm holding.

Luke plucks the stuffy from my hands as we stand in front of the woven basket. "I had one as a kid. Smaller, but the same type of starfish."

"Oh, yeah?"

"Yeah, I lost it. Well, I don't think it was lost. The foster parents didn't want me anymore, told my caseworker I wasn't a good fit for their house, so one day she came in to help me pack." I pause, taking the stuffy back from his hands.

"But I couldn't find my starfish. His name was Finny, which is funny because starfish don't have any fins. I had it for so long, I don't even remember where I got it. It may have even been mine from before, with my parents."

I sigh. "Anyway, I'm crying because these people don't want me and I've lost my favorite stuffy. All my shit is in black bags, and I have no idea where I'm going next or who those people are. If they will like me or how they will expect me to behave or if I can even act happy cause I'm not. I'm angry and scared. The caseworker tells me the foster mom, I don't even remember her name now, will look for it. I knew that was a lie. Pretty certain one of her kids kept it. I never saw it again."

A ball of lead drops into my stomach, souring the fries. Tossing down the stuffed starfish like it burned me, I mentally swear I'm not going to have a breakdown here in this nice, cheery family store, especially in front of Luke.

Sucking in a deep breath against the tightening in my chest, I glance at him. That dark, flat look dominates his face as his eyes narrow on the starfish like he could stab it. "You could get it," he says.

I shake my head, my eyes taking in the shape of him and all the little details of his face: the slight crow's feet, his perfectly trimmed mustache, and his favorite gold chain that dangled above me while we fucked not long ago. I admire the soft curve of his lips and the way he always slicks his hair back, but it's still wavy and curls at the ends. I memorize his face even while he staunchly stares at the stuffed animals. "No, you learn that for one reason or another, you just can't take everything you care about with you," I explain.

With that, I turn and walk over to the table with a hodgepodge of beaded jewelry boxes and shot glasses, not seeing the objects in front of me.

I can feel Luke's eyes on me. Picking up one of the jewelry boxes, I fidget with it a moment before moving on, allowing my feet to take me to the rotating stand of magnets. Spinning the carousel, I see pictures of dolphins, crabs, fish, and flip-flops fly by, all advertising the abundance and fun of White Cove.

A purple-and-pink picture of a sunset catches my eye. In the middle of it sits the rock formation Luke took me to. The image is soothing and romantic in a sort of whimsical, once-upon-a-time way. I pull the magnetic image away from the metal.

My eyes meet Luke's over the tables of stuff. "I found what I want."

It's dark by the time we get back to the store after a quiet walk along the beach and dinner. Luke decided we should go shower to wash away the sand. The hot water was amazing, but the mirror revealed my back was more scratched up than I thought from leaning against the rocks during our lovemaking session.

I check the clock as Luke cuts the engine—nearly ten pm. The radio continues to play "In and Out" by Blonder.

"You've been quiet this evening. Penny for your thoughts." Luke pulls out his pack of cigarettes. The paper crinkles as he pulls one out and lights it. The glow of the cherry and the smoke makes the car hazy before he rolls down the windows, letting in a fresh breeze of air.

"What happened to my pervy guy?" I tease. "You've been so... dare I say, romantic today?"

"Oh, the dirty Daddy short-shorts and slut muffin stuffing session weren't enough filth for you?" He stares out the windshield. "She cusses, lets other men fuck her, and now she wants me to be rough and gross with her... I've created a monster."

He grins back at me and reaches over to pinch my cheek. "You picked up slutting fast, didn't you?" Laughter worms its way up my chest as I turn ten shades of crimson.

"I love how embarrassed you get, especially after you were all into it. It's like the minute you're not coming on my hand or someone's dick, you remember you do have some shame. And that fact just makes me want to tie you to one of those dining room tables inside and fuck with you until you squirt all over it. Then, I'm going to stick my cock up your tight ass because I know it will feel amazing around my dick. How do you feel about anal?"

I sputter as the images smack into my brain. Blinking them away, or at least trying to, I realize I have made an error. "I made a mistake. You can relax, pervy Luke. I clearly don't know what the fuck I'm asking for."

Luke howls with laughter in the seat next to me. Grabbing me around the neck, he kisses me soundly and bites my lip, sending sparks of lust zipping into my pussy.

"Too late, caramel drop. Pervy Luke wants to play and you're in trouble." He clicks his seatbelt off and begins to crawl onto my side of the car. Laughing, I quickly yank my car door open and slide out as Luke snatches at my hair. Reeling me back into the seat, he slides his hands up under my shirt and bra to squeeze my tits. "These melons are just begging me to suck on them." He bites my shoulder.

Abandoning all hope of escaping him decently, I slip out of my shirt and bra, letting it rip over my head and leaving me crouched down topless just outside of his car with dumbfounded Luke holding onto my clothes. "Huh, fitting. That's how I found you the first time," he says. I sniff in his direction and toss my hair. Covering my nipples with one arm, I walk proudly to the back door and open it with the spare key.

A whistling catcall sounds behind me, and I stick my tongue out at him and point. "Don't forget our bags." He rolls his eyes and quickly opens the car door, slamming it with a, "Fuck the bags." He stalks toward me. Laughing, I quickly rip open the door.

I'm down the hallway in two seconds and hiding in the furniture, with Luke right behind me, yanking off his clothes.

You Better Run, Girl

CARMELLA

We pass out in my bed a couple hours later, hot and sticky, totally eliminating the shower we just took. My pussy is tender from so much abuse. I blush at the thought that eventually he is going to sell this bed to some unsuspecting customer who will never know I took the store owner's cock doggy style while he recorded it.

Luke's soft snores beside me bring a smile to my lips. The white glow of the digital clock reads three am as I slip from the bed and pull on some clothes, avoiding the used vibrator and dildos that litter the narrow pathway next to it. Rethinking, I snatch them up and decide to wash them after I go pee rather than in the morning before the store opens.

I startle at the loud *crack crack crack* sound from outside and glance back at the large windows at the front of the store. Nothing moves. I glance at Luke, who's still snoring away. *Must have been a car backfiring.*

Pushing open the bathroom door, I get a chuckle out of the sight of myself: wavy hair knotted and tousled, sleep shorts and Luke's tee shirt on, my arms laden with a bright assortment of colored silicone cocks. A warm feeling spreads in my chest and a sense of... contentment. Happiness.

Maybe even a little relief that for now, it's okay to be... stationary. Soon, I'll have to move, but not just yet. I revel in the feeling and dump the cocks in the sink, shaking my head with laughter at our earlier ridiculousness.

Smiling, I slip into a stall to do my business.

Muffled shattering glass snaps my head up. *What the fuck was that? It sounds like it came from outside.* Heart pumping, I strain my ears as I yank the shorts up. Silently letting myself out of the stall, I check the glass on the bathroom window. Intact. Cracking it open, I lean out and look down the drive that runs next to the shop, checking out the glass on those windows. Everything looks normal. From where I lean out, I can make out the black Escalade parked out front. No one gets out, but the hair on the back of my neck stands on end. *Weird.*

There's a heaviness in the air, and my skin prickles like my body is picking up on something my mind is too slow to process. *I should wake up Luke.* Padding over to the bathroom door, I wrap my knuckles around the handle.

Luke's scream rips through the air. "RUN, CARMELLA!" The pop of gunfire goes off in the other room, making me jump away from the door. Heavy foothills run up the hallway, followed by another set. Shaking, I take a step back.

"FUCK! MOTHERFUCKERS!" Luke yells. The sounds of more crashing comes from behind the glass mirror. *Luke's bedroom.* More breaking glass. Several people are running now. Muffled, aggressive voices fill the hallway. "Fucking grab him and shut him up. Bring him out here and find the fucking girl!" a deep voice orders.

My knees tremble as if plugged into an icy current. Shakily, I suck in air. *Think. Where to hide. Oh God, Luke.* I spin as panic begins to set in and I freeze. I'm horrified about what's happening in the hallway, for Luke, for me, for what could happen. There is nowhere to hide.

Thick, heavy hits and groaning come from the hallway. More thuds. A hushed, harsh voice laughs. "That's what you get, bitch."

A heavy thud slams into the wall connected to the bathroom, followed by silence. Dread creeps across my skin in the void of noise. I can hear myself sucking in ragged breaths. Slapping a hand over my mouth, I manage to get my feet to move and scramble across the bathroom. Crawling inside the cabinet under the sink, I shove aside cleaning bottles, my makeup, and bite down on my knuckle as tears spill down my face. My mind races a million miles ahead of me. *Where are Luke's friends?*

A low moan softly fills the air, and the sounds of something being dragged fills me with dread. The hot wetness of my tears cools on my face as I curl my body into a ball. My bladder threatens to give out as the bathroom door creaks open and footsteps shuffle in quietly.

BANG! I flinch.

A bathroom stall is slammed open and a man chuckles. "Girly, c'mon out. We already know you're here." Silence. "Come out now and make this easy on yourself." Cold sweat drips down my back and an uncontrollable tremor shakes me.

"Take those two," another deep voice orders.

Silence.

BANG.

BANG.

BANG.

Silence.

I shake as my lungs cry out for air.

"Fuck, the window is open," a deep voice says.

"You think she got out?"

"Greene, go tell Jay and take a couple guys; see if she's hiding outside."

The bathroom door opens and shuts.

The darkness of my place under the sink closes in around me. *This is just like all those times you hid from Gloria's boyfriends when they were on a binge. Just breathe and let it out.* I repeat the phrase a couple times in my head, willing my body to obey.

"Fuck, man, look at all these cocks. You think they're all for her? I need a girl like that," says one voice.

The deeper voice replies, "Na, he's a fuckin' fag. You see how fast he went down? Wearing all that fucking jewelry, I bet he likes it up the ass."

BANG. I jump. *That's the last stall. Please don't let them look in here. Please God, don't let them look in here.*

"You don't know. She could be putting more than one in each hole."

"You watch too much porn. Real bitches don't do that."

"Yeah, they do."

"Name one."

I squeeze my eyes shut as tears leak down my face. *Please don't let them find me. Please.*

Silence.

"See, exactly my point. C'mon, she's got to be around here somewhere. Let's go check the other bathroom."

The bathroom door creaks as they shuffle out and it thuds closed.

Gulping down air, I stay quiet. Voices from the show floor echo back to me. My ears strain to catch the words, but they're too muffled.

I need a phone, and I need to call the cops. Cops... fuck. I can't call the cops. *Can I? Will they know it's me? Will they want to talk? Fuck.* I squeeze my eyes shut and pull at the roots of my hair as frustration and helplessness rocks me. *Fuck me. Fuck my life. Fuck my fucking aunt. Fuck. Fuck. FFFFUUUUCCCCKKKK!*

Luke. He could be dead. Cold dread wraps its icy fingers in my belly. He needs help. My whole body trembles as fear turns my bowels soft. *Think.* Luke was in his bedroom when they got him. *Was he coming to get me?* Running. Running to get his gun. *The gun.* My eyes snap open.

I need the gun.

The gun is in the nightstand. The bedroom is right next door. *Get the gun, look for the phone. Help Luke. That's the plan.*

Roughly wiping my tears, I crack open the cabinet door and look out. I'm alone. Quietly, I slide out onto the floor and sneak over to the wooden door. Wrapping my hand on the handle, I freeze and look up.

The silver door closer—the one that has squeaked every day since I got here—floats menacingly above my head. I pull it open slowly and a low creak fills the air.

"Did you hear that?" a voice asks from the kitchen down the hall. I curse and gently let the door fall back into the frame. *Fuck.*

I glance back at the window. *It's farther from the gun but closer to a phone. I could get help. Have someone call it in. Luke, please don't die.*

Pivoting, I'm up and scrambling out the window. The black Escalade looms up ahead. *Maybe they don't know? Maybe they were playing music and didn't hear anything?* Staying low, I sprint to the passenger side door. *Oww, what is that!* Sharp pain lances through the soles of my feet. The broken glass cuts into my flesh before I see it shining on the parking lot ground. The passenger window is shattered. I look inside the Escalade and nearly scream. My stomach rolls up on me and I puke on the concrete. There is a hole in the temple of boring guy's face and chunks of brain and hair clinging to the inside of the vehicle. Dark blood hemorrhages from his nose like someone liquified the inside of his head. Shock is frozen on his face as he slumps in his seat. Rikki sits on the other side, and I think for a minute he could be sleeping if it wasn't for his sightless open eyes and the glistening wet shirt stuck to his stomach.

"Hey, I found her!" a voice yells, and I whip around in time to see a shadow hurtling toward me from the back of Luke's. Adrenaline floods my system as I push away from the car and run across the broken glass, no longer caring what happens to my feet. Pain shoots up my legs from my soles and I know I'm leaving behind a bloody path as I run. "Fucking bitch, get over here," the man behind me yells, close enough I can hear his labored breaths. The closed businesses fly by me as my legs pump, putting distance between Luke and me. *Lose this guy and get help!*

I weave in between businesses and alleyways, hiding and limping when I can until I can't see my pursuer anymore. I no longer care about the hamburger I'm making out of my own feet. I suck warm, wet, salty air into my lungs. Rounding the corner of the block, salvation appears. The neon of the gas station glows white and green with hope as the words *Open Twenty-four Hours* flash in the window. I limp across the parking lot.

Ripping open the front door, I hobble inside, startling the night clerk. "You have to help me!" I cry out to the middle-aged man behind the counter. His soft face is contorted by shock at my sudden appearance. "What happened?" he demands.

My chest heaves as I suck in another breath. He looks down at my legs and I follow his line of sight to the blood I've smeared all over the white-tiled floor. The sight sends more pain up my legs and I gasp. "There's a man following me. He's coming. Call the police!"

The man nods and, instead of reaching for the phone, pulls a gun from behind the counter. "Get away from the door," he tells me, motioning me to move deeper into the store. When he puts a phone to his ear, I hear the click of the safety being switched off. My body shakes as I limp toward the cold drinks. The clerk starts filling in the details of our situation to the cops. My mind races ahead again. "Tell them people are dead at Luke's Furniture. Two." I gulp. "Maybe three. They are several men with guns." The clerk's face pulls into a severe frown as he repeats the information, and I can feel the shock of the night slipping over me. I lean against the wall next to the drink coolers.

The ding of the store door opening startles us both. Spinning, I find the barrel of a gun pointed at me, my pursuer having finally caught up. "You have definitely made this harder than it needs to be," he growls. Movement flickers out of the corner of my eye as the clerk jerks his gun up at the man standing just inside the door. "Put it down now," the clerk orders, and my pursuer swings his gun toward him, taking aim.

Crack! A gun goes off and I scream as the man that chased me here falls to the ground and doesn't move, a puddle of blood slowly forming around him. "I... I shot him." The clerk pants into the phone. "He was going to shoot me. Oh God, I shot him." My back hits the cooler doors, the coldness from the glass leaching through my shirt, as I slide down to the floor. Sobs wrack my chest as the red fluid grows around the downed man and the smell of copper fills the air. I wrap my arms around my legs, hugging myself into a ball. I can't stop the tears.

The clerk rounds the counter and turns to me, phone pressed against his ear. The kindest honey-colored eyes I've ever seen look down at me. "Help is on the way. They're coming. Are you hurt?" My chest heaves in a way I can't seem to control and I nod my head. He tries to make a soothing hand motion but ends up just moving the gun in my direction, and I flinch. I think he realizes his mistake because he puts the gun on the floor as my gaze dances between him and the dead man.

He crouches down to my level. "Hey, it's going to be oka—" Bang! The clerk glances down as a growing red circle appears in his abdomen before he falls to the side with a groan. Someone is screaming and my mind recognizes that it's me. Behind him on the other side of the broken spiderwebbed glass door stands another man. He pulls it open, the bell going off above his head, and pauses surveying the scene. "Fucking hell, it's a mess in here. Jay is going to be pissed."

"Stop screaming!" he snaps, and I shut up at the sight of the pistol in his hand. His dark eyes burn into me from the depths of the black hoodie pulled up and framing his face. He pulls a phone out of his pocket and hits a button, and it goes through almost immediately. "I got her, but we have a problem. Dave is down and I have to clear the convenience store down the road. I killed the worker." He pauses for a minute. "Well, someone get down here and pick us up." He shoves the phone back in his pocket and points the gun at me. "You and I are gonna walk out of here nice and easy and then you're gonna get into the car without a peep. You hear me?"

I'm frozen as he approaches and grabs me by the arm, hauling me to my feet. My legs shake as he drags me toward the doors.

A deafening gun shot goes off in the silent space and I cover my head as my captor howls and stumbles into me, knocking me to the ground. "Motherfucker!" the man yells. Turning, I see the clerk lying on his side, gun in his outstretched hand, his other one pressed to his wound. He groans the word, "Go," at me before pulling the trigger again. The shot goes wide, shattering the already cracked glass door next to me and missing the man in the black hoodie.

I'm out the door and running directionless as screams and more gunshots go off behind me. The only thought keeping me going is to put enough distance between the bodies and me. Panicked, I keep going through the night until a light looms up ahead, and I find myself lurking in the shadows at the back lot of Luke's before I snap out of it. Guilt rears ugly in my head. *I got that man killed. I brought these guys to his store and then I left him.* Sobs rack my body. I shove down my mind's attempt to recount the number of dead I've seen tonight. I'm cold. Really cold. Like somehow, the drink cooler has taken up space inside my chest and spread outwards. Thoughts race faster than my consciousness can hold on to one, like sand sifting through my fingers.

Luke's sits still and silent. There are cars in the back I don't recognize. An engine revs and lights flash as one flys into the back lot, and I shrink down behind the thriving ivy that attempts to overtake a fence and part of the shop's roof. In the shadows, I watch as a guy hops out and runs inside.

Luke. My original idea comes back to me. *Get to a phone and help Luke. I've done all I can for the first part. Now the second.* My eyes scan the back parking lot and I try to come up with a plan to save us both.

TROUBLE IN PARADISE

LUKE

Darkness blurs my vision as I crack open an eye. Pain lances through my head. I blink and realize it's not darkness clouding my sight, but blood. I can taste the bitter, metallic flavor on my tongue. My knee doesn't seem to be working correctly, and I remember I've been shot.

"I think he's coming around," a disembodied voice says over me.

Shattering glass, figures flooding into the show floor, the gun going off and the immediate pain in my leg, the resulting brawl—one I lost in my own bedroom—as I tried to get to my gun, all of it rushes back to me. Including the beat down in the hallway before they dragged me out here. I take a shallow breath and realize my ribs are fucked.

A feminine giggling catches my attention. *Carmella?* My brain reforms after getting fucking scrambled. Fear and bitter disappointment band my chest. I wasn't fast enough to get the gun and my girl... *Where is my girl?*

Another giggle. Much closer. My stomach knots.

"Did you forget about me? I didn't forget about you," an unknown feminine voice says, and something strokes my cheek. I focus in on her.

Black pigtails and a punk-rock-goth aesthetic on a lithe, pale body that stands on black platform boots bends over in front of me. Her face comes into focus through the blood.

"Wednesday." I try to spit out the wad of blood in my mouth and realize my cheek is swollen inside. "You know, it took me forever to get the stink of you off my dick," I croak.

Wham. Pain splits me in half and I ball up. My breath escapes and doesn't return as my diaphragm seizes and my ribs protest the beating. The big motherfucker beside me retracts his fist from my stomach. Four swastikas decorate the knuckles that have rearranged my innards.

My lungs whistle and wheeze as I suck in precious oxygen. Another fist cracks across my cheek and the force nearly snaps my neck. *I'm going to have a serious case of whiplash.* Lightning blossoms across my vision and blood pools in my mouth. Black dots threaten to consume my sight and carry me away.

"Shut your fucking mouth. Don't talk about my girl like that," the big motherfucker says.

My chin settles against my chest as the world swims. *His girl?*

"Sorry, dude, but your girl's a skank whore," I retort.

Wednesday is there in a flash and slaps me across the face. "Fuck you," she spits.

"And you wanted the sausage. We did this already. You scream at me. I don't care. Blah, blah."

Another slap. Compared to the punches of the big motherfucker beside her, her slaps are like butterfly kisses. *I could do this all day.* Black spots hover as pain blossoms in my head and nausea rolls around my stomach. *Never mind. I might have a concussion. She should probably stop hitting me.*

The big motherfucker pushes her behind him. His shaved head gleams in the lights cast from the back of the store. His gravelly voice drags across my nerves. "I'm sure this must be very confusing for you."

"Yeah, let's say for argument's sake that I'm a little lost." Panic spikes as adrenaline dumps into my bloodstream. "Were you the navy SUV?" I ask.

"Yep, that would be us. I'm Jay."

"And my men?"

He chuckles. "Dead. They didn't even know what hit 'em."

Nausea rolls up my stomach as I glance out into the night through the front windows. Guilt over Rikki and Casper cuts through me. *They were good men. Sasha is going to be furious.*

Jay continues talking. "We met that night at the club, ya know. I almost had you out the car door, if it wasn't for that fancy kick you got me with." He glances back at the three men standing around us. "We thought about coming and fucking you up that night, but it wasn't worth the effort, not after watching you pull a gun on that girl. Things change though," he says, slapping me affectionately on the cheek before pinching my face between his hands. "Funny thing is, we still aren't here for you." He pushes my head, snapping it backward.

"If I remember correctly, I nearly had you with the front of my car." A rough cough burns my throat.

Jay nods. "You're a real funny fucking guy. Tell me another joke, funny guy."

I open my mouth to say something about his mother, but he punches me in the face and I black out momentarily before I swim to the surface again. Blood dribbles down my lips from my nose.

One of the men tosses the big guy a phone, and he catches it lightly, clicking on the screen. Panic crawls around in my chest as I struggle against the straps holding me to my own fucking used furniture. The chair rattles but doesn't give. *Fuck, what a time for something I sell to actually hold up.* Panting, I swallow. "Listen, you are fucking with the wrong man. You've picked a fight you won't win. Sasha will kill all of you for fucking with his business."

"Who the fuck is Sasha?" Jay asks, looking at Wednesday, then at his men. I watch them shrug and confusion pours through me. My mind races as I realize they aren't here for the cash in the shop. They may not even know about it if they don't know Sasha.

A looming feeling of dread takes up residence in my body. "Why are you here?"

Jay thrusts the phone in my face, and a photo of a younger, smiling Carmella shows up on the screen. He looks down at her picture. "Cute, isn't she? I bet she's sweet as pie." He leans forward to whisper in my ear, "Between us guys, I think it's only fair if I get a taste. After all, you already helped yourself to mine." My mind blanks at the horror of what he is saying.

"If you fucking touch her, I am going to kill you," I snarl. He leans back and we make eye contact. Emptiness stares back at me as he grins. "I believe that you believe that."

At a normal volume, he adds, "I was going to ask you where the girl is, but my guys are rounding her up as we speak. She's a slippery one, got around my boys and ended up outside. If it wasn't for your fancy camera system, we probably wouldn't have found her at all."

The phone lights up and buzzes in Jay's hand with an incoming call. "I got to take this," he says, standing.

Fear roots and twists me up inside. *They wanted Carmella all along. But why? And why wait to take her?*

"Fuck!" Jay yells, startling us all. He narrows his eyes on me as he listens to the other person on the phone and looks at his men. "Benny, get down to the twenty-four seven now. Dave went and shit the bed but we got the girl," he orders. Jay speaks back into the phone. "Yeah, we are on our way." He hangs up and rubs his forehead.

"Which stop?" Benny asks.

"The one down the fucking road, you idiot. Now go!" Benny hightails it out the back, leaving just four of us now.

"What did Dave do this time?" Wednesday asks in a bored voice.

"Dave's dead and Bones killed the guy at the counter." A ripple moves through the group. *Oh, so dead bodies piling up wasn't part of the plan.* Wednesday gives a low whistle and shakes her head. "Poor Davey, how did they even end up down there?"

"Fuck if I know. Alright, let's wrap this up and get the fuck out of here." Jay pulls a gun from his back and moves toward me.

I shake my head, which is an immediate mistake. "You're making a bad choice. I work for the mob."

That brings Jay up short. "You're making a lot of enemies here tonight, and over what? A girl?" I goad.

Jay crouches down in front of me, considering me like he somehow sees me in a new light. "If you work for the mob, then we both know that girl is worth a shiny nickel for anyone who can retrieve her. So let's not play."

He waves the gun in front of my face. "Is that why you've been keeping her to yourself? I nearly shit when I realized I knew exactly where my next paycheck was and you, of all people, had her. It made me downright giddy." He straightens up. "But I think you had the right idea, holding out instead of handing her over. This half upfront, half when she is delivered, is horseshit, making us play the waiting game until we could confirm it was her. Getting the first payment took so long, it fucked up a lot of good opportunities to grab her earlier and now look." He gestures around. "It's a big fucking mess."

My mind races ahead and gloms onto all the details he just volunteered. I decide to play along. "Yeah, I didn't trust the guy to come through on the second payment, so I kept her around and asked for more. I'm surprised he paid out for anyone else to come and get her. How much did he give you? Probably not as much as he gave me."

Jay pulls out a butterfly knife, spinning it open, and the blade gleams threateningly as it slices through the light. "How much did he give you?" he counters.

I play on his greed and throw out a number that's sure to piss him off and increase my chances of living a little while longer. "Ten grand in cash."

Wednesday makes an unfair sound and stops her food. "That's fucking crap, Jay! It's way more than we got!" The knife stops spinning. Rage leaks into his face. "That son of a bitch. I knew he was holding out on us. Change of plans," he announces to the group. "We take the money and the girl."

The knife plunges down into my thigh. The sound of Wednesday's giggles mix with my screaming as Jay twists the knife in my wound. "You're gonna give me that money. Right. Fucking. Now," he grinds out between clenched teeth. *Death might be preferable to torture,* my mind offers unhelpfully.

"I'm not giving you fucking shit." I hiss and spittle blows out between my teeth.

He twists the knife again, and I scream until my voice is raw. Wednesday is all but clapping and jumping up and down in excitement like a maniac. She coos, "Let me have a turn with the knife, baby." *This bitch is level-ten crazy.*

I turn on her, snarling, "Listen, you stupid cunt." A fist rams into my stomach and I puke, forming a nice little puddle of red and yellow on the carpet Carmella works so hard to keep vacuumed. *Probably a bad sign that there is blood in my vomit.* Pain radiates throughout my whole body. *Sasha was right. I fucked Wednesday. I like them crazy. I've brought down hell on both our heads for trying to keep Carmella, while all my mistakes roam about freely. She was better off running when she could. Hanging around with me is only going to get her raped or killed.* I cough and spit the acidic taste from my mouth.

A shadow moves over me and Wednesday's nails dig and tear into my face, pushing into my eyes. The scratches burn. I pull my face back as she digs into my eyelids. "Call me a fucking cunt...," she seethes. She's suddenly lifted off me. The one who tossed the big dude the phone has a hold of her, dragging her backwards and making calming noises. He tells her to chill out, that Jay has this under control.

The back door of the store opens and slams shut as Benny comes running in, panting. "We got problems. Bones is dead. I can hear sirens. I was there for a second before I split. The girl is gone. We need to get out of here."

"I say when we go, and we aren't going until we at least get the money," the big guy snarls. He rounds on me. "This is about to get worse for you." The knife flashes as it's pulled out of my leg. Blood arches and splatters across the floor. A scream rips from my throat. "Tell me where the cash is!" Jay roars.

"Just cut off his dick and let's go look for the money ourselves, Jay," Wednesday whines.

He points the knife at her. "Shut the fuck up." Jay looks to the other men. "Start searching. See what you can find."

A sudden flood of lights from the front parking lot illuminates the dark storefront, and the shrill cry of a car horn makes everybody jump and flee toward the shadows.

"Who the fuck is that?" Jay bellows as the horn continues to blare into the night. "Greene! Rags! Go check it out. Hurry."

The two men slip toward the front quickly.

"They're coming!" I yell, hoping Carmella or whoever just came to my aid hears me. A backhand blows across my face. The world tilts as my vision warps and readjusts. Another wave of nausea rolls upon me, making me feel shaky and clammy. A band of tape is pressed over my mouth. *Great, now when I puke, I'll just suffocate and die.*

The blaring horn cuts off, leaving a terrifying, crushing silence. I can barely lift my head as I stare toward the front and think the worst.

One of the men appears from the dark, holding a piece of wood, followed by the other. "No one was there, just a board wedged between the dead dude's chest and the horn. Benny's right. I can hear sirens. We're out of time."

A car alarm goes off at the back of the store. The anti-theft device I put on my baby wails into the night. "Fuck this, cops are going to be here any minute," one of the men says. A couple of the guys mutter their agreements. I can hear the glass crunch under their feet as they move around nervously.

"Bunch of fucking pussies," Jay snaps.

I watch the crimson stain grow on the carpet under me and blood flow freely from my thigh. *I hope he didn't nick something vital.* My hair is wretched to the side. "Talk," Jay says.

If this is to be the end, then it will end on my terms. "Suck my fat fucking plaster blaster and choke on it, just like your girlfriend did, you Nazi piece of shit."

There is a moment of deep satisfaction as I watch Jay's nostrils flare wide and the look of murder cross his face, but it's cut short by the white-hot pain blossoming across my chest as Jay's blade slices me open like a Christmas ham. Darkness crowds my vision as I watch my shirt and skin peel apart, revealing muscles and tendons. Blood pours down onto the floor as my vision shutters. The world tilts and the last thing I'm conscious of is Jay's voice. "Grab him and let's get the fuck out of here."

To Be Continued.

Acknowledgments

I would like to give a big thanks to everyone who was involved with the creation of Trash Daddy. I'm so thankful for your support.

The legal plot wouldn't have come together without your help and knowledge, Lyssa. Without you, I would've spent countless hours of legal research and still would've gotten it all wrong.

Also, I probably would've given up out of frustration and been seduced into a new project without your encouragement and experience, Regina. Thank you for being a sort of mentor and sharing your tricks and tips.

To my Lover, thanks for always making me laugh, even when I didn't want to, and for being my own personal trash daddy. You helped shape Luke's voice more than you probably know.

I am truly blessed to have so many great people in my life.

About the Author

Jenni Tayla has always enjoyed themes that are sexually inappropriate, dark, and occasionally cross over to the extreme. A lover of action-adventure, fantasy, and horror movies, she tends to fall asleep during rom-coms and feel-good flicks. It's arguable that she doesn't find happiness to be the most compelling emotion. Chronically avoidant, she's been an avid reality escapist all her life, thanks to being introduced to the Harry Potter Series when she was twelve. But despite being a devourer of stories, she didn't pick up the pen to write her own until she was thirty-one and then decided to embark on the perilous path of self-publishing. Some would say she only knows how to do things the hard way. She would reply that, technically, her "doing things the hard way" is just her ADD, plus a willful nature, and she didn't ask for their opinion anyway. When not writing, her day job is as an Environmental Specialist for a Native American Tribe. She and her partner are raising twin daughters and hope that one day, they will strike fear into the hearts of men and earn the title of being terrifying, just like their mom.

Milton Keynes UK
Ingram Content Group UK Ltd.
UKHW012313060524
442290UK00005B/345